I0666740

# Lost Souls

# of the

# Hinterlands

A novel by Larry Carr

Barkwood Press paperback edition 2015

Also from Barkwood Press

Apotheosis

In the Den

Custodial Rites

Fate Accompli

To my niece
You weren't meant for this world
I hope to meet you in the next

## Prologue

He felt … Nothing. There was nothing to feel.

He wasn't even sure he was conscious. He thought that he might be having a dream; a numb, disorienting dream that had him spun in a cocoon of paralyzing emptiness.

He told himself to wake up. He told himself to open his eyes.

He opened them and saw … Nothing. There was nothing to see. Everything was as black as tar.

A sense of panic rushed through his mind like an electric current. He couldn't see. He was blind.

Then he thought: Have I always been blind?

He didn't know, and that scared him.

He thought about his name, about his life, about who he was, where he was from, his family, what he did for a living, but every question he posed came back without an answer.

What was his name? He couldn't remember.

Where was he from? He didn't know.

What did he do for a living? He …

He remembered the sirens and flashing red lights of a firetruck. He remembered ducks in flight, in a perfect V formation, their quacking voices filling the sky. He remembered chocolate chip muffins and a tall cup of coffee. He remembered … she had blonde hair … and red leather seats … and a number two pencil with a dull tip.

He wondered if he was dead.

He wondered if he was in a coma.

He again told himself to open his eyes, but again he saw nothing. No shapes. No colors. No light. There was only darkness.

He considered his other senses.

He felt the heat of the sun on his face and the gentle caress of a warm breeze. He intuited the size and shape of his body by experimentally touching his arms, his legs, his head, his face, and though he perceived these things, and perceived his own touch, nothing felt familiar to him, nothing felt real. It was like he was fondling a mannequin in a storefront window display.

He tried feeling around him. His hands struck solid ground, and he scratched his fingers in the earth. It was hard, rough, rocky terrain, gritty and warm to the touch. Yet still he could not see, and that terrified him.

He tried his voice, but only a rasping croak escaped, the sound of a small animal in pain. He tried it again, attempting to say Hello. It came out, "Oowoo," like he had a mouthful of marbles. He thought about marbles: round, colorful, glassy balls that you shot in a ring. He recalled playing marbles, but ... he ...

He remembered ice cream and nacho cheese, and the feel of cold water. The high, pointed spear of a church steeple and endless taps of beer flashed in his mind.

The faint scent of salt caught his nose, and after that the sound of a faraway voice. He heard the voice clearly, but not the words spoken.

Then he heard a voice closer to him.

"Hello," the voice said. It was female, and there was fear in it.

"Hawhoa," he answered back. Then he said it three more times, quickly, desperately, striking notes of panic.

"Hello?" the female voice said again. "Who's there? Who are you?"

His mouth was so dry that it was hard for him to form words. "I don' kno," he managed. "I can' see. Um bline. I can' see nuttin!"

"I can't see either," the woman said. "Who are you?"

He carefully worked himself up to his knees and reached out his arms, searching for anything. "I don' kno," he said. "I don' rahmayber."

"I don't remember either. I don't remember anything. I just woke up here. But I don't know where *here* is. And I can't see, and I don't know my name, or who I am, or ..."

She began to cry.

"Me, too. I jus wok up. Jus a minit awgo."

"I don't understand," the woman said, sobbing. "I don't know why I can't remember anything. Not my name. Nothing. And I don't know why I can't see. I don't know why I'm blind."

"Mey eader. I don' kno why."

The sound of approaching footsteps drew their attention, and the woman frantically called out for help: "Hello?! Hello?! Who's there? We need help. We can't see. Hello!"

She received no answer, yet the footsteps continued. There were numerous sets of them, too many to count, and the closer they got, the louder they got, until they sounded like a small battalion on the march.

The woman began yelling. "Who's there? Who's there?" Then:

"Somebody help us. Please. We can't see. We don't know where we are. We don't know *who* we are?"

The footsteps came to an abrupt stop, and a man's voice said, "Grab the stones." His voice was fast and harsh, the voice of man who had age and hard miles on him.

"Hello?" the woman called out desperately. "Who are you? Please, can you help us? We need help."

The man who had just woken up blind and dumb could sense someone close to him; he could smell the general funk of sweat and humanity in the air, could hear the soft rush of heavy breathing all around him, could feel the suspicious eyes of strangers looking him up and down. He wanted to stand up, but without his sight to guide him, he felt unsure of his balance. Instead, in a calm and reasonable voice, even though he was fit to burst, he said, "Plea, sir, can oou hepp us?"

He felt a hand on his shoulder … and then he felt himself falling back. "Ay!" he cried out right before hitting the ground. Then he heard the woman scream. He screamed, too, for help, for mercy, for someone to please tell him what was happening.

"Take what they've got and get them to the boat," said the man in charge. "The other one, too. And make it quick. This side of the shore worries me. Haunted here."

The blind man called out, "Wait! Wher are we? Who are oou? Pleas. Someun tock to mey!"

No one spared him a word.

Instead, invisible hands began accosting him; they pinned him to the ground, they rifled through his pockets, they pulled off his clothes. He shouted curses at them and struggled to get away, but they held him down and stripped him bare.

They did the same to the woman, who screamed throughout, yelling out things like, "Stop!" and "Rape!" and, "Please God! Help me!"

As this was happening, the man in charge gave a speech, his coarse, unfriendly tone adding to the horror of his message.

"Worry not, you shan't be harmed, not by my men. We care not for your stinking bodies. You're cargo. Cargo like the stones. Like meat. Like silks and hides and fish. You're cargo we shall deliver. As for your clothes and personal items, you'll need them not where you're going. You'll need nothing but the rags we give you to wear and a strong will. There's a long journey ahead. Save your strength and your hope. You'll need both."

## One:

The sky was dense and tar-black, as it always was at night. There were thousands of stars up there but no moon, which cast an ominous spell over the vast desert of Hinterland. A small fire made of weeds and grass and the occasional stick crackled and threw off faint light, projecting half-shadows on the ground. Three men were gathered around this modest blaze; three men and one demon.

The Demon Kin had roamed the desertlands for ages, and the men who passed through this seemingly endless tract of sand and rock did their best to avoid them. They could possess a man and drive him mad; and they worked magic, powerful, ancient magic that could steal a man's soul and send him running to his grave.

One of the men, an old hand named Calrick, spat on the ground. Then he took a swill from his cask, drinking down mouthfuls of the foul cider his wife made for him. He grimaced a little at the taste, and spat again.

The demon spoke. "You folk look rough on the edge. The desert is hard land to walk." It had a strong, abrasive voice, a voice you felt as much as you heard. "Is not for all."

"It's not the desert, it's the work," said Dol. Like Calrick, he was an old hand from Meridon, in the far southwest territories of Hinterland. He was mostly a desert dweller now and it showed. In just a few seasons the desert had etched itself on him, giving him a hard, lean, weathered look. He had been good-looking once, with flowing brown hair and a strong chin, but those days were gone now. A thick, scraggly beard hid most of his face, which had grown old, and his eyes were a sad shade of blue. On his belt was a sword made of the finest steel and a leather whip. He was deadly with both, though neither could harm the demon. "Not pleasant work, stealing and strong-arming other men."

"Then do it not," said the demon.

Dol shook his head. "We do the work because we need the pay."

"As has been and always shall be, so make nothing of it, vandalos, unless you savor to be on the other side."

Dol hated being called a vandal, especially by the demon, but that's exactly what he had become. Once a promising land filled with life and love, laughter and children, Meridon was now a wasteland, not unlike the desert itself. And a man had to do what a man had to do to feed his family and make his way. You could call that justification if you like, but you also could call it necessary. Either way, Dol didn't much care for it.

"You lied to us," he said to the demon.

"Surely no. All sides are square, vandalos."

"What of the lakas? They roam this desert free. We see them. They haunt us nightly on the plains."

"Lakas have been here since before your time began."

"There are more now," Calrick put in. "And they are eager to fight."

Within the shadows that made up the demon's face, its eyes flashed yellow. "Surely men such as you can handle lakas."

"You averred they wouldn't bother us none whilst we did your work," said Dol. "Lest you forget."

"They bother you?"

"Of course they bother us!" snapped Alde, Dol's son and the youngest of the group. He was only eighteen in years, but he was tall and strong and fierce, with a natural disposition for violence. With his wild, shoulder-length blond hair, handsome features, and smooth cheek, he looked more like a boy than a man, but those who hailed from Meridon had no choice but to grow up fast. He did not care for the desert, and he did not trust the demon.

"If they bother you, kill them," the demon said. It nodded to the sword on Dol's belt. "That'll do it quick and well."

"To kill 'em you got to get on 'em, and I ain't keen," replied Calrick. "They stink, and if they bite you, or scratch you, you turn to dust."

"Are you keen on sleep terrors?" the demon asked. "Or do you rest quiet here in these lands?"

Dol shot the demon a look.

Calrick spat on the ground.

The sleep terrors that plagued them when first they adopted the desert as their home were gone, but now their waking-thoughts were braided with the madness of the Kin, which could send a man quickly to his death.

The desert of Hinterland was no place for the callow or faithless.

"Truly," said Dol. "And many thanks for that. But lakas were part of the accord, too, and nothing's changed."

The demon wavered before them like a black flame. Most Kin were phantom creatures, dark spirits cloaked in shadows and gloom. They had neither height nor weight, neither arms nor legs; they had no discernable faces or bodies. Their only distinguishing feature was their yellow eyes, which shined hauntingly in the dark.

"You want lakas dead but that I cannot do," it said. "They are of the desert. The desert is part of them, and they are part of it."

"You promised," said Dol.

"I lied," replied the demon. "We do such when occasion calls. And often it does."

"You cannot be trusted!" Alde barked, his youthful temper getting the best of him.

The demon shot him a look, its yellow eyes flashing, and young Alde whelped in pain and disgust.

"Hey!" Calrick shouted. "He's just a kid!"

"He must learn his place," the demon hissed. It then filled Alde's mind with another shock of disturbing images, causing him to close his eyes, clamp his hands on his head, and wail in misery.

"Enough," Dol said in a calm but stern tone, and the demon released its hold on the boy.

"He's your boy, vandalos. Aye. You need teach him to keep his tongue. Or I will."

"He's a good kid. Only young."

"A foolish child," said the demon.

"He'll be a leader of Meridon one day."

The demon knew that not to be true but said nothing of it. A leader, yes, but not of Meridon.

"You can't do anything about the lakas?" Calrick asked.

The demon's mystical form shifted and a moment later a small leather pouch hit the ground at Dol's feet. "Calto root. Potent magic. That should keep them off you. Send them moaning to the mounts."

Dol picked up the small leather pouch. He hefted it in his hand, and smelled it. There was no discernable odor, but his eyes began to water.

"Powerful," the demon said. "Don't burn it or eat it, and keep it from your eyes lest you wish to turn blind."

Dol dropped the pouch on the ground, away from the small fire.

"You have offerings for me, vandalia?"

Dol glanced at Calrick, and Calrick moved to his pack. He knelt, pulled out a small bag, and returned to the fire.

He hated this part. It wasn't just the deal with the demon that bothered him, but the exchange, too. There was something unnatural about it.

He made sure the small pouch was tied-off before tossing it over to the demon, and a shiver ran down his spine as he watched it disappear in the shadows that blew around the lingering figure in black like the flames of a fire. A moment later, something came back, appearing from where the small pouch had disappeared. A large rucksack clattered noisily when it hit the ground at Calrick's feet.

"Many goods, all for you," the demon hissed. "Gold, fire and seeds, steel and medicine, as agreed."

None of the men made a move for the sack, knowing that would be taken as an affront. Not that it mattered. Even if the demon shorted them, there wasn't anything they could do about it. The deal was in the demon's hands, and the cards dealt were always in its favor.

Dol had grudgingly struck the deal more than three years ago, when times were at their worst for him and his. And while the demon had lied about the lakas, and a couple of other things, too, it had kept true to most of the pact. The sleep terrors were gone, and they were gaining riches.

"What of the stragglers we gave?" the demon asked. "Are you making good use of their unwanted bones?"

Dol snorted and looked away, disgusted by the question.

In a plain yet bitter voice, Calrick said, "They'll do."

"All do and all must," replied the demon. "Such is life."

Neither man liked taking stragglers as prisoners, but assets were assets, and manpower and womenfolk were, practically speaking, coveted assets in Meridon, especially since the scourge. They'd only gotten three so far, two men and one woman, but two of them — one of the men and the woman — were of sound age. The woman had already been claimed in marriage, and the men had been assigned to work.

"It's not their world," Dol said, "and they know it."

"It's as much theirs as yours," replied the demon. "If your conscience won't allow it, take them not. Otherwise."

Dol said nothing to that. Calrick, too, kept silent.

Alde had a couple choice words in mind, but he wisely bit them back, having yet to recover from the horror-images the demon had shoved through his brain like hot steel. He had never experienced anything like it before and never wanted to experience anything like it again.

The mystical form of the black ghost wavered hypnotically, and the flames of the fire seemed to darken in its shadow. "Rest up, vandalia," it said. "Big days to come and we need be in front of them."

"I was actually thinking we could use a break," replied Dol. "I'd like to see the rest of my family. My wife. My homestead."

"You will work when work is needed. And when I say."

"There are other bands. You've made other deals. Micah and his slave for you. Nalon, too."

"Aye. They do. And they work when work is needed, and when I say. As you and yours will."

Dol had no good answer for that, at least not one that would make a difference. He had spent less than sixty nights at home over the last three years. He missed his wife and kids, and he missed his homestead, but the Kin didn't care about things like that, and the demon, at least for now, was calling the shots.

"Can we at least return to Meridon?" Dol asked respectfully.

"Go your way for now, vandalos," the demon said to him. "But when I call, you must answer."

"Any idea when that might be?" Calrick inquired. Like his friend, he also missed his home and family. It had been far too long since he had known the warm touch of his wife.

The demon's dark, billowing form appeared to grow in size, and its eyes flashed yellow. "I know nothing of time, vandalos," it said with a hiss. "Your kind seeks to measure it, not mine."

The meeting was over. All that had needed said had been said, and all that had needed exchanged had been exchanged.

In its harsh, abrasive voice, the demon said, "Until again, vandalia," and as it had materialized out of thin air, it vanished the same way. One moment it was there, its darkness swelling and flowing amidst the low-licking flames of the fire, and the next it was gone.

Alde waited a few ticks before making his opinion known. "I don't trust that cursed thing," he said reproachfully. "It lied to us."

"That it did," replied Dol. "Yet it kept its word about the sleep terrors. And we are increasing our wealth."

Calrick took a seat on the ground and unfolded the rucksack. Dol crouched down beside him and began picking through the materials. There were steel daggers and blades, chips of gold and silver, fire-flint, tobacco, various seeds and spices, and vials of potent medicinal elixirs. These were important belongings, assets of need and want in Meridon, and they made Dol and his clan wealthy by comparison.

"Fold it up," he told Calrick after taking a quick inventory. "Morning will be on fast and we need rest."

Calrick did as told, packing and folding the rucksack with great care. He was older than Dol by a year, though he looked younger. His cheeks and chin were spotted with a scant beard and his fair brown hair had started to go gray, but there was still light in his eyes, which cast on him a youthful glow. He had been a simple farmer once, tending huge fields of wheat and corn, rye and barley, but then the scourge hit and the ground in Meridon turned to stone. Even the forests, the great river Potami, and the lakes seemed to die, becoming barren and desolate. Poor and starving, with a family to feed and care on, he'd had little choice but to take up a blade and join his friend in the desert. Now they were vandals in league with Kin, working a crooked deal for the return of their once fertile land.

Dol reached into his vest pocket and pulled out his pipe and tobacco. He loaded it, put a spark to it, and puffed until smoke began to rise.

When Calrick finished with the rucksack, he did the same, taking a seat at the fire while he smoked.

Alde was the only one who did not indulge.

The flames of the fire danced like serpents, and the desert grass crackled and spit. It was the only sound to hear in the desert at night, unless there were lakas or yenas about. Lakas were the most bothersome; those vile creatures moaned like sick sheep, their toneless voices a haunting song in the dark.

Dol pulled a silver flask from his pack. He unscrewed the cap, took a draw, and handed it to his son. Drinking with the menfolk was Alde's favorite part of walking the desert, and he often exaggerated how much he drank when he talked to his friends back home. He also liked to tell them fantastical stories about demons and lakas, and he never failed to embellish the details, opting for a more sensational slant. And he would grin wide and happy whenever he saw the envy in their eyes.

He took a swig, and then another, before handing the flask back to his father. The cider was strong, and Alde grimaced at the fire it lit in his chest and belly. Yet it was a far better drink than Calrick's cider; that stuff could eat through rock.

"I'll take first watch," Dol said as he stared out at the impenetrable darkness of night. There was nothing to see, and that worried him. He knew there were lakas and yenas out there, and the fire would tempt their interest. Not to mention the Herders they had robbed.

"Guess we'll see if this stuff really works," Calrick said, referring to the pouch of Calto root the demon had given them.

Dol grunted in agreement, and took another drink. "Long day ahead tomorrow. Best be getting our rest or we'll pay for it."

Somewhere in the black distance, the first laka moan rose above the soothing crackle of the fire. Young Alde flinched, and searched the dark horizon for movement. He didn't see anything, but he knew they were out there, staggering, wanting.

Dol handed the flask to him and said, "Drink, boy. It'll calm you."

Alde never had to be told twice. He downed a couple snorts, and then a couple more. When he was good and dizzy, he lay for bed, trying not to think about the lakas and yenas in the desert, or the terrible hallucinations the demon had forced through his mind like hundreds of shards of glass; fiercely mangled hallucinations of war and lust, hate and fear, family and flesh, shadow and bone. They had mixed together in a seductive orgy of madness that had left him with cold skin and a painfully hard erection.

There was meaning and truth in those dark visions, a meaning and truth he did not understand, a meaning and truth he wanted to understand but for fear, for it both tormented and tantalized him. These twisted thoughts plagued him under the desert sky until oblivion stole him away, and when he dreamed, he dreamed of death.

**Two:**

They came to shore on a big boat manned by the river-folk. The river-folk had numerous boats, though only one was large enough to cross the great watery divide that wrapped around all of Hinterland like a giant serpent. The river Potami was narrow in some spots, wide in others — as wide as a sea — and often treacherous. There were rapids and rocks to contend with in the south, violent storms and maelstroms up north, and unpredictable currents that made navigation a dart throw. Not to mention the beasts that lived in the deep waters, some of which could swallow a man whole.

At Vernon, the river was more of a bay, though its waters flowed just the same. The other side could not be seen, and its depths had yet to be measured. A few people still fished the waters there, but they rarely filled their nets, and most of what they caught was not worth the effort. The best fishing was up north, beyond the archipelagos of Boreal, the lands the river-folk called home. There they had fish six feet long and plenty tasty.

It was far worse off the coast of Meridon; those dark waters were now cursed. The fish there had five or six eyes, some had two tails, others had no scales. There were snakes, too, hundreds and hundreds of aggressive river-serpents slithering on and below the surface of the water, ruthlessly searching for anything to bite. Some were more than twenty feet long, while others were highly-venomous. Rarely a moon spun a cycle without a kid getting killed down there.

The river-folk were a motley crew beholden to none but the Angeloi. Many believed it was because they lived on the water. They didn't speak much, and they routinely kept to themselves, treating outsiders with tacit scorn and suspicion. They weren't known to be violent, but they weren't to be trifled with either. They could fight.

The captain of the big boat, Movin, was a perfect specimen: small and wiry; strong and direct; surly and hard-working. His feet were flat and usually bare, his skin possessed the sun-dappled texture of dying citrus fruit, and his eyes gazed out at the world in a permanent squint. Bearded, with thick hair, a broad nose, and a smile absent a few teeth, he wasn't quite ugly, but he was close enough to pass.

He had one job only, a job that had been bestowed upon his ancestors by the Angeloi generations ago: usher the stones and blind fools from the far shores of Potami to the town of Vernon. They got to keep as booty whatever trinkets they found there, everything from clothes and jewelry to books, musical instruments, and odd coins. They sold most of it in the towns along the river, cashing in, as all in Hinterland were known to do, on death. They weren't rich, and their way of life was anything but easy, but they were free and wanted for nothing.

Movin skillfully pulled the giant ketch into the dock at Vernon while his crew prepared for debarkation.

The crew at the dock, bossed by a stern, one-armed man named Eront, rushed about like mice, securing the old wooden vessel to the dock and readying the notch for the gangplank.

It took only three minutes for the first crew member, Alto, to come ashore. Alto was Movin's brother, and he led the way down the plank with great agility, making sure it was safe.

"All's well on the dock," he called up to the ship in a husky voice, and a few moments later the cargo appeared.

There were three of them roped together by their hands and waists: an old man with sparse gray hair, bowlegs, and a wrinkled face; a frumpish, middle-aged woman with big eyes and reddish-brown hair; a wiry young man with dark brown skin and the shadow of a goatee. The old man looked wary, the woman looked exhausted and demoralized, while the young man appeared more curious than anything else.

Led by the old man, they walked hesitantly down the plank, making sure of their balance. The three of them had arrived on the far shores five days ago, blind, scared, and utterly confused. Their sight had returned to them in stages: first they saw only shades of light and dark; then they began to see colors and shapes; by day three they were able to make out objects and faces that were close to them. These things appeared blurry and faded in their eyes, but it sure beat the alternative. A couple days later and the blurriness was gone and they had redeveloped depth perception.

Now they could plainly see the full scope of Hinterland.

Like their vision, their fear and confusion had also increased.

Everything they had the river-folk had taken from them. Their funeral clothes had been replaced by worn leathers that fit them shabbily and chafed their skin. The woman had had her jewelry taken (three rings, two bracelets, a watch and a pendant, all of high quality), the old man had been made to give up his rings and his pocket watch, and the young man had had his necklace stolen. But that was the least of their concerns. They still had no idea who they were, where they were, or what might come next.

15

"Old friend," Eront said to Movin, showing him a hearty smile.

The ship's captain shook the harbormaster's hand and said, "Eront." They were not friends only business partners, and Movin suffered no pretense otherwise. Truthfully, he didn't much care for Eront, though he knew he had no choice but to deal with him.

"Three?" Eront said with a note of surprise. He glanced at the sad, frightened faces of the three stragglers the captain had brought to his dock. He was not impressed.

"And a hundred and eighty-nine stones on top," Movin added.

Eront licked his lips. "A hundred and eighty-nine? A large haul."

"Aye. My biggest ever."

The harbormaster studied the stragglers a little more closely. He felt bad for them; dead souls lost in limbo, doomed to walk the desert before reaching the Great Stone Temple on the other side. And then what? No one knew for certain, but the old tales were not encouraging.

They all had the same desperate look about them, like beggars without a hat. You could see it in their eyes; they had no clue where they were or even who they were, and it terrified them. They could speak and hear, feel and see, touch and taste, but they could not understand, and though they possessed memories of their old life, some of those memories being quite specific, they remembered nothing about themselves or the cruel twists of fate that had brought them to the shores of Hinterland.

Perhaps it was better that way, thought the harbormaster.

Sometimes the truth is too heavy to bear.

"Any gear or goods for sale?" he inquired, his mind seamlessly moving to profit.

Movin nodded once. "As always." He pulled a small leather pouch from his belt and drew open the string. "Baubles," he said with a scowl, though he understood quite well how popular baubles were in Hinterland. Him and his made a fair wage on the garments and baubles of the dead.

He moved to Eront's post and emptied the bag, spilling out a few rings, a couple bracelets, a couple necklaces, and two timepieces. They were all made of either gold or silver, and some had gemstones for decoration. Some of these gems were green, some opal, others red. And then there were the clear, bright, glassy stones known as diamonds. Those were most in demand, and Movin never sold one for less than full value.

"Very nice," said Eront, sifting his one hand through the treasure, his rough, gnarled fingers standing out like blood on a wedding gown.

Movin watched him with suspicion. He did not think him a thief, but nor did he trust him. He trusted only himself and his crew, as was the way of the river-folk.

He found a ring, a plain gold band, and handed it to Eront. "Payment," he told him. "The rest are for sale."

Eront took the ring and eyed it greedily. He brought it up to his mouth and bit it, wanting to taste the gold.

"It's true," said Movin. "No need for worry." He then raised his hand and motioned to his crew.

Three deckhands rushed over to the captain, each of them lugging a satchel over their shoulder. They presented their haul, and ran off without so much as a glance at Eront.

"The souls of the dead," said Movin, opening one of the satchels to reveal a load of small, odd-looking stones of different color and shape. Some were round and gray, some were oblong and brown, others were jagged and black. "Count them to make sure."

Eront nodded. "They shall be counted," he said. "One hundred and eighty-nine, correct?"

"Aye. Any less or any more, you tell it. We'll be here for the night. My crew want for rest and dry land, drink and company. And we need to go to market for goods."

"Of course," said Eront. "The ship shall be watched."

The two men shook hands, signifying the end of the deal, and Movin made his way up the dock to dry land, on his way to see Daglan for payment. Later, he would spend some of that payment at Sana's.

Eront, meanwhile, motioned for one of his runners. To specify, he called out, "Weslan. Here. Now."

The boy Weslan hurried to his boss's side.

"Find someone from the Council of Elders and tell them that a new ship has come in," Eront told him.

Weslan nodded obediently and ran off.

On the far side of the gangway, the three slouching, bedraggled souls lost in a new world glanced around nervously and chittered amongst themselves. They asked questions that had no answers, and made comments that meant nothing.

Where were they?

How had they gotten there?

What was this strange world?

Where were they going?

Was this going to be there new home?

"It's going to be okay," the woman said in a voice absent faith. She was tall and thin, and not so long ago she had been beautiful. Now, with her pale cheeks and sunken eyes, she resembled a fresh corpse in a casket.

The young man nodded and said that he believed that, too. This was not so much false bravado as simple courteousness. The truth, he believed, was much more unpleasant, but he had been taught to respect his elders.

The old man had no such misgivings. He had a pretty good idea what was happening, and if he was right, things weren't going to be okay for a long time, if ever again. He said this to the others, bluntly.

The woman chose to ignore him and said, "Last thing I remember ... " But her words ceded to silence when her memory failed, and despair stole what little light remained in her eyes.

"It was Christmas, I think," said the young man.

There was some agreement from the woman, and the three of them spoke for a while about the holidays, mostly about food.

But that discussion soon faded, too, like all the others they'd had since arriving in Hinterland, replaced by silent consternation and an underlying sense of hopelessness. And those feelings grew in depth as they were led off the dock like slaves, roped together and pulled along in a world they did not recognize or understand.

## Three:

Lizzy could see the fish in the water, its silvery skin reflecting blue and green in the bright morning sun. It was dancing with the bait, inching up on it then jerking away, then swimming back around.

She held the trawl pole still and made not a move.

Lizzy liked the hunt, be it for fish or game. She had patience that belied her fourteen years and skill that rivaled many of the young men in her village. Barely a teen, she already was deadly with a bow, and she could split a hare's eyes from thirty paces with a slingshot.

The fish circled around tentatively, delaying the inevitable. It was hungry and would eat ... and then would be eaten. It was only a matter of time, and Lizzy had no problem waiting.

That's when she heard a noise behind her, the uneven rustling of footsteps in the high grass that surrounded the pond. Someone was sneaking up on her. She wasn't scared, knowing most likely it was her older brother or one of his stupid friends. They always tried to scare her, or throw dung at her, or push her in the water.

She remained a statue, holding her pole perfectly still, waiting either for the fish to take the bait or the mischief-maker's reflection to appear on the surface of the water.

It was a calm day and sunny, and when her brother Jonno reached the crest of the bank, the faint makings of a smile cut her face. His reflection wavered transparently in the still pool, and got bigger as he got closer.

He wasn't very good at sneaking up on people. It was the same reason why he wasn't very good on the hunt.

He routinely had gotten the best of Lizzy when she was young and naïve, a little girl with more curiosity than wits, but she since had learned his tricks and he no longer could surprise her.

He crept forward, and she held still, watching him on the water.

He hesitated for a spell, like a tiger in the bush ready to pounce on its prey. Lizzy saw this, and to bait him, she jiggled the pole a little and said, "Come on, fishy, bite!"

It worked, because the next moment Jonno sprang forward, intending to push his little sister in the pond. But at the last moment she spun away, and his momentum carried him into the water with a splash.

"Dammit!" he shouted at her. "You no-good gypsy-girl!"

"Serves you well," Lizzy replied with a smile. "You can't sneak on me, Jonno Carpana. You tramp around like a boar."

He waded out of the shallows and onto the bank, where he shook a hand through his bramble of dark hair and wiped off his face.

Jonno was a short, slender, handsome boy of seventeen, the eldest child of the Carpana clan. Unlike Lizzy, he had a playful, foolish, immature nature, and always seemed to be either causing trouble or finding it, much to the chagrin of his father, Yondo.

"You heard me sneaking?" he said on a sour note. He sat on the bank and pulled off one of his boots, spilling out water.

"Saw, too," Lizzy said, smiling tartly.

Jonno looked at the surface of the pond, which now was rough and choppy with the waves he had made. But he could see how the bright morning sun reflected off the water and it occurred to him then that Lizzy had seen him all along. She had played him, and he felt like a fool.

"Not fair," he said, and pulled off his other boot.

"As fair as trying to sneak and throw me in," she replied. "Lucky I don't tell father. He'd tan you good."

"Whatever, gypsy-girl," Jonno said with a snort. He put his boots back on and strapped them tight.

"And you scared the fish. One was about to bite."

Jonno glared at his little sister. She was his sister in name only, not blood. She had come to the family as an infant, when Jonno himself was only three. She had left on the docks by the river-folk, and there were times, like now, when Jonno wished they would have thrown her over the side. Nor was she so little anymore. She was growing like a weed, and if she didn't stop soon, she surely would pass him by. Only fourteen years old and already more than five and a half podes tall. She was as gangly as a skiachtro, but uncommonly fast and athletic. Quite strong, too, for a girl. When games of sport were played, she often matched up with boys her own age and older, and routinely bested them, much to the embarrassment of their fathers.

"Ma said to fetch you," Jonno said, finally getting around to why he had come. "Said it was urgent."

"But I've only got two fish," Lizzy replied.

Jonno shrugged as if he didn't care. "Suit yourself, gypsy-girl. I gave the message, and you heard it."

Lizzy watched as her brother stalked off soaking wet. She didn't much care for getting the best of him, but the last year or so he had become so unkind to her. Her ma had told her it was because of the change a boy goes through, and that soon she would change, too.

"He's becoming a man, and soon you'll become a woman," her ma had explained. "It's part of growing up."

"Dad is a man and he don't act so," Lizzy had replied.

That's when her ma had told her how boys took longer to mature and become men, and how even the well-respected and much-feared Yondo Carpana had acted a fool for a couple of years.

She said everyone had to go through it.

Lizzy hoped her brother would grow out of it soon. She missed the old Jonno, the funny, friendly Jonno, the big brother who used to show her around town, play with her, take care of her, make her laugh.

She returned to the lake's edge and pulled her stake from the ground, lifting from the shallows the two fish she had caught. They wouldn't make for much of a meal, but she could always return later, when the sun was down and the air was cool. Her dad and his mates were presently on a hunt in the southern woods; perhaps they would come across a boar or a pheasant, maybe even a buck.

Should there be such a blessing, Lizzy prayed.

Good meat had been scarce in Hinterland for generations, ever since the Great War had ravaged the land, laying waste to man and beast alike. Dozens of species had been eradicated, and those that had survived had lost many of their numbers. Large game was as rare in Hinterland as an easy day, and while plenty of small game could still be found scurrying about, it was never enough. Sheep were tended for their wool and sometimes their meat, goats were raised for their hides and their milk, and chickens made for a nice dinner, though their eggs were far more valuable than their breasts and thighs. But farmed animals didn't reproduce very well, which made killing them a dangerous prospect. The unwritten law in Vernon was one-for-one: you killed one goat or sheep or chicken from your pen for every one that was birthed. This made hunting and fishing imperative for survival. Farming, too.

In Vernon, one of the largest settlements in Hinterland, potatoes and beets grew best. They could usually count on cabbage, lettuce, tomatoes, and beans, too. Wheat and rye were sporadic; some years they stretched for the sun, while others they barely broke the dirt. Tobacco grew well enough, and they had a smattering of apple, pear, and fig trees that

21

occasionally produced. Patches of grapes and berries showed up in the long summer months, and while most preferred to use them for wine and pies, Lizzy loved eating them off the vine.

Set on the great river, Potami, at one of its widest and deepest points, Vernon had been a fisherman's paradise in the days of old. But the schools of spinners and sharps that once had populated its warm waters had all but disappeared, leaving nets empty and boats in drydock. Another painful and unfortunate consequence of the Great War.

The Carpana's were better off than most when it came to food. Lizzy's ma, Gabriella, baked tasty breads and pies, and they had three sheep, six goats, and a dozen chickens in their barn. They also had a large garden on their land and two fig trees. There were several ponds to the east of them, and a lazy stream that ambled along the eastern and southern edge of their property. They were blessed. But nothing satisfied the belly quite the same way as a chunk of fresh-roasted boar meat.

For now the fish would have to do. It was a scant catch, but some was better than none, and her ma had ways of making the most of things.

That in mind, Lizzy slung her trawl pole over her shoulder, picked up her stake and bucket, and started for home.


Yondo Carpana was a Herder, an honored Voukolos in the town of Vernon, as liked and respected as any. He had dark brown eyes and dark brown skin, and kept a trim beard on his slim but handsome face. His brow was as flat as a creek stone, his hair black and thick.

Like most in Hinterland, he toiled day and night, working hard to keep a roof over his family's head and food on their table. That was when he wasn't walking the desert, escorting the souls of the departed across the red waste that separated Vernon from the Great Stone Temple. These difficult labors had left him with a lean, powerful build, with rope-like muscles and a straight back. He wasn't that tall, but that didn't make him any less formidable. Jonno was already as tall as his father, and it looked as though Lizzy soon would pass both of them by, yet very few in Vernon ever thought to challenge the Herder. He was fierce, whip-fast, and knew how to fight. The few times that men larger than him had tried him, they had woken up wishing they hadn't.

Gabby was his woman, the matron of the family. Short and thin, kind and smart, she and Yondo were very much in love and made for a good pair. She was a true beauty, with smooth olive skin, straight black hair that hung to her breasts, and narrow eyes the color of coal-ash. She was a good mother to their children, teaching them how to read and write, work and think, and she was a good wife to Yondo.

They had three children.

Jonaton Lee, tabbed Jonno, after Gabby's grandfather, was the eldest. He had dark skin, only a shade lighter than his father's, dark eyes, and full lips. He was intelligent, good-looking, athletic, but he had a loose tongue, a careless attitude, and a propensity for mischief. Yondo wanted the boy to be tougher, more serious, more focused, because that's what made for a good man and trusted Herder. If Jonno could not become these things, if he failed to become a Herder and live up to his father's example, it would be an embarrassment to the family name.

Lizzy was the middle child in age. Gabby and Yondo had been trying to add to their family for more than to two years when a strange, pale, orphan girl was unexpectedly brought to their door on a stormy Spring night. They had accepted her completely and without hesitation, believing her to be a gift from the Angeloi. They gave her the name Elizabeth Layne, and Gabby doted on her like a mother hen.

Lastly, there was Dalla, the baby of the family. She, too, had dark skin, dark eyes, and dark, brambly hair, just like her brother and father. Dalla had been considered a miracle at the time of her birth, which occurred close to eight years after Lizzy had been gifted to them. It was a difficult pregnancy for Gabby, and the girl was born a full moon early. But both mother and baby survived, and Dalla showed no ill-effects. She was a happy, healthy kid of six years, with great depths of curiosity and a smile that lit up her face.

That was the Carpana clan in full, and though Lizzy was not blood, a truth anyone could see just by looking at her (she had pale skin, gray eyes, long brown hair), they treated her as nothing less. She had their name, and she had their love.

What Yondo had was news that would affect the whole family: a spot on the next trek had opened up and Jonno was going to get his chance. He was grown enough to travel the desert, so long as he was properly supervised, and by age he was the next in line. If pressed, Yondo would have said the boy needed more time, more training, more mettle, but Dock's son, David, who usually went with them, had an injured foot and could not walk.

Yondo made the announcement at dinner, and Jonno pounded a fist on the table and shouted out jubilantly, excited to finally be getting a chance to walk the desert with his father. It was a dream come true for him.

Gabby, on the other hand, was not pleased. "He's just a boy," she said. "The desert is no place for a boy."

"He's seventeen and grown," Yondo replied. "And he won't be alone. Dock and I will be with him."

"He's too young," Gabby protested. "There are demons and lakas and wild creatures in the desert."

"I'll be fine," said Jonno, a clear note of teenage exasperation in his voice. "I'm not a child so don't treat me as one."

"Don't sass your mother," Yondo told his boy. "That's not how you prove yourself a man."

Gabby looked at her boy, then she looked at her husband. "Yon?" There was an imploring tone to her voice, highlighted by a mother's worry. She wore the look, too.

Yondo understood her concern; he was concerned, too. Jonno may have been a man by law but he was yet a boy in manner, and the desert was no place for a boy. But time passed, and times had changed. No matter the danger, they needed more men in the desert. Though he had always told Gabby that they would make all decisions concerning their children together, Yondo understood it was ultimately his call. In the Hinterlands, fathers decided the fates of their sons, as mothers decided the fates of their daughters.

Jonno was young, sure, but Herders started young. Yondo himself had started when he was only sixteen. He said this to Gabby, and then added, "David is eighteen and has been out a dozen times already. That is the way, and there's no stopping it."

"And what of us?" Gabby said as Dalla and Lizzy silently observed. "You're comfortable leaving three women alone?"

Yondo smiled kindly at her. "The three of you are hardly helpless. And there are menfolk about should you need them."

"What of vandal attacks?"

"There's never been a vandal attack in Vernon."

"And there were none never in the desert ... until there were."

Yondo sighed. "I know," he said. "But the extra coin will help, and it's eventual. If not this time, it'll be next time, or the time after that. And the vandals don't harm, only steal."

"I never wanted him to be a Herder."

"Mom!" Jonno cried out petulantly. "It's what *I* want."

Yondo shot his boy a disapproving look. "Jonno," he said, "you and your sisters go out. I need to talk to your ma alone."

"But father," Jonno whined.

"Now!" Yondo said, and there was nothing in his tone that suggested he was interested in having a debate.

Jonno got up without another word and skulked away.

Lizzy looked at her mother and said, "What of the table?"

"It'll be here when you return," Gabby said to her.

Lizzy nodded obediently and took her little sister's hand. "Come, Dalla," she said. "We'll make a fire for the night."

Dalla smiled happily and went with her big sister.

When the kids were gone, Yondo got up and walked around the table, to where Gabby was sitting. He put his hands on her shoulders and began massaging them in a loving, reassuring way.

"You don't think I know your ways, Yon," she said to him, but made no move to stop him. "It'll take more than this to change my mind."

"You're upset. This relaxes you when you're upset, does it not?"

She said nothing. It felt good.

"You can't protect him forever, Gabriella," Yondo said to her

"Ha!" she snorted. "I can damn well try."

"I'm going to be with him. He's not going to be alone."

"The Kin is in the desert. You said they've been more active lately."

"Aye. But they're thwarted easily enough with the old words."

"What of lakas and yenas? Fanny said Sev used to have nightmares about lakas. Vena says Winston has them still."

Yondo went, "Mmmmm," as if agreeing, though for him it was more about understanding her concerns than agreeing with them. He had had nightmares himself when he was a young Herder, though mostly about the Kin, those evil black ghosts that haunted the sandy waste betwixt Vernon and the Great Stone Temple. The desert was hard ground to walk, but when you knew what you were up against it made things a lot easier. And no one knew better than Yondo Carpana.

Instead of telling her that, he said, "He's going to start sometime. He's been training hard. It's inevitable."

"I didn't want this for him, Yon. Not the life of a Herder. It's too dangerous." There was genuine fear in Gabby's voice, the untamable fear of a mother. "Every time you go I worry that you're not going to come back, and now I have to worry on Jonno, too."

"Don't I always come back," Yondo said.

"He could be a Smith or a Tanner. He could work on Mecklan's farm."

"A common hand?" Yondo snorted. "No. Nor a Tanner. I am a Herder and he is my boy. He shall be one, too."

Gabby looked back over her shoulder at him. "It's not the life for Jonno," she said. "You know it as sure as I."

"We won't know for certain until he's out there," Yondo said, even though part of him believed his wife was right. Jonno was a good kid, a smart kid, a strong kid, but he lacked common sense and character. He wasn't serious enough, and wasn't steady under pressure.

Yondo attributed most of that to the winds of youth, remembering well that he had hardly been perfect at that age. Time, the desert, and life in the Hinterlands would eventually harden Jonno, he believed. He was hoping that an actual trek in the desert might get that started.

"I'll be with him, and Dock'll be there, too. And if it's too much too fast, he can set out until he's older. But it's time to find out."

Gabby let out a sigh of defeat. It was over, and she had lost. She had voiced her opinion and concerns, but Yondo had made up his mind. A boy was his father's responsibility, as Dalla and Lizzy would be hers. She would decide when they were ready to work and ready to marry; she would even have a say in who they married. But Jonno's fate lay in Yondo's hands, and Yondo was a Herder. In Hinterland, that meant Jonno would be a Herder, too. It was the way.

"You'll watch him close?" she said. "Night and day?"

"Of course," said Yondo, still massaging her shoulders. "He's our boy."

"When do you leave?"

"Two days from now. On the morn."

"Two days? So soon? The last Herders to leave aren't back yet."

"They're do back any day. And a new consignment came this morning. We go when they come in."

"But two days?" Like a true Herder's wife, Gabby started thinking practically. "I need to bake bread and make more jerky. And you'll need extra water from the well, and another pack and bunk."

Yondo said he was aware. "There'll be time for that tomorrow," he told her. "Tonight we should take comfort." He bent over and kissed her neck, and she sighed again, deeper this time. "Only two nights together before I'm gone a moon." He kissed her neck again. "What I need is my woman."

Gabby smiled blissfully. With her eyes closed, she leaned back, tilted her head up, and waited for him to kiss her proper. He did, and she kissed him back.

**Four:**

Peck raised his bow and focused his aim as the first snow of the year fell in heavy clumps. It was hard to see more than thirty or forty steps in this weather, but the wapiti stood out like a fire in the night. It stood five podes high, and its massive crown rose up another two. Peck had seen stags this big before, but his father or his uncle had always taken them. The shot had to be perfect.

"Aim for the heart," his father, Loman, whispered to him. "Wait 'til it turns to the side. The shot'll be clean."

Peck knew that already, but said, "Yes, father," all the same. And he waited for what felt like an eternity, his bow raised, the string pulled back to its tensest point.

He was only fifteen in years, but he was strong enough for the hunt; he was strong enough to hold the bow steady for another five minutes, if that's what it took.

Peck was tall for his age, with broad shoulders, long arms, large hands. He surely would grow to be a big man someday, over six podes if he was anything like his father and uncle. Curly brown hair crowned his head and his upper lip had begun to develop the slightest hint of a mustache, but his cheeks and chin were still perfectly smooth. He could not wait for the day when he could grow a full beard. In the northern territories of Boreal, a beard was a sign of virility and strength. Most men, including his father and uncle, had one.

"Be still. It senses us," whispered Titus, Peck's uncle. With his smooth mahogany skin, dark brown eyes, full beard, and stalks of wild brown hair, he looked so much like his big brother that some thought them twins. They were the exact same height and build, too. The only real difference between them was three years of wear and tear ... and a missing tooth. Loman had had a bottom incisor knocked out in a fight when he was yet young and wild.

Peck nodded to let his uncle know that he understood.

The wapiti lifted its massive head and looked around. The trees, mostly pines and cedars, were thick in this part of the forest. The sky above was a dark, endless gray that blotted out the sun.

The snow had only been falling for a short time but already the ground was covered. Leaves and limbs were coated white, giving the scene a dream-like mood.

The good news was that there was no wind.

Everything was silent. It was as if the snow had suffocated all sound.

Peck waited patiently, his eyes tracing what would be the arrow's flight. The wapiti dipped its head again and started grazing, eating what little grass it could find.

Loman tapped his boy on the shoulder. "Be ready. It's going to move."

Peck nodded once, keeping his aim straight. A few seconds later his patience was rewarded when the wapiti turned to the side, presenting him a clear shot. He did not hesitate.

The arrow zipped between the trees and through the snow, making not a sound until it pierced the hide of its target. The wapiti let out an agonizing howl and took off on a dash, bounding through the forest in a mad panic, not realizing that it was already dead.

Loman and Peck darted off after it. Following the trail of blood in the snow, they found it a short time later, lying on its side under one of the many skyscraping pines that populated the Great Northern Wood. It was yet alive, though just barely. Every snorted breath it took marked itself in the air. Loman pulled a knife from his belt and handed it to his boy.

Peck didn't care for this part. The killing he didn't mind; he'd taken the lives of countless hares, marmots, polecats, and beyos; he'd even killed a few small stags and boars in his time. But with them the arrow had always done the work. It was easy that way. The animals were dead by the time he found them and all he had to do was gut and skin a corpse.

This was different. Usually the blood he got on his hands was cold; today it would be warm. A pool of it under the wapiti's front legs had already melted through the snow. The striking difference in color – the virgin white of the snow and the primal red of the beast's blood – caught Peck's eye and made him think about the wisp-thin threads between life and death. Here one moment, gone the next.

This was part of the hunt, and his father was waiting.

The animal let out an anguished grunt; the sound of life coming to an end. It tried to move, but didn't have the strength.

"Do it," Loman told his boy. "It's time."

Peck moved forward reverentially, his father's silver blade glistening in the snowy forest. He knelt down beside the wapiti and laid a gentle hand on its stomach. "Easy there," he said to it when it snorted and tried to buck. "Easy now."

"It's suffering," Loman said. "Do it. It's mercy."

Peck looked the great beast in the eye, as his uncle and father had taught him, because it showed respect, respect for life and for death, and in the depths of those big black animal eyes he saw its spirit depart ... and he saw, in a blurred reflection that etched itself in his mind, the length of his own life and how he would die. It was a vision he had had before.

He then thrust the knife into the side of the wapiti's neck and yanked it across, severing its main artery, taking its flesh for good. The beast stirred and let out a muffled, guttural yowl, then died still and silent in the snow under the pines.

Loman placed a hand on his boy's shoulder and said, "A good kill."

Peck said nothing, only nodded. He was consumed by the warmth and oily richness of the animal's blood, which filled the air around them with a subtle metallic scent and stained his hands from finger to palm.

He stared at his hands for a long moment, marveling at the violent color of the blood, then wiped them on his pants and stood.

"Won't be easy lugging this beast back to camp," Loman said. "But worth it." He gestured for his knife.

Peck wiped the blade on the sleeve of his shirt, so that now both his shirt and his pants were marked by the kill, and handed it back to his father, who began the arduous chore of gutting the animal.

They camped at the western edge of the Great Northern Wood, in the cover of a strange outcropping of rocks and tangled hedges. It was where they normally camped on their way home from a hunt. The heart of the Great Northern Wood was a four-day trek from their village, and the outcropping marked a halfway point.

They had just finished dinner, and their fire was burning low. Loman and Titus were smoking tobacco, their bootless feet kicked up after a long day on the trail.

Titus said to his nephew, "Fetch some more wood from the pile, boy, and throw it on."

Peck did as he was told. He brought back an armful of the branches and twigs he had gathered before dinner and dropped them on the ground. He then picked up a couple of the bigger pieces and began carefully placing them in the flames. The fire welcomed the sacrifice with a hiss, growing stronger and brighter.

Peck picked up the iron prod they used to stir the fire and poked at the charred wood, moving some of the larger pieces around to let more air circulate. The fire crackled, and a wild scatter of orange embers surged upward, rising high into the blackness of the night. Peck idly followed their ascent, but then his eyes moved to a patch of stars in the heavens.

"Ever wonder what's up there?" he said.

Titus looked at his nephew, and followed his gaze upward. "Nope," he said. "Got plenty worries here on the ground, boy. Don't need to worry myself with lights in the sky."

Peck stabbed the iron prod into the earth and took a seat. He had eaten his share and now could feel the weight of sleep pushing down on him, made all the heavier by the warmth of the fire. "Dad?" he said.

Loman glanced at his boy. "Yeah?"

"What happens to animals when they die?"

Skepticism twisted Loman's face, which glowed golden in the firelight. "Animals?" he said, and turned to his brother.

Titus smiled, and then laughed. Loman laughed, too.

Peck felt stupid for having asked the question, but the thought had been on his mind ever since he had taken the wapiti's life. The stain of the beast's blood was still on his hands and the rich iron smell of that blood yet haunted his nose. He had eaten its flesh, as was the custom, but only after he'd had his uncle cook all the taste from it.

"You think too much on things that matter not," Loman said. He had yet to get used to his son's strange way of looking at the world, and often he wondered if it meant the boy was cracked.

Peck was an unusual child – there was no way of getting around that. He had been so ever since his mother and two sisters were slaughtered in the most savage way. Almost nine years had passed since then, but it was clear to see the boy had yet to fully recover. He had been there that night, had seen it happen, and though there was nothing he could have done to stop it, he yet bore the weight of guilt.

"I think I saw the wapiti's spirit leave its body," Peck told his father and uncle. "It trembled, and vanished."

Titus and Loman exchanged a look, and Titus said, "Aye, might be you did. Everything has a spirit, and the hand of death takes all sooner or later, man and beast alike. But it's nothing to fear or worry on."

Peck said, "I don't fear death, uncle. It's life I fear."

Loman puffed on his pipe. He loved his boy dearly and had always done everything he could to provide for him and keep him safe, but damn if the kid wasn't off the edge. Peck constantly asked questions about death and what happened to people after they died, and he wanted to go to the desert and see lakas and demons. He was fascinated by tales of the Kin and took every opportunity to soak up knowledge on the occult.

Loman understood this likely had to do with him having witnessed the murders of his mother and sisters. Only six at the time, it had proven to be too much for him. He had had terrible nightmares for years; he had them still, from time to time, screaming in his sleep.

He had referred to the savages who had committed the acts as, 'Blood Creatures,' describing them as four men with scarred, crimson faces and empty gray eyes. They had come when Loman and Titus were on the autumn moon hunt with the other menfolk in the village. A posse caught up with them ten days later on the skirts of Boreal, near the northernmost border of Vernon. When found, the men were naked, disheveled, and confused. They kept talking about being cold inside, and claimed they had no memory of the attack.

They couldn't even give their own names when asked.

At trial, Peck bravely identified them as the assailants, but also made note that they were different. Their faces were different and their eyes were different. Gone were the awful scars and the dark red tint of their skin, and their eyes were normal colors, not the cold dead color of stone.

The men were convicted and sentenced to death. Because he was the husband and father of the slain, Loman got to choose the manner of punishment, as was the way. He decided the men should be beaten to death, and on a cold, rainy morn in the middle of the autumn moons, the four men who had raped and murdered the women of the Lett clan were savagely beaten with clubs.

Peck had been given permission to watch the execution but had chosen not to. Loman and Titus had gladly participated, taking out their pain on those who had caused it.

"An animal's spirit goes where it goes," Loman told his boy.

"And our spirits?" Peck inquired. It was not the first time he had asked this question, and he was determined to keep asking it until he got an answer that satisfied him.

"Someplace better," Loman said to him between puffs. "Now sleep."

Peck nodded and laid back. That was the stock answer, the same one he got all the time, yet he could not accept it. No one ever gave it a name, this someplace better, and if a place didn't have a name, then it didn't really exist.

"You shouldn't think of death when you have life," Titus told his nephew. "It's bad luck."

Luck was something else that Peck didn't believe in. Things happened, bad and good, and most of the time, from what he could tell, there was no sense to any of it.

The wapiti he had killed had walked the forest in the morning, and in the evening it had been his dinner. Nine years ago, on the morn of the first full moon of autumn, his mother and sisters had baked bread and pies. And later that evening, soon after the sun had set, savages broke into their hut and murdered them.

What did luck or fate have to do with that?

Peck had no idea.

**Five:**

The silhouette of the tallest building in Vernon filtered through the dull gray distance, slowly becoming real. This filled Aglan with hope.

He and Largo had been walking wounded for three days now, leaning on each other for balance and support. They walked at night mostly, when it was cooler, and twice had survived laka attacks. Thankfully, the mindless creatures were unarmed and moved deliberately. Largo had been scratched by one but as yet showed no signs of turning to dust.

"Look. There," Aglan said, pointing ahead. The steeple of the church stood out against the dusky desert sky, evoking a call to faith. Next to it, the block outline of Sana's Saloon took shape, evoking a different call. Everyone in Vernon worshipped at one or the other; many at both. "We're almost home, friend."

Largo was in far worse condition than Aglan. He had taken two bolts from a crossbow: one in the leg and one in the shoulder. That had been fifteen or sixteen days ago, on their way to the Temple, carrying 119 living stones. The yena attack had happened three nights ago, on their way home, and they had been very fortunate to survive. Both of them had sustained several bites and gashes in their battle with the wild dogs, and again Largo had gotten the worst of it.

A well-built man with a strong back and sturdy legs, he currently was dragging bone across the hard desert floor, one leg pulling the other along, his odd stride marked by single footsteps and a long, jagged trail. His sandy blonde hair lay flat on his head and the straggly hairs of his beard were caked with sweat and blood and grit. He looked ready for a funeral pyre.

"We're almost there," Aglan said to him, hoping to inspire a strong kick to the finish. He had thought they would never make it, yet here they were, no more than two miles from home.

"Water," Largo croaked. "I need a drink." He barely had any voice left. He barely had enough strength to speak.

Aglan stopped, pulled their canteen from his pack, and shook it. There were perhaps three or four swallows left, and they would be piss-warm.

"Sip," he told his friend. "We have to make it last."

The sun had set an hour before, yet a faint reddish hue still clung to the horizon, lending a small amount of light to the eye. Darkness would come quickly, and the cold with it. And with darkness would come danger. They didn't have to worry about lakas this close to town; the nightwalkers lived deep in the desertlands, among the rocks and caves, and they roamed free in the blowing sands of the Dustbowl, where they seemed to come out of nowhere to attack. Closer to town, though, where the desert gave way to more fertile land, their numbers were few.

At night, this close to town, yenas would be the bigger problem.

Lakas didn't eat food; they seemed to exist on the dust and dirt of the desert. But yenas, like all beasts, needed food to survive, and good food could be found closer to the towns of Meridon and Vernon.

Another yena attack could spell the end for them.

"Only two miles to go," Aglan said after taking a sip of tepid water. He capped the canteen and slung it over his shoulder. "Maybe less."

Largo gasped heavily. His mouth hung open like a busted door and his pale, desert-chapped lips trembled.

He peered into the dying light of dusk, trying and make out Vernon, the town he and Aglan called home. He thought he saw the steeple of the church, but then it vanished.

"Where is ...?" he said, his voice a dry, breathless rasp.

"Don't talk," said Aglan. "Save your energy." He was younger in age than Largo and larger in build. Tall with broad shoulders and thick arms, he was a fine physical specimen. His dark skin and full beard served him well in the desert.

He heaved a shoulder under one of Largo's shoulders and wrapped an arm around his back. "Come," he said, steadying him. "Time is wasting."

"No time," Largo croaked. "No time in the desert. Nothing here but sand and sun and death."

Aglan paid him no mind and began walking for the both of them. He stepped one foot forward and dragged his companion along with the other. It was going to be a long two miles to Vernon. At their current pace, they would not make it there until morning.

At least they were on flat land now. There were no more hills to climb, no more large rocks or sloping dunes to navigate, no coarse shrubs to catch their feet and send them sprawling.

Two miles of hardscrabble lay between them and home.

Two miles of hardscrabble ... and one demon.

The demons that roamed Hinterland had names, but those names were not known by men and women, They thought to call all demons by the same name: Demon. And all of them together were known as Demon Kin.

The demon that found Aglan and Largo slogging through the desert, beaten and bloody and next to dead, was known by some as Mar, and it was as old and powerful a demon as there was in Hinterland. It had been around before time had started and planned on being around long after it ceased. It had broken men into pieces, torn women to shreds, and twisted children into unmanageable knots. It had killed many, both in the flesh and the spirit, and had no thought to stop.

It appeared out of the ether behind the two Herders, unbeknownst to them, and followed behind for a spell, watching them struggle.

This was great theater, and Mar allowed it to go on.

"Can't wait to see my Jena again," Aglan was saying as they stumbled across the hardpan. "She makes a fig pie fit for a king, and after the kids go down for the night, she'll treat me like one."

Largo said, "A good woman is a blessing," in a voice made weak by all the hardship the desert had dealt him over the last thirty days and nights.

"We'll have a bath, her and I, and then ..." Aglan let that sentence stand, allowing his imagination to pick up the thread. He couldn't wait to see his sweet Jena again, and the kids, too.

"Two miles more and you'll get to see your clan," he said, hoping to encourage Largo. "Betty and Lell and Anna. Bet they miss ya, Lar. They need their pop. Put that to your mind."

Largo thought about his kids: Betty was twelve and growing fast; Lell was ten and sure to be a Herder like his old man; Anna was only three, but already she looked so much like her ma.

Largo thought lovingly of his late wife. Lulu had passed a couple years back, shortly after giving birth to Anna. She had wasted away to nothing from a fever that would not to break. He missed her deeply.

He thought about leaving his kids alone in the world, leaving them without a father or a mother to lean on. He expected to die soon, before making it home, and the idea of his kids being orphaned put an ache in his heart. He felt he only had a few more breaths left in him. He was cold and exhausted, and he couldn't feel his legs anymore. Worse yet, his vision had all but forsaken him, leaving him nearly blind. He couldn't see Vernon for nothing; all he could see was a barren, colorless expanse that seemingly went on forever, or didn't exist at all.

"My little ones," he said, scratching out every word. "My kiddies."

"You'll see them again," Aglan said to him. "Worry not, we're almost there. I can see the steeple. Sana's place, too. Good ol' Sana and her sallies. They'll be pleased to see you."

"I need you ... I ... You have to promise ..."

Those few simple words stole Largo's wind, leaving him red-faced and wheezing. He staggered forward and almost fell, and Aglan nearly went down with him.

"Easy, Largo. Easy now. A little longer, brother. We're almost there."

Despite his size and strength, Aglan had begun to flag. He had done most of the work the last couple days and the effort had taken a toll. He didn't know how much longer he could drag Largo and maintain his stamina, and he wondered if it might not be better to leave him and return with help. "Look," he began, about to suggest that very idea.

He never got the chance, though, as Mar, having seen enough, finally spoke. "You know," said the demon, startling both of them, "I wouldn't do that if I were you. An idea, sure, but not a wise one. The desert is no place for the wounded and weak."

They turned around together, their weary bodies advancing in the slow, juddering, awkward movements of marionettes. Largo's left foot clipped a rock and he lurched from Aglan's grasp and crumbled to the ground. A feeble groan escaped him, and he rolled over on his back.

Aglan regained his balance after a wobbly step and turned his attention to the dark figure before them.

"Yenas in these parts will look to make a meal of him," said the demon. "A feast of flesh and bone and blood."

"Demon!" Aglan cried out, drawing the short-blade from his belt. The vandals had taken everything else, leaving him and Largo with barely enough to protect themselves.

The demon laughed at the ridiculous show. "What do you plan to do with that, Voukulos," it said, and vanished. A moment later it reappeared behind him. "And now?" it added mockingly.

Aglan wheeled around, his sword still drawn. He knew it was useless against the dark spirit, but instinct was hard to ignore.

On the ground, Largo gasped for air.

"Set it down and we'll talk," the demon said, its ghostly body wavering elusively. The effect was hypnotic, and Aglan, wide-eyed and shaky with exhaustion, grudgingly obliged.

"Time to deal, Voukolos, you think? No point dying to yenas little more than two miles from home."

"We're not striking a deal with a demon," Aglan shot back. "No how."

"Rather die than live? Jena and her bath not worth the price? Sounds like you might think to reconsider."

Aglan shook his head defiantly. "No! Go from us, demon. Be gone! Or I shall mouth the words of old."

A sinister laugh came from the demon. "Deal or die," it said.

"I would rather die."

There was a moment of silence, and the demon's eyes flashed. "Have your way, while you can, Voukolos." Its eyes flashed again, and Aglan instinctively looked over his shoulder. In the distance he saw movement, the low, fast, purposeful movement of a pack of yenas on the hunt. Their eyes glowed pale gray in the dark and their paws kicked up sand. They were coming hard and fast, and all that Aglan had to fight them off with was a small blade and a badly wounded friend.

"Easy to think on it," the demon said with a hiss. "One thing to die, Voukolos, another to be eaten."

They could not survive a pack of yenas. Neither of them would survive. Largo's death would be mercy, but Aglan knew that he would suffer. He would be gnashed to the bone and eaten like a scrawny polecat. That was no way for a Herder to die.

Then the demon said, "Aye, it is done, and wisely," and its eyes flashed yellow again. Its smoky essence vanished in the night.

"What's done?" Aglan shouted, not understanding. "Hey! Demon!" But his voice was heard only by Largo and the charging yenas. He peered through the darkness at the coming attack and readied his blade for battle.

"Largo?" he said, calling to his friend. "Can you stand and fight? Yenas are coming. We need be strong."

He watched, somewhat astounded, as his severely-wounded friend worked himself to his feet. A testament to the will and character of a true Herder. The desert was no place for someone keen to quit, and Largo was as tough as any in the ranks. "Here, take this," Aglan said to him, handing over his short-blade. "I'm in a better way. Give me your dagger. I can fight yenas well enough with it."

Largo took hold of the small blade. The steel was coated in dirt and dust, hair and blood, the remnants of a disastrous trek through the desertlands. The blade was chipped in places, and part of the hilt was broken.

"Quickly. Your dagger," Aglan said, gesturing frantically. "They're closing on us."

Largo showed his friend an unnerving smile void of humanity. Then, as fast as a snake, he pulled his dagger from its sheath and plunged it in Aglan's heart.

Pain and shock twisted Aglan's face, making him an ugly sight. Blood spurted from the wound when Largo pulled the dagger free, and the Herder's knees buckled. He went down in a heap, and gapingly mouthed, "But ... I ... I ..." The rest of his message was drowned in blood, and he gurgled his last breaths.

Largo wiped the dagger on his pants and re-sheathed it. He pulled the scabbard from Aglan's belt, attached it to his belt, and slid the short-blade inside. Noticing the canteen on the ground, he grabbed it, unscrewed the cap, drank what was left, and dropped it next to his fallen friend. He then sniffed and looked out at the desert.

The yenas were close; no more than thirty strides away. They were moving steadily, driven by the unremitting single-mindedness of the hunt. Soon they would fan out and circle their prey, and then they would gradually contract that circle until they were close enough to begin their well-choreographed attack.

Only tonight no attack would be needed. Dinner had already been served. Aglan was a big man with good muscle; the yenas would get their fill and most likely go to bed with meat still on the bone.

Largo gazed out at the night. It was fully dark now. The dim lights of Vernon could be seen in the distance.

He started walking.

Largo Kelsman made it to town a short time later, before the moon was at its zenith. He had heard the yenas start on Aglan's corpse and had turned around to watch them feed. They had ravenously ripped at the Herder's dead body, taking out chunks of flesh, chewing it with their heads down and their hackles up. A couple of the wild desert dogs had glanced up at him between bites, their eyes glowing grayish-white in the dark, but not one of them had thought to move on him. He was protected now.

The square was empty when Largo staggered in on weary legs, but the lights at Sana's were still bright, and the sounds of music and merriment could be heard within.

He dragged himself up the plank steps of the saloon, pushed through the batwing doors, and stood there, looking around aimlessly, a mangled, filthy mess painted in blood and dirt.

The first words burst out of Linny the liar, one of the younger sallies that trolled the floorboards at Sana's infamous saloon. She always watched the door for incoming customers, anxious to greet anyone who might have a few spare coins in their pocket.

She saw Largo and let out a scream that stopped the music and turned all attention on the Herder.

Morris, the town doctor, stood from his stool and took a couple of clumsy steps forward. "Largo?" he said questioningly. "You okay?"

Every eye in the place was fixed on the Herder, all of them watching him as he stood there with a blank face, not saying anything at all and slightly tottering back and forth. Then he collapsed.

Doc Morris, a rapidly-aging man with a rapidly-expanding midsection, rushed to his side and checked his pulse. "He's alive," he called out. Then he said to the men close by, "Help me get him to my place. He needs attention."

Four men helped carry Largo Kelsman out of the saloon and across the square to Doc Morris' office, while a crowd of onlookers followed behind, chattering incessantly in hushed tones. The name Aglan was mentioned more than once.

"You need help, Doc?" asked someone from the crowd.

"Yes. Go and fetch me Lona," Doc Morris replied. "And hurry."

The four men carried Largo inside and carefully lowered his limp body onto the doctor's table, taking care not to touch or bump any of his wounds. The Herder didn't move, and one of the men, Aron, asked if he was dead.

"Hardly," said Doc Morris as he went for the tools of his trade. "He's breathing and his blood is pumping."

Though Largo looked three-days dead, his chest continued to rise and fall at a steady pace, indicating life, and blood continued to seep from his many wounds. The men stood around and watched as Doc Morris began cutting free Largo's tattered clothes.

"On all the souls of the dead!" one of the men exclaimed when he saw the damage that had been caused by one of the crossbow bolts the Herder had been shot with. The wound was charcoal gray in the center with an angry red welt the size of a fist around it.

Another said, "Ain't never seen nothing like that before."

"You should leave," Doc Morris told them. "Go on now. Go get Lona.

I'll need her."

The men gladly left, and Doc Morris got back to work, cutting away the clothes that Largo wore. He noticed two crossbow bolt wounds, a couple nasty gashes from either swords or knives, and numerous bites and scratches from yenas.

"Just what did you get yourself into?" Doc Morris said aloud. "You've been torn to shreds."

He went to the table where he kept his surgical instruments and picked up two cutting blades, a pair of pinchers, a long, flat, dull object called a presser, and bandages. Next, he moved to his desk, opened the bottom drawer, and pulled out the bottle of shine he kept there for emergencies. He found a glass, filled it almost half way, and dropped the blades and pinchers in. Then he took a good long swig of the foul liquor, wincing at the taste of it.

It was then his daughter, Lona, arrived. She was yet young and demure, and the sight of Largo's naked manhood made her blush and look away, more so than all the blood and wounds did. She was nineteen years of age and had yet to be promised, though there had been many offers made for her. Her long blonde hair and blue eyes were a draw, as was her womanly figure. But she was Doc's first and favorite child, and he could not bear to let her go.

She was too good for the practice.

"Father?" she said, hesitantly stepping into the room.

"No time for modesty, girl," he told her. "This man is dying. Some of his wounds look infected. We need to work fast."

Lona never had to be told anything twice. Up close, she could smell the liquor on her father's breath, but that wasn't anything new. He drank often, and heavily. It would be her hands that were steady, and she didn't flinch when he handed her the cutting blade.

"You cut exactly where and how I say, girl. You hear?"

"Yes, father," she replied, bristling with excitement.

She loved doctoring, especially operating, and lately she'd been getting more opportunities to practice. Her father was getting up in age, and one day soon the office would be hers. Some of the women in town already asked for her when they came in.

"Here," Doc Morris said, pointing a sausage-like finger at the wound on Largo's chest. "Cut two inches worth on either side. Half an inch deep. Don't be afraid to push down."

41

Lona did as told with clear eyes and hands as steady as stone. The incision she made was perfect, and with a quick tug she removed what was left of the bolt. She then meticulously went about cleaning, sterilizing, stitching, and bandaging the wound. From there, she tended to the gash on his leg before moving on to the many bites he had sustained.

Largo didn't stir once during the entire procedure, which lasted well into the night. He just lied there, as still and silent as the table itself.

When Lona was done, Doc Morris handed her the bottle of shine. "For your nerves, girl," he told her.

"My nerves are fine," she replied, handing it back to him.

"Suit yourself." He tilted the bottle and took a couple glugs.

Lona, meanwhile, retrieved a sheet from the cupboard and covered Largo's naked body. And she stayed by his side until the morn, routinely checking his pulse and his breathing, making sure his condition remained stable, while her father snored loudly at his desk, passed-out drunk.

## Six:

Largo slept until late morning the next day. When he woke, he gave a fractured account of what had happened to him and Aglan in the desert, speaking vaguely about the vandal ambush near Domboll, the laka attack on the plains, and the yenas that finally had finished off his valiant partner.

"He saved my life ten times," Largo said. "He was a true Voukulos."

Though some of his story was garbled and there was much he could not account for, the Elders saw no reason to doubt him. Largo Kelsman was known as a good man and trusted Herder, and it was obvious he had endured quite enough already.

The other Herders were angry, and many of them swore revenge on the vandals. Lakas were mindless creatures, unaware of their desires and actions, while yenas were animals driven by a primal need to survive. It made no sense to seek revenge on creatures such as that. But the vandals? They were men, made of the same flesh and bone, beholden to the same basic principles of life. Surviving the desert was hard enough without having to worry about being attacked by your own kind.

By Largo's word, the vandals had taken eighteen of the ninety-one disembodied souls the Herders had been carrying and most of their weapons and supplies. Weapons and supplies had value in Hinterland, but not the souls of the dead. What the vandals wanted with them the Herders had no idea. But those on the Council of Elders assumed the worst, which meant Kin.

Comprised of thirteen revered members of the community, one each from the eleven respected guilds in the town of Vernon – Smith, Farmer, Herder, Lawman, Doctor, Presbyter, Miner, Craftsman, Judge, Mason, Tanner – and two appointed adjuncts, the Council of Elders made the laws and governed the land, and their word was final.

An emergency meeting was called by the Herders because something had to be done. Another trek was due to start, a big one, and they didn't want to take any chances or lose any more people.

As one of the most respected Herders in Vernon, Yondo Carpana was looked to for answers. His reputation gave his words weight, and before the Council of Elders he spoke them with passion and intelligence.

"Vandal attacks cannot be taken lightly," he said in his deep baritone voice. "These thieves from Meridon are stealing not only steel but stones and stragglers. We cannot let that stand."

There was a general air of agreement from the other Herders.

Yondo continued.

"But violence is not the answer. Revenge serves no one but the Void. I believe we need send an envoy to Meridon to see if a truce can be arranged. The loss of life cannot be tolerated, and the theft of souls is a serious crime. Those responsible must be made to stand trial and suffer consequences. Perhaps a reward can be offered for the capture of these raiders. Meridon is in distress. An offer of gold could persuade them."

Esai, a former Herder with an unblemished record of service, stood and cleared his throat. He had retired from service years ago and now was one of the Adjunct Elders on the Council. With his soft belly, sparse red hair, and spotty beard, he didn't look like much, but there had been a day when he was one of the fiercest Herders in the ranks.

"Yondo speaks well," he began, his voice quiet but clear, "but I'm afraid we're past such measures. This is now the sixth attack. We cannot suffer another one. The Kin we know. They haunt the caves and roam the desert. They have magic and cunning, and sadly some folk fall for their charm. Meridon is a sad testament to that. The land and water there have lost life, and the folk remaining have become criminals and fiends. An envoy would be a waste of time, I believe. They have no order there, no reason, no respect, no law. They no longer have a court or council. You all know me. I am not a man of violence. But they must be stopped."

"We can switch our route, change our schedule, go in larger groups," suggested Rone Evers, another experienced Herder. Due to his bad knees and advanced age he no longer walked the desert, though he was more than ready to strap on his boots again for this matter. "We can walk at night, pitch camp in the day. We've done so before."

"I say we *must* strike back," said Esai. "And soon. Inaction makes us look weak, and weakness will always be preyed on."

"I don't think that wise," replied Olvin. He had been the leader of one of the treks that had suffered a similar fate, going back almost a year. They had been ambushed at night near the mounts and had had no choice but to give their attackers what they demanded. Food, steal, and medicine had been taken that evening; two stragglers and eleven stones, too.

"One of ours is dead," Esai reminded everyone. "We must respond, and we must do so decisively."

Lester, the Elder of the Smiths, stood to speak. He was an older man of great thickness, with a heavy beard and strong hands. He served violence, and it was violence he wanted done. "I don't make blades for them to swing," he said, his voice jarringly loud. "They have stolen our steel, *my* steel, *steel* I have sweated over, *steel* I have poured my heart into, and I want them punished for it."

Jeb, the Elder of the Miners, the richest faction in all of Hinterland, had a different mind. "I understand Lester's anger," he said politely, "but the theft of goods, no matter what they are or what they're worth, can be tolerated. Goods can be replaced. But not the theft of souls and stragglers. That we cannot stand for. Yet we must be wise about how we go about it. We have laws for a reason."

"Who has those souls now?" replied Esai. "I think we know. It's not the vandals from Meridon."

A wave of hushed muttering coursed through the room, and the word 'Kin' touched every ear present. There was no doubt the Kin was behind these attacks, but to what end no one could say. What did demon spirits want with inanimate souls? What could they possibly want with stragglers? They usually could find weak-willed men and women to possess and do their bidding without having to kidnap them. Meridon was proof of that. So why go after the dead from another world?

There had to be something more at work.

"It's not as simple as that," said Yondo, his voice drawing a hush from the crowd. He had yet to be attacked, though he had started to worry about it, especially now that Jonno was set to join the ranks. The vandals were no joke; to a man, they were good with a bow and handy enough with steel, and they lied in wait like serpents. "They use the hills and rocks for cover, and they attack at night, in groups of three and four. They'll not be easy to defeat."

"Then we need to send a group of Herders to greet them," said Horace, another Elder. With his powerful build, wild ginger hair, and bestubbled face, he looked more like a miner or blacksmith than a lawman. But he was Vernon's High-Sheriff, and as such he had no patience for crime. "Esai is correct. Action must be taken or we'll appear weak. I say we find the men responsible, bring 'em back here, and swing 'em on the gallows."

"They're not lakas. They're smart," said Yondo. "If they see numbers not in their favor, they'll disperse."

"Two groups then, of four men each," suggested Dock, one of Yondo's oldest friends. He was a man in his middle age, not yet forty in years but closing fast. Handsome and fit, he had dark brown hair, a thick, bristly mustache, and aqua blue eyes. His skin once had been fair but now was the color of rich leather. The desert had taken care of that. Like Yondo, he was not a big man, but he could fight. He and Yondo had walked the desert together many years, and now their sons were ready to join them. Dock's oldest already had.

"Two groups?" said Daglan with a note of interest. "Tell me how."

"One taking the stones and stragglers," Dock explained, "and another hunting the vandals. Separate paths. Separate agendas."

"You're talking about hunting *men*," said Yondo in a disapproving tone. "That is not our way."

"Nor is it our way to allow violence to go unchecked. One of ours is dead. That is murder."

Yondo seemed surprised by Dock's opinion, but he also understood it. That's what made this dilemma so difficult: there was no singular right answer, only a number of imperfect ones from different perspectives, none of which were likely to work.

Even so, Yondo remained hesitant to agree. Hunting usually led to killing, in his experience, and the prospect of killing men, even thieves and killers, was not something he was keen to do. He made this known to the group.

"I respectfully disagree," said Hamar, the Elder of the Millers and the youngest on the Council. He was a tall, thinly-built man with long blonde hair and a thick mustache. All the women thought him good-looking with his high cheeks and soft blue eyes, with his dimples and pointed chin, and he did his best to give them all a shot. He possessed a deep drawl that slid words together slowly but precisely, in a manner that was easy to listen to, and he laid it out there for those gathered in the hall. "I get that violence mostly leads to more violence, but to do nothing would be dereliction of duty. They've taken stones and they've taken steel, and now one of ours is dead. I say we track 'em, catch 'em, and bring 'em to town." He nodded to Horace. "A hangin' sounds right to me. Been a while since we had one round here."

"I agree," said Lester, and a couple other voices chimed in support.

Esai looked at Yondo and said, "I'm afraid they know not of peace, old friend. If they did, reason and compromise would be the way. They have nothing to lose, and that makes them dangerous. I do not wish violence, either, but the people of Meridon have fallen on hard days. The ones that remain are either strung on flower-root or bent on chaos."

"If we attack, chaos we will give them," Yondo reasoned.

"I'm afraid there's no other way," said Stu, an aging former Herder and the Council's other Adjunct Elder. His bright green eyes were a beautiful sight, even on an old man such as himself. His flat yellow-brown hair, bowed legs, and missing ear not so much.

"No other way," Esai echoed.

Most in the crowd agreed with nods and words of support.

It was then Daglan spoke. No member on the Council held power over any another, but Daglan was the oldest and most respected of the group. He had been a respected Voukolos for many years, before age and aching joints had caught up to him. He had walked the desertlands, had battled demons and lakas, had shepherded countless souls to the Great Stone Temple of the Angeloi. If anyone's opinion mattered, it was his.

"The Kin have roamed the desert forever and always will. They're tricky bastards, relentless and cruel, and have drawn some of our kind away. But mostly we've learned to deal with them. They cannot hurt us physically. They are powerless spirits if we do not let them in. But the vandals *have* let them in. They are men, and men *can* attack us. They can hurt us, and, as we've learned, they have little value for life. The vandals, they've been twisted by the Kin, and what's left of them is madness. If they not be thwarted, they'll only grow stronger and bolder.

"Souls are our charge," Daglan went on, his old but robust voice rising, capturing his audience in full. His glorious white hair and beard gave him the look of a sage or prophet, and that's how many in Vernon viewed him. "They are why we Herders cross the desert. By decree of the Angeloi we were given this charge. How much longer will we be trusted if we lose more? How much longer will the Angeloi show us preference?"

"The Angeloi haven't been seen for generations," said Horace. "Many believe they are gone for good. I am one of them."

"Perhaps," said Daglan. "But that does not give us cause to shuck duty. We are trusted to shepherd souls and stragglers across the desert to the Great Stone Temple. It will always be our duty, and we will always respect that, whether the Angeloi are here or not. And if the vandals of Meridon insist on preventing us from doing our job, if they insist on attacking us and stealing what they have no business stealing, then I say we have no other recourse but to strike them down."

Nodding heads and whispers of agreement filled the room.

But Yondo still could not agree. He abhorred violence, believing it a means that yielded only greater violence. The vandals had attacked them, and now they were preparing to attack the vandals. And then, down the line, the vandals would attack them again. The circle would continue to grow, and every rotation would produce more death.

Many would be sent to the Void before their time and it was all because of the Kin. Yondo was convinced there was a larger, more sinister plan at work, and he believed that striking peace was their best option. He also knew that tempers were high and vengeance was wanted.

"Friends," he said, "I cannot disagree with anything Daglan has said. He is wise and always speaks true to his heart. But if indeed the vandals are doing the bidding of the Kin, and all here surely believe that so, it stands to reason they have the support of Kin. If that's true, they'll not fall for common trickery, and we will fail to flank them, no matter our number. I say we take the vandals a truce and offer them peace. Perhaps we can convince them to turn their backs on the Kin and seek a better way."

"And let them get away with murder?" said Esai, his voice thick with scorn. "Let them cause blood and death to ours with no consequence?! Let them steal our things?! Let them steal the souls of the departed?! I'm shocked you think that way, old friend."

Yondo took a breath. "You misunderstand me," he said, remaining calm. "I said nothing about letting them go without consequence. Those responsible must be brought to justice, and that justice must be severe. I only mean to forgo violence."

"And I say the time has come to embrace it. I'm afraid the death of our dear friend Aglan demands it. Or do you want to tell his family we're going to do nothing."

Dale, the Judge in town, stood to speak his mind. He was old and gray and hunched over, with cloudy blue eyes and a face full of wrinkles, yet he was as wise as anyone who called Vernon home. As Judge, it was his duty to make sure justice was properly served, and he had been doing so for the last forty years.

"We have laws for this very reason," he said, his voice rattling out of his chest. "The law is the bedrock of our way of life and we must respect it. Without it we are animals."

"Aglan is dead," piped Stu. "What does the law say of that?"

"That those responsible be brought to trial."

"Do you honestly believe the vandals will let us bring them to trial without a fight? Not likely."

"I know I've mentioned this before and it's been voted against," said Yondo, again taking the lead. "But perhaps it's time to speak with the Monks. Perhaps they could be of assistance. Maybe they know why the Kin want souls and stragglers, and maybe they can help those who are under their sway." Yondo found the Presbyter with his eyes and said to him, "Avarno, you must have friends at Lockhead? I'd be interested to hear what they had to say on the matter."

The town's Holy Man, who was quiet and small of build, with a bald head and smooth face, nodded once and said that he did. "I can send word with one of my pigeons. They fly true and fast."

"An interesting thought," added Olvin. "I can make inquiries, as well. I know a Monk. He might come if I send word."

"I do not care for that idea," said Esai. "Monks have their own way and we have ours. I'm not interested in their thoughts on this matter. This is our domain, our responsibility, not theirs."

"I agree," said Stu. "The Monks have their own responsibilities."

"It involves the Kin," said Yondo. "They know more about them than we do. I think we should at least consult them. Maybe one of theirs can walk the desert with us."

"They used to do that all the time," added Olvin. "I think it a fine idea."

"Can you get one of theirs here in two days?" said Esai derisively. "Because that's when we leave." He looked at the Presbyter. "Do your pigeons fly that fast?"

"It's time to accept that we're alone in this fight and must safeguard ourselves from the scourge of the Kin," said Daglan. "If the vandals wish to side with demon spirits, then we must treat them like demon spirits."

"I side with Daglan and Esai," said Stu. "We need a show of strength."

Many in the crowd agreed with him, and one man shouted out, "They want a fight, give 'em a fight!"

That was met with raucous approval, and while Esai chuckled at the response, Daglan raised his hands for quiet. When finally the noise died down, the old Herder spoke.

"I believe we need to find these criminals and bring them here, and the best way to do that is track them and catch them. We've done so before and can again." He then turned to Avarno. "As for the Monks, I'd prefer to leave them out of it for now. Let's first see if this plan works. If it does not, we can send word to them. No need to trouble them just yet."

Avarno nodded respectfully.

But Yondo still had doubts. "We take ten or more to the desert," he said, "and they won't attack. Not if the Kin, who see all without being seen, are with them. Or it could be they're baiting us. Could be a battle they want, and when we go, they strike with numbers, crippling our ability to shepherd souls, not to mention protect our homes and lands. It is a flawed plan."

"I doubt as such," said Esai condescendingly. "The vandals are fiends and thieves."

"Fiends and thieves who've gotten the best of us in the desert numerous times," replied Yondo at once. "Do not underestimate them."

Esai had no response for that.

But Daglan did. "This is an ugly situation," he said, that robust voice of his grabbing hold of the room. "We cannot afford to turn on each other, and we cannot afford to be lax. All the plans we've discussed have flaws, and none of them, I fear, will be successful without violence. I think what we can all agree on is that something need be done ... and that the stones and stragglers are our top priority."

"Aye," said Esai, nodding.

Most of the other Elders agreed, as well, as did those who had come to listen and observe.

"The Kin are with them," said Olvin. "And I'd bet my last chink they're giving those stones and stragglers they steal to the Kin."

"We all know it," said Rone.

"The Kin care nothing about them," said Stu. "The Kin care only about helping themselves and hurting us, and they'll do what they feel they must to win. They'll side with yenas or vandals, murderers or Monks."

"Well put," said Mengin, an old time Herder with many treks under his belt. His hair had begun to turn gray and wrinkles marked his once-handsome face, but he still walked the desert, and walked it well.

"We need to bring them to justice!" Esai declared. "The Angeloi are gone. We'll get no help from them. And the Monks have their own problems to worry on. We stand alone in this fight and must defend ourselves. We do it right, we can wipe them out for good."

"Exactly," agreed Stu. He turned to the Herders, who were sitting together near the front, and addressed them directly. "This is a matter of honor and pride, as well as duty. Because of them, Aglan was food for yenas and Largo barely survived."

There was more agreement from the Council of Elders, as well as the general assembly, but not so from the Herders. It was one thing to protect yourself from trouble, another thing entirely to instigate it. Yondo made his opinion known, and a few of his friends, Mengin and Olvin included, echoed him.

But many of the others liked the idea, including Daglan, who said, "The vandals must be thwarted. One Herder has been killed because of them, another badly wounded. If we do not stop them, they will not stop, and they, along with the Kin, will grow stronger. I agree with Stu and Esai. We must act."

"Count me on that side," declared Alek, the Elder of the Craftsman. "We should go for them now. We cannot allow our next trek to be compromised."

"Agreed," said Lester.

Ned, the Elder of the Masons, concurred.

Daglan nodded approval, and many in the room followed his lead, adding words of consent.

"The matter has been discussed appropriately and now must be brought to a vote. What say the Council?" Esai called out. "All in accord with attack, raise a hand."

Daglan's was the first to go up. Stu, Ned, and Lester raised their hands, too, as did Esai and Alek. In all, ten of the thirteen Elders voted for an attack, which made the decision final. The only Elders who did not vote in favor were Dale, Vernon's Judge, Avarno the Presbyter, and Jeb, though only Avarno voted against it; Dale and Jeb conceded by not voting either way. That made the final tally all but unanimous.

"It is thus settled," Esai called out to the crowd. "On our next trek, which shall go in two days, we'll look to strike back at the vandals." He turned to Yondo. "We know you don't agree with the decision, old friend, but we know you'll abide it."

Yondo nodded. He had spoken his mind; now he would do his duty.

"That said, we prefer you lead the walk, for you are our best. Choose eight Herders to go with you, the strongest and truest we have. Plan your route and strategy accordingly. Make it sure, and leave nothing to chance."

The meeting ended soon after the vote, and Yondo reluctantly went about his work, choosing among the Herders of Vernon the men he trusted most. Then, with the help of Daglan and Esai, they went about devising the foundation of a plan, discussing everything from the safest route to travel to the best way to track the vandals.

Yondo still thought it a bad idea, and Mengin and Olvin agreed with him, but none of them could dispute the fact that something had to be done. They had to guard the souls of the departed, and they had to protect themselves.

The planning took hours, and Yondo would not return home until well after supper.

He brought with him bad news for his boy.

Jonno was pouting in his room. He had been pouting for two days now.

Yondo had broken the news to him after the meeting, explaining the need for a change in plans after what had happened to Largo and Aglan. Even so, Jonno had stormed out like a petulant child. He was still acting like such, frowning and moping around, not talking to anyone.

This juvenile display upset Yondo but not Gabby, who was pleased her boy would not be walking the desert. Yondo, meanwhile, was again disappointed by Jonno's fast temper and lack of maturity. Gabby had been right: Jonno was not ready to be a Herder. He was almost full grown yet still a child in many ways, and the desert was no place for a child, especially in times like these, with Kin and vandals about.

Yondo was sitting by the fire, smoking a pipe, mulling these thoughts, when Lizzy walked in the room. "Dad?" she said, sitting next to him. "You're leaving tomorrow morning?"

"Yes, my dear," he told her. "Soon after breakfast."

"Lots of stones to carry ... and three stragglers."

"Aye. Close to two-hundred, between stragglers and stones."

"That's a lot, isn't it?"

"I suppose."

Lizzy was silent for a spell. She gazed deeply into the crackling orange swell of the fire, her eyes transfixed by the seductive dance of the flames.

Yondo puffed on his pipe and waited patiently for his daughter's next words. He knew more were forthcoming.

He didn't have to wait long.

"I hear this is to be a dangerous trek," Lizzy said. "I heard whispers of what happened to the others. One dead, another almost."

"All treks have their dangers, girl," Yondo told her. "But worry not, there are nine of us going. I'll be fine. The vandals aren't that tough."

Lizzy smiled faintly. "I know," she said.

"Then what has you troubled."

Lizzy shrugged. She had words to say, but she didn't want to say them. She knew she would, but she would have preferred not having to.

Yondo said to her, "Go on, girl. Tell me what's on that mind of yours. You came here to talk. Talk freely."

Lizzy nodded, and set her mind. "It's the Kin," she said at last, her voice barely above a whisper. She didn't like mentioning the Kin for fear they would hear her and mark her for possession.

"It was vandals that got them," Yondo told her. "Yenas, too. We're planning on fixing that."

Lizzy was quiet for a spell. Then she shook her head. "No. It's the Kin," she said. "I know it. And so do you."

Yondo nodded pensively. "Aye," he said. "I'm sure they're part of it."

"They're behind it all," Lizzy said with absolute certainty. "They sow it and reap it."

Yondo smiled faintly, and thought: if only I could put Lizzy's mind and spirit into Jonno's body; I'd have something fierce to work with then, a true Voukolos in the making.

"You listen well, girl," he said to her. "And you're right. But vandals aren't Kin, only men, and they need be stopped so we can walk the desert safely."

"They'll come at you," Lizzy said to him, sure of it. "If not this time, next time."

"Aye. It's been that way forever."

Lizzy fell silent once more, thinking about what she wanted to say next. She stared into the fire and went with, "Something bad is in the air. Something evil. I feel it."

"You worry like your mother," Yondo replied in good humor, though his thoughts mirrored hers.

Meridon had fallen, the vandals had gotten bold in their attacks, and lately there had been reports of strange occurrences in the wild, tales of possession, fearsome giants, and monsters made of man. Tales not substantiated, yet believable nonetheless.

Making matters worse, the Angeloi had been gone for more than ten generations, leaving the fortune of all those in Hinterland on the wheel. And fortune had not been kind.

"You always say that mom's too smart for her own good," Lizzy reminded her father.

Yondo pulled his pipe from his lips so that he could laugh. As whiffs of cherry-scented smoke ascended around him, he said, "I think *you're* too smart for your own good."

Lizzy smiled wanly, pleased by the compliment, though not so much by what it meant.

"My sweet girl," Yondo said to her, "I've got no choice but to go. I'm a Herder. It's my sworn duty." Here, his eyes narrowed and his expression took on a more solemn edge, and when he started speaking again, his voice was a notch deeper. "If you remember anything I say to you, remember this: no matter the circumstances or possible consequences, no matter the people or deeds involved, it is our duty to always do what we can for good. Not only what we have to do, not only what we should do, but more. The beginning and the end mean nothing, child, only the labyrinth between. That is where we find our true selves."

Lizzy nodded to show that she understood, but she remained silent.

Yondo took advantage of that silence, drawing smoke from his pipe.

Then Lizzy said, "You'll have more stories when you return?"

"With three stragglers on foot? Most likely."

The stories were Lizzy's favorite part. Not the stories of lakas, yenas, and Kin, which was what Jonno preferred, but the stories from the mouths of the stragglers, those lost souls on their way to the Great Stone Temple. Those were the stories that captivated her imagination and set her mind racing on edge. Stories from the world she herself had come from.

The One True Living World had rules, rituals, and magic all its own, with a language similar to their common tongue but filled with color and verve. They had different clothes, different shoes, different baubles; they had different customs and different religions. It was all so fascinating.

"Can you tell me one now?" Lizzy asked her father. "The one about the woman who flew around the world like a bird. Or the one about the great queen who ruled a nation."

Yondo smiled at his little girl. She had such innocence, such fire, such enthusiasm; she was sweet and kind and smart, and all of life interested her. He hoped she would stay that way forever.

"What say I tell you of the great flood, child," he said.

Lizzy nodded excitedly. She had heard that one before, but it was one of her favorites. It came from To Theiko Kylindro, the Divine Scroll, which had been written by the Angeloi themselves many generations ago, back when Hinterland was their home.

The pages of the Divine Scroll were filled with the most magnificent tales; tales of the Godhead and Holy Trinity; of angels and demons; of the Great War to come between the flesh and the spirit.

Lizzy desperately wanted a copy, but Yondo had not yet been able to obtain one for her. Books were a rare commodity in Hinterland, and To Theiko Kylindro was the most sought after text in the land. The original, believed to possess the power of the Angeloi, was hidden away somewhere at Lockhead, under the protection of the Order of Monks.

"If we're going to do this, I'm going to need more ale," Yondo said, standing. "And more wood for the fire."

He moseyed to the kitchen to fill his cup, while Lizzy hurried out to the woodpile to fetch a load. She returned a short time later with as much wood as her skinny arms could carry. She dropped it on the floor next to the hearth and began wedging some of the smaller pieces into place.

"There," she said, as dozens of orange and yellow embers sparked to life. They rose from the flames and disappeared up the shoot. "I'm ready."

"Me, too," agreed Yondo, and eased back in his chair with his ale and his pipe. "And if you're good, and it's not too late, perhaps when I'm done with the story of the great flood, I'll tell you about the time the river-folk brought over a little pink girl with blonde ringlets and deep lungs."

This was a reference to Lizzy herself, and she protested with a note of childlike embarrassment. "Dad!"

"You *were* a pink little thing," he told her with a playful look in his eyes. "As pink as a baby pig. And you definitely had deep lungs."

"Stop," she said, her cheeks ripe with a blush. "Tell me of the flood."

"Of course, my little skiachtro." That was his nickname for her, his lighthearted term of endearment. It meant Scarecrow.

He took a drink and puffed on his pipe, and Lizzy curled up at his side, ready to be entertained.

Yondo usually liked the start of treks. There was excitement in the air; the excitement of adventure; the excitement of the desert itself, with all the challenges and beauty it had to offer. He didn't often admit it, but he loved the desert; he had always loved it, from the first time his father, a Herder himself, had taken him camping there as a boy. That first night under the stars had laid the foundation for what was destined to become his purpose. He loved his family more than anything; they were number one in his life, and there wasn't anything he wouldn't do for them. But being a Herder was a close second. It was who he was as a man.

Normally a team of two or three Herders made the trek across the barren, rocky terrain, escorting the stragglers and living stones from one world to the next. This time, however, nine of them would be going, and there was a strong possibility of trouble.

The possibility of trouble was a constant in the desert, with yenas and lakas, sidewinders and scorpions, demons and the unforgiving elements, but rarely did they leave Vernon looking for it.

And when you went looking for trouble …

Gabby would have made mention of her fears but she was happy enough that Jonno wasn't among the nine going. Jonno, meanwhile, continued to pout in his room like a petulant child, still not understanding why he couldn't go.

"I can handle myself," he whined when his father came to say goodbye to him. "You've seen me with a blade. I'm not a kid anymore. And if I go, there will be ten of us."

"I know you can handle a blade, and I know you're not a kid," Yondo told him. "But this trek is different. The Council has spoken, and I haven't a choice. They want experienced fighters. They want men who've been there before. And I agree."

Jonno issued a resentful snort.

Yondo pulled him in for a hug. "Despair not, my boy," he said to him. "You'll walk the desert soon enough."

Jonno sniffed and said, "Sure. Next time. Always next time." The scorn in his voice was as rich as the chorus of a song, but Yondo chose to ignore it. He had more pressing concerns.

At the door, Lizzy and Dalla presented him with a gift: homemade potato bread and figgy pie. They had four large fig trees on their land, so figs often were included in Gabby's recipes … sometimes to disastrous results. There's only so much you can do with a fig.

Yondo thanked them kindly and placed the items in his pack. Then he gave his girls hugs and kisses. "I'll be back before you know it," he promised them. "Take care of your mum for me while I'm gone. You know how she gets."

Gabby smiled nervously, while Dalla's thin little smile perished under the weight of sorrow. She hated seeing her father leave, even more than she loved seeing him return.

Lizzy's face, conversely, was clear of all emotion. It was perfectly blank, and the deep, faraway look in her eyes gave Yondo a bad feeling.

"Be careful," she said to him. "Take heed. Promise?"

Yondo nodded solemnly and gave her another hug. "I'll be back with more stories, skiachtro, and we'll talk."

Yondo moved to his wife next. She was troubled, but kept a stiff lip. "Listen to your girl," she told him. "They come, you protect yourself."

"You women worry too much," Yondo said to them. "I need go before you make *me* worry."

"So go then," Gabby told him, teasingly gesturing to the door.

Yondo grabbed her by the waist, pulled her close, and kissed her. It was a passionate kiss, a lover's kiss, and while Lizzy politely looked away, Dalla blushed and went, "Woooooooooo."

Yondo told Gabby that he loved her, and after she told him the same, the Herder unexpectedly scooped up Dalla and said, "You like that, eh?" And he started pecking her sweet little face with kisses while she squirmed and shrieked with delight.

Gabby laughed.

Lizzy laughed.

Dalla continued to shriek and giggle.

When she'd had enough, Yondo put her down, and she wiped away all his kisses with the sleeve of her shirt.

"When I come home," Yondo said, wagging a finger at her, "more of the same for you."

She giggled and told him, "You'll have to catch me first."

He faked a move toward her, and she shrieked and ducked behind her mother's skirt.

"Don't hide behind me," Gabby said, moving away.

It was like this most times Yondo left for a trek, though this time was a little different. Instead of sadness, there was a genuine sense of menace in the air, as real and unpleasant as the desert heat. Yondo felt it plainly, and he could tell that Lizzy and Gabby felt it, too. For Gabby, this was nothing new; she always worried on him when he went on a trek. But the fact that Lizzy felt the same gave Yondo pause.

Not that that would stop him. He had a job to do and would do it. He would cross the desert with stragglers and living stones because he was a Herder and that's what Herders did. It was his duty, set down generations ago by the Angeloi, and he was loyal to his word.

He left his family and walked into town alone with a large pack over his shoulder and weapons on his belt: a long-blade made of good steel and his unique double-bladed knives. Dock would bring his bow and daggers, Molt his trusty axe and spear, and the fourth member of their group, Edgar, Molt's nephew, a young man of only twenty-two, his crossbow and short-blade. They would be well-armed and well-prepared.

Half a rote after leaving his homestead, Yondo strolled through the batwing doors at Sana's Saloon, the normal meeting place for Herders about to embark on a trek. He was the first among his kind there, and he ordered an ale from one of Sana's girls.

"Big trek," the pert young sally said when she set the wooden mug down in front of him. "Best of luck to ya."

Yondo nodded and said, "Thank you, dear." He then took a swig and pulled out his tobacco pouch.

The rest of his team arrived shortly thereafter, looking fresh and ready for action. They all partook of ale and tobacco before gathering up the stragglers and heading off to the rough, unforgiving terrain of the desert.

Four men armed and looking for trouble.

Five more would come later and follow after them, walking the westward path with a different agenda.

Only one of them would ever see the town of Vernon again.

**Seven:**

You never knew how many or what sort of stragglers you might get, and they rarely failed to surprise. Most of them had plenty of wits left, though they carried no personal memories of themselves or their loved ones. They could tell you who the President of the United States was (one of the major leaders of the One True Living World, Yondo had learned), and which teams had won the World Series, the World Cup, and the Super Bowl (just three of the many sporting championships held there), but they could not recite their names nor any details of their own lives.

Yondo couldn't imagine having to go through something like that: you die in one world and wake in another, but this new foreign world you've come to is merely a gateway, a harsh passing ground made up mostly of desert and fear. The stragglers would find no home here; their home lay beyond the red rocks and sandy waste of the great desert, beyond the five mounts that pierced the clouds. O Megalos Naos tou Petrinon Angelon awaited on the other side of the mountains. The Great Stone Temple of the Angels. That's where the Tall Man dwelled, deep in the underground tunnels of that ancient shrine. He collected the stragglers and the stones, and in tribute gave gold and blessings.

It was a peculiar arrangement; at least Yondo had always thought so.

It had been a long day – the first day of a trek always was – and the three stragglers were already down for the night. The long walk and the unremitting desert sun had taken the life right out of them.

The campfire rustled, giving off heat and faint light.

Yondo had drawn first shift, and while the others slept, he kept watch for lakas and yenas. There normally weren't many of either where they had pitched camp, but you had to keep an eye out nonetheless.

It was quiet, and that quiet seemed to go on forever.

Yondo reached for one of the three satchels and carefully undid the drawstring. After all the years he'd spent on the herd, after countless treks and adventures, surviving confrontations with Kin and the perils of the desert, it was the living stones that most fascinated him. He pulled one out, mostly dull green and gold in color, and hefted it in his hand. It was surprisingly light, warm to the touch, and its colors subtly changed, darkening in some places, fading in others, like the scales of a fish in water.

None seemed to understand the difference between the stones and the stragglers; not even the old scrolls or the journals of the prophets gave a definitive answer as to why some souls came across incarnate while others, the vast majority, more than a hundred to one, came across as living rocks. Not that it mattered for they all went to the same place. They had a date with the Tall Man, sometimes referred to as the Dark Shadow, because a shadow was all that had ever been seen of him. And from there it was off to the Void. Everything was different in the Void, or so Yondo had heard. Old lore stated that everything was in the mind on the other side of the veil, including the body, which seemed unnatural to him.

He remembered showing one of the stones to Lizzy a few years back, and a smile overcame him when he thought about how wide her little eyes had grown at the sight of it. She had asked to hold it, and when he had told her she could, she had not hesitated to take it in her hand. She had handled it with wonder and reverence, mesmerized by its odd colors and utterly intrigued by the warmth and soft glow it produced.

They *were* beautiful, thought Yondo. Some more than others. He occasionally wondered what his might look like.

Lizzy had asked him the same question that day.

"Does my soul look like that, too?"

"They're all different," he had told her. To which she had replied, "I hope mine is red and green and white."

Yondo carefully placed the stone back into the satchel and stood. He searched the blackness of the desert for life and found exactly what he expected to find: nothing. There was nothing out there.

That would change soon enough. They were on the first plateau, where everything was clear and flat and wide open, where you could see a threat from half-a-day away. Two days from now they would reach the outer rim of the dunes, where wild blowing sands were known to drop visibility to almost nothing. Even slow-moving lakas could get the drop on you there.

After that would come the red rock mesas, where the terrain was much rougher and far more dangerous, and where there were plenty of places for vandals to hide. That would be when things got serious.

This was the easy part.

The hard part, Yondo knew, lay ahead.

"Is it always this damn hot here?"

This question had come from the salty old man with stone-gray hair and a pale raison face. He had proven to be the slowest moving straggler of the group, and Yondo had taken it upon himself to keep the old moaner walking at a steady speed. He had his work cut out for him.

"Aye. It's a desert," he said.

"It's blistering hot. Like an oven. I should be wearing sunscreen. Do you have sunscreen? I'm guessing you don't."

Yondo had heard about sunscreen from previous stragglers, all of whom had seemed concerned about the power of the sun. The idea of a cream that protected the skin from burns intrigued him, but Hinterland didn't have department stores with beauty counters. Boysens when mixed with callack paste worked well enough to sooth a burn, but Yondo didn't think that remedy could prevent one.

"No. No sunscreen," he said.

"I'm getting a terrible sunburn," the old man complained. "Look at my arms." He thrust his arms in Yondo's face. "Look how red they are."

The man's arms were red, but they didn't look burnt. Yondo said as much to him.

"I know my body," the old man replied with a brusque tongue. "I know when something's wrong. I can tell. Are you telling me I don't know my own body?"

The old man had started complaining soon after the trip had begun and had yet to stop. It was only day two, but his incessant carping made for bad feelings and short tempers.

He was walking with Yondo now, the two of them more than forty paces behind the others, all of whom had grown tired of his constant negativity. In the desert, morale was important. Patience even more so. Yondo Carpana was a patient man.

"You don't know about this, obviously. You're black. I'm fair-skinned and old. It's different for me. The sun burns my skin. Did you know you can die from sunburn?"

Yondo didn't know that, and he doubted the veracity of it. He didn't say that, though. What he said was, "Many of your color have walked the desert and none of them burned. Our sun doesn't burn the skin."

"What kind of sun doesn't burn?" replied the old man "I never heard such a thing. That's what a sun does – it burns. It's a ball of damn fire. You feel how hot it is? I can feel my skin cooking. My face is probably as red as a strawberry."

Yondo looked at the man's face. A slight sheen of red could be seen peeking through the pale wrinkles that made up his aged countenance, but it hardly looked troubling.

"Your face looks fine, sir," he said, maintaining his patience. "The sun'll be down soon enough."

"And then the cold comes."

"Aye. The temperature drops."

"This blasted weather is enough to chap my hide. Literally. I still don't know where we're going. And I don't know why you can't tell us where we're going? We have a right to know."

"We've told you where we're going. We're going to the Great Stone Temple on the other side of the desert."

"The Great Stone Temple?" the man said bitterly. "What does that even mean? What sort of hell awaits us there? I have half a mind to run off."

"Not wise, unless you're keen to be dinner for animals."

The man stopped walking. He was sweating and breathing heavily, and his small brown eyes were rimmed with a look of exhaustion. "I need a break," he said. "And water. I need water."

"We're already lagging behind," Yondo said. "We need to get moving."

"I'll get moving *after* I've had some water," said the man. "Two days of this nonsense with twelve more to come. I'm old and I'm tired. I'll be lucky to make it there."

Yondo uncorked his waterskin and handed it over.

The man took a drink and sneered. "Warm," he said. "Like piss. I don't suppose you have wine?"

"I've got cider," Yondo said. "You promise to keep your step, tonight at the fire I'll favor you with some."

"Hard cider?" the man inquired with a note of interest.

"Truly. My woman makes it from pears."

The man gulped down a couple more mouthfuls of water. Some spilled on his chin and ran down his neck. "Warm like piss," he grumbled.

Yondo took back the waterskin, wiped the mouthpiece, and drank. Then he corked it and slung it over his shoulder.

"Come. We need to pick up the pace," he said, starting back up. "Can't break until we reach the other side of the steppe."

"I don't like walking in this heat," the old man spit back at him. "My feet are killing me. It's excruciating."

Yondo didn't know that last word, but he imagined it meant something unpleasant. Everything the man said came out on a sour note, as if his tongue had been soaked in vinegar.

"It's hard, I know," Yondo said to him. "But this is where you are, and it's what you must do."

"I could stop right here and refuse to move. How about that?"

"Sure, you could do that ... and be eaten alive by either yenas or lakas, whichever find you first. Pray it's the yenas."

"This blasted world!" the man grouched. "Yenas and lakas? Whoever heard of such things." He hadn't seen any yet, but he had heard the gloomy moans of lakas last night, and one of the other Herders, Dock, had tried to explain to him what they were. It sounded to the old man like they were zombies or mummies, though apparently they were made of sand. And the yenas he figured were hyenas or something similar. He wasn't keen to cross paths with either species, truthfully.

"We're dead, ain't we?" he said, refusing to stay quiet. "I know enough to know that I'm dead. Just say it already. Go on. You can tell me. It's not like I can do anything about it."

"The dead don't talk," Yondo replied. "And you don't shut up."

The old man snorted angrily. "Maybe I will stop right here," he said, and stopped walking. "I've never been treated like this in my life."

Yondo grabbed the man's elbow and said, "I'll walk you if I must."

The man yanked his arm away. "I'll do it myself, thank you."

"Fine. But you have to move. We have ground to make up."

The man grumbled something under his breath, then started walking again. A few steps later he said, "You were serious about that cider?"

"Yes, sir," Yondo said. "Best in the land."

"And I can have some?"

"Enough to ease the aches of the day."

This idea seemed to please the old man, and miraculously his pace increased.

## Eight:

"You see it?" Manly whispered to his partner.

His partner said nothing; he merely looked over at him with a glare in his eyes that would have stopped a yena in its tracks.

That was Kelt's way. He thought that talking was an overrated form of communication, especially when it came to answering stupid questions. Of course he saw the thing that Manly was speaking about; they'd been tracking it through the sparse woods that surrounded the lands east of the Dark Forest for three days now.

"It looks to be alone," Manly said. Conversely, he did not view talking as an overrated means of communication. He talked quite a bit; enough for the both of them. "They're known to walk alone."

Kelt agreed. The coarseness of his beard and the narrow squint of his pale blue eyes showed him to be well into his middle age, which made him one of the most experienced Monks in Hinterland. There wasn't much he hadn't seen or done, and he bore the scars to prove it.

"What do you think?" Manly asked.

Kelt sniffed the air like an animal. Something didn't feel right to him. They had been tracking the flesh-eater for three days now and not once had they gotten this close. They were no more than a hundred steps away from it; before today, three hundred steps was as close as they had gotten, and even that distance had felt somewhat perilous.

Now they could hit it with a rock.

Sarkofagoi were rare creatures. Rare and incredibly dangerous. They looked entirely human; they walked upright on two legs, they had arms, hands, fingers and feet; they had human faces and human hair. They looked exactly like men, moved exactly like men, but they were not men. Men didn't stand more ten feet tall and weigh more than five-hundred pounds. And men didn't eat human flesh.

Old lore said they were the children of the Kin, the bestial offspring of unholy communions between Kin and humans. They were soulless, mindless, flesh-hungry monsters hell-bent on blood and destruction. Supposedly they had been killed off by the Angeloi in the first Great War, and since none had been seen in Hinterland for more than five generations, no one thought to doubt that.

But old lore wasn't right about everything, just like most prophecies never came to pass. Eccentricities of the truth mixed with fear and want and embellishment rarely fade away; it is more likely they grow in size and strength, becoming behemoths.

Kelt knew better, of course, for he had seen at least three of them, one of which he had helped kill. It was a battle he would not soon forget, which was why he was reluctant to attack.

His partner, driven by the wild winds of youth, had a different mind. "Come," he said. "When will we ever get a look this good?"

Manly was a fresh young man in his early twenties with long brown hair, soft brown eyes, and a clean, handsome cheek. He barely looked old enough to have hair on his legs, yet like all Monks in service he was a highly-skilled warrior, deadly with an array of weapons.

Because of his age, he tended to be impatient and eager to kill. He had always wanted to be a Monk, like his uncle before him, who had died on the job a year prior to Manly passing the trials and joining the ranks as an apprentice. It was the most dangerous profession in Hinterland, and there weren't many who could handle the rigors of it. You had to be strong, tough, fast, faithful, sharp-minded, and willing to suffer great pain. You had to be able to survive long stretches by yourself, sometimes going weeks without seeing another person. Most importantly, you had to be able to put the horrors you routinely witnessed out of your mind.

Monks were not permitted to marry or have children. They called no one place home and held no possessions other than those needed for their work. They walked the land in search of the evil things that didn't belong, the demons and spirit-beasts that attacked the soul as well as the flesh, killing both. And when they found these things, they fought them.

Hinterland had gotten far more dangerous the last few generations, and Kelt wondered how much longer it would be before the evil things took over. Meridon had fallen. Demon possession was on the rise. People were becoming more violent, more lustful, more selfish.

There had been a mass suicide at Hornock last year, the likes of which Kelt had never seen before; sixty-one people from the small fishing village had taken their own lives under a harvest moon. They were nothing but bones and teeth by the time they were found, and their blood had turned the soil black. Then there was the man from Lowber, north and west of the Dark Forest, who murdered twenty-seven people, including fifteen women and six children, with an axe. Now the Sarkofagoi.

For generations there had been no sightings of them, leading people to believe they were either a myth or an extinct race. Kelt knew otherwise, of course, having fought one before, years ago, but his kind preferred to squash rumors, not feed them. Fear, the grizzled old Monk knew, was a far more dangerous enemy than a few random Sarkofagoi. But now word was going round. Whispers from the wilds up north told of giants twelve-feet tall with unnatural strength and an insatiable appetite for human flesh. They supposedly lived beyond the remote reaches of Hinterland, where not even the Great Serpent River flowed, far removed from any towns and large groups of people. Though lately sightings of the monstrous creatures had become more frequent in Boreal.

What had started out as a spook story had quickly become a genuine threat, and Kelt and his kind were out to end it as swiftly as possible.

"I'll double back and flank him to the right," Manly said in a low voice. "When I'm in position, I'll draw his attention and you take the first shot. You're better with a bow than me. Then when it turns to find you, I'll take mine. Could be we end this with little effort."

"Arrows have little effect on them," replied Kelt. "Unless you get them in the eye or neck."

"Then aim for its eyes or neck," said Manly. "You're a crack shot."

Kelt shook his head in a show of mild exasperation. The bravado of youth was only trumped by its foolishness.

"Come on. It's now or never," Manly said on a whisper. "You ready?"

Just then, Kelt felt something, and he held up a hand and said, "Wait."

Manly did not want to hear that. "Wait? For what? This is it."

Kelt squinted into the deep brush. There was nothing there to see, so far as he could tell, but he felt *something*. A presence. A *dark* presence.

For a Monk, the weapon that need be sharpest was the mind; it was responsible for keeping them alive far more often than their blades or bows. A Monk had to learn to trust his or her fears and feelings, no matter what, for often they were right.

Time and experience had taught this lesson to Kelt.

"For now we wait," he said. "And watch."

Manly let out an audible sigh of disappointment, yet offered no words of dissent. He didn't like watching and waiting (it seemed to him that's all they did most days), but he understood that he still had much to learn. If it had been up to him, he would have attacked the beast head on, going at it with speed, blunt force, and unswerving determination. Of course, that very attitude had contributed to his father's untimely demise.

There was a reason, he reminded himself, that Kelt had survived so many battles and so many years. Old Monks were as rare as old virgins in Hinterland, and their wisdom needed to be respected.

Manly repositioned himself and set his eyes on the creature before them, studying the way it moved, taking note of its impressive size, the span of its arms and the length of its stride.

'Know your prey before you think to attack it.'

That was one of Kelt's most frequently used idioms.

Manly fought back his more primal urges and endeavored to comply.

All plans are subject to the spin of the wheel and the unpredictability of the breeze, making them as delicate as fine crystal.

While watching and waiting, measuring their target, Manly and Kelt witnessed the flesh-eater lift up from behind a stack of wood and rocks what looked like a young woman. Manly pointed and said, "Did we really miss that? Was she there the whole time? Because I didn't see her."

They had been spying on the Sarkofagos for most of the day and hadn't once caught sight of the body the creature was presently stringing up by an ankle from a sturdy limb. From where they were hiding, there was no way for them to tell if the woman was still alive; she wasn't moving, and her body was unnaturally pale, but that didn't mean she was dead.

Many of the old tales surrounding the Sarkofagoi had to do with them raping young women. They were known to kidnap young maidens for the purpose of sex, and to kill and eat any menfolk who took exception.

Manly said, "We have to do something. I'm not going to sit here and watch that thing cook and eat someone, dead or not."

Kelt agreed, though he remained wary. Something felt off to him.

He leveled his stare on the hanging body, watching it for signs of life. It may have been impossible to tell whether or not the young woman was alive, but it was plain to see she was naked. Her pale skin glistened in the dying light of the sun and her full breasts hung seductively. Her large, round nipples and thatch of black pubic hair stood out strikingly against the silvery gloss of her flesh, making her seem all the more real.

If the stories were true …

Kelt stopped himself there, before his mind wandered aimlessly into the horror-scope of his imagination, where the terrible things he had seen and experienced still lived.

Best to stay in the light and leave the dark in the dark.

After securing her, the flesh-eater made its way back to the woodpile and started to build a fire. It did so with surprising care and efficiency, bringing to mind more human qualities.

"We have to do something," Manly said, urging his mentor. "Elsewise it's going to eat her. Or, if alive, rape her."

Kelt agreed. Whatever odd sense he felt mattered not. A woman's life was on the line. Or, if she was already dead, they could at least preserve her corpse and give her a proper burial.

"Double back," he told his young apprentice. "We need to know if the girl is alive. If she is, she's the priority. I'll attack the thing first, from the front. Then you can join from the side."

Manly nodded that he understood, and a moment later disappeared in the woods. When you were hunting beasts and demons on their turf, the element of surprise was paramount.

Kelt caught a glimpse of Manly a short time later, creeping down the right flank, moving slowly but with purpose. As yet, the Sarkofagos hadn't noticed him; it seemed more concerned with the fire.

No more than twenty steps away from the hanging body and Manly still couldn't say if the woman was alive or dead. She wasn't moving, her skin was pale but not blue, and it was impossible to tell in the diminishing light if she was breathing or not. If she wasn't dead, Manly thought, it was only a matter of time.

She was naked, that much was certain, and there were bruises and marks of blood all over her body. Her hair, shiny and jet black, shielded most of her face, leaving Manly to question her age. He put it at anywhere between twenty and thirty-five.

The young Monk glanced in the direction of his partner and gave him a signal that he was in position and ready to attack. Kelt understood and readied his blade. Before he stepped out, though, he indulged his intuition and gave the sparsely-wooded dene one last glance. He saw nothing of interest and reluctantly set his worry aside. It was just the thought of death that had him anxious, he told himself. Same as it ever was and would be.

He readied his short-blade and stepped out into the open. He was three steps down the slight grade when the flesh-eater's eyes looked his way. It saw him and stood tall, its height rising to almost twelve feet.

The damn thing was wide, too, with long, muscular arms, thick legs, and a torso that looked like it had been carved from the trunk of an oak. Kelt had only clashed with one Sarkofagos in all his days, and that one had been smaller, less formidable. Even so, it had taken him and another Monk, Benno, nearly two hours to kill the thing. Benno had suffered a concussion and three broken ribs in the battle, while Kelt had walked away with a broken wrist and a broken jaw.

As Kelt continued his slow but steady approach, the flesh-eater made it known that it was ready for a fight. It banged its chest with a massive fist and let out a yowl that echoed far into the woods. It was then that Manly reached the woman. He stayed with her long enough to determine that she was merely unconscious, not dead, and then moved on the beast from behind, drawing his sword as he closed in.

The beast charged Kelt, and Manly sprinted after it.

Kelt kept his short-blade, while with his other hand he pulled the whip from his belt. When the beast was no more than thirty paces away, he sent the whip slashing through the air with an effortless flick of his wrist. The tip of the whip was braided with spikes, and when those spikes tore into the beast's face, it let out another yowl, this one in pain. Kelt drew the whip back and flung it again, but the beast avoided its bite this time, jerking hard to the left as the whip snapped just inches from its ear.

Kelt was forced to toss the whip aside and draw his long-blade. He cut at the beast once, missing it, and then again, leaving a small gash on its arm. Then he dove out of the way of a massive fist.

Manly joined the fight, swinging his sword violently, hacking and slashing at the beast with the unrefined power and speed of youth. But all of his attempts missed and he was forced to back off.

Kelt retook the lead, circling left. Manly circled right.

The Sarkofagos stood at center, glancing back and forth between them, waiting for one or the other to charge and swing.

It looked completely human, only much larger. Its bearded face had a sculpted cut and its skin was the color of dying corn husks; its eyes were black, its mouth as thin as a knife blade, its nose large and flat and bent. Covering its lower half, from waist to knee, were a pair of torn pants that looked three sizes too small, while on its huge feet it wore makeshift boots fashioned from animal skins. Its torso was uncovered, showing off well-defined musculature and dozens of scars, the remainders of battles fought against great and terrifying enemies.

"Kalogeros," it said in a bone-rattling voice. "Go and live. Stay and die."

"Can't go," Kelt replied. "You kill and eat folk. We can't permit that."

"I kill and eat food in my lands," the Sarkofagos said, gesturing to the wild around them. "You want not become, you need go now."

Kelt gave his partner a look, and Manly nodded back. They would attack at the same time: one from the left, the other from the right; one high, the other low. It was a well-choreographed dance that all Monk teams employed with great proficiency.

Kelt tightened his grip on his weapons. The Sarkofagos said to him, "Not wise, Kalogeros. I am a king. You cannot beat me." A split second later, the giant swooped down, picked up a rock the size of a melon, spun, and threw it at Manly.

It was an impossibly fast motion, too fast for even a trained Monk to react to, and the sound the rock made when it struck Manly square in the face was the sound of death. Blood splattered, bones broke, and the young man's body went limp and collapsed to the ground.

"Noooooo!!!!" Kelt screamed when he saw his young apprentice fall. His voice boomed through the halcyon valley like thunder, clattering off the trees, echoing on and on. He charged with anger and hate, swinging both his swords at the flesh-eater, going at it with unrestrained vigor.

But the Sarkofagos avoided most of his metal, dancing away from him with speed and grace that was quite unnatural for a creature so large. The few blows the Monk actually landed were glancing blows at best, blows that barely drew blood from the flesh-eater's hide-like skin.

Kelt was undaunted, though, and continued to attack, his swords a blur of glinting steel in the dimly-lit dene. He missed badly with a looping slash, but then landed a solid kick to the flesh-eater's midsection. The blow had little effect, though, and before long Kelt began to wane.

Somewhat strangely, the flesh-eater did not capitalize on the Monk's exhaustion; it merely stepped back, giving the winded hunter time to recover. "You're not mine, Kalogeros," it said, its voice and face all too human. Eerily and terrifyingly human. "You're to be hers."

Kelt didn't know what that meant until the flesh-eater moved away and the naked woman, who only moments before had been hanging upside down from a nearby tree, stepped forward.

"Kelt the great. It is your day."

She was clothed now, barely. The thin, silken frock covering her body did little to conceal her feminine form, and she boldly moved forward, knowing that Kelt would not be able to resist her. Or, if able, that he would not survive the ensuing fight.

"Daimonas!" Kelt mouthed with disdain. "In flesh!"

The woman threw her head back and laughed. "Aye," she said, and ran a seductive hand along the curve of her right breast. "In flesh."

First a Sarkofagos, and now Kin in flesh.

The Kin had been banished from the flesh and made to live in the spirit at the end of the Great War. As black ghosts, they were all but impossible to kill, and they could appear and vanish instantly. They could possess a body and get them to wield a sword or seduce an unsuspecting fool, or they could haunt their heads and fill them with thoughts of uncontrollable madness, rage, and lust.

Their banishment had not lasted long; perhaps three generations. They once again possessed the power and influence to take flesh for themselves. They were easier to track, easier to trap, and easier to kill when in flesh, but they were also much more dangerous. In the flesh, they could kill their victims themselves. They could wield a sword with their own hand and cut a man in half. They could seduce a Presbyter or rape a bride. They looked perfectly human but were so much more; so much stronger and faster; so much more persuasive and cunning.

Kelt knew this better than most, but he was not one to cower. "You can't tempt me, demon!" he said with snarling conviction. "Try if you must, but it's a waste of time."

The woman smiled sweetly at him, like a girl in love. "Kelt, dear," she said, "time means nothing to me."

"Until there's none left," replied the Monk.

"My string is endless, little man. Yours ..."

Kelt was a proud man, and the demon was pricking at that pride. But he also was a smart man, and he knew the demon was right. He had given all he had against the flesh-eater and it, in turn, had barely broken a sweat. Beyond that, the demon-girl could cause him all sorts of trouble; she easily could beat him in the flesh, armed or unarmed, or she could turn the forest against him, calling out to the animals and bringing to life the trees. The Kin had such power.

"Fine. What do you want?" Kelt asked her. "You must want something or I'd be dead already."

"Quite true, Kalogeros," whispered the demon in flesh. She drew near, her naked body a tease beneath the transparent cloak she wore. "I'm Saliel," she said, "and you are trespassing. These are our woods, not yours. You don't belong here."

Kelt glanced at the motionless body of his young apprentice. He'd had no chance to confirm Manly's death, yet he knew the boy had breathed his last. He may have failed to save his life, but he was not willing to leave him to the savage whims of the Sarkofagos. Not without a fight.

"Fine. I'll leave," he said, trying to sound casual. "But I want him. He deserves a proper burial."

"No," said Saliel plainly. "There's a price to pay."

"Easy words when you're the one collecting," replied the Monk.

Saliel smiled sweetly, and reached to touch Kelt's cheek.

He slapped her hand away, and the flesh-eater growled menacingly.

"Such malice," Saliel said with sublime mockery. "Such hatred in you."

"Call it what it is," Kelt replied. "And I have."

"I've roamed these lands far longer than you, Kalogeros. And will long after. It is inevitable."

"Perhaps. It seems this is not my day."

"But it is, dear. Or rather it can be."

Kelt offered no reaction, which took some effort. The demon was dealing in the usual way, offering a life of death in exchange for life. It was a slanted deal that many had made in the past, and had they a soul afterwards they would have regretted it.

"You and I can walk this dene together," Saliel said, going on. "Make it ours. Live for pleasure and love."

"Love? Ha! No love can come from you," Kelt said.

"You know not of love until you've known me, Kalogeros."

Kelt laughed a little, yet he could feel his mind starting to turn. He had to stay strong. He had to hold tight his faith. "I wonder how many dead men have said those words?" he said, boldly looking her in the eye.

"Thousands," she replied, smiling wickedly.

"Sorry, but I lean not to possession. You should know that well. Death is but a step we all must take in our walk."

Saliel's beautiful face twisted with contempt. "You speak of death with a cold tongue. It's not what you think, Kalogeros."

"Then tell me," Kelt said. "Tell me of death."

Saliel smiled again, a look so lovely on her face. "I am as real as you, Kalogeros. I am flesh. Feel if you like." She closed her eyes and arched her back seductively, offering the Monk her body. Her nipples, dark and erect, showed through her sheer frock.

Kelt's eyes grew wide with desire, but he refused to touch her.

Saliel relaxed, opened her eyes, looked at him. A thin smile lifted the corners of her perfect pink lips. "You want me," she said. It was not a question. "You want to touch me, to have a way with me, but you won't allow it. You stop yourself. You deny yourself pleasure for the prospect of pain. So utterly foolish. Yet it is so."

Kelt remained silent. He would have called her a liar, but then he would have been the liar, not her. Everything she had said was true. There was a desire in him that he hadn't felt in years, if ever, and he didn't know how much longer he could stifle it.

"Change is here, Kalogeros," Saliel went on, her voice a tempting whisper, as soft and soothing as a warm evening breeze. "This world has been forsaken. Soon there will be nothing to protect."

"Until then," Kelt said.

"Why die when you can live? And live well. There is no reason in that, Kalogeros. No reason but pride."

"Reason bends to truth, not the other way."

Saliel smiled. "I do not wish to possess you. I only want to make peace."

Kelt howled laughter, which drew a snarl from the Sarkofagos, though only a look of mild indifference from Saliel. "A demon offer of peace?" He glanced at his fallen partner, lying as dead as the stone that had violently claimed him. "Tell Manly of peace," he said. "Or his father. Or mine!"

"Aye. Exactly," said Saliel. "No need to fight and die when you can live and breathe free."

"Under your sway, and you decide. No freedom in that."

"We celebrate freedom, Kalogeros. It's your kind who abhor it. You put up fences, make rules, make judgments. It's you who hunt and kill us." She slowly traced a delicate finger around the outside of her full breast, then beneath it. "It's you, Kelt of no clan," she said to him seductively, "who will not take comfort in this soft, warm flesh."

Kelt directed his gaze away from Saliel's supple young body and set it squarely on her eyes. "Not for me, darling," he said as unholy thoughts raced through his head and made his blood hot. He remained strong, though, refusing to forsake his spirit for the unrepentant cravings of his flesh. "Not for me."

Saliel sighed dramatically. "Suit yourself, Kalogeros. Choose your way and want, which is death. If I see you again, on the other side, don't say I didn't warn you."

"Not my style," Kelt told her.

"We shall see about that."

It was near impossible to withstand a demon this close by. They could read your thoughts like words on a page, and even put thoughts in your head that you would have sworn were your own. They were devious and sinister, and this one, despite her outward beauty, was no different.

Kelt had come up against many Kin in the past, and he had been trained to recognize and withstand their power. But most of the Kin he had fought had been spirits, either black ghosts or men and women possessed. This was only his third encounter with an actual demon in flesh.

He was determined not to fall for her tricks, and, more importantly, not to let her in his head. She was angling to get in there, had been angling since her first words; probably, Kelt figured, even before that, since he and Manly had first arrived in the forest. That's most likely what he had sensed – the unholy presence of the demon circling them, looking for a way in. But he would not allow it, and he would not submit to her.

Saliel had begun to realize that it was pointless to try and turn the stalwart Monk, but she liked to have her fun. This was foreplay for her, the succulent buildup to what she hoped would be a satisfying climax, and she licked her lips in anticipation.

What she had been unable to glean while having her fun was that Kelt had a surprise for her. He had been waiting patiently to spring it, waiting for the Sarkofagos to present him with a better angle. As soon as it did, the old Monk wasted no time.

He had kept his blades in hand, though he had let them fall to a non-threatening position. His posture also indicated passivity. So the flesh-eater was not ready for an attack, certainly not one from more than twenty steps away. But that's what it got.

Keeping his thoughts hidden from the demoness, Kelt hurled his long-blade through the air like a dagger. The blade pierced the flesh-eater's groin area, just below the hip, going into the bone, and the beast cried out in agony and fell to the ground.

With the Sarkofagos wounded and Saliel frozen in shock, Kelt reached into his bag of tricks and pulled out a handful of the only substance Kin were known to despise: Salt.

He threw it at her, hard, then turned and ran, bounding through the forest with all the speed his legs could manage. He didn't look back and he didn't slow down, and as he ran, he spoke the old words in his head, the words that all evil things hated. Even so, he fully expected the demon to appear out of nowhere and run a sword through him.

She's playing with me, Kelt thought as he continued to race through the woods, not worrying about how hard his heart was pumping, not listening to the unnatural hum in his ears.

To give hope where there is none – that was their cruel, wicked way. To give you just enough rope to hang yourself … while making you think that hanging might just be a good idea.

Kelt ran and ran, and he didn't stop running until he was unable to draw another breath. His heart pounded in his chest, his brain pounded in his skull, and his lungs felt like they were on fire. He could feel the blood rushing through his veins like a raging river.

He collapsed to his knees and struggled to suck in air. Some time went by before he finally caught his breath. He stood.

The forest seemed empty to him, an eerie wasteland of brown sticks, dull colors, and dead earth. He searched for movement, any movement, but didn't see any. The demon hadn't chased him down and he couldn't figure out why. Unless the salt had stopped her.

Or maybe it had never been about him.

He squinted into the pale light of dusk, searching for the demon Saliel or the mighty Sarkofagos. He was certain they were out there, watching him, waiting to attack. But they never came for him, and after some more time had passed, the Monk found it possible to relax. He unscrewed his canteen and gulped down three mouthfuls of tepid water, then poured the rest of it over his head.

The water was refreshing, but it did nothing to ease his soul. His partner was dead and there was a demon in flesh and a monstrous Sarkofagos in these woods.

It seemed to Kelt that there were more evil things every day. While the Order of Monks had decreased dramatically over the last couple of generations, the evil things they hunted had increased.

Especially the Kin. Whispers of the Kin had since become screams for help, and the Monks could no longer match the demand.

It wouldn't be long before things really got bad.

Unless the Angeloi returned. They would set things right.

Breathing normally now, with his strength returned, Kelt capped his empty canteen and checked over the forest one last time. Then, holding strong to his short-blade and keeping close to cover, he made double-time through the woods.

## Nine:

Peck slogged on, moving at a pace that had become automatic. His uncle and father followed six paces behind him at the same speed, their feet lifting and falling in a strange and almost perfect rhythm. Clusters of animal skins were strapped to Peck's back; they'd take what they wanted of them and trade the rest at market. Loman and Titus, meanwhile, pulled a sled loaded with more than four-hundred pounds of meat and bone.

It had been a good trip and they had plenty to show for it. Sixteen kills, which would net them plenty of trade and more than a winter's worth of good meat for family and friend. It had been their best hunt in years, prompting Loman to suggest they go north beyond Old Settlers' Gap every year, to where the cedars dominated the Great Northern Woods.

Peck didn't much care about how good the hunt had been; he just wanted to get back to his hut and his bed, where he could sleep with a roof over his head and solid walls around him. He wasn't like his father and uncle, who weren't happy unless they were outside, sleeping under the stars, cooking over a fire. They liked dirt and grass and the stimulating smell of nature. Peck liked it, too, until it came time to sleep; then he preferred to be inside, under a roof, with all the comforts of civilization.

With their current load, they were at least seven days from Greenhorn. It was hard lugging so much weight through the northern forests of Boreal; the terrain was hilly and rough, with a lot of fallen trees and large rocks, and they were forced to go around steeper grades and thick woods. Things would smooth out for them once they crossed the Forse River and caught Hunter's Trail. There were a few small villages on the trail where they could stop and take rest, maybe even get a dry bed and a hot meal cooked by someone else.

Peck had yet to go hungry a single day in his life let alone a week or longer. Both Titus and Loman liked to talk about the great famine that had ravaged Boreal when they were kids. "Hundreds died of starvation," they would say as a means of a warning. Then invariably one of them would point a finger and offer up a favorite line: "Food is a blessing and must be thought of as such."

Peck agreed, but since the deaths of his mother and sisters he no longer thought much about blessings. It seemed to him that things just happened, be it a famine or a good hunt. Eventually there would be another famine and more people would starve to death, and in time another boy's mother and sisters would be ravaged and murdered. Everything had a time, and time had everything in the palm of its hand.

"We'll set camp outside the Strawlands tonight," Loman called out, and Titus said, "Sounds good to me, brother."

The Strawlands was nothing more than fields of unruly thistle bushes and wild maize. The stalks grew high but produced little, and though the crop was edible, the kernels were as hard as stones and didn't soften much after boiling. And the taste, even with a generous amount of salt, was stomach-turning. Many a man had broken a tooth on Strawlands corn, and many more had suffered excruciating intestinal distress.

The stuff did not digest without a fight.

"About how far is that? Four rotes?" Peck inquired.

"About that," replied Titus. "Why, boy? You getting tired?"

Peck snorted out a laugh. "I was thinking of you, old man," he said.

"How swell of you, boy, but this old skylos is just fine. I could walk all night without a break. Not like you and those tender feet of yours."

The sad truth was that Peck *was* tired and his feet *were* sore, not that he'd ever admit it; especially not to his uncle, who liked to playfully razz him about everything. They had been walking across rough, hilly terrain since lunch and he was toting not only the hides from their hunt but also a lot of their gear. Though it was more than that when he really thought about it. He'd been walking for close to a full moon now, trudging over all sorts of ground, in all sorts of weather, always with extra weight on his back. Nearly a full moon, sometimes called a month, of sleeping under the stars or in cramped, cold, makeshift hovels; nearly a full moon of hard earth for a bed and only his arm for a pillow; nearly a full moon of listening to his uncle and father snore and fart like sick beyos.

Peck didn't sleep well in the wild. Whenever he returned home from a long hunt, he would hibernate the entire first day, locking himself in his room and burying himself under the covers. He couldn't wait to do that again. He couldn't wait to build a small fire in the hearth, crawl into his bed, and sleep.

"Stop! Look!"

Those whispered words had come from Titus, and the intensity and urgency in his voice influenced Peck and Loman to listen.

"What is it?" Loman asked his brother. "Where?"

"There." Titus pointed to the line of trees flanking them to the right.

They were more than two miles away, but clearly visible.

Those trees stood at the edge of the Dark Forest, one of the four haunted grounds of Hinterland. There were things in those woods that defied logic; that made your skin prickle and your hairs stand on end; that turned the mind over and over again, until it was soft and muddled.

It was said Kin dwelled there and only fools dared its borders.

Titus and Loman, like most folk in Hinterland, avoided the Dark Forest like a plague, choosing instead to hunt the lands to the north and east. They didn't venture into those haunted woods where evil seemed to dwell, and when they circled around them, they were mindful to keep a safe distance.

Peck especially didn't like the Dark Forest, called Skoteino Dasos by the ancients. He thought it stunk of death and decay.

"I don't see anything," Loman said, straining his eyes. "What is it?"

"Not sure. I saw ... something."

"Boar? Bear? Haller?"

"A bear, perhaps. A big one. Up on its hind legs."

Peck searched the tree line where his uncle had pointed. The hairs on the back of his neck were standing and he could feel the awful chill of the scaredy-bumps all down his arms.

He didn't see anything, either, but he'd had plenty of nightmares about the evil things in that place.

"I think you might be losing your wits," Loman said to his brother.

"Some would say I never had any in the first place," Titus replied.

"*I* might say that," Peck joked.

Titus bent at the waist, pulled up a handful of tall grass and weeds, and tossed it at his nephew, who turned and ducked. Some of it caught in the boy's curly brown hair and clung to his shoulders, and Titus laughed.

"Feeble old man," Peck said to him playfully, brushing it away.

"Hairless squat of a toad," Titus replied.

"You two," said Loman, shaking his head.

They started walking again, though Peck couldn't stop himself from glancing at the forest's edge every so often, searching for whatever it might have been his uncle had glimpsed. He never saw anything, yet he couldn't get rid of the uneasy feeling that *something* was out there, watching them, following them. Skoteino Dasos was known to be haunted ground, as it was known to be home to large, predatory animals.

Peck said nothing of it, though, knowing too well the reaction he'd get from his uncle and father. They already thought him mad; he didn't need to strengthen that opinion.

So on he walked, and they followed behind.

Peck let the firelight dwindle down to almost nothing before adding a few more small twigs to the pile. The flames lapped gently at the new food, tasting it first, then contentedly consuming it.

Peck added a couple small branches next, carefully slotting them in here and there, making sure not to suffocate the flames. The fire grew in strength, and the tender bark crackled. It was the only sound that could be heard in these woods. Peck wasn't sure how he felt about that.

Quiet was good at home, in his bed, with walls and a door to protect him from the outside world. But out here, in the middle of nowhere, with who knew what lurking in the darkness, Peck couldn't bring himself to trust the quiet. It felt wrong to him. It felt suspicious.

He had drawn the third shift on watch, the morning shift, which had allowed him to go to sleep soon after pitching camp and eating. That had been fortunate considering how tired he had been after walking all day. His uncle had taken the first shift, his father the second, which was the most difficult of the three; it was a tough ask indeed to sleep for three hours, wake and be alert for two, then shut down again and fall back asleep. Loman had that sort of constitution, though.

Peck usually took the first shift because that was the easiest and safest of the three. Over the years, the second shift had proven to be the most dangerous; there was more activity when the moon was at its zenith and the night its darkest. The third shift could be a mite spooky at first, but it also was the most beautiful. There was nothing quite like watching the red sun of Hinterland crest the horizon and bathe the morning in warm, wondrous colors. Judging by the position of the moon and the soft gray shine of the night sky, Peck figured he had maybe a rote to wait.

Some had taken to calling a rote an hour, but Peck was not yet among them. Minutes were the newest unit of measurement he was most familiar with. According to the Monks, who studied these things, there were approximately sixty minutes in a rote, twenty-eight rotes in a day, and 392 days in a rota, or what most now called a year.

Seconds and minutes and hours, days and weeks, months and years, decades and centuries. It was all very confusing, and had yet to catch on everywhere. Most folk chose to ignore the intricate measurement of time, preferring instead the ancient practice of observing the seasons. Spring and Autumn, Winter and Summer. A rota equaled one rotation of the seasons, though no one had ever thought to number them; no one other than the Monks. According to them, Hinterland was in its 968th rota.

Peck's uncle Titus had something called a timepiece. He had gotten it years ago from one of the river-folk, after saving the man from a wolf. It still worked, though Peck, like many of his ancestors, couldn't understand the need or want to measure time so precisely. Seconds and minutes and hours? What did they matter? A second passed by in a snap of fingers.

Day and night mattered, and seasons were important enough to mark the passage of; even months were worth noting, as they were counted by the moons. There were thirteen of them in a rota, but only four of them had a name. The Harvest Moon was the tenth full moon of the year; the Sowing Moon was the third; the Summer Moon, often called the Silver Moon, marked the middle day of the seventh month. And lastly there was the New Year Moon, which officially ended the year.

Measuring things had become the newest phenomenon in Hinterland. Time was measured, land was measured, and, most significantly, wealth was measured. Chinks of gold and silver recently had been assigned specific monetary values based on weight, and gold, silver, and copper coins were now commonly traded across the land.

Peck understood the need to measure wealth and land, but to him it was a strange practice indeed to measure something that only existed in theory. There was no arguing that time passed, and time went on, but to call it anything other than time made little sense to him.

The timepiece, if nothing else, was an interesting gadget. It was made of gold and its face had odd symbols on it. It was those symbols, called Roman numerals, that marked the passing of time. The face itself was round and flat, with a thin glass covering, and was attached to something like a chain, only it was called a fop. There was an hours' hand, a minutes' hand, and a constantly-rotating seconds' hand.

His uncle was fascinated by the mechanics of it, and often called it his most prized possession, though he rarely carried it with him. It never told the correct time anyway.

Peck thought it a trinket.

Loman thought it a waste of good gold.

No matter what they thought, it seemed the measurement of time was now part of life. Most homes in Boreal, especially those in the civilized villages like Greenhorn, had at least one timepiece, be it a sundial or standard clockface. Craftsmen had learned not only how to build them, but also how to adjust for the time difference, using the ones that had been brought across by the river-folk as templates. And the merchants had understood how to turn a profit selling them.

Peck still didn't see the point. The sun rose in the morning, marking a new day, and fell at night. Seasons passed, and the rotas, or years, passed with them. What did it matter if it was four of the clock or half-passed six of the clock? What did it matter if it was the 857th rota or the 968th? Life was all about the moment, and the moment was all that mattered. And time did not exist in the moment.

His father, like most in Hinterland, felt the same way.

The fire began to dwindle. Peck poked at the orange embers around the base of the stack, causing the flames to rise and the embers to glow. Then he stopped and listened, for a faint sound had caught his ear. It was a sound so faint it might have been carried by the breeze, and he moved away from the crackling fire so he could better hear it.

It wasn't an animal sound, and it wasn't a sound of nature. It was unlike any sound Peck had ever heard before, and he stood perfectly still and set his mind to listen.

Soft. Sweet. Seductive.

To Peck, it sounded like the lullaby his ma used to sing to him when he was a boy, and a warm feeling of comfort spread through him. It was like someone was pouring honey-milk in his ear.

He listened to it raptly, dreamily, allowing its melodious hum to swell in his head. He felt numb all over, and the rest of the world fell away.

Then, as it had begun, it ended. That sweet, soft, mellifluous song faded to silence and what remained was the sound of the wind soughing through the trees.

Peck remained perfectly still, waiting for the song to return.

But it didn't. It was gone.

It was then Peck realized his eyes were closed. Shortly after he opened them, he came to a second realization, this one much more disturbing: he was no longer at camp with his father and uncle; he was now somewhere in the middle of the Dark Forest, and he was alone.

A storm of panic assailed Peck. The Dark Forest was dark in the middle of the day, with the sun high in a bright, cloudless sky; at night it was pitch black. The impossibly high trees in the forest blocked out all light. Peck looked up but could not see even a single star.

He was about to call out for his father and uncle but fear stopped him. There was no telling what evil lay in these woods and he saw no point in calling attention to himself.

The wind gusted, rustling the leaves on the trees and blowing back his thick brown hair. He dropped his chin and turned his face away. Then he heard something move behind him. He wheeled on a dime, peered into the black, saw nothing.

There was nothing to see.

He focused his eyes on the dark and they slowly began to adjust. Soon enough he could make out the trunks of nearby trees, their thick outlines barely visible against the interminable black that surrounded them. Their branches and leaves remained camouflaged by the night, along with the rest of the forest. Peck knew it was out there, though, alive and silently hostile, looming like a giant predator.

The wind gusted again, even harder this time, and again Peck heard something move behind him.

"Who's there?" he said, fear straining his voice.

No answer was returned, and Peck reached for his sword, convinced he would need it. He gasped inwardly when he realized it wasn't in its sheath, and that gasp turned as dry as dust when he discovered that his knife wasn't on his belt. He was alone and unarmed in the Dark Forest, with who knew what lurking in the black.

Then an encouraging thought struck him: it was a dream.

To solidify that thought, he put it to words: "It's a dream," he said. "Just a dream. That's all. I'm asleep at camp. It's a dream."

He told himself to wake up, but it didn't work. He tried again, yelling those words in his head, but nothing changed. He remained in the forest, and the invisible terrors of the forest remained in him.

Peck was no stranger to bad dreams; he'd been having them for years, ever since the brutal attack on his mother and sisters, an attack he had witnessed firsthand. And those dreams had gotten worse over time, leading him farther down a bleak and terrifying path.

It occurred to him that he would be forever doomed to suffer sleep terrors. Worse yet, those visions had begun to torture him in the light of day. The faces of the things that had killed his ma and sisters haunted him like death haunts the infirmed, often making him wonder if surviving that attack had been worth it. Something had been opened in his mind that night, something terrible that frightened Peck down to his soul, and there seemed to be no way to close it.

But this was no dream. He was no more asleep than the forest itself, and the forest never slept.

He glanced around in the hope that more of what the forest held would reveal itself to him, but the darkness remained impenetrable. He figured that he could either wait for the night to end or he could try to feel his way through the woods, using his other senses to guide him. Not that he had so much as an idea of where he was or a clue as to which direction he should walk. But he was too anxious to just stand in the dark like one of the many trees of the forest, stand there like helpless prey, scared and skittish, fretting every little noise.

He looked down; he could see the ground well enough, and he could make out the shape of his legs and feet. It was something, he told himself, trying to be positive. It was a start.

He picked a direction and started walking.

"Peck!" The shout reverberated in the quite forest, ricocheting off the trees and traveling on and on. "Peck!"

Loman Lett had awakened just after dawn, and shortly thereafter had discovered his boy was missing. Peck wandering off was not an uncommon occurrence, but four hours had passed without sight of him.

Peck liked to go off on his own at home, but never on a hunt. Hunts happened in strange lands, and Peck was not one for roaming alone in strange lands. Especially not so close to the Dark Forest.

"Peck!"

"Peck!"

Titus's voice carried better, but Loman's held more emotion.

"Where the hell could he be?" Loman asked.

Titus shrugged and said, "Don't know."

"Something got him. Something had to."

"Don't think like that, brother," said Titus. "He probably went for a piss and got distracted by a squirrel. You know how he is."

Loman hated being a doomsayer, but it came natural to him. He was someone who had already lost his wife and two daughters to unspeakable violence. Peck was all he had left, and now the boy was gone.

"He likes to wander, but not like this. He would not go like this."

Titus grasped his brother by the shoulders and looked him square in the eyes. "We don't start back until we find him," he said. "The hides and meat mean nothing. Only Peck."

"Thank you, brother."

"And we'll find him. He couldn't have gone far."

"Peck!"

"Peck!"

"Can you hear me, son? Where are you?!"

"Peck!"

Presently, Peck was more than seven miles away and traveling in the wrong direction. He needed to be going west or south; instead, he was walking north.

At least now he could see his surroundings. The sun had come up about an hour after he had started walking, and though the Dark Forest was always dark, even at midday, there now existed a faint aura of light to help guide him.

It was really quite a wonder, this dark, haunted place. The trees were nearly as tall as mountains, and the flowers and bushes were thicker than black honey.

Peck had spotted a couple animals he had never seen before, and they had looked at him much the same way that he had looked at them: with a mixture of curiosity and suspicion. They had been small animals, different but not completely unlike hares and squirrels. They were nothing to fear, at least not on sight. Peck was fairly certain he didn't want to run across any large animals that called the Dark Forest home. For one thing, he was alone. For another, he was unarmed.

He kept his eyes alert, searching the shadows and verdant underbrush for movement. He gazed into the treetops for predators, knowing that's where the really big arachnids and serpents dwelled, their bodies perfectly camouflaged in an endless tangle of branches and leaves. There were venomous creatures in this place, and a variety of poisonous plants, too. The hands of death were all around.

Peck's initial plan had been to make it back to camp before nightfall, but he was fairly certain that was a lost cause. He had been walking for rotes without so much as a hint of human life or a clue as to which direction he was going. He kept telling himself that soon he would come to a break in the forest, yet it was half a day later and he was still tramping through the bush and bramble of the dark woods, as lost and hopeless as ever.

He was desperately hungry and thirsty. The hunger he could ignore, but not the thirst. He needed to find a stream or pond soon or he was going to start waning.

To pass the time he tried singing songs, dusting off some of the old campfire ditties his father and uncle often sang on hunts, usually after a few too many ciders. But he lost interest in that quickly, realizing the sound of his voice drowned out the sound of the forest. As much as he was looking for trouble, he was listening for it, too.

"Most times your ears will alert you to prey before your eyes," his father had taught him. "Ears hear in every direction while eyes only see what stands before them." That was good advice well remembered. He wasn't the predator out here but the prey, but he assumed the same reasoning applied.

He scampered up the crest of a small hill, stopped, and looked around. He saw the same things he had been seeing since the sun had first come up and meekly penetrated the forest's dense canopy: berry bushes and shrubs, plants and brightly-colored flowers; he saw mammoth trees and hanging vines that looked like they might be great demon snakes; he saw shadows that seemed to move as soon as he pulled his eyes from them.

He again considered calling out for his uncle and father, and again was scared off by the thought of what else might hear him. That's when he first remembered what his uncle had claimed to have seen only yesterday when they were skirting the edge of the Dark Forest: a large beast stalking the tree line. It had spooked Titus something awful. It had spooked Peck even more and he hadn't even seen it.

'Imagination sketches a more vivid picture than reality.'

Where had he heard that? Peck knew the words, but he couldn't recall the source. Maybe they were his words? Or maybe they had belonged to his mother? According to his father, she had had a skewed way of looking at things, too. No matter. The last thing he wanted to come across was the creature his uncle had seen.

He turned left, taking in more of his surroundings, staring through the ethereal mist that forever clouded the forest, giving the darkness an added layer of mystery.

A shadow moved, then disappeared.

Peck stared at that spot for thirty unblinking seconds but saw no other movement. Finally, he blinked. Nothing changed. He blinked again.

That's when something small and purple caught his attention. Not just one small purple thing, but dozens of them. They looked like berries.

It was indeed a berry bush, and its limbs were polluted.

Peck started down that way at once, led by his stomach, which was empty and growling. Though desperate to eat, he moved carefully, not wanting to give himself away. The prospect of food exhilarated him, but not so much that he forgot about where he was or what dangers may lie hidden in plain sight.

'Let your guard down for a moment and it might be the last time you ever get a chance to.'

There was no question about those words; they were his father's, and he had heard them more than once.

Move too fast and you could step on a snake or alert a nearby bear to your presence.

Peck liked berries, but he didn't want to make them his last meal.

The small hill he had crested bottomed out gradually, giving way to level ground. The earth was softer under his feet here, the plants a little sparser, and there was a path. He stopped and looked for tracks in the dirt, animal or human, but found none.

The berries on the bush were akin to the boysens normally found farther south, in southern Boreal and northern Vernon. They were slightly larger than boysens, and there was a reddish tint to their purple skin, but they possessed the same bumps and oblong shape.

Next to the berries, Peck recognized the leaves of peanut plants. There must have been fifty of them clustered together, and he grabbed one by the stalk and ripped it from the ground. A web of roots came out, and a smile spread across the entire width of his young face. He liked berries and would eat his share, but he loved nuts.

He began pulling plants one after the other, with both hands, until he had at least fifty of them. He then began the arduous process of plucking the nuts from their roots and wiping them clean of dirt. He sampled a few while he worked and found them to be somewhat mushy and tart, though still tasty.

He collected a hundred or so before shifting his attention back to the berries. He picked one, smelled it, cautiously licked it. The same sweet taste he remembered from the pies his ma used to bake tickled his tongue, and he popped it in his mouth and chewed.

It was delicious.

He picked a couple more and ate them. He cleaned off a full branch and started on another. He decided to eat his fill of berries now. The nuts needed time to dry out; he could have them for dinner.

He still needed water, though.

That's when he saw a huge white bird swoop down and alight on the branch of a nearby tree. It was a magnificent bird, with glorious white feathers, large black eyes, and a slim, sharp beak. Peck had never seen anything like it before. It was beautiful and majestic, a creature to admire, but all he could think was that it probably would make for a great dinner. Pheasant had always been one of his favorite meals, and wild chickens were tasty, too. This bird looked meaty enough to fill his belly.

He watched it for a while, and the bird watched him back.

Peck glanced down at his feet, searching for something to throw. A rock would do the trick. He spotted one a few steps away.

The bird squawked loudly, and when Peck looked at it, it shook its bird head at him. Then it went on staring.

Peck put that somewhat human display out of his mind and went for the rock. He grabbed it, stood tall, and began slowly working it around in his hand until he had a good throwing-grip.

The bird squawked again, shook its head again.

Peck stopped and looked around. Something didn't feel right.

"Weird times ahead," the bird squawked, and Peck nearly fell over with fright. "Not for killing me. Friend not foe. Friend not foe."

Peck's eyes went so wide they threatened to burst from his skull. "A talking bird," he muttered to himself.

The bird answered him in its unique bird voice. "Talking bird, talking bird," it screeched. "Where? Where? Talking bird."

Peck stared at the remarkable creature and went, "Ummmm."

Then, before his eyes, the bird's color changed from white to gray, then from gray to black, and then back to gray again.

Once more, Peck went, "Ummmm." He dropped the rock at his feet, convinced that he was going mad.

The Dark Forest was a mysterious place, and Peck had heard many tales from people who had dared its land, including a few from his uncle and father. There were beasts and demons and monsters that called the haunted woods home. There were ghosts and aberrant creatures looking to kill and feed. But talking birds?

Peck wasn't sure if he should kill it or ask it a question.

Then, impossibly, he noticed that the forest had begun to move against him. Vines reached out for him. The branches of nearby bushes curled around his feet. Trees leaned over him menacingly.

There was a brilliant flash of golden light, and a shadow rose up from the ground, swelling like a storm cloud.

Peck tried to scream for help but his voice failed to break the air; it echoed inside his skull like the shrill cry of a dying animal, slowly fading away after every fear-laced resonation.

He screamed again when he saw the shadow-thing rise high above him. The bushes took hold of his ankles and anchored him to the ground while the vines wrapped around his wrists and stretched him tight.

He screamed again, and again, and again, louder each time, and though he never heard his voice, he felt the vibration of it in his head. It was positively deafening.

It felt like he was being torn apart, and he threw his head back and roared with all his might.

More shadows appeared, dozens of them; they danced rhythmically to the sound of the drums pounding in Peck's head. Behind those drums came screeches of agony and shouts of anger, and behind them oozed the whispers of ancestors long gone.

This is it, Peck thought. This is where I shall die, in the Dark Forest, alone, at such a young age.

No one knew where he was, and no one knew where to look for him. He feared his body would never be found, that the animals would devour his flesh, the earth would take his bones, and the forest would consume his spirit. He feared that he would become a phantom of the grove, forever haunting the evil wood of the Dark Forest.

That's when he noticed the bird again, still perched high on its branch. Its feathers were white once more, and it seemed to be smiling.

"Talking bird! Talking bird!" it squawked, and then flapped its wings and took to the sky, leaving Peck on his own.

The darkness of the forest overcame him.

**Ten:**

Dol shook his head. "It's suicide," he said.

The demon's ghostly body wavered hypnotically in the dying light of dusk. It had been patient long enough. It had been patient for generations as man spread across its lands like rats, claiming them as their own. The time had now come to take it back.

"You lack trust, vandalos. Have no faith."

"Faith? What faith? You're a demon," Dol said, as if he needed to remind the shadow-spirit.

"You want have faith in a river snake or yena? Faith is faith, vandalos. I have it. Do you?"

"What you ask is suicide. There are nine of them. You said yourself."

"No. There are four, and there are five."

"And we are three."

"Trust, vandalos," said the demon. "We will not lose. I'll not allow it."

Dol stared off in the distance, where he could see the faint orange aura of the campfire they had going. Calrick and Alde were over there, likely wondering why the demon had wanted to speak with him alone.

Dol knew why. "My boy is sixteen," he said. "Aye, he's strong, but not yet ready to go against trained Herders. Not at those odds."

"Who says he must? Do it right, with my aid and wit, and he'll suffer not a scratch. None of you will. On my word."

Dol sighed. "Next time," he said. "We're tired."

The demon's amorphous body billowed, and in its dastardly sibilant voice came forth these words: "I care not you're tired, vandalos, and want no excuses. The plunder will be worth it, and the time has come."

""What of Micah and his?" Dol said, looking to bargain. "They are four and better rested. And I'm sure they'd be happy for the extra coin."

"Micah and his will serve, too. All hands needed for this one. Do not presume to question me and mine, vandalos. Only do as I say."

Dol sighed again, more deeply this time. It seemed as though they were destined never to make it home. They were less than two days from their village, but the demon wanted them to return to the interminable heat and emptiness of the desert. Dol didn't want to go.

"They'll be ready for us," he said. "You said yourself. Two groups, armed and wary, prepared to fight. Even with Micah and his we're likely overmatched."

"They're not ready for me," the demon replied.

"You can't fight. Not for fists or knives."

"Who says it? Only you. But you will change that. The time has come."

Dol didn't need to see the demon's face to know it was smiling. This was the play he had known was coming, but now that it was here, he no longer wanted to play.

He had agreed to the arrangement of his own freewill, taking it upon himself to look after his clan by any means necessary. But when you make a deal with a demon ...

He knew he could not renege ... unless it was a slow, painful death he wanted; and not just for himself, but for his whole family.

"Does it have to be now?" he asked. "Things are good."

"Things are *not* good," the demon hissed. "Haven't been good for more generations than you can count. Time has come for change, and you need choose what side you're on."

Dol said nothing. He knew what side he was on; he had made the choice and sealed the pact with blood. His blood. Yet he still had trouble believing it. He had turned his back on mankind and sided with Kin. He was a traitor.

"Bad times are coming," the demon went on, its voice droning in Dol's head, making it hard for him to think. "Most will perish, but some must live. Live by our favor. That will be you and yours should you play the cards dealt you."

"Bad times been here long before now," Dol said mournfully. "We've lived them for years."

"You have air in your lungs and blood in your veins, vandalos. Your family, too. Is pride worth the risk?"

Dol remained quiet. The demon's voice continued to buzz in his head. The deafening echo it generated actually caused him pain.

"A wave of madness and carnage soon will come, vandalos. You best be on the right side when it hits or it'll be regret that puts you in the ground. You and yours."

Dol knew what the demon was doing but he wasn't strong enough to stop it. He knew the old words, but he hadn't the faith to say them. On his lips they were babble.

"The pay?" he asked, hoping to ease his concerns with the thought of treasure.

"More than ever," replied the demon, its eyes flashing yellow. "Food and medicine, steel and gold. And the best seeds for purple flowers." It watched for and found delight in the greedy look that flashed on Dol's desert-worn face. "And more, vandalos," it said, going on. "Chinks and coins, silks and all. Meridon will be reborn. With us."

Dol tried to apply thought to the demon's terms, but the undercurrent of its voice continued to drone in his head, delivering a constant vibrating noise that kept nudging him into swells of confusion.

"Say it and it will be, and we'll go. Decline and I will find another. And what then of Meridon? What then of your line?"

Dol had already made up his mind; he had made it up two years ago, when first he had struck the deal, when he had looked into the pale yellow shine of the demon's eyes and agreed to serve it. That night he had comforted himself with lots of whisky and the idea that, despite the cost, it had to be done. It was the only way.

In only two generations, Meridon had gone from a thriving population of 60,000 down to roughly 25,000, and of those 25,000, at least seven out of ten were men; of those men, more than half were either old and past their prime or fiends lost in the daze of the purple flower blossoms. They needed an influx of good men, good women, and children, and for that they needed supplies. They needed crops and animals, medicine and weapons, chinks of gold and silver for trade.

They needed the help of the Kin.

"I knew the day would come," Dol said in a tone stricken by defeat. His shoulders were slack, his eyes cast down on the red rock of the desert. He was the image of a beaten man. "I just thought I'd have more time."

"Time doesn't exist," said the demon. "It is a trick."

"Will it hurt?" Dol asked.

"Yes," the demon replied. "You will know true agony, vandalos, yet not feel a thing."

Dol stared into the billowing shadows that made up the dark spirit. "What do you mean?"

"You are the best of your kind, vandalos. Well-respected among your people. A leader. Makes no sense to take you. But your boy."

"No!" Dol said at once, shaking his head defiantly. "Not Alde. That was not the deal."

"It has been decided," replied the demon. "Or I can go."

"You want to possess my boy?! No! I won't allow it. The deal was for me, not him."

"The deal was for your blood," said the demon. "He is your blood."

"That's not what I agreed to!"

"Aye. It is. And so you know, vandalos, it's not possession I seek. It's something different, and you will have to give it."

"I'll not give it," said Dol. "Never."

"You will or you won't," said the demon. "Perhaps it's Micah I should barter with. Lay this fig at his feet."

"Not Alde. He's a good kid."

"He's a fool and a barker, weak-minded and soft. But a fine specimen. Of good blood and good bone. He will do."

Dol shook his head again. "No. There's got to be another way."

"Always there are other ways, vandalos. But this is my way, and it has been decided."

Dol loved his boy deeply. Alde was his first born, and he had big plans for him. It was he who had struck the deal with the demon, but it would be Alde who reaped the benefits. That's what Dol had thought when he had offered his blood. The demon would take him, and Alde would take his place, becoming Meridon's leader. But it seemed the demon Mar had a different idea.

The thought of sacrificing his boy broke his heart. He couldn't imagine looking at Alde and knowing there was a demon inside him, that his oldest child was nothing more than a suit of meat for a Kin. But it would be the end of his clan if he turned his back on the deal he had struck. He knew that as well as he knew his own name. The demon had promised prosperity and the return of Meridon, and it had promised Dol a long life and fruitful lineage. It also had implied that if the deal was broken for any reason, Dol could expect Meridon and the remainder of his clan to fall on even harder times. His home had already been ravaged by famine, addiction, disease, and poverty; the only reason there was any hope at all was because of the deal he had brokered.

Meridon was far from its glorious past, but some crops and game had returned to the land, and not as many people were sick and starving. As for the purple flower blossoms, generally referred to as mumba buds, Dol was intrigued. The hallucinogenic properties derived from the root of the plant had been the cause of much strife in Meridon, but it also had been an excellent source of revenue. Mumba buds produced amazing medicinal and intoxicating effects, and every village in Hinterland sought a steady supply. He who controlled the mumba bud market would be rich beyond his wildest dreams.

With the seeds the demon had offered, Dol and his could begin to rebuild Meridon's struggling economy, which had bottomed out more than two generations ago; coincidentally, that was when their purple flower crop had first begun to dwindle, leaving them with just enough product to meet their own needs, which quickly went from medicinal to recreational.

Dol had watched many a friend lose their mind and soul to mumba buds. It was one thing to aimlessly slip into the void, yet another to get stuck there. Many in Meridon had been unable to find their way back from the shadows the dangerous, mind-altering drug cast; they shambled about like lakas, all but dead to the world, their minds and bones and flesh slowly rotting away.

Then again, Dol reasoned, the weak always found ways to fall.

"I beg you, take me, not my boy," he said. "I'll go willingly and serve you well."

The demon's shadowy form expanded like a blast of dark smoke. Its eyes flashed yellow. "You serve me well enough as yourself, vandalos," it said. "We all have a part. You have played yours. Now it's time for your son to play his."

"But why Alde? There has to be someone else."

"Your blood is old, vandalos. Your wife's, too. Your ancestors trace back to the start of Hinterland. That is rare. I need old blood but a young body. Your son fits that shape."

"But I have to give him? That is the way?"

"Aye. That is the way."

"Then I don't consent."

"Is that your final word, vandalos?" said the demon. "A word that will lead to consequence. And graves."

Dol now realized that he had been played into a corner. Either step he took would lead to death.

The demon had been right about Alde: he was a good kid, a fine and noble specimen, but there was weakness in him. Not physical weakness; though only sixteen, he was nonetheless as big and strong as a bear. But emotionally, psychologically, he had his share of flaws. He was impatient and headstrong, arrogant and wanton. The boy was susceptible to the demon song, and Dol couldn't help but wonder how long it might be before Alde fell on his own.

"You have three under roof," the demon said. "Two more than this one. Two more to protect and love."

Dol said nothing. What could he say.

"And your boy, he will be king."

"No. *You'll* be king," replied Dol miserably. "He'll be what you wear."

"Matters not, vandalos. The deal you made is in blood."

Everything hinged on this decision, and Dol felt himself relenting, felt himself leaning towards sacrificing his boy to the Kin. He could still hear the demon's words echoing in his mind: "Say it and it will be."

The desert sky was black and the red sand seemed to have turned to ash. Dol gazed off into the distance, picking up the faint orange glow of their fire. His boy was there, likely worrying about him, wondering where he was and what he was doing.

What he was doing was betraying his son, his family, his fellow man. What he was doing was serving Kin. The pain that thought caused him wrenched his face into an ugly mask.

The demon delighted in this. "So?" it said. "What shall you say?"

It was an impossible choice with a simple answer: one boy for a country of them; one boy for riches and health; one boy for a return to prominence and power. All he had to do was agree.

But could he trust the demon?

He looked into the yellow shine of its eyes and saw the jagged bones of death rise up. He saw lakas and yenas and dead friends; he saw his clan and the sprawling fields where his home once had stood. What he didn't see was color. There was no color at all in those blade-like yellow slits, only shades of gray. Shades of gray from which there was no escape.

And behind it all he saw the relentless advance of the Kin, like smoke rising from a fire that could not be extinguished.

"What say you, vandalos?" the demon said with a hiss. "Death or life? With or without? You call the coin."

Dol of Meridon closed his eyes and answered.

**Eleven:**

The girl was smiling and giggling, and Peck felt embarrassed. He wasn't sure why he felt embarrassed; he was bathed and clothed, and he didn't have anything smeared on his face. He checked it anyway, wiping at his mouth and under his nose with the back of his hand.

Yet there she was, looking at him and giggling. Then he realized that she wasn't looking at him at all; she was watching a small, dark-skinned girl play hop-jump-spin. Then the girl herself took a turn, and Peck was mesmerized by the effortless grace and agility with which she moved.

"Would you like a turn?" she asked him, and Peck froze in place. She could see him, and the force of her eyes struck him dumb.

"Hello?" she called out. "It's not that hard. If you've got two feet."

"I know a bird that talks," Peck told her. It was all he could think to say. "It changes colors, too."

"Birds can't talk," the girl told him, and the little dark-skinned girl laughed and laughed.

"No. Honestly," Peck said. "It talks. It knows my name."

"You're strange. Where are you from?"

Peck was about to answer when a gust of black smoke rose up from the earth and enveloped the girl. She was there one moment, gone the next, and all that remained when the smoke cleared was the little dark-skinned girl playing hop-jump-spin.

"Noooo!!!" Peck cried out.

The girl returned moments later, though now it was apparent she could no longer see him. She was somewhere else, somewhere far off and dangerous, surrounded by devious men and dark spirits. She was skinny and young, and they were pulling at her, pulling her this way and that way, trying to pull her apart.

She fought back valiantly, but the darkness overcame her and she disappeared again.

Then Peck saw his mother and sisters; they were floating a few feet off the ground, and they looked down at him with grim, unfriendly faces.

"Son?" his mother said, her hair golden brown.

"Pecker," chimed his oldest sister, Alise. That was the nickname she had given him when he was just a babe.

"Look. It's Peck," said his other sister, Tama. She had the same golden brown hair as her mother.

"Mom? Alise? Tama?" Peck replied, astonished by the sight of them.

"They can't hear you."

This unexpected voice came from the direction of the twisted maple tree to Peck's right. He looked but didn't see anyone there, and when he turned back to find his mother and sisters, they were gone.

"Dammit!" he cursed.

"Peter Lewan Lett! What did you just say?!"

It was his mother again. She glared at him with condemnation, and Peck's boyish cheeks flushed red with shame. "You can see me?" he said to her. "You can hear me?"

"I know I didn't teach you that word. I expect you heard it from your Uncle Titus. He always had a vulgar tongue."

Peck stared at his mother's ghostly face. "Mom? Is that you?"

"Of course it's me. Who else would it be?" She wet her thumb with a lick and went about cleaning the dirt off his face. "I swear," she said to him, sounding slightly annoyed, "if there's muck to be found you find it. Don't you wash anymore?"

"Mom!" Peck said, lurching away from her overbearing attack. It was what she had always done when he had dirt on his face, and he, in turn, had always pulled away from her. He remembered that it had been especially embarrassing whenever it happened in public.

"Cursing? Not bathing? Getting lost in the woods? I swear, boy, what are we going to do with you."

Peck looked around. "Did you see a girl here?" he asked.

"A girl? And you with mud on your face."

"I'm right here, Pecker," his sister said to him.

"Not you, Alise. Another girl. With dark hair. Skinny."

His mother frowned disapprovingly and shook her head. "You promise me you're going to start bathing more often. You hear me, boy?"

"That's probably what happened to the girl," said Alise, grinning mischievously. She was as pretty and pert as ever. "She probably caught wind of your stink. Do you sleep with boars now?"

"He doesn't smell like a boar. He smells like the woods," said Tama, who had always been kinder to him. "Like nature."

Out of the corner of his eye Peck caught a glimpse of the girl with long, dark hair. She was running away from something but he couldn't see what. She vanished again, but reappeared moments later. Now she was falling.

Falling. Running. Fighting. Whoever this girl was, she was exciting. She was also surrounded by darkness.

"There!" Peck cried out, pointing.

His mother and sisters looked. "There what?" said his mother.

"Pecker's losing his mind. Pecker's losing his mind," Alise sang out.

"It's because he's lost in the woods," Tama put in.

"Look. Right there," Peck said, still pointing. "She's walking through a swamp and there are all sorts of evil things watching her. Snakes and ghosts and birds. Can't you see?"

"Pecker's going crazy. Or maybe he's in love."

"Alise, stop harassing your little brother."

"He started it."

"Peck, dear," his mother said to him. "Are you alright? You look sad."

His mother and sisters were real; he could see them, he could hear them, and his mother had touched him. All the same, there was something undeniably wraithlike about them. They were noticeably faint, and they seemed to possess little if any substance.

"No. I'm not alright," he said. "I'm lost in the Dark Forest. Or maybe I'm dead. Am I dead? Because you're dead."

"We're not dead, honey. Just gone. As is the way. Maybe you need some food. You're not acting right."

"Mom?" Peck said, his heart welling with emotion. Tears began to run down his cheeks and a lump lodged in his throat, preventing him from saying what he wanted to say.

"Mom," he croaked, trying to force out the words. "I wanted to ... I mean, I think I need to ... I ... "

But she was already gone. His sisters, too. They had vanished before his eyes like specks of dust, leaving not a trace behind.

The young girl was nowhere to be seen either.

"Lost his beans, lost his beans," something squawked. Peck thought it had to be the white bird, but instead it was a fat groundhog. "Bean soup. Look at all those beans," the groundhog squawked.

"There's a white bird in these woods," Peck said to the animal. "Do you know it?"

The groundhog waddled off in a rush, seeming spooked. Then the trees started to move. Their leaves rustled and their branches bent to the will of the wind, but it was more than that. They appeared to take steps, shuffling left and right, slowly rearranging themselves in the forest. Their trunks coiled and their roots writhed in the ground like snakes.

Then one of these trees said to Peck, in a voice decidedly female, "Shhhhh, child. Tell no one. We switch for the sun and the moon. And who should know? Makes it hard for folk such as you to find your way."

"Wait!" Peck cried out. "Where's the girl with dark hair?"

The tree laughed, and then the other trees joined in. Together, they made the sound of a powerful wind whirling through a canyon.

"Shhhhh," the lady tree said. "Tell no one and you can have some syrup. Straight from the tap."

Peck looked around, searching for the girl with dark hair. There had been something special about her, something mesmeric and fascinating, and he wanted to talk to her more. He wanted to know her name and where she was from.

But the trees were pushing in on him and the sky was falling. He heard rushing water and a thunderclap so loud that it hurt his ears.

He had wanted to tell his mother and sisters that he was sorry. He had wanted to beg their forgiveness because he had been unable to stop the attack that had claimed their lives.

*"Leesy's little brother is fat and happy, Leesy's little brother runs 'round the barn. Leesy's little brother makes chicken head music, Leesy's little brother lives on the farm."*

This odd little ditty rained down from the treetops, and the sound of it reverberated in Peck's head, taking him back to his youth. It was the same song his sister Tama used to sing to him when he was just a babe, and at the end she would lovingly bop his nose.

Peck started to cry.

The bushes started to cry.

Then it started to rain.

The sky turned red, flowers wilted on the vine, trees turned to ash. Raging fires burned here and there, and screams of anguish emanated from the flames, crying for mercy. They were the screams of millions of dead babies, and Peck heard every one of them.

"Why is this happening?!" he wailed. "Why?!"

He wasn't expecting an answer, but he got one. From a redbird.

"Time to fly south, kid. South ho!"

Peck looked at it and said, "Do you know a white bird that can talk?"

The redbird shook its head.

"What about a girl with dark hair?"

The redbird shook its head again. Then it said, "I know a monkey that thinks it's a man. I know a beyo that thinks it can fly."

Peck had no reply for that.

Then the redbird said, "The dark-haired girl is a friend."

Peck's eyes lit up. "Really?" he said, excitement raising the timbre of his voice. "What's her name? Do you know where I can find her?"

The redbird flapped its wings. "Tell me your story and I'll tell you mine," it said. "Tell it full and honest."

Peck started at the beginning.


The Dark Forest had an ethereal charm in the daytime. At least Kelt had always thought so.

He hadn't escaped the flesh-eater and demon-woman so much as they had let him escape. They most likely could have run him down if they had wanted, but Kelt never questioned good fortune, especially when it favored him. He never questioned bad fortune, either, though he did mourn the death of his friend.

Manly may have been a man by age, but really he was just a boy. And now he would go to the Void a boy, alone and much too soon. Kelt had seen far too many of his friends go to the Void too soon. He would go there one day, wherever *there* was, yet he couldn't help but wonder how he had survived so long.

Was it fate? Fortune?

Hinterland was rooted in death, and those roots were connected to everything. But now it seemed it might be cursed by death, too. Death had begun to change the color of things, first from white to gray, then from gray to black. If things kept up like that, it wouldn't be long before all of life was in the dark.

Kelt opened his waterskin and drank. It would be another ten days before he was home; ten days to reflect on the perils of the Dark Forest and his friend's untimely demise; ten days to question his decisions and relive the terrible, tragic memories of his life; ten days of nagging doubt, solitude, and loneliness.

When would it finally end?

The leaves on the trees rustled in response to a stiff breeze, and Kelt peered skyward. The trees were so tall, so magnificent, so old. As old as Hinterland itself. The Dark Forest was a stunning and beautiful sight in the dim light of day, but no less deadly.

Danger lay everywhere in these haunted woods, and he had chosen to walk them. He had walked them yesterday; he was walking them today; he would walk them again tomorrow.

But why, he wondered? Why should he choose to dare this ground?

The old Monk took in and slowly released a deep breath, enjoying the crisp, earthy scent of the forest despite all the evil it held. He then started walking again. After only a few steps, he sensed movement high and to his left, and his eyes shot that way.

It was a bird, a large bird with pure white feathers, and it was flying his way. The bird began to dive, and Kelt instinctively reached for his short-blade, just in case it had an idea to attack.

But instead the bird swooped away, choosing to land on a low branch of a nearby tree. It then looked at Kelt and squawked.

The Monk stared at the magnificent winged creature as if it were a work of art. Its feathers were gloriously white, its eyes black and keen, its wings large and powerful. Unlike Peck, Kelt had no thought to kill it. Why would he? It was spectacular.

He took his eyes off the great bird and started up again, moving quickly across the forest floor. The bird let loose a mighty squawk then, stopping the Monk in his tracks. When Kelt looked up at it, it squawked again and took flight, landing on the next tree.

Kelt thought little of the display and started walking again.

The bird squawked even louder, and once more took flight, traveling effortlessly to the next tree.

A ridiculous thought then occurred to the Monk: he was going in one direction; the bird in the other. He decided to test his theory by taking a few steps toward the bird. He did this cautiously, watching for a reaction from the strange and beautiful creature. What he got in return was something completely unexpected: the bird nodded its head, flapped its wings, and flew to the next tree. It then looked back at the Monk and squawked again.

Kelt was astounded. The bird wanted him to follow.

But should he?

It was widely known Kin could control animals. They could control some humans, too, those with weak minds and corrupt souls, though that took more energy and effort. Animals, with their lack of intellect and hard-wired instincts, were ideal targets for the Kin, who often used them to do their bidding. They could influence a bear or even a wolf to attack someone, and those were mammals with decent brains. A bird would be easy pickings for them.

The possibility that this was a trap could not be dismissed. The bird might be leading him back to the demon-girl and flesh-eater. That would be a truly wicked plot, though hardly unprecedented.

But intuition told Kelt that wasn't the case.

Instincts were far more important than any weapon a Monk carried on his belt, and Kelt's instincts told him that the bird could be trusted. There was something pure and gentle about the creature, and the old Monk found himself curious. And if it was a trap?

Kelt had never had a death-wish, unlike so many others in The Order. He enjoyed life, for the most part, and fully intended to fight for it until his dying breath. But he was a Monk, a warrior, a battler of demons and monsters, and danger came with the territory. You had to take a chance every now and again, had to put fear in your pocket and cut against the grain. It was part of what his kind did.

'Logic only gets you so far in life. Every once in a while you have to step foot into the unknown. That's what faith is.' His former mentor and friend, Monroe, had taught him that.

In deference, Kelt hiked up his boots and let the bird lead him through the Dark Forest.

The bird flew from tree to tree and Kelt followed it, talking to himself more than he would have cared to admit. His mumbled words circled around the point of his possible insanity for following a bird through the Dark Forest. He uttered the words, "I must be out of my mind," close to a dozen times during the march. "I'm actually following a bird," was another sentence he used frequently. They often were paired together.

He went up and over a hill, and the bird took wing again, landing on the branch of a large pine tree. It squawked, and Kelt followed it.

He had started this trek with his sword in hand, prepared to fight should the enigmatic fowl be leading him afoul. But he had long ago sheathed his blade, believing the bird could be trusted.

Trust a bird? He *was* cracking up.

Regardless, the bird seemed friendly enough.

But where was it leading him? That was the question.

Kelt started down the grade, walking sidestep for better balance. As he walked, his eyes scoured the landscape for danger. You had to be alert at all times in the Dark Forest, and you had to be ready to fight.

At the bottom of the hill he angled left, heading towards the bird. He saw a berry blossom bush and a small patch of peanut plants to the right, and farther off he glimpsed a walnut tree. Those were his favorite, and it just so happened that he was feeling a bit peckish. He decided to take a detour but made it only three steps before the bird squawked at him.

He looked back over his shoulder and said, "I'm hungry. Cut me slack."

The bird squawked again, even louder this time.

"Relax! I won't be long!" Kelt cried out. Then, mumbling under his breath, "Now I'm *yelling* at birds. If the others find out they'll retire me for sure. Maybe lock me away."

The bird squawked one more time, and when Kelt glared at it, it rose up and angrily flapped its wings.

"What do you want, you stupid bird?!" the Monk shouted.

It was then a strange noise from the brush, ten or twelve paces away, drew his attention. It sounded like a whimper and was followed by a raspy snort. His blade came out in one smooth motion, the fine metal singing as it scraped against its sheath.

Large boars were known to populate these woods and they could gore a man with their tusks. It hadn't sounded like a boar, though.

Some rustling sounds followed, and then a madcap laugh.

A laugh? That meant … it was a person.

Kelt cautiously followed the sounds and eventually came to the bare foot of a young man. His dirty toes were wiggling triumphantly while the rest of him remained hidden beneath the tangled branches of a berry bush.

"Hello there?" Kelt said in a friendly voice. "I come in peace." With his blade, he carefully moved aside some branches of the bush, revealing a frightened boy with red stains all over his mouth and chin.

"Aaaaaaahhhhhh!" the boy screamed in a high pitch and scrabbled away.

"Wait," Kelt said. "Hold on."

"Bumbler! Bumbler!" the young man cried out, a raving, terrified look in his eyes. "Mad Bumbler!"

Kelt understood what was happening: the wilderberry bush, the red stains on the boy's face, the fear and mania in his eyes – he'd foolishly eaten the berries, which had intense hallucinogenic properties, and now was swinging loose from high branches.

Kelt backed away, not wanting to frighten him more.

Suddenly, the white bird squawked, and Peck spun around to find it.

When he saw it perched on a nearby pine, his eyes welled with joy.

"You're back," he called out to it. "Thank the stars you're back!"

"Brought help," the bird replied with a squawk.

The squawk was all that Kelt heard. Peck heard the words.

He looked at the sword-bearing stranger and showed him a demented grin. "You found my bird," he said to him. "Many thanks, good sir."

"He found me," Kelt replied. Then, pointing, he said, "You ate the berries from that bush?"

Peck nodded excitedly, his demented, red-stained grin adding color to his madness. "The peanuts weren't dry yet," he said. "I like peanuts best, but they weren't dry."

"Aye," Kelt said, smiling kindly. "Peanuts are good."

Peck went, "Ha! Ha!" as if Kelt's words had been a joke, and then he swung back around to the bird. "Can he help me find my pa?" he asked it.

The bird flapped its wings and said, "He's a Monk."

Peck turned his attention back to Kelt, though now there was an expression of awe on his young face. "You're a Monk?" he said to him. "How did you know that?"

"The bird told me. He talks."

Kelt looked at the bird. So far as he could tell, all the bird could do was squawk; annoyingly so. But the last thing he wanted to do was shatter the illusions of a boy on wilderberries.

"I know," he said. "He told me to find you."

"Really?"

"Really."

Peck started to sob. "I lost my father and uncle," he said through his tears. "We were hunting, and then I was alone in the forest. I saw my dead mother and sisters, and there was a girl, she was falling. At least I think she was falling. She was very pretty and very ..." He paused and glanced around nervously. Then he said, "I can feel the color of my skin changing." He looked at his forearms. "I can't see it," he said, "but I can feel it."

Kelt offered him another kind smile. He had never experienced the effect of wilderberries, but he had run across a few who had. They could make a mind go stark wild.

Peck reached up and grabbed a fistful of his own hair. "I can hear it growing," he said, pulling on it. "My hair. It's growing. And my skin is changing colors. And the mosquitoes think they're poets and the spiders hate everything."

"Very true," Kelt said.

The bird squawked, and Peck threw it a glance. Then he said to Kelt, "Ovince says you're here to help me."

"Ovince?"

"The bird's name. He looks like an Ovince to me. Yes?"

Kelt looked at the strange bird again. "Sure," he said. "Ovince."

"You're here to help?"

"That's right. I'm here to help."

Peck jerked his head back and swatted wildly at the air. "Can you stop the mosquitoes from buzzing?" he said. "They make no sense and their poems don't rhyme."

The effect of wilderberries was purported to be not only powerful but long-lasting, and it seemed like maybe this kid had consumed quite a lot of them. It was obvious that what he needed most was rest.

Kelt sheathed his sword and said, "Would you like a drink?"

Peck was overcome with joy at the prospect of water. "Yes! Yes!" he cried out. "Water, please. Cold, wet water."

The Monk uncorked the cap of his waterskin and approached the boy. He handed him the skin, and Peck slugged down six or seven mouthfuls of the tepid liquid, spilling it all over himself as he did.

He moaned in delight when finished. "So good," he said, and greedily gulped down more. "Refreshing," he added.

The Monk took the waterskin from him, capped the mouth, and slung it over his shoulder. Then he pointed aimlessly up into the trees and told Peck to look. When the boy did, the Monk clocked him upside the head with a stiff right hand, knocking him out cold. Kelt was kind enough to catch him before he fell, and he lowered him gently to the ground.

The bird squawked approvingly.

"Was that okay?" Kelt called out, only half-sarcastically.

The bird nodded its head, flapped its wings, and took to the sky.

**Twelve:**

The Croppings was a field of desert grass and shrubs that had cropped up along the banks of a small tributary that flowed to the Basin. The Basin was the lowest point in the desert, and all the natural water funneled down to the reservoir. Rumor had it that the reservoir was more than sixty feet deep and contained all sorts of fish and interesting water life, though no one had ever confirmed that. There also was plenty of green at the Basin, the only green that could be found in the desert. Fruit and nut trees, thick shrubs, flowers of different bloom, and real grass grew out from the shoreline of the reservoir, bringing to life a verdant oasis in the middle of a sea of red sand and waste. But no one dared venture there. The Basin was home to packs of yenas. Scores of them gathered there, along with desert rats, buzzards, turtles, sidewinders, and even lakas.

The land surrounding the Basin made for a fertile hunting ground for yenas. This would be one of the more dangerous nights they spent in the desert. The yenas most likely wouldn't attack such a large group, but they almost certainly would come sniffing around, panting hungrily on the skirts of the camp, waiting, hoping for a lone piece of meat to wander too far from the safety of the herd. The whitish glow of their eyes and their taunting laughter would haunt the darkness all night.

Molt built a fire, and after dinner he pulled from his pocket his prize possession. He had bought it from the river-folk long ago and had taught himself how to play. It was called a harmonica, and Molt had gotten pretty good at blowing campfire songs. He preferred a slow, mournful pitch, what the dour old man called, "the Blues." These tunes fit the night well, becoming part of the mood.

As he played, the others talked and drank cider.

The topic eventually swung around to baseball, which happened often at the campfire. Rarely a trek went by without someone discussing the sport. Yondo had learned about different games from the One True Living World, games like soccer, basketball, hockey, football and lacrosse, but it was baseball that fascinated him most of all. They had a game exactly like soccer, called Laktisma, and another one called Traps that combined some of the elements of basketball and lacrosse. But for Yondo, baseball seemed truly unique. He wanted to learn as much as possible about the game so that one day they could play it in Hinterland.

Presently, the young man, whom they were calling Jacko, was drawing in the sand with his finger.

"Babe Ruth, now there was a ballplayer," the old man put forth. He'd already had three snorts of cider and was teetering happily on the edge of drunkenness.

"You never saw Babe Ruth play," Jacko shot back at him. "You're not *that* old."

"No. But I know about him. Read about him enough." The old man, who had chosen the name Franklin for himself, turned to Yondo. "He used to pitch *and* hit. And back when he played, players would maybe hit six or seven homeruns a year. But him, the Babe, the Bambino, he'd knock out fifty or sixty."

Yondo nodded as if he understood such feats were impressive. Then he said, with a modicum of uncertainty, "A homerun is when the batter hits the ball over the fence?"

"Exactly," said Jacko.

"And a grand slam," Franklin added, "is when the batter hits a homerun with the bases loaded."

The game sounded very interesting, but also quite complicated, much more so than Traps, the object of which was to fling a small disc through a two-foot ring that stood eight feet off the ground. Teams consisted of seven players, the field was circular, and it certainly was a contact sport, unlike baseball.

"I never cared for baseball," the auburn-haired woman said. They were calling her Audrey, after her favorite movie star, Audrey Hepburn. "I preferred basketball. A lot more action."

Jacko, Audrey, and Franklin took turns explaining basketball to the Herders while Molt blew low, soulful music from his harmonica. They interrupted one another, talked over one another, and generally disagreed on the nuances of the game.

Yondo lost interest quickly.

Soon after the sky darkened to black, the first moans of lakas broke in the distance, seeming to drift in on the wind. The screeching yelps of yenas weren't far behind, and Audrey said, "I don't like dogs?"

Molt said to her, "Worry not. They'll poke around some, but they won't get too close. They like easy meat."

Something had been on Jacko's mind since getting off the boat in Vernon. He had forestalled asking about it earlier because he had wanted

106

to get to know the Herders a little better, perhaps develop a rapport with them. The one he trusted most was Dock, and as the warmth of the fire died down, but not the warmth of the booze, he made his way over to the handsome yet grizzled desert-walker and struck up a conversation. He started off with some small talk about lakas.

"Near as we can tell," Dock said to him, his blue eyes glinting in the firelight, "they're part of the desert. Don't see 'em nowhere else. And when you cut 'em, only sand is spilled. No blood, no bone. Just grit."

"You don't know where they come from?"

"Nope." He took a swig of shine and offered some to Jacko, who gladly accepted. "They were here long before us, and likely will be here long after. Where they came from, well, you'd have to ask the Angeloi."

"The Angeloi?" Jacko said. "You mean ... *Angels?*"

Dock nodded meditatively. "That's what your kind calls 'em."

"There are angels here?"

"Used to be, according to old lore and the prophets. But even if that's true, they ain't been seen in generations."

Jacko licked his lips; the dry desert heat had chapped them something awful. Then, staring out at the empty black, he said, "We're dead, aren't we? You can tell me. I can take it. Franklin and Audrey think we are, and I agree with them."

"Dead men don't talk," Dock replied evenly. "But you're gone from your world, that's sure."

"This is the afterlife then?"

"After what?"

"After ... *life?*"

Dock seemed puzzled by the notion. "This is life," he said. "Another stage of it. *After* what came before, and *before* what will come next. If that helps you any."

Jacko gave that a moment to sink in. Then he said, "So why can't we stay here? You know, in Hinterland? With all of you?"

Dock looked the young straggler in the eye. "Because that's not the way," he said. "You come here, but you're not to stay. You have your own place to be."

"The Great Stone Temple?"

"No. That's where we take you. You'll go somewhere else after that."

Jacko took another drink of shine before handing the bottle back to Dock. "And where's that?" he asked.

Dock offered the young man a casual shrug. "Don't know. Never been. No one here has. Not our place."

"But you've heard tales?"

"Sure. There've been plenty of stories passed down, from too many generations to count. But stories often lean to fiction, and the older those stories get, the less truth you find in them."

"What if I run?" Jacko said on a whisper, not wanting the others to hear. He had been convinced by Franklin and Audrey that they were on their way to a place called Purgatory, and Franklin, a one-time devout Catholic, had painted a rather grim picture of what awaited them if indeed that was true. Supposedly Purgatory was a place of trial and suffering, and Jacko didn't much care for the sound of that. By comparison, Hinterland seemed a good fit. He had seen a couple of attractive women back in town, and he was quite sure that he could get used to no electricity or running water so long as he had enough food and drink.

"Run where?" Dock asked him, looking around at the barren sweep of the desert. "There's nowhere to run to."

"You could give me a sword, some food and water, and I could … " He let that suggestion hang, wanting to see if it would take.

It would not. "You'd not last a day on your own," Dock told him. "The yenas or lakas would get you, and you don't want that. Trust me."

"What if you took me back to town? I wouldn't cause a fuss. I swear it. And I can work. I'm a hard worker. Honest."

"I believe you," said Dock. "But it's not allowed."

"Why? Who says?"

"It's against the law." Yondo's words, though softly spoken, struck like a fist to the chest. He had come up behind them while they were speaking, his steps as silent as the stars in the sky. "And, more importantly, this is not your world."

Dock looked up at his fellow Herder and smiled. "Our young friend here has got hot feet. Wants to run."

"I was only asking about, you know … *things*," Jacko said to Yondo, conspicuously avoiding the Herder's gaze. It wasn't that he was afraid of Yondo, but he was more timid around him than the others. There was something about the short, dark-skinned Herder that awed Jacko, making him feel more like a child than a young man.

"Can't let you go back to Vernon, and to turn you loose in the desert would be a cruel act."

"You can run if you like," Dock added. "More than a few have."

Jacko looked at him. He suspected there was more to that statement, and when Dock didn't go on, he asked him about it.

The Herder's lips twisted up beneath the bristly hairs of his mustache, and he slowly shook his head back and forth in an ominous way.

"We tracked each of them down, as is our job," Yondo said. Then, with an unmistakable note of gravity, "Found two of seven alive. The other five, we found what was left of their bones. And you don't want to know what old lore says about the fate of those who die in this world but are not of this world. It's not pleasant."

Jacko had never been a poker player, and the frightened look on his boyish face showed that. He glanced at Dock, hoping to see a playful smile on his lips, indicating that Yondo was only joshing, or at the very least laying it on thick. But Dock's handsome face showed a grim expression, and Jacko's posture sagged.

"No getting out of it then?" he said despondently.

"Why do you want to get out of your own life?" Yondo asked the young man. "This is just another part of it."

"I know. But ... I mean ... I don't know."

"A wise man prepares himself for but fears not what lies ahead, for nothing is etched in stone."

Jacko had no reply for that bit of sagacity.

"Forgive my friend," Dock said with a smile. "The desert makes him poetic. Or perhaps it's the cider."

Yondo laughed.

Jacko laughed, too, but it wasn't a natural laugh.

Sensing the young man's gloom, Dock handed him the bottle of shine. Jacko took it, gulped down a couple swallows, and handed it back. "I've heard stories about where we're going," is all he said.

It was then that Molt and Edgar came back to the fire. They had taken a leisurely stroll around the perimeter to make sure all predators were at a safe distance. They had heard a few moans from lakas but hadn't seen any. The yenas were out there, loitering in the dark, their whitish-gray eyes dancing like firebugs. Uncle and nephew had tossed a dozen or so stones in their direction, driving them back.

"All's safe for now," Molt reported. He was not a big man, but he had survived the desert for twenty years. His orangish-red hair had started to fade; so too the feeble beard that clung to his cheeks and chin like creek moss. Yet his deep brown eyes remained as sharp as ever.

"I hate the Croppings," said Edgar. He looked so much like his uncle that some in town whispered that Molt must have stolen away his brother's wife for at least one night. Edgar, only twenty-two years in age, was taller and thinner than his uncle, but possessed the same orangish-red hair, deep brown eyes, high cheeks, and pointed jaw. They even had the same voice. "Here and the Dustbowl."

Jacko looked at Edgar. "How old are you?" he asked him.

"Twenty-two years, give or take," replied the young Herder.

"That's all? You look older."

"It's the desert. It ages you."

Edgar turned and walked away then. It wasn't rudeness that made him go but consideration. Of all the tasks a Herder had to preform, the hardest for the young ones was often conversation. Answering questions was easy enough, and passing small talk was no problem, but you had to be careful not to say or ask the wrong thing.

Human nature had nearly caused Edgar to ask Jacko the same question that had been asked to him: 'How old are you?' But the young man wouldn't know his age any more than he would remember his name, and that might depress him. 'In the desert, saying nothing is better than saying the wrong thing,' was the mantra his uncle, among others, had beat into his head, and he had taken it to heart.

"I think it's probably time we get some rest," Dock suggested, speaking mainly to Jacko. Both Aundry and Franklin had already taken off their boots and climbed under their blankets. Casualties of Gabby's pear cider, Dock's shine, and miles of hard desert terrain, they were ready for sleep. "Sun rises early, and we must, too."

Jacko agreed without fuss; he was ready for sleep, too. He had asked some of the questions that had been on his mind for the last couple days, and though he hadn't gotten the answers he wanted, he had learned a thing or two. Now he craved a few quiet minutes to put his thoughts in order, which wouldn't be easy after all the alcohol he'd consumed. Dock's shine had his head spinning in circles, and those circles increased in speed soon after he laid down his head, making coherent thought impossible. Shortly after that, those circles stopped completely when sleep overtook him. The next thing he knew, it was morning and the desert was waiting.

Franklin was already complaining.

**Thirteen:**

Gabby needed romas and Elizabeth wanted to go to the market. Lizzy liked going to the market, seeing all the people, looking in the shops and stores, shopping for things she might want when she had money of her own.

They lived on the outer skirts of Vernon, along the trailhead of the northern pass, about four miles from town. They were close enough to walk there without trouble when they needed something, and far enough away to maintain their privacy. Not that they ever needed much. They had most of what they needed to survive on their own land. Nine stremmas with a field of small crops (beans, taters, corn, wheat, onions, carrots, lettuce and peppers), numerous fruit trees and berry bushes, and even a walnut tree. They also had a dozen chickens and eight goats. But for whatever reason, their dirt would not sprout tomatoes.

Lizzy took with her a single silver coin, two dozen eggs – whatever the store owner preferred she would give as payment – and her little sister, Dalla. It used to be Jonno escorting Lizzy to the market, taking her to town, showing her around, teaching her where things were, who to deal with, how to pay. Now it was Lizzy escorting Dalla, and Lizzy loved the responsibility. Dalla just loved being with her big sister.

It was midday when they arrived, fresh from a walk in the warm sun. Dalla had chittered on most of the way, asking her big sister all sorts of questions about life, the desert, the stragglers, and what it was their father actually did on treks. As usual, Lizzy answered her sister's many questions patiently and thoroughly.

At market, Lizzy showed Dalla how to choose the best tomatoes. She picked them up, she looked them over, she gently squeezed them.

"You want them firm," she explained, "but not hard."

Dalla picked one up and gave it an experimental squeeze. "What's the difference between firm and hard?" she asked.

Lizzy inspected the bushel of tomatoes, found one that was not quite ripe, and grabbed it. "Here," she said, handing it to Dalla. "Squeeze this one, and then the one you have."

Dalla did as told, and though she didn't really feel a difference, she nodded thoughtfully and said, "Yeah."

"Firm is a touch softer than hard," Lizzy said. She pointed out a small area of the roma that was green and added, "And there'll be no faded patches like that. It'll be red all around. That means it's good and ripe."

"Red and firm," Dalla said. Then, feeling confident: "Can I pick a couple? I should like the practice."

"Of course. This is going to be your chore someday."

Dalla fingered through the bushel, looking for the brightest romas she could find. She spotted one, but when she picked it up she thought it felt a little mushy. She squeezed it a couple times, then handed it to Lizzy and asked for her opinion.

"You're right. This one is a little soft. But mom is making gravy, too, and soft ones are good for gravy. Find one more of these, and then pick a couple firm ones. I'll go get the yeast and salt and flour."

Dalla got to work, and Lizzy tramped off down the aisle. The salt, yeast, and flour were just around the post, which allowed her to keep an eye on Dalla. That had been the one order Gabby had given her before sending them off: don't let your little sister out of your sight. It was the same order that Gabby had always given Jonno.

Lizzy got what they needed and returned to Dalla, who was diligently picking through the bushel of tomatoes. She had set aside four romas, and when Lizzy got there, she asked her to assess them.

Lizzy put the salt, flour, and yeast in the basket, picked up and squeezed the roma tomatoes one by one, then smiled at her little sister and said, "Perfect. Let's go."

Dalla beamed from ear to ear with pride.

Up front, they set the items on the counter.

Big Loti, the owner of the store, stopped his whittling and showed the girls a friendly face. It was a wide face with a wide nose; his lips looked like fat slabs of mutton and his eyes drooped as if he were tired. If not for his glorious white hair, he would have been the ugliest man in Vernon.

"The Carpana lassies," he said to them happily. "Out shopping, I see."

"Yes, sir," said Lizzy.

"Yondo's on a trek, no? Off in the desert for a moon."

"He is. Mom's making noodles and bread tonight."

"Wonderful."

"It's my favorite," said Dalla.

Big Loti gave the items on the counter a quick scan. "Payment?" he asked. "Or credit?"

"Eggs or silver," Lizzy replied, with Dalla closely watching. She was impressed by her big sister's composure and confidence, and wanted to learn how to be just like her.

"I'm not sure two dozen eggs are enough," said Big Loti meditatively.

"The eggs aren't enough?" Lizzy said.

They were, more or less, but had Lizzy not questioned him the way she had, with a note of skepticism in her young voice, he might have said 'no' and asked for the silver. But honesty was paramount in Hinterland, even when dealing with children, and it was never wise to cross the kin of someone like Yondo Carpana. Not over a couple of eggs.

"Sure, sweetie," he said to her, his fat lips spreading into a smile. "Two dozen eggs should cover it. Even up."

"They're fresh this morning," Lizzy told him. "And large."

"You always have the best eggs."

"We have the best chickens."

Dalla happily pointed to a couple of the eggs and said, "Those ones are from my chicken, Ezzie."

"They look good," said Big Loti.

"They are. Ezzie's good and fat, so she lays good eggs."

Big Loti gave the girl a wink. "I'll have the missus fry 'em up tonight with some onions and peppers."

Dalla smiled big and bright.

"You need anything while Yondo's off, you let me know," Big Loti told Lizzy. "Anything at all."

"We will. Thanks, Loti."

The two girls left the store and started across the square. There were quite a few people around, shopping and working, hanging about and talking. It gave the town a nice energy.

Lizzy said 'Hello' to those she knew or to those folk who said it first to her, and even Dalla chimed in a couple times.

A girl they both recognized – Molt's eldest daughter, Alana, who used to sit them when they were young – stopped and asked them where they were going.

"Home," Lizzy told her.

"Heard Jonno's peeved about being let back," Alana said. "He was anxious for his first trek."

"Jonno's peeved about everything these days," Lizzy replied. "On account of him going through the change from a boy to a man."

Alana laughed a little, and Dalla joined in with a smile. "Boys are a strange lot," Alana said. "But fun. Tell him I said, 'Hi', and that his time will come soon enough."

Lizzy said she would, and her and Dalla continued on, going past Doc Morris's place, the Smith's place, the jail, the food silo, and Marjory's Dress Shop, which they had visited on the way in, taking time to gaze at all the wonderful clothes plump yet pretty Marjory and her plump yet pretty daughters wove from the fine threads the silk traders and river-folk brought them.

"Come," Lizzy said to her little sister in a conspiratorial tone. "If you promise not to tell mum, I'll let you peek in the window at Sana's. Just for a moment."

This was an enticement that Jonno had bribed Lizzy with in the past: a look inside Sana's infamous saloon, where the menfolk in town went to drink and listen to the songs of Ava and Eva, the beautiful twin sisters with beautiful voices and shapely breasts. They wouldn't be singing now, but there'd most likely be some men in there, drinking and acting up.

Lizzy remembered overhearing an argument there once, an argument with some pretty colorful language, the likes of which Yondo had forbade her from ever repeating. But mostly it was old men sitting at the bar, drinking and socializing with sallies half their age, hoping to get them to drop their scanties for a couple of lousy copper coins. Nevertheless, Sana's was an enticement, and young Dalla accepted the idea enthusiastically.

Lizzy looked around to see if anyone who knew them or their mother was watching, for the town had eyes everywhere and folk were only too keen to point out the mischiefs of children. After determining the coast was clear, she grabbed her sister's hand and led her up the steps of Sana's porch. Loud voices emanated from inside, and suddenly there was a burst of laughter, six or seven different voices joining in amusement.

Lizzy pulled her sister over to a small window that showed into the main part of the saloon. She peeked first and saw two young women surrounded by a circle of men. They all seemed to be enjoying themselves quite a bit, and it appeared innocent enough to Lizzy, who moved aside and told her sister to hurry up and look.

Dalla did so, a grin as wide as the desert on her face. When she finally pulled herself away, her big brown eyes were bulging, and with a resounding note of awe she said, "So that's where mom and dad used to go to dance?"

"Aye. Long ago."

Lizzy quickly stole another glance for herself, peeking through one of the clean streaks in the glass. This time it was her eyes that bulged, as the two women had their tops pulled up, revealing their naked breasts. Shouts of approval from the men folk echoed out while the women danced and swayed seductively, playing to the crowd. Celebratory pats on the back and a call for another round of drinks followed.

Before Lizzy could turn away, she regrettably caught the eye of a man she knew, someone who just happened to work with her father. It was Largo Kelsman, the Herder who'd been injured and left for dead on the last trek. He looked beat to dirt and half-wasted, with bandages on his head and a sling over his shoulder. His lame leg was resting on a stool.

But that's not what piqued Lizzy's interest.

Largo looked … *different*. Scary different.

Lizzy would have sworn to the Angeloi that she was seeing things, but other than Largo's busted-up face, which appeared unnaturally dark and oddly distorted, everything else looked normal. Everyone was spot on: Dalla looked right; the people in the street looked right; the other people in the bar looked right. It was only Largo. He looked …

"No!" Lizzy chirped with some volume when Dalla went in for another look. She pulled her sister back, saying to her, "We need be going. You had a peek. Now it's time to go."

The rasp in her sister's voice surprised Dalla, though she thought little of it. She had had a peek, and though she hadn't seen anything interesting, her youthful curiosity had been satisfied. She'd seen inside Sana's Saloon, and her and her sister now had a secret.

They started away in a rush, down the steps of the old saloon and out into the square. They stopped, however, when a voice from behind called out to them: "Carpana girls?"

Lizzy reluctantly peered over her shoulder.

Dalla turned full around.

It was Largo Kelsman. He was coming towards them, limping badly, his unsteady balance aided by a cane. Out in the light of midday he looked even worse. His face was a mess, cluttered with angry bruises and freshly-stitched scars. But it wasn't the bruises and scars that struck Lizzy like a bolt; it was the dark, ghostly visage hiding behind those bruises and scars, staring out at the world through Largo Kelsman's pale brown eyes.

Lizzy secured the grocery basket in the crook of her left arm. With the other she took her sister's hand.

"Girls?" Largo said, giving them each a look. His eyes gravitated to

Lizzy, and there they stayed until she looked away from him. "Yondo's out in the desertlands. I just got back."

Lizzy nodded and said, "Yes." She could not bring herself to look at him again for fear of what she might see.

Dalla saw no threat at all, and said to the wounded Herder, "Our pa never comes back all beat up like that."

"*Dalla*," Lizzy hissed, and squeezed her hand.

But Largo laughed good-naturedly and said, "That's because he's a better Herder than me, sweetie."

He reached out to touch Dalla's cheek, but Lizzy yanked her away from him, hard enough to make Dalla cry out, "Hey! Ow!"

Largo set Lizzy with a suspicious look, but Lizzy turned away from it. "Sorry, but we must be going," she said, and hastily dragged her little sister off. "Come now, Dalla. Ma's waiting. We must get back."

"Tell your ma I asked about her," Largo called out to them as they went on their way. Then he added, "I'll be praying for your dad. I know what it's like out there in the desert."

Lizzy gave no reply. Nor did she look back, at least not until they were well out of town. Then she looked over her shoulder every twenty steps or so to make sure that Largo wasn't following them. She set a fast pace and pulled Dalla along with her, nearly causing the girl to fall more than once. This drastic change in demeanor made Dalla worry, and she asked her big sister what was wrong.

"Nothing to worry on," Lizzy told her, trying to sound natural but coming off anxious. "We need to get home is all. Ma is waiting and you know how she gets when we're late."

Dalla accepted this answer yet still was worried. She could sense something was wrong, but she didn't question her sister again. She just did her best to keep up.

As for Lizzy, she didn't slow down until their house was in sight, and she didn't let go of her sister's hand until they were safely inside.

Lizzy held her secret the whole day, but the weight of it eventually wore her down. She broke shortly after her evening chores were done, while Jonno was out with his friends and Dalla was studying her letters. She brought it up while Gabby sipped at her evening tea.

It wasn't an easy tell, and understandably there was a lot of hemming and hawing at the start. Lizzy didn't know what she had seen, and she wasn't sure how to properly describe it. More than that, she wasn't even sure that she believed it herself. But she had to tell someone.

When she finished, Gabby fixed her with a very parental look. Lizzy had seen that look before, many times; it was a look Jonno received often, usually after he said or did something stupid.

Lizzy had a pretty good idea what would come next.

"Honey," Gabby said to her gently, "I'm sure it was just the bruises. I heard he got beat up pretty good. Heard he nearly died."

"It wasn't the bruises," Lizzy told her. "There was something *behind* his face. Or inside it. I don't know how to explain it right."

"Okay," Gabby said, remaining patient. She knew Lizzy well enough to know when something had her spooked. She also knew that not much spooked her anymore. "What was it then?"

Lizzy thought about what she wanted to say, then, after some hesitation, in a voice so quiet it couldn't even be called a whisper, she spoke. "A demon maybe."

Gabby smiled politely at her daughter. "No. Not a demon, child," she said. "They don't work in such ways."

"But they do," Lizzy protested. "They possess people. The preacher said so. Dad, too."

"Aye. That's true enough. But when someone's possessed, you can tell. They're mad with hate and lust. They can't hide it. Your father visited Largo before he left and said nothing about it. And your father is a Herder. He knows of the Kin."

Lizzy sighed. "But it was there, ma," she said. "Honest. I saw it. I'm not making it up."

"I believe that *you* believe you saw something. But I think maybe your eyes played a trick on you. It can happen in the sun."

A shred of doubt crept into Lizzy's mind. "Maybe," she said, suddenly unsure of herself. "But ... He ... "

"For all the whispers and rumors, possession is rare, child. Haven't had one here in years. Last one was Delric, I believe, and he was half mad to start with. He killed three people, then himself. Largo's a Herder. It's near impossible to turn the mind of a Herder."

"But he was attacked. He was weak. Maybe he didn't have a choice."

"A Herder will always choose death over possession."

Lizzy opened her mouth to speak more, but nothing came out. Doubt had her firm in its hand now and she was no longer sure what to say or think. She would have sworn on her life that Largo had a demon in him, but her pa had seen him and had said nothing of it, and her ma was making sense. Demons possessed the weak and the wanton, and Herders were neither. But she had seen *something*.

There were people out there who supposedly could see things that others could not; they could see through the veil of reality into the shadows of the dark places, where the Kin and their kind hid from the world. *To Vlema*. The Sight. Most folk considered it a falsehood spun by diviners and witches, nothing more than a sham put forth to fool fools and make money. Of those who did believe in it, many thought it a curse, a sign of communion with evil spirits.

Lizzy wondered if perhaps she had the Sight.

"Look, we can't do much for it now," Gabby told her. "Yondo's gone twenty-five more days and nights, along with many other Herders. But if you like, we'll stay away from town, and away from Largo, too, at least until Yon returns. Then we'll tell him about it and see what he says."

Lizzy nodded respectfully. "The Kin make people mad?" she asked.

"They drive them to fits. Make them do terrible things. Did Largo *seem* odd or different to you? Did he seem dangerous?"

Lizzy's broomstick shoulders lifted and fell with a shrug. "Don't know. Maybe. I don't really know him."

"He just *looked* different?"

"Aye. He looked ..." She wanted to say he had looked evil or possessed, but doubt stole her confidence and instead she said nothing. A sad look dragged her lips into a frown.

"Come child," Gabby said to her, and pulled her close. She grabbed the brush off the table and began running it through her daughter's wild tangle of long brown hair. "I'm sure it was nothing, but if you're really worried, I can go and visit him tomorrow. I can take him food. Largo's a widower and would appreciate a hot pie."

"No!" Lizzy said with a start. "Don't. Please." The brush caught in her hair then, and she winced when her mother yanked it through the knots. "Owww," she said, reaching back.

"If you would brush it fresh from your bath it wouldn't get so tangled."

Lizzy hated brushing her hair. She wasn't overly fond of baths either, but they served a purpose. She actually preferred bathing in the creek at the end of their property, but Gabby had forbidden her from doing so anymore, saying it was unladylike. It was dangerous, too. Lizzy hadn't bled yet, but she had begun to blossom.

"Just stay away from him, okay?" Lizzy said. "I don't want you going anywhere near him. Promise me."

Gabby set down the brush. She touched Lizzy's chin and gently guided her head around until they were looking at one another. And when she gazed into her daughter's deep gray eyes, she saw fear and worry and sorrow, emotions quite unnatural to Elizabeth Layne Carpana.

Jonno was one to be swayed by fear and things imaginary. Even Gabby herself had been known to give too much way to unnecessary worry. But Lizzy? Lizzy was as playful as an otter pup yet as keen as a hawk. She seemed to possess an innate sense about people, an innate sense about the world around her, and more often than not was right.

There was something in those smoky gray eyes of hers that spoke of a terrible truth and suddenly Gabby was concerned.

"Okay," she said. "I won't go near him. I promise."

"Good," Lizzy said. "We can wait for dad to come back."

Gabby said that sounded like a fine idea. Then she picked up the hairbrush and started combing through her daughter's wild nest of hair again. "I swear," she said with a note of jocularity in her voice, "I think you literally tie your hair in knots just to spite me."

"It just gets that way on its own," Lizzy said. "There's so much of it."

"Well, I know how to fix that." Gabby grabbed a handful of locks and playfully called out, "Say the word and I'll chop it all off."

"No," Lizzy said, pulling away. "I like it long."

"Then brush it, girl. Or it's a bald head for you."

Lizzy giggled, and Gabby laughed and started brushing again.

**Fourteen:**

Peck heard the crackle of a fire. He felt its heat on the back of his neck. He smelled smoke and ... *charred meat?*

He thought of the white bird, and he thought of his father and uncle. He thought of the white bird because he had dreamt of the white bird. He thought of his father and uncle because he had lost them.

He was awake, but he kept his eyes closed for a time. He wasn't sure where he was or who he was with and he wanted more information. There were smells and sounds he could interpret that might give him a clue. He was quite good at putting clues together. Such as ...

He heard faint sounds of breathing and chewing but no talking, which likely meant that whoever had built the fire was alone. He heard crickers, too, those noisy little pests that kept him up all hours with their constant screeching. Hearing them meant it most likely was nighttime; it also meant he was probably no longer in the Dark Forest. As for what he could smell, the charred meat captured all of his attention. It smelled rich and tasty, and he was so very hungry.

Another detail he gleaned was that the heat from the fire was warmest on his back. That meant he was facing away from the flames.

That thought in mind, he hazarded a glance, opening one eye just a slit. It was dusk; he could tell by the color of the light; more gold than red. He saw before him rocks, grass, and bare land, leading him to determine, as he had suspected, that he was no longer in the Dark Forest.

Then he heard a strange voice say, "You're awake. Good."

Peck didn't move. The voice was both familiar and unfamiliar to him; he couldn't place it, but he knew he had heard it before.

"Come now, boy, you must be hungry. You've been out for more than a day." Then: "If I meant you harm, boy, you wouldn't be free. You'd be shackled tip to toe. Or you'd be dead."

Despite that logic, Peck remained still. He slowed his breathing and shut his eyes tight. He didn't know who this man was or what he might want, and he wasn't about to make things easy on him.

Then the tantalizing scent of the charred meat found his nose again and he thought that he should at least consider a proper introduction, perhaps even some polite conversation ... polite conversation along the lines of: 'Could I maybe have a piece or two of that meat?'

And so Peck slowly turned over, lifted his head, and set eyes on the stranger who had spoken to him. The man appeared to be around the same age as Peck's father and uncle, perhaps a little older, and he possessed the same salient, hard-etched features they possessed, letting it be known that he made his way on the land with equal parts hard work and character. His nose looked as though it had been broken a couple times, and there was a scar aside his right eye. His shoulders were broad, his back straight. His bearded chin was solid and his hands were like paws.

It was the man's attire that was most interesting, though. He wore the gray robe and rawhide boots of a Monk. And on his belt Peck noticed the traditional weapons of that Order: a knife, a short-blade, a set of daggers. There was no long-blade or whip visible, but Peck saw an empty sheath for a long-blade and a clasp where a whip might go. That left little doubt in Peck's mind that this man was a member of The Order of Monks.

"Feeling better?" Kelt said. "Quite a journey you took, I imagine."

Peck's memory had yet to return in full. He remembered the hunting trip with his father and uncle, he remembered hearing a melodious song, he remembered following that song and getting lost in the Dark Forest, and he remembered the talking bird, Ovince. He had scant memories of dreams that included his ma and sisters, and also a dark-haired girl running from shadows. He had even scanter memories of berries and peanuts, and of trees that talked and moved through the forest.

There was little sense to make of these dreams as far as Peck could tell so he put them out of his mind. Instead, he concentrated on the pounding thump in his head and the deep rumble in his stomach.

"Is that rabbit?" he asked. There were dozens of questions queued up in his head, questions about The Order of Monks and the mysteries of the Dark Forest, questions about demons and magic and dark spirits, but it was hunger that leapt to the fore.

"Have at it," Kelt said. He pulled his knife and offered it to the boy.

Peck didn't have to be told twice. He grabbed the knife, reached over the flames, not the least bit worried about burning his hands, and sliced off a chunk of meat. He blew on it a couple times, then popped it in his mouth. It burned his tongue and the insides of his cheeks, but he chewed and swallowed it anyway.

"Eat your fill, boy. I have more." Kelt promptly skewered the skinned carcass of another hare and carefully situated it over the bustling fire.

Peck sliced another piece from the fully-cooked one. "I'm so hungry," he said as a means of apologizing for his lack of manners.

"I would think so."

"Would you like me to say a prayer first?" Peck asked, believing that's what a Monk would want. "Do it proper?"

"Do you know any prayers?"

Peck's face went blank. His ma had made him say prayers at bedtime every night, and also over every meal, but his father had made no such demands after she had passed. In the Lett house, all faith had died with the women. It had been years since Peck had rehearsed one.

"Not really," he said, looking somewhat embarrassed. "I mean, I know a few prayers to the Angeloi. The shorter ones. I used to say them every night, actually, but it's been a long time since then."

"You look far too young to say it's been a *long time* since anything," Kelt replied. "Anyhow, you've got no need to worry on prayers, boy, proper or otherwise. I gave thanks whilst skinning them."

Peck took another piece.

"So, who are you? From Boreal, I assume? You've got that look."

Peck nodded while he chewed rabbit.

"You're a mite young to be roaming the Dark Forest by yourself."

"I heard a song and followed it into the woods. Then I got lost."

"Ahh. And the berries?"

"The berries?" Peck searched his memory. "Oh, right," he said, remembering. "I found a berry bush. Peanuts, too. The berries were very sweet. I ate a lot of them."

"What else do you recall?" Kelt asked him, the slightest hint of a grin etching itself on his face.

"Well ... I ..." Peck hesitated, unsure of whether or not he should mention the talking bird. He did not want to come off as insane, especially to a Monk.

Kelt helped him out. "How about a talking bird? You remember a talking bird, boy?"

Shame warped Peck's face. He looked away from the Monk and said, "Ummm ..."

"Poetry reciting mosquitoes? They ring a bell?"

Peck's awkward shame morphed into confusion. "Poetry mosquitoes?"

"Walking trees?" the Monk went on. "Prophetic bumble bees? Grumpy spiders? A pretty girl with monsters chasing her?"

Though he recalled few details, Peck had a good idea of what the Monk was talking about. "My dreams," he said. "I had dreams about trees walking in the forest and a dark-haired girl being chased by shadows."

"Maybe dreams. Maybe hallucinations," Kelt said. "Those berries you ate were hallucinogenic."

"Hallucinogenic?"

The Monk nodded, and spun the rabbit half a turn. "There's a powerful toxin in them. They'll make you see things that aren't there. Make you remember and then forget things you never knew."

"So then ..." Peck wanted to inquire about the talking bird, but once again embarrassment made him reluctant. There had been no talking bird, he now realized. He had been hallucinating.

He tried again. "I was ... My dreams, they felt so ..."

They had felt so real, yet strangely he couldn't remember very much about them. He remembered the white bird, and he remembered seeing and speaking to his ma and sisters. And of course he remembered the girl with dark hair. Her face was etched in his brain.

"Are you alone?" Kelt asked him.

Peck broke free from his doleful ruminations and shook his head. "No. My pa and uncle are with me ... *were* with me. We were on a hunt."

"You don't know where they are now?"

"Looking for me, I suppose. We were at camp and I heard ... *singing.*"

Kelt nodded as if this made sense. "Skoteino Dasos calls to some folk, and its call is hypnotic."

"Yes," Peck agreed. "Hypnotic. It was like I was in a trance."

"Where did you lose your kin? Any thought on that?"

Peck swept his gaze across the land ... and he realized he had no idea where he was or which direction he was facing. He glanced up at the sky, trying to figure his way by the morning sun.

"North is that way," Kelt said, pointing left. "The northern border of Boreal is there," he went on, his finger traveling farther left. "The Great Northern Woods are to the south and west, three days from here."

Peck picked out a point in the general direction of the Great Northern Woods and said, "About there, I'd say. Along the rim of the Dark Forest." Then, remembering something, he added, "We last set camp in the Strawlands. Do you know where that is?"

"Aye. It's more than a day's walk from here." Kelt pointed due west, at least thirty degrees from where Peck had pointed. "That direction."

"I have to go there. Now. I have to find them. They won't go home without me, and they have hides and meat for the winter. It was a good hunt. Families are depending on us. I have to find them."

Kelt showed a brooding sort of look; he had the right face for it. There was wisdom in his eyes and strength in his jaw. "Can you handle a blade, boy?" he said.

Peck nodded, said he could.

"There're evil things in the Dark Forest, dangerous things, and I can't safeguard you and myself."

"I'm a good hunter," Peck said.

"Ever encounter a Sarkofagos?"

"A what?" Peck asked. He had never been good with the old tongue.

"A flesh-eater."

Peck's eyes widened considerably. "No," he said. "Why? Are they in these parts?"

"Aye, they are. How about Kin?"

Peck's eyes took on a different shape; a different shape and a different shade. Kelt noticed it right off and said, "You've seen one?"

Peck looked away from the Monk, choosing instead to stare out at the red shades of morning. "I think so," he said in a quiet, reflective voice.

Kelt turned the rabbit again. "We've got some time before we can eat this one," he said. "Why don't you tell me what you saw, boy, and I'll tell you if it was a demon."

"Well?" said Peck when he had finished. "What do you say?"

The story was astonishing, but not shocking. Kelt had heard similar tales from others during his days as a Monk; violent, bloody episodes that made little to no sense when held up to the light ... but not so in the darkness, where the Kin did dwell and dance. It wasn't murder for money or passion or revenge; it was murder for the sake of murder, violence for the sake of violence, cruelty for the sake of causing pain that would endure long after the blood and bodies had gone cold.

Rare, random, and completely unpredictable.

"Sounds like possession to me," Kelt said. "It's a test of sorts."

"A test?" Peck asked. "How so?"

"There's a lot not known of the Kin. The Sarkofagoi have returned to these parts, and demons once more are taking flesh. That's what I was running from when I found you: a Sarkofagos and a demon woman in the flesh. They killed my partner."

"I'm sorry."

Kelt shrugged indifferently, but the lambent glow of the fire betrayed his true feelings. There was sorrow on his face and pain in his eyes. He had liked Manly; to lose him at such a young age was a tragedy. "Thank you," he said in a soft voice. "He wasn't much older than you."

Life in Hinterland was hard, and Kelt wasn't sure how much more he could take. It seemed to him that the inexorable force of momentum was on the side of the Kin and the only thing standing in its way was time.

"What sort of test?" Peck asked.

Kelt broke free from his somber thoughts and refocused his mind. "The Kin's been getting stronger," he said. "Old Kin are coming back, and New Kin are coming out of the wood."

Peck was confused. "New Kin? I thought Kin was Kin?"

"Kin are Kin, but there are Old and New. Old Kin are more powerful and dangerous, and they have dwelled here since the dawn. They and the Angeloi came here together, and it was their war that nearly destroyed this world."

"And the new ones? Where do they come from?"

"The Old make them from us. Possession is the most common way to do it. Others they trick with a deal too good to be true. A small number are born by them."

"Born by them?"

"Aye. They can easily seduce us, and while they struggle to procreate, it's not impossible."

Peck was aghast. He didn't know what to say.

The Monk went on. "The New aren't as strong or cunning, nor can they control people or animals, but they're powerful nonetheless. They're stronger, faster, and harder to kill than we are, and they are vessels of true darkness."

"And they're from here?"

"Some are. But this is not the only world. There are others. Demons can come and go in these worlds like walking through doors."

"You've been to these other worlds?" Peck asked.

"Me? No. We cannot cross such divides, except in death. And in death, only your soul survives, not your flesh."

"I don't understand," Peck said. "How can you know there are other worlds when you've never been to them?"

This simple query brought a smile to the Monk's bearded face. "Good thought, boy," he said, nodding appreciatively. "For one, it's written in the Divine Scroll, and the Divine Scroll came from the Angeloi. For another, strung demons have confessed it. They're out there, only we don't know how to get to them. It's like how stragglers and stones come across Potami with the river-folk. Where do they come from? How do they get here? It's a mystery. One not meant to be known. Yet."

Silence followed for what felt like a long moment. The fire was slowly dwindling, but the sun's face was up and bright, adding color and warmth to the day. To the east, the first trees of the Dark Forest could be seen, while to the west and south the view was more scenic.

The Monk took a drink of tea while Peck thought about what he wanted to say. He went with, "They're big, right? Flesh-eaters. I've heard they're big. Ten podes tall." His voice was edged with the curiosity of youth, and there was a wide, eager look in his eyes.

"Some are twelve podes," Kelt told him. "And they're as thick as oaken trees and just as hard."

"And you fight them?"

"Aye. But it's not easy fighting monsters so big."

They were surprisingly quick, too, thought the Monk. On top of that, they were highly-intelligent. Not only could they speak the common tongue, but they could put together words and thoughts better than most men. That made them incredibly dangerous.

"I can quote lore, boy," Kelt said as he stared at the flames, "but lore is just that. The Kin play all sorts of tricks, and that includes spreading lies as lore. They spin webs and salt their words with the truth, and before you know it you're lost."

Peck nodded as if that made sense. Then, wanting confirmation, *needing* confirmation, he said, "You believe it was Kin that killed my ma and sisters?"

"Sounds like it to me," Kelt told him. "If not them, their influence."

"What do they want with us? I don't understand. What could they have possibly wanted with my ma and sisters?"

Kelt sighed. That was not an easy question to answer. Even so, he gave it a shot. "This was their world once," he said. "Before we ever came here. They want it back."

"And the Angeloi?" Peck asked.

"There are writings not included in the Divine Scroll that state the Kin and the Angleoi lived here together as equals. Then we came along and the Angeloi began showing us favor. It has been said by many that that was the cause of the Great War."

"Do you believe that?"

The Monk gave the boy a genial smile, then he spread his arms in a way that showed off his robe. "Aye, it is a comfortable garment," he said. "Stylish, too. But I don't dress like this for comfort or style. This is my way and I live it. But it's not my concern where the Kin come from or what they want. I know them to be true, and I know them to be evil. My only want is to stop them."

A grim look darkened the depths of Peck's eyes. In the amber glow of the fire, he looked haunted. "After everything that happened to my ma and sisters," he said, "I want to stop them, too."

"Easier said than done, boy. They kill easy and die hard. And they've got more tricks than you can count."

"But you *can* kill them?"

"Demons? Aye. Anything can be killed."

"But *you've* killed them?"

The Monk had been asked this very question hundreds of times; there wasn't a town or village between Casping and West Farm where he hadn't been made to speak on it. He had loved answering it in his younger days, when the job and his spirit were still fresh and new, before he'd been hardened by nine-thousand days and dark nights. But now it was more of a nuisance than anything else. Everyone wanted to know about his battles with Kin, and everyone had a battle they felt compelled to share with him. But with Peck, he felt no such inconvenience; he actually wanted to tell him the truth about things.

"Yes," he said plainly. "I've killed demons."

The boy was impressed. Monks were solitary men who kept no friends or family, who came and went like the wind and rarely spoke a word, yet they were widely revered, even idolized, throughout Hinterland. Peck dug in his heels and lobbed another question: "How many have you killed?"

Kelt didn't have to think about that; he knew the count by heart. There were three slashes on the back of his right shoulder, one for each demon he had slayed. He told the boy exactly that.

"Only three?" Peck replied, surprised by the low number. He had thought it would be much higher given the Monk's age.

"They're not easy to find, and even harder to kill," Kelt told him. "They are survivors, cunning and strong."

"But … Only three?"

"Aye. Only three. And I was lucky all three times. You twig, boy, most of what we do has little to do with killing Kin, despite whispers and rumors. We aim to help folk in need. That is our true mission. And while we may not *kill* many Kin, we chase a lot of 'em off. It's called 'Exorkoun' in the Divine Scroll. When there is a demon inside someone, possessing them, we pull it out. This does not kill the demon, but it does save the soul of the man or woman possessed. And that is more important. We also pray in communion, leave blessings behind that ward off evil spirits, and kill monsters made of man."

"Like flesh-eaters?"

"Aye, like flesh-eaters. But I've only killed one of those. That's what people want to hear about, though. Kin and sarkofagoi. The soul-struck and possessed." A faint smile lifted the corners of the Monk's mouth. "No one cares to hear a campfire tale about an old man in a robe reciting prayers," he said. "And I can't say I blame them."

Peck smiled back. Then he said, "Still. It has to be hard."

The Monk stared into the pulsing heart of the fire. "This has been a world in decline for many years," he said in a faraway voice. "A forsaken world lost in darkness. War is coming. I don't know when, but it's coming. And it's a war we cannot lose."

Peck said nothing. What could he say?

The Monk went on: "The Kin have increased in number here, and they have become emboldened." He thought about the seductress in the woods, the sable-haired beauty who had toyed with him, and he thought about the giant that had killed his friend. "Meridon is gone, and the lands in the far north are wilder and more dangerous than ever. So too the haunted lands here. The Dark Forest, the Marshlands, the Dustbowl, the Dillies."

Kelt shook his head in disappointment. For every victory he had celebrated in the cassock, there had been three or more defeats to mourn. "Evil is a disease," he said, his voice one with the song of the fire. "Once it gets hold of you, it rarely lets go. Meridon is an example of that. The Kin have been here since the start of time. I don't often see them, but I feel their presence. It's growing by the day.

"There are other stories that were left out of the Divine Scroll, ancient stories of unknown origin, that claim the Kin and Angeloi are one in the same. Brothers and sisters in spirit and flesh. These same stories claim there was a war well before the Great War in Hinterland, and the Angeloi

128

who lost were cast down here. It was them that became what we call Kin."

Peck was blown away. He was hearing things he had never imagined possible, and the sharp edge of the world had left him with a rather vivid imagination. The Kin once had been Angeloi? The idea seemed ridiculous.

Then again, the more he thought about it ...

There had been an old man in Boreal, old man Tucker, a crazy old goat who used to go on about demons and the forces of evil, about the Angeloi leaving Hinterland generations ago, about the world being forsaken, about scourges to come. Everyone said he was a fool gone mad on shroom tea and idlewood bark, and they cursed him, and mocked him, and beat him.

Peck had been a boy of ten when Tucker was killed, and though no one ever spoke openly about how it happened, rumors nevertheless abounded. They were the kind of rumors spoken in hushed, fearful tones, as if such words might breathe life into something unspeakable.

Those stories had made Peck think about what had happened to his mother and sisters, but when he had asked his father about it, he had been admonished, severely.

"You do them a great insult by mentioning them in the same breath as that lunatic," Loman had told his boy that day before sending him off to bed without supper.

But now ...

Peck thought about what he wanted to say next, which one of the thousand questions currently swimming in his brain he most wanted an answer to, questions about the Kin and the Angeloi, questions about his ma and his sisters, but all he could think to ask was, "How many worlds are there?"

The Monk shrugged his shoulders and spat in the fire. "Five? Eight? A couple dozen?" he said vaguely. "Hard to say. Wish I had more answers for you, boy. I've heard tales of other worlds beyond the Great Stone Temple on the far side of the desert, and I've heard tales of other lands past the Great Serpent River. But tales will make you chase, and no one that I know has ever been. What I *do* know is that we are more at risk now than ever before, the Kin is bolder and more in number, and Hinterland is slowly falling."

Another question rose in Peck's head and he quickly blurted it out, not wanting to forget it: "How do you fight them? The Kin? How do you kill them?"

Kelt had been posed that particular query by hundreds of people, all of them hungry to hear about great and bloody battles with evil spirits and ghastly monsters. He had a stock answer on the cuff, a simple, believable, boring response that hinted at the truth but downplayed any theatrics, only he didn't want to use it with the boy. He felt the need and the want to speak freely with him, so he did.

"Most demons are spirits, so there's no flesh to harm. You have to kill the spirit by making it flesh, which involves a trap and hours of prayer. It's a difficult and dangerous ordeal, and often fails. When it doesn't, when the demon is caught, you take its head and burn what's left of it."

"What kind of trap?" Peck asked.

"A trap of flesh and blood. We use animals mostly. A few times we've trapped them inside people, when there was no other way. Those people were long gone by then. Beyond saving. There are divine sigils involved and numerous prayers. It takes a lot of effort and a lot of belief, and still we fail way more often than we succeed."

Peck wanted to know more but he didn't want to push. The Order of Monks was a mysterious rank, and their methods were steeped in tradition and secrecy. They rarely spoke to anyone outside their Order, and to become one of them you had to renounce everything but your first name.

"Instead of talking about demons," Kelt said, not letting the silence between them grow, "why don't you tell me about this girl of yours? You spoke of her quite a lot in your sleep."

"Girl?" Peck said, somewhat confused. "You must mean my mother?"

"You called her Dasha."

"Dasha?" Peck had no idea what the Monk was talking about. "My mother's name was Hilde, and my sisters were called Alise and Tama."

"You kept telling her to run and hide, that there were shadows trying to kill her. You told her to hide in the garden and to trust no one, neither friend nor foe."

"Oh. Her?" Peck said, remembering now. The dark-haired girl from his dream. "I don't know her. She was just a girl in a dream I had. Or maybe it was a hallucination. I don't know which one it was." Yet he remembered her face exactly, just as he remembered everything she had done and said.

"Sounded important," replied the Monk. "Oh well, no bother. Dreams can be omens, they can show us our desires and fears, and they can be nothing more than madness. What of your mother and sisters? You dreamt of them, too?"

Sorrow took full command of Peck's young face. "Aye. I wanted to ask them to forgive me for not being able to help them," he said. "But they vanished before I could tell them."

Sensing the boy's pain, Kelt said, "There's nothing to forgive, I'm sure. Not many out there can stand against three possessed bodies, and you were only a child. If you had stood and fought, they would have killed you, too. You do owe them a debt, though. Your ma and sisters, that is."

"What debt?"

"You're alive, boy, so you must act it. It'd be an insult to them if you let their deaths ruin your life. That's not what death is about. They've moved on, as must you."

Peck nodded thoughtfully. That was the same message his pa and uncle had been trying to hammer into his head the last eight years. Peck had always known they were right, of course, yet he had chosen to ignore their advice, instead giving way to guilt and pain. Or maybe it was more about shame? He wasn't sure, but once again he'd been confronted with the truth. This time by a Monk.

"I know," he said. "But ... I ..."

He had more to say but couldn't seem to find the words. He always struggled finding words when he needed them most; they got mixed up or lost somewhere inside him, and then before he knew it the moment was over. Anyway, he thought, what words could possibly alleviate his pain and regret? What words could make him feel whole again?

Fortunately for Peck, he was with someone who didn't put much stock in words. Kelt valued integrity and privacy over communication, and he could tell the boy wasn't ready to unburden himself.

"We should probably try to get a few miles in today," he said with a glance to the sky above. "Are you okay to walk?"

Peck nodded. "Aye," he said. "I can walk."

"We'll go west, toward the Strawlands. We'll skirt the edges of the Dark Forest but won't go in."

Peck said that sounded good.

"Hopefully we'll find your pa and uncle near where you left them. But if they think you went into the Dark Forest, we might have to go in, too. Is that okay with you?"

Peck said it was. Then he added, "So long as you know where you're going, because I don't."

"Aye, it's easy to lose your way in there," said the Monk. "But I have a pretty good sense of direction."

"I'm with you," Peck said. "I'll do what you say."

"Good. You can start by dousing the fire. I'll get things packed up and ready to go. It's a good day. I'd like to get ten miles in if we can. That'll make the walk that much easier tomorrow."

Peck agreed. As the Monk went about packing up their gear, Peck laced up his boots and got to work. He removed the skewered carcass of the second hare from the fire, carefully setting it aside. There was still good meat on its bones, and he was still hungry. He then started kicking dirt on the flames.

While he worked, he thought about his ma and sisters, and he prayed for his pa and uncle. The Monk had been right — there was nothing his five-year-old self could have done to stop the attack on his mother and sisters. There should be no guilt on his plate for that. But not so for his pa and uncle. If something happened to them, there was no one else to blame. It would be his fault alone, and that was a heavy truth he did not think himself strong enough to carry.

Hopefully, he wouldn't have to.

**Fifteen:**

Dol, Calrick, and Alde stood back to back to back, their blades drawn, their muscles tense, their eyes focused and squinting. They were sweating and bleeding and sucking in giant gasps of air.

Dol had denied the demon Mar, telling it that he would not sacrifice his boy. To his surprise, the demon had vanished without another word. But now it was back, after two nights of tenuous peace, and it had brought with it familiar faces: the faces of Micah and his clan of desert-raiders. Only it wasn't Micah, Mitch, Oleg, and Mayer that stood before Dol and his; it was their bodies and their faces, but not them.

They had been ... *changed*.

Dol wasn't exactly sure what had happened to them, but whatever had happened, it had turned them into mindless monsters. Micah and his were gone, and their bodies now belonged to the Kin.

As for their souls ...

The one that looked like Oleg circled left. The one that looked like Mitch circled right. The ones that looked like Micah and Mayer stayed perfectly still. None of them said a single word or even made a sound; they just stared blankly from eyes that held not a glint of humanity.

It was terrifying. Even worse, it seemed they could not be killed.

Dol had stabbed the one that looked like Mayer in the chest, straight through to the hilt of his short-blade, yet the man who once had been Mayer was still standing, still fighting, looking no worse.

Behind the men, in the near distance, a pack of hungry yenas had gathered. There were at least nine of them. They were watching the fight with great anticipation, eager to feast on the outcome.

Behind the yenas, its black, sinewy form gently wavering in the heat of the desert, was the demon that Dol had denied.

"Micah. I know you can hear me," Dol pleaded.

Dol and Calrick had been pleading with the other group of vandals since the start of the confrontation, but they had yet to receive a response from them. The men who used to be their friends, who used to work and hunt and drink with them, showed no signs of recognition or care.

It seemed all they understood was violence.

"Dammit to hell! They're not armed!" Calrick shouted in frustration. "I don't care what they are! Monsters! Demons! We can take them!"

Calrick was right – the men *weren't* armed. But they weren't exactly *men* either. They looked like men; they looked identical to the men from Meridon that Calrick and Dol had known their whole lives. But they were not those men; not anymore. They were unnaturally fast and strong, and incredibly efficient in their movements. They attacked in unity, and were even more patient than lakas. Beyond that, blades seemed to have no effect on them, and they weren't even the least bit winded after a lengthy battle.

Dol said, "We attack together. Calrick, you take the left. I'll take the right. Alde, you stay between us and watch our backs."

The vandals moved forward in unison. The men under the sway of the demon Mar watched them with cold, dead eyes.

Calrick attacked first, swinging wildly at the man-thing that looked like Micah. It gracefully moved out of way, then dodged another attempt by rocking back and to the left. On balance again, it darted forward and slammed a heavy fist into Calrick's midsection. The vandal's eyes popped, and he dropped to his knees and doubled over.

Alde quickly stepped in and swung at the attacker he used to know as Mayer. He missed, and from behind he felt powerful hands grab him by the shoulders and pull him back. He spun around with his blade leading the way but cut only air. His second swing made the same empty sound.

Dol tried to help by keeping the other two at bay, but they were merely toying with him. One danced in and then back while the other did the opposite. They moved swiftly yet methodically, with great poise and grace, until Dol didn't know which way to turn or look.

A fist struck him on the jaw and put a universe of stars in his eyes. He wheeled around to counter with his blade but stumbled off balance, nearly falling. A second fist dug into the soft meat of his lower back, making him grimace in pain. He turned again, and then again right away, hoping a double move might catch one of them off guard. But his attackers were ready for him, and all he got for his effort was a fist to the back of the head and a mouthful of sand when he hit the ground.

All three vandals had been felled, but their attackers didn't go in for the kill. Instead, they backed away and stood perfectly still, staring mindlessly ahead with their vacant eyes.

"We can't beat them!" Calrick huffed in frustration. "They're mocking us." He found the demon and called out, "Finish us already, you bastard!"

The demon's laugh was an evil hiss that pricked their ears.

"What sort of evil did you do to them?" Dol shouted.

The demon said nothing.

"I don't understand," Calrick said as he cumbersomely rose to his feet. He was winded and bleeding, and his left eye was nearly swollen shut. "We made a deal. We had a pact."

"Deal is done on your friend's word," the demon replied.

"Dad?" Alde said questioningly. "What is it talking about?"

"It's Kin, boy. Kin lie," Dol said, unwilling to speak the truth. The truth was just too much to admit, even to his boy.

Especially to his boy.

"I need a body without a soul and it's your debt to pay, vandalos."

"Dol?" Calrick said, seeking an explanation.

"And I told you no!"

"So you did. And here we are."

"What the hell is it talking about, Dol?"

"Dad?" Alde said again.

Dol knew it was over. Whatever his friends had become, it seemed they could not be killed, at least not by manmade weapons. Even if by some act of fate or fortune Dol and his somehow managed to kill them, a ravenous pack of yenas waited in the wings, hungry for a fight and flesh. And behind it all, pulling the strings, was the demon Mar.

It would get what it wanted or it would take their lives.

"You can have me, not my boy," Dol said, still trying to bargain.

"You want to end up like your friends?" the demon said to him. "You want your bodies to forever walk in the dark? Your eyes to see no color or life? What will your wife think when your body and face return from the desert to rape and murder her?" The demon hissed with sinister glee. "How the wheel spins, vandalos. Make the choice and live."

"Dol?!" Calrick shouted. "What does it want?! Speak it!"

Suddenly, Alde wailed in a voice filled with terror. He collapsed to the ground and began spasming.

Dol rushed to his side.

"Alde? Alde?" he cried out, shaking him violently. "Alde?!" He glared at the demon with great hatred. "What did you do to him?! What dark magic is this?! Release him!"

The demon vanished into thin air without word and the attackers, the monsters that once had been men, converged on the wounded vandals.

"Dol!" Calrick shouted, calling him to attention.

But Dol's focus remained on his eldest child, who was convulsing in the sand and dirt of the desert. Alde's face had begun to turn blue, while spittle and a string of incoherent syllables flew from his lips.

Dol smacked his cheek and called out his name in a panicky voice.

The boy's eyes were clamped shut, his face wrenched in pain. His skin was the pale blue color of the first winter moon.

"Alde?! Dol cried out again, shaking him harder. "Alde?!"

"Dol!" Calrick shouted. He presently was more concerned with the attackers than Alde's condition. They would be no help to the boy dead.

"Release him!" Dol cried out to the demon. "Release him now!"

"You the same," the demon replied from the dark, and its ghostly-form once again took shape. "Release him to me and live."

Dol glared at the demon. "Bastard!"

"Not me, vandalos," it replied. "I know my line is pure."

Dol looked down at his boy, who continued to spasm and shake on the hard desert floor. He then turned his eyes to Calrick.

"What is this, old friend?" Calrick said to him. "Why are we here?"

Dol offered no reply. Instead, he looked at the men who had once been his friends: Micah and Mayer, Oleg and Mitch. They were shells of men, as dead as sand and stone, as dead as the lakas that mindlessly roamed the desertlands looking for flesh to corrupt. Whatever the demon had done to them had come straight from the root of evil. Dol couldn't imagine his body walking around without him inside it, and that made him think about the twisted fate the demon had in mind for Alde. How could he possibly do that to his boy? How could he live with himself after?

"Speak the word with truth!" the demon said, its terrible hiss of a voice filling Dol's head with contempt. "Speak it!"

"Dol?" Calrick said in a desperate way. He still had no idea what was happening, and he was scared.

"I say it and we live?" Dol said to the demon. "And not like them."

"You live," the demon replied. "Well and strong and good, with all you need. Your families, too."

Dol glanced down at Alde; the violent spasms had stopped, but the boy continued to shiver as if freezing cold, and his sweat-soaked face was still unnaturally pale. It was hard for Dol to comprehend that this would be the last time he ever saw his son alive. He began to sob, his chest heaving. "Angeloi! Help me!" he cried out at the top of his voice.

"There are no Angeloi here," the demon said to him. "But for me."

Dol lovingly touched his boy's cheek and feathered back his long blonde hair. "Forgive me," he said, tears streaming down his face. Then, in a voice choked with regret and pain, he gave his word.

"I give him. He was mine but now is yours."

"No!" Calrick shouted. "Dol!" But it was too late.

The demon's eyes flashed yellow and it disappeared.

A moment later, Alde of Meridon was reborn as Amaros, one of the Nine Elders of the Kin.

## Sixteen:

Titus and Loman hadn't done much talking since Peck had gone missing. There wasn't much to say other than platitudes and empty sentiments, and those wore thin fast. Peck was gone, and after more than two days of searching for him they had yet to find a single clue as to his whereabouts.

Titus had promised Loman repeatedly that they would find him, that everything would be okay, but he no longer believed those words any more than his brother did. They were expert trackers, but the Dark Forest was an impossible warren, as large and confusing as it was dangerous. They had followed the boy's trail into the woods easily enough but had lost it soon afterwards. As far as they could tell, his tracks doubled back twice, then disappeared. And Loman would have sworn on his skin that the tracks had changed from one time to the next, and the forest with them.

Titus told his brother to eat something.

"I'm not hungry," Loman replied. He had lost his wife and daughters to violence, and now his only boy was missing in the dreaded Dark Forest.

"I still don't understand," said Titus. "What could have happened?"

Loman had been over it in his head a thousand times and still it made no sense. Peck had disappeared in the night, with nary a sound made, with no signs of a struggle. The only set of tracks from the camp to the forest had belonged to the boy, and they had gone cold in the pines. It was like he had up and vanished into thin air.

"We're not going to stop looking until we find him," Titus said. It was about the thirtieth time he had made this claim.

Loman gave no reply.

"You have to eat, brother," Titus said to him. "I know you don't want to, but another day in the Dark Forest will tax you. Mind and body."

Loman knew his brother was right, but the smell of the meat turned his stomach. He couldn't imagine eating it without throwing it up.

"Later," he said, and reached for his pack. He pulled out his tobacco pouch, carefully twisted a roll, and set flame to it.

Titus, meanwhile, stabbed a piece of meat from the pan with his knife. He blew on it a couple times before taking it with his teeth. He would not let good food go to waste. He stabbed another chunk, and another after that, and while Loman smoked, he polished off their breakfast.

"Seems I'm cursed, brother," Loman said as Titus tidied up. "First my wife and girls, now my son. What could I have done to deserve this?"

Titus had no good answer for him, and did not try to make one.

"I've nothing left. Nothing." Then, realizing who he was with, he quickly added, "Only you, brother, and I'm thankful for you, truly, but it's not ..." He trailed off then, fighting back tears.

Titus didn't need to hear any more words, and he certainly didn't need an apology. Loman Lett had already suffered more pain than most ever would, and it seemed more was coming.

It was hard for Titus to see his brother in such anguish, but even so, he did not try to console him, knowing all too well that words often proved futile. Sometimes life beat the shit out of you and there was nothing you could do about it. And sometimes, before you even had a chance to heal, it came around and beat the shit out of you again.

Titus had been there for his brother after the deaths of Hilde, Alise, and Tama. Never had he seen anyone so disconsolate. And rightfully so. How they had died was appalling: raped and murdered in their own home; left for dead with their naked bodies beaten and their throats cut.

Loman's only solace was that they had spared his boy. His thirst for vengeance was briefly quenched a few days later when he got to take part in the execution of the men who had done it. He and Titus swung the clubs that rainy morn, breaking the bones and bashing the skulls of the men who had raped and murdered three defenseless women, two of them under the age of thirteen. Their howling, agonizing deaths had heated Loman's blood but had done little ease to his mind. Though justified, their deaths had been nothing but more death in a world full of it.

Now his boy was gone.

"It's the forest," Titus muttered, his eyes staring at the dark wood to the north. The pine trees, tall and thick of branch, looked menacing in the morning mist; a giant fence meant to keep the good folk out and the evil things in.

They had set camp away from the lingering specter of the Dark Forest, in the mouth of a small grotto that offered shelter from wind and rain. Loman had stayed on watch all night, unable to sleep. He had hardly slept or eaten since Peck had gone missing and the effects showed on his face. His dark eyes were glassy and sunken, and his cheeks held no color. He was running on instinct, on pure heart-sick adrenaline, and that wouldn't last long.

Titus was worried about his brother, but he knew there wasn't anything he could do for him … short of finding Peck. Finding the boy alive and well. The problem was that they had to go back into the Dark Forest to look for him.

Titus fixed his gaze on the thick brush and tall pines that made up the boundary of the infamous wood, his otherwise reasonable mind fretting the dangers that lay within. Some of those dangers were real, others imagined, but they all had a place.

They had searched there the last two days and hadn't crossed paths with anything abnormal or dangerous. But Titus feared that only meant they were due.

Odds were a strange bet, the hunter thought to himself as he absently watched the storm clouds gathering over the forest, threatening to drench their day with a wet and sloppy rain: they're in your favor one way or the other, no matter how you wager; but they're against you just the same.

"We should get a jump," Loman said, his voice slower now. He looked ready to keel. "There's a storm brewing."

"Rain or snow?" Titus said. "Personally, I'd rather see snow. Maybe that way we could find some tracks."

"Aye," agreed Loman. "Either way we have a long hike ahead."

"I'd feel better if you ate something first."

Loman didn't bother saying a word; he just gave his brother a look. It was a look that said more than a thousand words, many of them the four letter variety.

Titus nodded in return and finished tidying up the camp.

Soon afterwards they were on their way back to the Dark Forest.

A stingingly cold rain had started falling soon after they had entered the Dark Forest, coming down gently at first then gradually getting harder. The rain had no effect at all on the Monk, who had spent many years walking in all sorts of weather. He used to wonder how many miles he had walked in his day, but the thought rarely occurred to him anymore. Some time ago he had decided it didn't matter. His feet had covered much of Hinterland but they would never cover it all.

Peck liked the rain; he always had. There was a cleanness to it, he believed. He often stayed out and let it wash over him, like a shower from the heavens. He especially liked it in the Dark Forest. The trees were so high, their branches and foliage so thick, that the rain played like a song; it spattered on the leaves overhead, making euphonious pitter-patter music, before gently dropping down as if being poured out of a watering can. It was cool on the skin, adding to the chill in the air, but Peck didn't feel cold. He didn't really feel anything.

He occasionally checked the trees for his fowl friend but caught not a glimpse of the big white bird he had named Ovince. That made him think about the dreams he'd had under the effects of the wilderberry blossoms. Were they dreams or delusions, he wondered? Did it make a difference?

He had seen his mother and sisters, he had talked to a white bird, and he had heard beautiful poetry recited by mosquitoes. All of it had been as real to him as the Dark Forest was now, and that's all that mattered.

And the dark-haired girl? He didn't know who she was or how she had invaded his visions; he didn't even know if she was real or not. But he could still see her face, plain as day. It was burned in his mind.

"We should be at the eastern rim of the Strawlands in a few rotes," the Monk called out. "We'll stay in the forest until then."

"Sounds good to me," Peck replied.

"Is there a chance they're looking for you on the skirts of the wood? If so, we can go that way now."

"Perhaps so," said Peck. "They don't like the Dark Forest much. But they're expert trackers, and I know they followed my tracks into the woods, which means this is where they're most likely looking for me."

"To tell a truth, I don't like the Dark Forest, either," said the Monk.

"Why not?" Peck asked. "Seems like a whole lot of nothing to me. I haven't seen an animal, big or small, in more than two rotes. And thus far we've not encountered anything evil."

"In terms of evil, night is different than day," Kelt said. "As for animals, you must be blind, boy. Not sure what kind of hunter you are, but twenty steps to your right, at the base of that pine, is a wapiti."

Peck's head turned automatically. He squinted into the rain.

"Your other right," Kelt told him patiently, and Peck swiftly turned his head that way, trying not to seem embarrassed. He scoured the bases of all the pine trees in that general area and finally saw the beast, catching but a glimpse of its stubby, white-tipped tail as it darted into the bush.

"They're all over the place," Kelt told him. "If you're looking. Beyos and squirrels and fatters. Lucies and horntails, too."

Peck hadn't been looking; not really. He had been walking on instinct alone, seeing only what was directly in front of him, and only seeing that vaguely, while his mind toiled away at thoughts too tangled to solve.

"Surest way to get dead in the Dark Forest, to get dead anywhere, really, is to be in your head when you should be in your body," said the Monk. "It's a strange conflation betwixt the body, the mind, and the soul, when you think about it," he went on. "The soul helps control the mind by setting boundaries, the mind controls the body, and the body tethers the mind and the soul to this world. The three coexist together, both independently and as one. Quite remarkable."

Peck rather liked that thought, and he gave it a moment to sink in. Then, remembering the wapiti he had killed, he said, "I saw a wapiti's soul leave its body. Is that possible?"

Kelt chuckled a little.

"What?" Peck said self-consciously. "Is it not?"

"*You* saw it, yet you ask me if *I* think it's possible," the Monk replied. "If you saw it, you saw it."

"I also talked to a bird yesterday, and heard verse from mosquitos."

Kelt chuckled again. "We're you tripping on berries when you saw the wapiti's soul?" he asked.

"No."

"There you have it then."

Peck stopped walking and turned around. "You ever seen anything like that?" he asked.

Kelt looked the boy square in the eyes and nodded. "Sure. Man *and* beast. You catch just a hint of it, a ghostly image of light and shadow, and you're not even sure what it is at first. Then it's gone." He snapped his fingers. "Like that."

"Yes," said Peck. "It's almost invisible, and then it is."

"Better watch, boy. Might have the makings of a Monk in you. A Monk or a Mystic."

"What's wrong with that? You're a Monk."

"Aye. But it's not an easy road to walk. And more often than not, it's a short one."

Kelt thought about his fallen partner, Manly. Too young to be dead, yet dead the boy was, gone from the world too soon, savagely cut down by a Sarkofagos. Kelt wondered how he could still be alive after all the things he'd seen and done, all the encounters he'd had with strange and evil things, all the battles and confrontations, the countless near misses and the endless twists of fate that somehow had twisted in his favor. It had to be luck, he reckoned, knowing that luck was a light that eventually would go out.

"Personally, I think it would be a good life," Peck mused. "Fighting evil across the land. Helping folk in need. I can think of worse ways to spend your life."

"Aye," said Kelt. "So can I. But I can think of better ones, too. A family. A home. Things to call your own."

They walked in silence for a spell, their soft, wet footsteps and the falling rain the only sounds between them. Kelt stayed three steps behind the boy, his steel blue eyes scanning the forest for danger, while Peck kept pace in front , his mind, not his eyes, doing most of the work.

He thought about the white bird, and he thought about his mother and sisters. He thought about Kelt's statement, too: the soul controlled the mind, the mind controlled the body, the body tethered the mind and the soul to this world. He rather liked that idea; it made everything seem a little less real, and for Peck there was a strange sort of comfort in that.

The Dark Forest suddenly didn't seem so dark anymore.

Loman had started to feel the effects of not having eaten anything for the last two and a half days. His stomach was empty, his legs weak. He said to his brother, "Can we stop? Have you any of that jerky left?"

"I do," said Titus, happy to oblige. He had noticed his brother's stride slowing but had not dared say anything about it. He knew his big brother would eat when he had to, and not before then.

Titus pulled his pack from his shoulder and took rest on a fallen tree. He dug through the pack, found the jerky, pulled out a rather large chunk of it, and handed it to his brother.

"Am I a pack of wild dogs?" Loman said to him.

"Eat what you want, save the rest," Titus told him. He pulled out a loaf of bread and offered it to his brother. "Here. Take some of this, too."

Loman took it, ripped off a piece, handed the rest back.

Titus took a bite and chewed quietly.

Loman took a seat on the same fallen tree and kicked out his legs, glad to be off his feet. "This place is a maze," he said dispiritedly. "I don't know if we're coming or going. I don't know where we've been."

"We continue to walk with the tree line always in sight," said Titus. "Peck knows to do the same. He's a smart kid."

Loman looked around. "And where is the tree line? I've lost it again." He pointed to the left. "That way?"

Titus looked that way. He didn't see the tree line. He didn't see anything but trees and bush and fertile growth. He looked in the other direction and found the same. "That way, I think," he said.

"You think?"

Titus consulted the sky but found no answers there. He could not see the sun, only small patches of blue. "This forest is a maze," he said.

"I know. I said that."

Loman gnawed at the jerky, and Titus took a bite of bread. They ate in silence for a while, nothing between them but the sound of their chewing. Then Loman said, "We're not going to find him."

It wasn't a question, nor was it a statement he wanted a response to. It was what he now believed.

"Don't say that," Titus told him. "Peck's smart. He's strong."

"He's been gone more than two days. We've looked all over for him. Either something got him, or he ran off on his own."

"He wouldn't do that," Titus said, even though that same thought had occurred to him, and more than once. Even so, he didn't really believe that Peck would run off without telling them. The boy was a bit on the odd side of the swing, but he loved his father and wouldn't dare be so callous to him. It was more likely that something had got him; there was no telling what sort of vile creatures lay in wait in the Dark Forest. If that be the case, it was probably best they didn't find him.

"I'm cursed, that's what it is," Loman muttered despondently. "It's the only thing that makes sense."

"You're not cursed," replied Titus, though it was hard to argue. Their parents had died in a fire when Loman was just thirteen and Titus ten. They had had a sister, too, younger by five years; she had died of the fever sickness before her third birthday.

"How else can you explain it? First, Maggie. Then our parents. Then my wife and girls. Now my son. And here I am, still breathing, left to deal with the ghosts of my dead."

"It's a cruel, violent world, brother, and getting worse. It's a wonder any of us survive very long." After a brief silence, Titus added, "And so far as we know, your boy's not dead, only missing. You know him. He gets a wild hair and goes. Perhaps he ventured into the trees for a peek and got lost. It wouldn't be the first time."

"Perhaps," said Loman. "But that doesn't ..." He stopped suddenly, his attention grabbed by something in the woods. His eyes narrowed to a squint as he stared hard into the verdant brushwood of the Dark Forest.

"What is it?" said Titus, looking in the same direction. "You see him?"

"I saw ... *something*."

"Something *human?*"

"Yes. Yes." Loman stood tall and fixed his eyes on the spot where he had caught a glimpse of ... something. Then he saw it again. "There!" he cried out, pointing. "Look."

"Aye. I see it, too," said Titus. Then, at the top of his voice, he called out for his nephew. Loman joined in, and the name Peck echoed among the trees.

The brothers started that way in a rush, darting through the bush and bounding over fallen timber like a couple of spry rabbits. And they both stopped dead in their tracks at the same time, with Titus slipping on the wet terrain and nearly falling. The thing they had been running to finally appeared in full, and though it was human, it was not Peck.

It was a woman, a really attractive woman in a short, sheer frock that did not fall far past her hips. She had wild dark hair and an unnaturally pale face, and both Loman and Titus thought she looked like an angel.

Her feet were without shoes of any kind, yet she walked with a lithe step, her bare, supple legs scissoring in and out rhythmically. There was something ethereal about her, something beautiful and divine, and the brothers Lett found themselves captivated.

"Miss?" Loman called out to her softly.

She looked at them for the first time, showing no fear, no inhibition. Her face shone in the dark light of the forest like a star in the sky, and a smile graced her lips. She had dark, smoky eyes, nearly black, and wasn't wearing a thing under that frock.

"Miss, are you all right?" Loman asked her.

She kept coming forward, and the closer she got, the more her feminine form took shape. She was absolutely stunning, and both Loman and Titus were rapt.

It was Titus who broke free from her spell first. "Miss? Have you seen a boy in these woods?" he asked her.

Up close, her eyes glimmered like the black glass of Meridon. They were positively hypnotic.

"Skoteino Dasos is no place for boys," she said to them in a soothing, mellifluous tone.

"We think he may have gotten lost," said Loman. Lust put a rasp in his normally deep voice, and the girl smiled demurely at him.

"What are you doing out here?" Titus asked her. "Are you lost? Do you need help?"

She was right in front of them now, no more than a step away. Because of the rain, her sheer top left little to the imagination. Her small but firm breasts clung to the gossamer fabric, seeming one with it, with her nipples erect and clearly visible. The Lett brothers were boggled; their eyes swollen and moist.

The young woman made no effort to cover herself, nor did she ask them to look away. She simply stood in front of them, boldly, blatantly, looking as ripe as a summer berry.

"I need no help. I live here," she said to them. "Skoteino Dasos is my home. What is your boy's name?"

Neither of them responded. They were mesmerized.

"I have a boy, too," she said. "His name is Salvon. My name is Saliel."

Desire held both brothers firm in its grip. Neither of them were thinking about Peck. They both had one thing on their mind, and it was the same thing, and it had built itself into a tempest.

"Sorry, but I've seen no boy here," Saliel went on. "Other than my own. Skoteino Dasos is no place for boys."

"No," Loman managed, while Titus meekly shook his head back and forth. He looked drunk.

"No place for grown men, either," Saliel said softly, and with either hand she touched and caressed their bearded faces.

Her hands were soft and warm and smooth, and their eyes lolled shut as wonderful fantasies stole their spines and wove webs in their lust-dampened brains.

"Had we seen a boy," Saliel said, continuing to gently stroke their bearded cheeks, "we would have killed him. And we have not killed any boys today."

That last part broke the trance the Lett brothers had been under with jarring asperity. Together they took a step back from the mostly-naked young woman.

"Who are you?" Loman demanded, his hand going for his knife.

Titus reached for his blade, too.

That's when they heard heavy footsteps behind them. Twigs and brush crackled beneath the weight of these steps, and the brothers swung around in unison, drawing their blades as they did.

And they saw ... the largest man they had ever seen. He had to be twelve feet tall and balance more than fifty stones. He was a mass of bone and muscle, and on his giant slab of a face rested an expression of anger and arrogance.

"My son, Salvon," Saliel said, making introductions. "Salvon, these men have lost a boy."

"We want no trouble here," said Titus, his breath heavy with fear.

"We want only to find my boy," added Loman.

"And now we want to find him, too," said Saliel, that soothing purr of hers now edged with menace.

"Young folk are tasty, tender, and sweet," said Salvon, his voice deep and rattling.

The Lett brothers had been in their fair share of scraps over the years, though most of those scraps had occurred in their younger days, when they were yet virile and strong. Still, they both knew how to swing a blade and throw their fists, and they both were good at it.

This day, however, they were badly overmatched. Neither landed a single blow, and both were dead in no time at all.

The forest did not stir.

**Seventeen:**

Lizzy wasn't sure why she hadn't thought of it before now. She needed to ask the soothsayer about Largo. If anyone would know about the Kin, it would be him. Only her mother and father had strictly forbidden her from ever going to visit the spooky old man with one eye.

"He's a known charlatan and spook," Yondo had told her after the soothsayer had offered to read the family's fortune one day. That had happened years ago, shortly after Dalla had been born.

"When you're full grown, you can do what you want and go where you please," Gabby had told Lizzy that day. "But I wouldn't take anything that man says to heart. You're likely to wind up dead."

Stories of the mysterious one-eyed hermit were whispered throughout Vernon with both curiosity and suspicion. Some said he had been a Monk; they said he had gone mad fighting demons and monsters in the Dark Forest; they said he had drunk too much shroom tea, a potent elixir that carried the mind into the haunted halls of the Spirit Realm, where demon whispers filled the ether like a song. It was widely known that a man could not keep his wits there long.

Most kept their distance from him, not wanting to associate with a possible madman and charlatan, while others visited him in secret, seeking his advice, his charms, his potions. Very few spoke to him in the daylight with respect or cordiality; most, even those who sought his gifts in secret, ignored him out of fear of what their friends and family would say. Others ignored him out of fear of what he could do to them, should he choose to be of that mind. To them, there was something frightful in that one eye of his, something that hinted at dark misdeeds seen and done.

Lizzy wasn't afraid of him. She was more curious than anything else. She would stare at him boldly whenever their paths crossed, and if by chance their eyes happened to meet, her two gray ones and his one blue, she would not immediately look away. Once she had even hazarded a nod to him, which he had kindly returned.

He lived in the middle of nowhere, thick in the boondocks, in what Yondo had once referred to as a hovel. Constructed mostly of limbs and stone and mud, it was set in the center of a dense wood of trees that led to the westernmost border of the Wildlands.

The strange atmosphere that surrounded the soothsayer's cabin acted as a dark force, keeping many a wanderer from his door.

Knowing she'd need a cover story, Lizzy told her ma that she intended to go fishing. She normally never lied to Gabby, but she believed this was an exceptional situation. Though she rarely lied at all, Lizzy practiced her deception with incredible attention to detail. She took her trawl pole with her, her bucket, and even woke up early to dig for bait.

The walk was easy enough by road, but Lizzy didn't want anyone to notice her. That left the long way around, across the creek and through the woods behind their property. One of the ponds she liked to fish was out that way, leading her to believe that lent further credence to her lie.

Near the end of the woods she came to a path that wound through a small field of wild corn. Farther in the distance she saw the top spears of the pines that guarded the land around the soothsayer's hut.

She walked at a steady pace, carrying her bucket and trawl pole with her. The wild corn grew thick here and gave off a sour odor that made Lizzy think of demons and other anathemas. Old lore said the Kin had cursed the corn after being driven out of their lands. Old lore said that all of Hinterland had belonged to the Kin once. But old lore said a lot of things, most of which could not be proven.

A narrow path had been cut through the wild corn by hunters, furriers, and travelers looking for a shortcut to Vernon. It was covered over in spots by dead husks and fallen stalks, which crunched and snapped under Lizzy's feet. She paid it little mind, though, as all her thoughts centered on the soothsayer and the questions she would ask him.

Would she have the courage to step foot across his threshold, she wondered? She also wondered what it might look like inside.

She had heard tales of exotic plants and dead animals, of creepy, crawly things kept as pets, of potions and magic elixirs, of ancient scrolls that detailed the true nature of evil. She had heard that the soothsayer liked to drink blood and eat human flesh. She didn't necessarily believe these rumors, but she had brought her double-bladed knives just in case. She also planned to keep a safe distance from the old man, and to politely refuse any food or drink he might offer.

These were the thoughts pestering her mind when she felt something sharp stab her lower leg, just above the ankle. Startled, she shrieked and jumped away. When she looked down, she glimpsed the tail of a serpent as it slithered off, disappearing in the field of wild corn.

The snake showed distinctive red and yellow stripes on a slender black body. A ringer. They were poisonous, their bite deadly.

Fear assailed Lizzy at once. Her leg began to throb and burn. Tiny veins of blood seeped from the two little puncture marks on her lower calf, and the skin around the wound started to swell and redden.

It was then her father's steady voice entered her mind. She had been with Yondo when something similar had happened to him.

'Stay calm, girl. Don't panic. You panic, your heart speeds up and the venom courses through the blood faster.'

Lizzy told herself not to panic, but she was afraid and in great pain. Then instinct and her father's words took over.

'Don't suck out the venom; it won't help. Keep the bite lower than your heart. Stay calm and don't think on the pain.'

The first two points were easy enough to follow. For one, Lizzy couldn't reach the wound with her mouth, so even if she had wanted to suck out the poison, she wouldn't have been able to. Keeping the bite lower than her heart was easy to accomplish, too; it was near her ankle, so it really couldn't get much lower. As for staying calm and not thinking on the pain? That was where she had a problem. The pain was rising hard and fast, surging through her body, and the bite itself was getting worse; it had already swelled considerably, and the red marks around the two puncture wounds had begun to turn black. She needed help.

Her home was more than three miles away; she didn't think she could walk that far in her condition. Merely standing upright was excruciating. The soothsayer's hut, on the other hand, was less than a mile off, and there was a good chance, Lizzy figured, that he would have medicine for such a bite. That's where she needed to go.

Urgency in mind, she hazarded a step ... and the agony that followed made her wince so hard that her face seemed to almost disappear.

"Vlasfima!" she cried out, issuing the one curse word common to her tongue. "I can't ..."

As soon as the word 'Can't' escaped her mouth she again heard her father's voice. This time there was no love in it at all. If there was one word that Yondo Carpana could not abide it was that one, and in Lizzy's mind his strong, fatherly tone dressed her down.

'Can't' simply would not do. She was not going to die alone in a field of wild corn, on the hem of a lie she had told her mother.

A serpent would not be the end of her.

With renewed determination, she pushed the pain out of her mind and took another step. The pain returned with a vengeance, but again she pushed it down, refusing to succumb to it. Another limping step followed, and another after that, and pretty soon she was walking.

Her leg felt like it was on fire, and the discoloration around the bite had begun to spread, crawling up her calf and bleeding down her ankle to the top of her foot. The swelling was so bad now it looked like her lower leg might explode. By the time she cleared the field of wild corn, the increased swelling and pain had turned her limp into an awkward stagger, making every step a desperate fight for balance.

She realized she was sweating profusely. A veil of perspiration covered her face and little droplets of sweat flavored her lips with the taste of salt. Her body was pouring out sweat, too, soaking the insides of her clothes. If that wasn't bad enough, her mouth was bone dry, her head was spinning circles, and her eyesight had started to fade. She could still see, but everything had a strange, colorless mist around it, and every time she blinked her eyes it got worse. First, things on the periphery began to disappear; then, things farther away faded from sight. Soon, all she could see was what was right in front of her. Thankfully that included the trees that guarded the soothsayer's remote hut.

She was a sweating, panting, limping, half-blind mess when she entered the woods. She still felt pain, but mostly her leg was numb now, which made walking even harder. Then her foot caught a root and she stumbled to the ground.

Part of her wanted to stay there, part of her wanted to let nature take its course, but that was the weak part of her, the cowardly part, and she would not allow it to speak its words. She could barely see, barely breathe, barely move, but still she refused to give up.

Though it was a struggle, though it caused her great pain, she managed to clamber to her feet. She made it only six more steps before falling again, this time landing face-first in the dirt.

She was well into the woods, but the soothsayer's hut had yet to reveal itself to her. Something primal told her that it was straight away, and that if she could make it only a little farther she would find it.

She was too tired and in too much pain to walk, so she worked herself to her hands and knees and began to crawl. And she kept crawling, through the dirt and mud, over rocks and roots that bruised and cut her hands and knees, until finally she saw it: the soothsayer's earthen hut.

Lizzy crawled up the steps of the porch, dragged her dying body to the door, and put her fist to it with as much strength as she could muster. And she kept knocking, faintly calling out for help as she did, until her poisoned-soaked mind gave way to the black.

The sun was still in the sky when Jonno returned home, though its time was coming to an end. When he saw the anxious look on his mother's face, the kind of anxious look only a fearful mother can show, he shrugged and shook his head. "I didn't see her anywhere," he reported.

"You went to all the places she usually goes?"

"Aye. The pond at the end of the property, the creek bend, even the marsh outside town. She wasn't at any of them."

Gabby was very worried now. She had started to worry a couple hours ago, when Lizzy had failed to show for lunch. It wasn't anything for her to lose track of time when she was fishing and hunting, or even when she was playing in the woods, but she almost never missed a meal, especially when Yondo was gone on a trek.

Lizzy had begun to take it upon herself to be the provider when Yondo was gone. Jonno handled the chopping of firewood and the heavy lifting, but it was Lizzy who usually did the hunting and fishing. She liked it more, and was better at it. And Jonno was at that age where he didn't like doing chores or being told what to do; he liked going off with friends, skinting with girls, sneaking hard cider.

Lizzy was the one who brought home fish and game, and Lizzy was the one who made sure the house was safe.

Dalla was worried, too. Lizzy had promised to take her to the docks the following morn to watch the boats.

"Where could she be?" little Dalla asked with a frown.

That's what Gabby wanted to know. She said to Jonno, "Watch your sister. I'm going to look for her."

"I looked for her already," Jonno said.

"And did you find her?"

"No. She's probably ..."

"Probably nothing!" Gabby shot back at him. "She's a little girl, and she's been gone all day."

"Not for the first time."

"Did you go into town?"

"Aye."

"Did you ask anyone if they'd seen her?"

"Of course. No one had."

This was not so much a lie as a shameful manipulation. Jonno had asked one person, a friend of his named Calvin, who had reported that he hadn't seen Lizzy in weeks. Not exactly a thorough search. His hike from fishing hole to fishing hole had been similarly haphazard.

Gabby wrapped a cloak around her shoulders and headed for the door. "I'm going out," she said. "I need you to watch Dalla while I'm gone."

"But I'm supposed to meet up with Calvin, Jessa, and Lina at Jessa's barn tonight," Jonno complained.

"You can meet them *later*. *After* we find your sister."

"This is so unfair. I have plans."

Gabby eyed her boy hard. "You stay and listen," she told him, "or I'll make it known to Yondo when he returns. We'll see how long it is before you get to see the desert."

"Mom!" Jonno whined. "It's not fair. The little gypsy brat goes running off and I get punished for it."

Gabby slipped on her boots. "She's going to get it, too. Worry not. But I need you to watch Dalla while I'm gone." She then pointed a stern finger at her son and said, "And don't call her that again. She's your sister."

Dalla watched as her mum left, and then looked at her brother. "You think Lizzy's okay?" she asked him.

"Of course she is. She's a brat. Like you."

"Nah-uh."

"She always pulls crazy stunts like this."

"I remember when you ran off and didn't come home all night," replied Dalla smartly.

"Shut up," Jonno told her. "And go to your room."

"It's not yet bedtime. It's not even dark out."

"Just stay out of my way or I'll tell ma you wouldn't listen."

A doleful look swelled in Dalla's big brown eyes. She said not another word to her brother and went right to her room. There, she threw herself on her bed and cried. Not because Jonno had been mean to her; she had gotten used to that. She cried because her two favorite people were gone from the house. She loved her ma dearly, but favored her father. They had the same dark skin, dark eyes, bristly hair. But even he took a backseat to Lizzy, who did everything with her, and who was perfect in her eyes.

They went on walks together, they did chores together, they shared a room and talked into the night. They had secrets, and they knew things about each other that no one else knew. And Lizzy had always been nice to her. No matter what. Jonno was only nice to her some of the time.

If Lizzy was gone …

Her tears doubled, and all efforts to stop them proved futile. She couldn't bear to think about what her life would be like if Lizzy was gone for good. Who would she play with? Who would she talk to? Who would be her friend and guiding hand?

If Lizzy was gone …

Dalla buried her face in her pillow and wailed.


Gabby walked swiftly, kicking up dust as she went. Her loose-fitting cloak whipped behind her like a cape.

She had checked the pond at the edge of their property, and then she had checked the creek bend. She had frantically called out Lizzy's name while she searched but hadn't received a single reply. Nor had she found any sign of Lizzy's trawl pole or bucket.

It was starting to get dark out and Gabby's motherly concern was intensifying. She was on her way to town to see the sheriff and ask around, and she planned to visit Largo, too, should no one have any answers for her. She wanted to see his face for herself. She wanted to see the look in his eyes when she asked him about her little girl.

Kids were safe in Vernon, for the most part. It had been years since the last one had gone missing. Willem and Cara's little girl, Dera, had gone to town one day for salt and was never heard from again. That had been ten or twelve years ago. Before her, there had been the boy from the Farot clan; he disappeared from his bedroom, only six years of age at the time. There had been others, of course, but Gabby couldn't recall their names. She was too worried to think on it more.

Lizzy was not a timid little girl by any stretch, but she *was* a little girl. Fourteen years of age, already a handful of notches over five podes, but as skinny as a sapling. No fear, though. Yondo had told Gabby years ago that Lizzy was the one they'd have to watch out for.

"Would fight a bear for a berry," had been Yondo's exact words that day, and Gabby had been unable to disagree.

She wanted nothing more than for her darling but stubborn daughter to grow out of her infuriating tomgirl phase, but as yet Lizzy had shown no signs of doing so. The girl was already better than Jonno with the unique double-bladed knives that were Yondo's weapon of choice. A design of his own making, they consisted of two fourteen-inch blades set three inches apart on a wide hilt. In the right hands they were deadly, and, according to Yondo, Lizzy had the right hands. It helped that she practiced with them all the time. She even slept with them by her bedside.

Even so, she was still a little girl, and little girls were vulnerable to men three times their size.

Gabby's biggest fear was that Lizzy had gone to confront Largo and Largo had taken exception.

Still, Gabby couldn't imagine Largo doing anything to Lizzy. He was a kind man by all accounts, and a friend to her husband. He was a respected father and Herder; not the type to hurt a child. Unless, of course, Lizzy had been right about him.

That thought got Gabby's feet moving even faster, and before long she found herself in town. She first stopped at the sheriff's office, where Horace and his deputies could be found, usually playing cards and shooting bull. They weren't in, though, and there was no sign on the door stating where they had gone or when they might be back.

From there, Gabby hurried over to Marjory's Dress Shop. But neither Marjory nor her eldest daughter, Ella, had seen Lizzy.

"She was in yesterday," Marjory told Gabby. "Her and your youngest, Dalla. They were *browsing*. That's what she told me when I asked if I could help her find something. 'No, thank you,' she said. 'We're just browsing.' And then Dalla said the same. They're so cute together."

Gabby would have smiled under normal circumstances, but not today.

Marjory, a parent herself, with two daughters, one near Lizzy's age, offered to help her look. Gabby protested at first, but Marjory insisted and Gabby eventually gave in, realizing it was pointless to argue with a mother when it came to the welfare of a child.

The two women split the town down the middle, with Marjory taking the shingles on her side of the street and Gabby taking the ones on the other. They met up outside Sana's having had no luck.

"No one's seen hide or hair," Marjory reported with a note of concern. "What do you want to do now?"

Gabby heaved a desperate sigh. Her eyes drifted to the batwing doors that led inside Sana's Saloon, and though the thought of entering that den of sin made her skin crawl, she believed that Largo would be in there, drinking and cavorting. She had come to see and talk to him herself, to look in his eyes and ask him about her little girl. She wasn't too keen to divulge that information to Marjory, though. Word in Vernon spread faster than fire in a field.

So she said, "I'm going to check the saloon. Maybe someone in there saw her. If you don't mind, could you try to find Horace or one of his men? No one was at the jail earlier. We might need to get a search party together."

"Good idea," said Marjory, who had a bit of a crush on the High-Sheriff. . "I'll go now."

"Thanks."

Marjory hurried off, and Gabby reluctantly climbed the steps of the infamous saloon, a mother's raw determination guiding her. It was still early in the night so the crowd was thin. There were a few sallies already tramping the boards, preparing themselves for festivities soon to come, and Jules, the guitar player for Eva and Ava, was sitting in the corner plucking strings.

Sana, the proprietor, a former sally herself, was holding court behind the bar, per usual, serving and entertaining the mostly male clientele. She had been a knockout back in the day, with long blonde curls, big blue eyes, small but pert breasts, and a shapely backside. Life had roughened her up a little, and age had put some wilt on what once had been a firm body, but she still had the blonde curls and the baby blues, which, along with her minxy smile and famously barbed tongue, was more than enough to get a few offers a night for her bed.

She held a bottle of cheap hooch in one hand and a smoldering pipe in the other, and was telling a story that highlighted the moral inflexibility of one of her newest girls.

"Needless to say, that's the last time he'll try that," she said with a saucy grin, and a burst of braying laughter rang out from her patrons. "Neither of them walked straight the next day," she added, red-faced with drink and amusement.

"Saves me from trying," one of the men called out.

"Two chinks of silver and I'll be your sweetheart," said one of the more forward sallies at the bar, a pretty young thing with large breasts and a round bottom.

"Here! Here!" one of the men shouted, holding up a couple chinks. The others roared approval, laughing and slapping the bar, while the young sally giggled and blushed bright red.

"Looks like a rough hump for Cara tonight," Sana called out, and her half-pickled patrons howled with delight.

Gabby ignored them. She scanned the faces at the bar until she found the one she was looking for. Largo Kelsman sat at the far end, his back against the wall. His gaunt but handsome face was as red as beet juice and still showed the bruises from his ordeal in the desert, but other than that he looked completely normal.

Gabby approached with a quick stride, and Sana's eyes widened when she saw her. "Gabriella Carpana?" she said with no small measure of surprise. "What brings you here?"

Gabby waited until she got to the bar to speak.

The others there, including Largo, greeted her kindly. The wife of Yondo Carpana was always shown respect.

She replied in kind, nodding and saying hello to everyone. Then she focused on Sana. "Any chance you've seen Lizzy today?" she asked her.

"That's your orphan girl, right? Pale skin? Long brown hair?"

Gabby hated when people referred to Lizzy as an orphan or a gypsy, though that was how many in town viewed her. She not only thought of Lizzy as her daughter, she had never introduced her as anything other. But now was not the time to take offense.

"Yes," she said. "Fourteen of age." She held a hand up at her full height. "About yay tall already. Skinny as a pole."

Sana shook her head. "No. Why?"

Gabby glanced at Largo, then said, "She's missing. Went fishing this morning and hasn't been back. We can't find her anywhere."

"Oh no."

"Where?" one of the menfolk asked.

"Not sure. She goes to the creek bend, sometimes the marsh pond."

"We'll get a group together," said Lew, the blacksmith's apprentice. "We'll find her."

"Surely," echoed a few others.

Largo said, "I saw her just the other day. Her and your other one. They were at the market."

Gabby had her opening, and she locked eyes with the wounded Herder. "You know of anyone out fishing today?" she asked him.

"I was out," said Fran, an older man with white hair and a white beard. "Was at the marsh all morning. She weren't there that I saw."

"What about you?" Gabby asked Largo.

"Would if I could," he said, holding up a crudely-fashioned crutch.

"Can barely get home and back."

"You know of anyone gone out to the creek bend?"

"Didn't wake early, and have been here since midday." Largo rose from his seat and stood with the aid of his crutch. "You talk to Horace?"

"He wasn't in. Nor any of his men. Marjory's gone to look for them."

"I believe they're escorting a haul from the mines," Doc Morris said. "Stones of value going to Boreal. There's not been a robbery recently, but it's wise to keep protection. His boy should be there, though."

With a hint of awkwardness, Sana said, "Arman? No. He's upstairs with Lessie. Said he had time to spare. I'll go and fetch him."

She disappeared in back, and Largo Kelsman stepped to the fore and took control of the room. "In the meantime, we'll get started," he said, speaking to all who were there. "Lew, Ric, Eddy – you boys go to the creek bend. It'll be dark soon, so take torches and lanterns with you. Marco, Al, Eton – you three take the marshes, just in case. Check the surrounding grounds, too. Mick, Owen, Alen – you search the woods to the east." He limped around the bar, his crutch clacking off the wood floor, marking his unbalanced stride. "Gabby," he said, "you should wait here for Arman. Sana will rustle him good and quick."

The men at the bar downed their drinks and went off in a rush. They made plans as they went, and almost all of them told Gabby not to worry, that they'd find her. But Gabby had something else on her mind.

Largo was right in front of her now, less than an arm away. She could clearly see into the depths of his pale brown eyes, and what she saw was … Nothing. There was nothing abnormal about his eyes, or his face, or his demeanor. He looked perfectly normal. Besides that, she noticed that his right arm was in a sling, and his left leg, while not splinted, was badly injured. Sure, Largo was a Herder, a big man with strength and deadly skill, but in his present condition it was hard to imagine him besting anyone in a fight. He could barely move.

"Come," he said, laying a friendly hand on her shoulder. "Have a drink. It'll settle your nerves."

Gabby felt nothing when he touched her; she felt nothing strange, nothing evil. "I can't," she told him. "I have to …"

"You have to wait for Arman. He's a good kid. Now come."

Largo awkwardly pulled out a stool for Gabby. "Sit," he told her. Then he nodded to Lita, one of the saloon's finest sallies, and said, "Apple brandy. Two fingers. On my tab."

"You don't have to …"

"Nonsense, Gabriella. You know how many times that man of yours has saved my wretched hide? More than I care to count. Not even sure I can count that high."

If something evil had Largo, Gabby couldn't sense it. He was beat up pretty good, and his cheeks possessed the rubicund shine of a man who'd had too much liquor, but other than that he looked fine. He was acting fine, too, not the least bit anxious or guilty; and he had taken it upon himself to get everyone involved in the search.

Lita produced a double-shot of apple brandy and Gabby, despite her initial protest, drank it straight down. Her nerves were thankful for the warm caress of the liquor, and though she couldn't fully relax, she found it a little easier to breathe.

"Better?" Largo asked her.

"I'll be better when I find my girl," she replied.

"We'll find her. We'll get the whole damn town looking for her."

Arman came spilling through the door then, pink-faced and damp with sweat, his shirt untucked and only half-buttoned. He looked nothing like his father, Horace, who had a full belly and a full head of ginger hair.

Arman was a stocky, handsome young man with short brown hair, a somewhat feminine nose and mouth, and rich hazel eyes. He had been enjoying himself immensely upstairs, and though he had pouted some after being interrupted, Sana's offer of a freebie had eased his complaints.

"Sorry," he said when he saw Gabby. "Shouldn't've left my post."

"Worry not on that now, boy," Largo told him. "Girl's been missing since …" He paused and looked at Gabby. "How long she been gone?"

"Early this morning. Just after sunup."

Largo turned back to the young deputy, who presently was tucking in his ruffled shirt. "Missing since dawn. Now I already sent teams out to the marsh pit, the creek bend, and the east woods. But there's still a lot of ground to cover. You have anyone with you?"

"The others went with my dad to guard the haul. They should be back in a couple rotes, though."

"Well round up who you can."

"I'll go with," said Jules, the guitar picker. "And we can stop and get my brother and my pa. They'll help."

"Thank you," Gabby said, touched by this outpouring of support.

"I'd go," said Largo, "but I'm afraid I'd only slow you down."

"Thanks. But we should have it covered," said Arman.

Gabby nodded, got up off her stool, and went for the door.

The two young men followed after her.

"I'll stay here, Gabriella," Largo called out to her. "And I'll be sure to send out anyone who comes in. And if they don't want to go, they'll have all the Herders in Vernon to answer to."

"Thank you much, Largo. You have my full appreciation," she called back to him. Then she pushed through the batwing doors and hurried off in search of her missing little girl.

Lizzy felt … Pain. A dull, constant ache in her leg.

She told herself to open her eyes, and after a couple experimental blinks, they snapped opened … to the sight of a frighteningly large owler on a perch, its wide orangish-yellow eyes staring down at her with benign interest.

Lizzy shrieked at the sight of the huge bird, and threw her hands in front of her face and shied away.

The bird blinked indifferently and turned its head.

Lizzy realized that she was in a bed, under covers, but it wasn't her bed and they weren't her covers. She looked around frantically, not yet remembering what had happened.

She was in a small, ramshackle hut, and she was alone. There was a fire burning in the pit. Above the flames hung a large cast iron pot of simple design. On the far wall she spied dozens of glass containers on homemade wooden shelves. A bright green frog was suspended in one of the jars; in another she saw what looked like a snake.

That's when her memory started to come back. The pain in her leg was from a snake bite. A ringer. She peeled back the covers to look at the wound but found it bandaged. It hurt, and her foot was noticeably swollen, but she remembered it being more swollen and hurting much worse before she had …

Before she had what?

Before she had …

It hit her then, and she knew where she was: she was at the soothsayer's hut, somewhere in the deep wood.

The last thing she remembered was limping into the sprawling forest that surrounded the old mystic's home, fighting pain, doubt, exhaustion, and failing vision. And now she was in a strange bed, in a strange house, with a rather large, docile owler looking down at her.

Aside from that . . .

Her leg felt moderately cool. She remembered it had felt like it was on fire soon after the snake had bitten her. And her vision seemed to be fine now; she easily could see across the room without any blurriness.

She looked around some. She had always been curious about the secrets this place might hold and now she was behind the curtain. The scene was not far from her imagination. She spotted a sleeping beyo pup near the fire, and saw a snake not unlike the one that had bit her confined in a large glass cage. There were more jars on a separate shelf near the door; some were empty, some were filled with different colored liquids, while others contained leaves and stems from various plants and flowers. There was a long table with an assortment of knives and tools on it, along with stacks of wooden bowls and mounds of exotic-looking powders.

Lizzy's mind began to run wild with thoughts of magic and mystery. She saw potions being made and fortunes being told; she saw incidents of sorcery and supernatural phenomenon; she saw the great mystical conflation betwixt the forces of good and evil.

It was positively toe-tingling.

Then the door squealed open and she saw the soothsayer.

He was old, bone-frail, pale-skinned. He had a nest of wild white hair and a gaunt face littered with stubble. His left eye was hidden by a leather patch. The other eye, milky blue in color, swept over to Lizzy.

"You're awake, girl," he said to her in a quick and raspy voice. He dropped the logs he had gathered from outside and they scattered on the floor near the hearth. "How's the leg?"

Lizzy stared at him, transfixed.

He said to her, "Hope Lolly didn't frighten you. She's a sight, and more than a little curious when it comes to your kind."

The beyo pup got up, padded over to its owner, and waited expectantly for him to scratch its back. The soothsayer obliged, and the beyo pup snorted contentedly.

"The beyo's name is Lolly?" Lizzy asked.

"No. The owler," replied the soothsayer. "The beyo is called Baba."

Lizzy didn't like to admit fear, but she felt some. She wondered what she must have been thinking to come here. This man was a mystic, a purported dark artist with strange and unexplainable powers, yet she had come to see him, and now was alone with him in his hut.

And not a soul in the world knew she was there.

"How's the leg, girl?" the soothsayer asked her again. He tossed a couple fresh logs on the fire, making it hiss and flame.

"Okay. I guess," Lizzy answered shyly.

He approached her with slow, awkward steps (it looked like one of his legs might be shorter than the other), and Lizzy instinctively withdrew from him, pulling the covers up to her chin.

"Come now, girl," he said, "no need for that. Fear collects too much garbage and then everything starts to stink. Anyway, who do you think patched you up? Surely not Lolly. Not with those hands."

The soothsayer was taller than she had thought him, and he possessed a very powerful air despite his age, his frail physical condition, and the quick, rattling way he spoke.

Then there was the eyepatch.

Lizzy endeavored not to stare at it, but she couldn't stop herself from wondering what that dead eye might look like. Perhaps that was the eye that allowed him to peer into the darkest corners of the Spirit Realm; perhaps it had been burned to ash by the things it had seen there.

She tried to focus. "A snake bit me," she said, feeling very childlike all of a sudden. "In the wild corn. I was ... fishing." She didn't think it wise to admit that she had been on her way to see him; not yet, anyway.

The soothsayer gave her a gentle smile. "Were the fish biting in the wild corn?" he asked. "What do you use for bait there?"

Lizzy felt stupid. She rarely lied, but usually when she did she was good at it. She rose up and gave it another shot. "I mean I *was* fishing, and then I ... was ... hunting. Hares."

The soothsayer let her have that one. "Got to watch out for ringers in the wild corn," he said. "They're everywhere, and they're not shy."

"How'd you know it was a ringer?" Lizzy asked him.

"From the bite. Their fangs are wider set and their puncture holes are smaller. Thank the stars for that. It limits the amount of venom they can put in you. Theirs is far more toxic than most other vipers. A thimble's worth can kill a grown man in less than twenty minutes."

Lizzy said, "I thought for sure I was a goner."

"I suppose the world's not done with you yet," the soothsayer told her. "Come now, let's see it."

Lizzy tentatively extended her wounded leg, and the old mystic crouched at her bedside to get a better look.

"Nasty buggers," he said as he pulled back the poultice. "I suppose you stepped on him? That's how it usually happens."

Lizzy nodded timidly. His hands were rough, his fingers knotted, his fingernails long and sharp.

"Ringers have killed more than a few in the wild corn. Gotta walk with your eyes as much as your feet."

Lizzy gave no reply. She found herself staring at his gnarled, earth-stained fingers, which stood out monstrously against the clean, tan press of her young skin.

"Should heal nicely enough," the soothsayer told her, resetting the bandage. "Got here in the nick of time, child. Time being what it is. Time and more time, always ticking, eh?"

Lizzy nodded hesitantly. Then she said, "It was really swollen. And it really hurt."

The soothsayer showed her a friendly smile. "Tough little girl, walking on a leg like that."

"Is that a ringer over there?" She pointed to the glass cage that held captive a snake that showed the same markings as the one that had bit her.

"It is," said the soothsayer. "Good eye, girl. Must make the antidote from the venom."

Lizzy thought about that and said, "The poison makes the cure?"

"Life works in mysterious ways, girl. Good and bad, light and dark, love and hate – they all connect together somewhere on the line. Never forget that." He got up and made his way over to the desk. "Would you like some cold tea?"

That simple query made Lizzy realize that she was very thirsty, and she nodded and said, "Yes, please."

The soothsayer poured her a glass, and Lizzy gulped down more than half of it before stopping for a breath. "I thought I was going to die," she said, and drank the rest.

The soothsayer filled her glass again. "Like I said, their venom is highly toxic. You're lucky you got here when you did. The black rot didn't have time to settle in."

"The what?" Lizzy asked.

"The black rot. The poison kills the tissue around the bite and you got no choice but to cut off the foot or leg or arm, whatever's infected. Skin turns black when it dies."

"That actually happens?" Lizzy asked, horrified by the thought.

"As often as death," replied the soothsayer.

"But that's not going to happen to me, is it?" The idea of losing her foot terrified her. "My leg's okay, right? I'm not going to lose anything, am I?"

The soothsayer let out a little chuckle. "You're fine, girl," he told her. "Worry not. I gave you medicine to help stave off infection, and the poultice has already started to work."

Lizzy relaxed, but still was worried. The prospect of death scared her less than the prospect of being crippled. She gazed down at her bandaged leg, trying to ascertain its overall health. She didn't see any black skin, which was a comfort to her, but the pain she felt now meant something different. It was far more concerning.

It was then that Lolly offered up a loud trill, and Lizzy's head automatically snapped to the bird.

"Truly," the soothsayer said to the owler. Then he said to Lizzy, "Lolly agrees that you have nothing to worry about."

Lizzy looked at the bird, then she looked at the soothsayer. She made no comment.

"So, Elizabeth Layne Carpana, what would you like to talk about?"

Lizzy flinched at the sound of her full name on the soothsayer's tongue. "How do you know who I am?" she said to him, more than a little surprised.

"You know me, don't you? And I know you."

Lizzy wasn't sure what to think about that. The idea that this strange man recognized her wasn't a shock, but the idea that he knew her full name certainly was. She didn't know how to respond.

The soothsayer filled the silence by again asking Lizzy what she would like to talk about.

It was a simple enough question, but uncertainty got the best of her.

Lizzy remembered why she had come, but she was no longer sure she wanted to talk about it with the soothsayer. Perhaps the snake biting her had been an omen and what she needed to do was run home. She wished she was there already, listening to her mother yell at her for lying and running off.

"You know, I've often wondered when you'd darken my door," the soothsayer went on, that old voice of his rattling out of his chest. "Always knew you'd search me out one day, truth be told, but I didn't think it'd be so soon. Thought you might wait 'til you were older. What age are you now? Twelve? Thirteen?"

"Fourteen," Lizzy said hesitantly.

Not only did this man know her name, he apparently had thought about her coming to see him. That was a frightening idea ... but hadn't she had that very thought many times?

"You're tall for your age," the soothsayer noted.

"That's what everyone says," Lizzy replied. "And who said I was coming to see you? I was fishing. Remember."

The soothsayer gave her a look. "Is that so? Okay. My mistake."

The beyo pup had wandered over to Lizzy's bedside and now was staring up at her with its black bandit eyes. She gazed down at it with a mixture of wariness and wonder, but kept her hands away. She had already been bitten by one animal today; she didn't need to add a second.

"Go on, dear, pet him," the soothsayer told her. "He's quite friendly, and his fur is soft."

Lizzy knew that beyo fur was soft; she had a blanket made of it. She also knew its meat was tart and gamey, and needed lots of cooking. It was best served in a stew.

The beyo whimpered a soft plea, and Lizzy, her curiosity winning out, as it almost always did, reached a cautious hand down and gave the little critter a scratch. It wagged its nub of a tail and snorted happily.

"He likes you," the soothsayer said. "Lolly does, too. I can tell by the way she looks at you. She's a great judge of character."

"Animals can't judge character," Lizzy said. "They're animals."

"Nonsense. Animals have greater instincts than we do. Ask anyone."

Lizzy removed her hand from the beyo and turned her eyes to the owler. "My dad has a saying," she said. "'Wise as an owl.'"

"They are very wise indeed. They see all. Now, as to why you're here, girl, really here, which is a question you've deftly avoided thus far. Would you like to tell me? Or would you rather have Lolly take a guess?"

Lizzy looked at the bird again. "Birds can't guess things," she said. Then, with a note of uncertainty in her young voice: "Can they?"

The soothsayer gave her a smile. "No. Not really."

Lizzy felt a good deal out of her depth. She was in a ramshackle hut in the middle of the woods with an old mystic who most people avoided, a huge owler with dangerous-looking talons, and a friendly beyo pup that wanted its back scratched. There were shelves cluttered with jars that held dead frogs and spiders, and at least three glass cases with live snakes in them. She was equally thrilled and terrified at the same time.

"Come now," the soothsayer said to her. "Don't be shy. You can ask me anything. I will answer truthfully … if I can."

Lizzy didn't know what to do. She had lied to her ma and had come a long way to see the old man, and she had nearly died getting there. If she didn't ask her questions, what would have been the point?

With slowly fading reticence, she said, "My mom told me that I'm not supposed to talk to you."

"Yet here you are, girl, talking to me. Funny how that works."

"Well … I was just …"

The soothsayer raised a hand for her to stop. "My name is Oreg," he said in a mannerly way. "It's good to meet you, Elizabeth Layne."

"Good to meet you, Oreg," Lizzy replied cordially.

"Now that we've been properly introduced, we can speak as friends."

Lizzy wasn't too sure about that, but said, "I suppose."

"Supposition is a thread that almost always ends up in knots, girl. Yes and no, however, rarely tangle."

Once again, Lizzy wasn't sure how to respond. A lot of what the soothsayer said went over her head. She knew the words well enough, but not his meaning.

Oreg said, "We're going to be here a spell, girl, so we might as well converse. Otherwise, what are we to do? We could play Checks, if you like. But I never lose."

Lizzy had heard of Checks, but she had never played before. She told the soothsayer that.

"Easy enough to learn for a whip-smart girl such as yourself. If there's time, I'll teach you."

Lizzy was interested in learning the game, but presently had more pressing concerns. "No, thank you," she said. "I think I need to get home. My mom will be worried."

"Aye. But it's a mite late for that," Oreg told her. "The sun has set. Not safe for a girl to be walking in these parts after dark. And on that leg, it's probably not wise to walk at all. At least not tonight."

Anxiety swelled up inside Lizzy, and she swung her legs over the side of the bed, saying, "I've been here all day? My mom's going to …"

That's when the pain struck her full, with all the blood rushing down to the wound, and she grimaced and pulled her legs back onto the bed. "Ow! Ow! Ow!" she whined. "It still hurts."

"Lie back. You need rest," Oreg said to her. "No way around it. No way around anything these days. Straight lines and circles all leading to the same nowhere. As for you, girl, I'm afraid you're stuck here for the night."

"No, I can't be," Lizzy said. "My ma's gonna tan me red for this."

"Then red it is, girl. Tan and red. But that matters not. You can't walk, and I can't carry you, skinny as you are. I'm an old man with old bones. It'll have to be tomorrow."

"But she'll worry herself sick. My pa's on a trek."

"I took care of it. Fret not."

"What? How?"

"I sent word to her by pigeon. They're annoying things and they shit everywhere, but they fly true."

"But ..."

"Relax, child, you'll be here for a spell. Then I'm guessing you'll be punished for the rest of your fourteenth year, and maybe into your fifteenth."

"Probably," Lizzy said soberly. And that would be after her ma tanned her bottom.

"So, that being true, wouldn't you think it a good idea to tell me the real reason why you've come? Who knows what life holds in store for us. You may not get another chance."

Lizzy recognized the wisdom in that statement. Not only would her ma dole out a harsh punishment for her rebellious act, Lizzy was fairly certain her pa would add to it when he got home. And he undoubtedly would forbid her from ever going to see the soothsayer again.

That meant that this most likely would be the only chance she got to ask her questions ... at least until she was out from under Yondo and Gabby's roof. And by then, she reasoned, what would be the point?

"Ummmm," she began, her hesitance stringing out that one syllable for a count of three. Then, summoning more voice, and more backbone, she said, "I guess I want to know about ... *the Kin?*"

Oreg flashed a meaningful smile, showing teeth that looked much too white for how old he was and where he dwelled. "You know," he said to her, "I had a feeling you might want to talk about that."

"Did Lolly tell you," Lizzy joked.

Oreg let out a full laugh. "Good one, girl," he told her. "I like that." He then stood, went over to the hearth, picked up a couple logs, and tossed them into the flames. "I'm going to make us a snack and some more tea," he said. "You hungry?"

Lizzy was famished, and said so.

"Appetite is a good sign that you're feeling better," Oreg told her. "As is making jokes."

A smile touched Lizzy's lips, and she leaned over the side of the bed and gave Baba a friendly scratch.

The beyo pup snuffled happily and wagged its little tail.

The town was out in force, and the name Lizzy was being shouted all over. Horace and his top two deputies hadn't returned from their job yet, and most of the women folk had stayed home with their young ones, but almost everyone else in Vernon was searching for Elizabeth Layne.

They split up in groups of four or five and scoured the countryside, using oil-torches and glass lanterns to light their way. Gabby searched with Arman, a Herder named Tito, Pauly, who was the Smith's oldest boy, and Ferdo, a miner and one of Yondo's closest friends. They soon made their way back to Carpana land, searching the marshes to the west as they went.

"My eldest, Olman, did this once," Ferdo said while the others called out for Lizzy, their mismatched voices echoing in the dark. "We found him with a busted ankle in the Dillies. You check the Dillies?"

"No. She's not allowed in the Dillies."

The Dillies was a desolate warren of black stone and ash that wove its way from the Wildlands into Vernon and down along the eastern rim of the desert. It was home to many small, murky ponds, though mostly they were frog ponds. Any fish in them were barely worth the effort. Lizards and snakes could also be found in and around those ponds, which was why Yondo had forbidden Lizzy from fishing there.

Lizzy had been forbidden from doing a lot of things.

Gabby told Ferdo that. Then she added, "Of course, that child lives to do things we've told her not to do. Wild as the wind, that one, and twice as unpredictable."

"We'll check them just in case," said Arman. "You don't have to go if you don't want," he told Gabby. "Can be quite dangerous in the Dillies, especially at night."

"If there's a chance my girl's there, I'm going."

"Fair enough."

"I want to stop home first. I need to check if Lizzy's returned, and I need to tell Jonno what's going on."

They continued to call out as they made their way back to the Carpana homestead, but their calls, like every other call presently reverberating across the countryside of Vernon, went unanswered.

The light from the oil-torches glowed bright orange in the dark and cast long, flickering shadows on the ground. And as the night continued to darken, so did Gabby's hope. They had covered a lot of territory but had yet to come across a single clue. The girl had been gone for more than half a day; there was no telling what might have happened to her or where she might be.

Gabby wasn't sure how those negative thoughts had managed to worm their way into her head, but as soon as she realized they were there, she banished them. Lizzy was alive and well, she told herself. Then she said it again, with more conviction.

"Up over the crest and you'll be home," Ferdo reported.

They climbed the crest and started down the other side, the light from their torches shining bright in the blanketing dark, marking them from miles away. They could see in the distance, here and there, the burn of other torches. Up close the torches flickered and churned, but from afar they looked like small, unchanging suns.

The wind had picked up over the last rote or so, adding to the damp cold of the night, and Gabby thought about Lizzy trying to survive the elements. The girl could catch her death of cold, or, if it got much colder, she could freeze to the bone.

No! It was unforgiveable to think such thoughts, Gabby told herself. What was the old adage her ma used to tell her?

*Think the worst and the worst shall find you.*

Lizzy was alive, Gabby told herself yet again. And she repeated that phrase over and over in her head, making it an anthem.

When they arrived at the Carpana home, Jonno met them at the door. "I guess you didn't find her?" he said with a hint of exasperation. The search for Lizzy was cutting into his personal time.

"No," said Gabby. "She didn't come home?"

"Do you see her here?"

"Don't use that tongue with me, Jonno Carpana," Gabby said to him, and added a hard look to let him know how serious she was.

"We're going to check the Dillies," Arman reported.

"Can I come with?" Jonno asked. "Better than sitting here."

"No. I need you here with Dalla," Gabby told him. "This is important."

"But I don't want to babysit," Jonno complained. "I can help. I know the Dillies. I've been through them a hundred times."

"I need you here."

Jonno threw his head back and let loose an exaggerated groan of disgust. "First dad tells me I can't go on the trek, and now you're telling me I can't go look for my sister. You know, I'm not a child. I'm a man."

"Jonaton Lee!" Gabby snapped at him. "Do as told. Please. This night has been hard enough already."

"But mom. It's unfair."

That's when Ferdo, who was burly and bearded, and spoke in a deep, manly voice, stepped in. "Listen to your ma," he said to Jonno, and much like when Yondo gave an order, there was nothing in the miner's words or tone that could be misconstrued.

Jonno pouted, but said nothing more, and Gabby went and changed into warmer attire. She also grabbed one of Yondo's blades, just in case, and told the guys to help themselves to any drink or food they might want. Waterskins were filled at the well and sticks of jerky were pocketed, and Tito took a snort of cider, claiming he needed it to keep the chill from his bones. Both Arman and Pauly thought that was a fine idea and shared a drink with their friend. Only Ferdo abstained.

They were about to head out when they heard scratching at one of the thatch-covered windows in the kitchen. Gabby rushed over there at once, frantically calling out, "Lizzy! Lizzy!" She threw the latch and opened the window wide, and a small, white bird flew in.

"Vlasfima!" Gabby exclaimed, swatting at it wildly. "Of all the madness! A damn bird!"

The pigeon calmly perched itself on the kitchen table and cooed.

"We don't have time for this," Gabby huffed. "Jonno!"

She planned to have Jonno get rid of the winged pest, by any means necessary, but Ferdo said, "Wait. Look at its leg."

Attached to one of the pigeon's legs was a small, rolled-up sheet of parchment, and around its neck was a black band.

"It's a messenger bird," said Arman. "We have one at the jail, though the damn thing has yet to learn how to fly true."

Ferdo approached the bird slowly, and the bird did not stir. He gently took hold of it in one of his large, calloused hands, removed the scroll from its leg, and set it back down. He then unrolled the scroll, revealing the soothsayer's message.

"What's it say?" Pauly asked.

Ferdo read it aloud for all to hear: "Worry not, Gabriella Carpana, your daughter is safe. She was bitten by a ringer in the wild corn. Fortunately, she made it to my cabin in time. I've cleaned and dressed the wound, and there's no reason to think she won't be fine. I would have brought her home to you, but I fear she's not yet strong enough to travel. You are welcome to come here for the night if you feel you must, but I assure you that she is safe and comfortable. Oreg."

"Oreg?" At first the name was unfamiliar to Gabby. Then it struck her like a stone. "That one-eyed mystic?!" she cried out.

"Aye. That's him," said Tito. "Oreg, the soothsayer."

"Oh Christous! What is she doing there? We have to go. Now."

"That's a five mile hike into some dark woods," said Arman.

"At least," added Ferdo.

"I care not of that," said Gabby. "I don't want her with that crazy old hermit. Not for a minute, and certainly not a night."

"He sent word so you wouldn't worry. I don't think he'd have done so if he had bad intentions."

"I don't care of his intentions," Gabby said. "Would you want Carolina staying with him for a night?"

Carolina was Ferdo's daughter, just a year younger than Lizzy. The answer Gabby received surprised her.

"Under the circumstances … Yes."

Gabby gawped at Ferdo in disbelief.

"I've met the man more than once. He's odd, sure, and doesn't smell all that fresh, but I believe him to be harmless."

"I don't care. I don't trust that charlatan, and neither does Yondo. I'm going. With or without you."

Ferdo nodded supportively and said that he understood. He then turned to the others. "Go back to town and tell those still searching that Lizzy's been found," he told them. "I'll accompany Gabby to the mystic's hut. I know the way well enough."

Arman said, "Are you certain? We can go with. It's no trouble. Those woods can be dangerous."

"No. It's fine. Go alert the others. No need to worry them more. And someone stop by my home, tell my wife where I'll be."

Arman, Tito, and Pauly agreed, and after saying their goodbyes they tramped off into the night, heading back to town.

Ferdo and Gabby, meanwhile, loaded up on supplies, including food, extra oil for the torches, and weapons, which Gabby insisted on taking. They went off in the opposite direction, walking north along the Traders' Road. They had a date with the soothsayer.

"The Kin is a weighty subject for such a small girl," said Oreg. "What made you risk life and limb to ask of them?"

"I think I saw one," Lizzy replied. "In a Herder named Largo. But my ma said my eyes were only playing tricks."

"Eyes have that tendency, child, though usually they can be trusted. Ears lie all the time because they hear what mouths say and lies come from the mouth. But your nose ..." here he raised a bony, crooked finger with erudite certainty "... you can always trust your nose. The *nose knows*. Remember that. Now, more importantly, what does your *mind* say?"

Lizzy took all that in as best she could. The soothsayer spoke at a herky-jerky pace, with an old man's rasp, which caused his words and syllables to collide at times. She filed his statements to memory and turned her thoughts to the question at hand. With the absolute confidence of a child, she said, "It was a demon. I know it."

The soothsayer nodded earnestly. "There are quite a few out there, and many can possess. What makes you think it?"

"Largo came back from a trek all beat up. He said vandals had attacked him and his partner in the desert and stole some of the living stones they had. And then later his partner was killed by yenas. So ..." Lizzy paused, thinking about how she wanted to phrase her next words.

The soothsayer helped her out. "So he was in distress, and people in distress are more likely to succumb to the Kin."

Lizzy nodded eagerly. "Aye. Exactly."

"The vandals stole souls?" Oreg asked her.

Lizzy nodded again. "Third time it's happened. My pa is leading a trek to bait them. The vandals, that is. To stop them."

A pensive look shaped the old, weathered face of the soothsayer, making a rather intricate spider web of his many wrinkles. "It's been coming for some time now," he said ominously. "And soon, I'm afraid, we'll be in the center of it."

"Center of what?" Lizzy inquired. "Something bad?"

Oreg ignored her question. Instead, he said, "This Voukolos you saw, what did the demon inside him look like? Can you describe it?"

Lizzy didn't have to think on that; she remembered the image vividly, in excruciating detail. The problem was that she could not forget it.

"It was ... Well, it was like he had another face behind his face. Hidden under the skin. It was scarred, dark red, and horrible. It looked ..." Lizzy stopped there, not wanting to say the word.

Again the soothsayer stepped in. "Evil."

Lizzy looked at him, and in her dark gray eyes the truth was revealed. Oreg patted her knee and said, "I think what you saw was real, child. I've heard such things before."

"You have?" Lizzy said. "Where?"

The soothsayer carelessly motioned his hand about, saying, "All over. Tales of demons are hardly scarce."

"But what does it mean? No one else noticed it. My sister, she didn't see anything. Nor the people in the saloon. Or those in town. His children neither, I assume."

"Aye. Most won't. Most can't."

"But ..." Lizzy sighed. After a long moment, she turned her sharp gray eyes on the soothsayer and said, "Does this mean I'm crazy?" There was fear in her voice, and worry on her face.

Oreg countered with a pleasant smile and another friendly pat on her knee. "Aye, child, that's precisely what it means," he told her. "Another way to put it is that you have *tou Mati Fantasma.*"

"Tou Mati Fantasma?" Lizzy questioned. She knew the old tongue well enough for a girl her age, especially the swear words, thanks mostly to her brother, but that phrase stumped her.

"Aye. What we used to call the Ghost Eye," Oreg explained. "More commonly referred to now as the Sight. Or, if you prefer the old words, which have a certain poetry: *To Vlema.*"

To Vlema. The Sight!

The idea thrilled Lizzy, but also terrified her. Not much was known about the Sight. Most people, her parents included, summarily dismissed it as nonsense, while others felt it a curse from the Kin. There were some who believed it a true and honest talent, a blessing not a curse, though mostly they were the sort that tended to be a bit eccentric themselves, people not unlike Oreg, who lived alone in the woods and spent their days with owlers and beyos and poisonous snakes.

The Divine Scroll mentioned the Sight numerous times, as did the letters and scrolls of the first prophet, Toman, but it was old lore that had generated most of the interest. Rumors and speculation passed down through the ages, fueling a fire that caused a lot of smoke.

Lizzy didn't know what to think.

Oreg sensed her ambivalence and said, "You're right to feel the way you feel, child. It's natural."

Lizzy flashed him a curious eye.

"A little excited, a little scared. It's how you should feel."

"My ma says the Sight ain't real."

The soothsayer smiled. "It's not. For her. But for you."

"Other people say it's a curse."

"It can be. If you allow it to be."

Lizzy wasn't sure how she felt about that.

"It's a powerful gift, if used right," Oreg told her.

"But what does it mean?"

"It means that most likely you're going to lead an interesting life, Elizabeth Layne Carpana. Difficult times lie ahead, and people like you will be at the center of things."

Lizzy again felt a mixture of excitement and fear. "What if I don't want to be at the center of things?" she said.

Oreg fixed her with another brilliant smile. "Fate has a way of putting you where it wants you, child, like it or not. And it's up to you to make your way from there." He leaned back in his seat, packed fresh tobacco leaves laced with various spices in his chestnut pipe, held a flame to the bowl and puffed away until a cloud of smoke gathered around him. "You didn't want to see Largo, did you?" he said.

Lizzy gave an awkward shake of her head.

"I'm guessing you didn't want to get bit by a ringer?"

"No. Certainly not."

"And you didn't want to stay here the night?"

Lizzy thought about that, and the conclusion she came to bothered her. "So I have no control?" she said.

"Quite the contrary, child. We have *all* the control. We just have to learn to recognize it, and trust it."

"What about the demon?"

The soothsayer puffed on his pipe, making more smoke. A pleasing aroma filled the hut, and Lizzy breathed it in deeply, thinking that it smelled like the Vernal bonfire they had every year in the town square. The beyo pup was curled up at her feet, sleeping peacefully. Above her the owler remained motionless on its perch.

"The demon left its mark on the man. That's what you saw. He was no more possessed when you saw him than you or I right now. But this Voukolos, he's a vessel now. The demon can see the world through his eyes from miles away. Can hear what he hears, feel what he feels. Can read his thoughts and know his intentions. And, if it so wants, it can possess him. It can take full control of his mind and body."

"So he's ... What is he?" Lizzy asked.

"The prophets called it *Psychika*," Oreg told her. "Soul-struck. His soul is still there, but it's been struck by the Kin. There are many varieties of it, leading all the way to possession."

A rather unnerving question occurred to Lizzy then, and she said, "So then the demon might have seen me when I saw Largo?"

The soothsayer met her stare and spoke the truth. "It's possible."

"So it might know who I am?"

"Aye. Possibly."

"Would it know that I saw it?"

Oreg's hunched shoulders rose and fell with a shrug. "Hard to say, child. But again, it's possible."

Lizzy felt sick to her stomach. A demon possibly had seen her and her little sister through someone else's eyes, which meant, at least according to Oreg, there was a chance it knew she had seen it. If that was true, it wasn't a stretch to think that it might come looking for her. She asked the soothsayer if this, too, was a possibility.

Oreg was impressed by her insight, yet casually waved off her concern. "Worry not, child," he told her. "Most likely it wasn't looking through the Herder's eyes at the time. Even if it was, the Kin have other interests." But even as he said it, he knew there was a chance the demon, if it had sensed her, would seek to find her. A young girl with *to Vlema*? That was a rare and valuable thing indeed, something to be treasured ... and feared.

"If you like," he said to her, "I can give you a charm. If you're not afraid of such things."

Lizzy shook her head. Afraid? She wasn't afraid. It actually excited her to think about possessing something magical.

"I can handle it," she told the soothsayer. "I'm not afraid."

"Probably best not to tell your ma about it, given her thoughts on such things. She might not approve."

Lizzy didn't like lying, but she really wanted the charm. "I won't tell her," she said. "Honest."

175

The soothsayer went to his workbench and began rifling through some of the drawers. After rummaging around a bit, he pulled something out and took it over to Lizzy. It was a necklace of sorts, quite crude in design: set in the center of an X made of dark wood was a small, black gemstone; two lengths of rope that had been braided together to form a perfect loop held the talisman in place.

Lizzy's eyes went as wide as the owler's at the sight of it. "What does it do?" she asked.

"Protection from the Kin. They won't see you so well."

He handed it to her, and she traced a finger over the small black stone. "I like it," she said. "Can I put it on?"

"Of course. It's yours now."

Lizzy slid it over her head and let it settle around her neck. It was made for a bigger person, an adult, but she figured that eventually she'd grow into it. She pulled it away from her chest and gazed down at it, captivated by the stone. "I love it," she said. "Thank you. But how am I supposed to hide it from my ma?"

"Keep it tucked in your shirt. Or in a pocket."

Lizzy said she could do that. Then she said, "So, are you going to take me home tomorrow?"

"No, child. No need for that. Your ma's on her way here as we speak. Should be knocking soon."

"What? She's coming here?" Lizzy exclaimed.

"Aye. I sent word and told her that you were safe, but she's on her way nonetheless."

Lizzy was confused. "But ... How do you know she's coming? Do you have the Sight?"

Oreg smiled once more, those perfect white teeth of his shining out through wrinkled old lips. "Don't need *to Mati Fantasma* to know a mother's heart," he said.

Lizzy sat back and sighed. "I guess the gig is up." She threw a woeful glance at the soothsayer. "That's what my pa always says when Gabby catches him doing something he shouldn't be doing. He said it's slang, from the stragglers."

"Aye. But what's the problem? You were going fishing, child. You got bit by a poisonous snake. My hut was closer than your home so you came here. That's all."

"My ma won't buy it," Lizzy said. "I already told her about Largo, and she's pretty good at putting two and two together. And she usually can tell when I'm lying."

"Fair enough."

Lizzy glanced down at the charm again. It had very little aesthetic appeal, but already it was one of her favorite possessions. It ranked right up there with her slingshot and the custom double-bladed knives her pa had given her on her last birthday. "I won't ever take it off," she said, and tucked it neatly into her shirt.

"That's good, child," Oreg said to her. "It only works if you wear it."

Ferdo pointed to a patch of densely wooded land. "It's through there, I believe. A couple hundred yards. Maybe more."

Gabby looked into the interminable blackness, interrupted here and there by the tiny, blinking sparks of firebugs. She held out her oil-torch, but the best it could manage against the swallowing black was a wan aura of trembling light. Darkness was different in the deep wood; it was darker, quieter, stranger. Gabby didn't much care for it.

"Sure you want to continue?" Ferdo asked her.

Gabby was staring straight ahead with narrow-pointed eyes when she said, "I'm sure." Right after that, she began walking, holding her torch in front of her like a drawn sword. Ferdo followed closely behind her, holding his torch at a more perpendicular angle. His short-blade he held like a drawn sword.

"I'm sure she's fine," he said as they traversed the heavily-wooded terrain. It was the fifth or sixth time he had said this, which diminished the message some. "Oreg is not a killer."

"No care for that," Gabby replied shortly. "I don't want him filling that girl's head with nonsense. She's got enough up there already."

"That's normal for her age."

"Perhaps. But Lizzy is anything but normal."

They walked on in silence for a while. Moving at a steadier pace, Ferdo eventually took the lead. He made sure not to get too far ahead, though; protecting Gabby was his top priority.

After moving past a thicket of pine trees and ruby bushes, Ferdo pulled to a stop and looked around.

"What is it?" Gabby asked him.

He pointed to the left. "A light," he said. "There. See it?"

Gabby held the torch away from her face and squinted into the darkness. "Yes," she said. "Is that it?"

"I believe so."

They went in that direction, and with every step the light got brighter and bigger. Eventually it took the shape of a small rectangle, and before long a modest hut began to emerge around that rectangle of light, nicely camouflaged by the surrounding woods.

The hut was made of wood and stone and earth, and though it was well-constructed, it appeared to lean slightly to the left. It had a sturdy porch and a squat chimney that billowed smoke up into the gnarled branches of the surrounding pine and willow trees. Gabby hadn't much of an idea what to expect, but so far as huts went, this one wasn't so bad. There was a door and windows, a chimney, a roof, a porch. She held her torch out in front of her as she approached, one step behind Ferdo.

They ascended the steps together, moving deliberately, keeping their footfalls quiet. No sound could be heard coming from inside the hut, but light from a fire could be seen flickering beneath the door jamb.

Ferdo looked back over his shoulder at Gabby. "Ready?" he said to her, sheathing his blade.

Gabby would have preferred he keep his blade drawn and ready, but understood why he couldn't. She then prompted him to knock, and took a good step behind him, just to be safe.

From inside, awkward footsteps drew near. Soon after they stopped, the door swung open at the hands of the soothsayer.

Oreg was first greeted by the rough, heavily-bearded mien of Ferdo; then, through the near-blinding glare of torch light, his one good eye locked on the lovely face of Gabriella Carpana. "Was expecting you," he said to her, stepping aside. "You can dowse your torches there," he gestured to a small barrel of water on the edge of the porch, "or let them burn out in the fire pit. Choice is yours."

Ferdo extinguished the torches in the water while Gabby rushed past the soothsayer and into the hut, searching for her little girl. She didn't have to look hard. Lizzy was sitting on a bed, her wounded leg propped up by pillows. She looked pale and scared and worried, and Gabby cried out, "Elizabeth," and rushed to her side. She didn't notice the beyo pup in Lizzy's lap until she was about to hug her. The sight of the animal made Gabby shriek and pull back.

The beyo looked up in horror, and curled into Lizzy for protection.

"What are you doing with that animal?" Gabby exclaimed.

"Everything all right in here?" Ferdo asked as he stepped lively into the hut. The high-pitched shriek had caught his attention and put him on alert. "Gabby?" he said, his gaze going back and forth between her and the soothsayer. "You okay?"

That's when Lolly, perched on the window sill above the bed, hooted loudly, causing Gabby to shriek again.

Lizzy was suitably embarrassed. "They're tame, ma," she said. "Look." She scratched the beyo behind the ear, and it nuzzled into her with a happy look on its black-banded face.

"It's a wild animal," Gabby said. "It can attack you."

"Baba? Highly unlikely," said Oreg. "Unless you count licks?"

Lizzy giggled. Baba certainly was a licker.

"You might as well not have walls or a roof," Gabby huffed. "You might as well live in a tree." She looked at her little girl. "Are you all right?"

"I'm fine, ma. Honest. Thanks to Oreg."

"That's a brave little girl you have there, Gabriella," Oreg said. "Bit by a ringer in the wild corn and made it all the way here. That takes strength and courage."

Gabby said, "Let me see it. We need to get you to Doc Morris." She stayed a few steps back, though, not wanting to get too close to the beyo or the owler.

"It's okay, ma," Lizzy said. "Honest. It hurts some, but the swelling's down and there's no black rot."

"Doc Morris has medicine he can give you."

Lizzy's cheeks bunched with a smile. "I know. He gets it from Oreg."

Gabby's head snapped around. Her eyes found the soothsayer.

"It's true," Oreg told her. Then he winked his one eye at her and added, "But what I keep here is far better."

Gabby was not convinced. "Let me see," she said again, yet again she made no move to get any closer. Then she said, "Put that wild animal down so I can look at the bite."

"Baba! Here!" Oreg chirped, tapping his leg.

Now Baba knew it was Oreg who kept a roof over his head and food in his belly, but he rather liked his new friend and was reluctant to leave her side. He exhibited this by waiting for a second, more stringent command. It was then that he grudgingly left the warmth of Lizzy's lap, jumped down from the bed, and padded across the floor to his owner, who promptly scooped him up and scratched him behind the ear.

Gabby, meanwhile, knelt at Lizzy's bedside so she could take a hard look at the ringer bite that nearly had killed her. The wound was dark red and swollen around the puncture marks, but there was no black rot and the rest of the leg looked normal.

"What were you thinking?" Gabby said to her. "I still think we need to get you to Doc Morris."

"You can do as you please," Oreg said, "but I wouldn't recommend moving her tonight."

"You want her to stay here, with all these wild animals and ... and ... who knows what else around?"

"It's safe here, Gabriella. I assure you."

"I'll vouch," Ferdo said, speaking up for the first time. "A ringer bite is nothing to play around with. Might be best to leave her rest for a spell."

"I'm fine here, ma," Lizzy said. "I've been here all day."

Gabby wanted to scoop up her daughter and carry her out of the soothsayer's cottage at once. Not just out, but as far away as she could get her. Only Ferdo and the soothsayer had a point: ringer bites were nothing to wave off, and asking Lizzy to travel five miles on a wounded leg, at night, after such a long and traumatic day, was not exactly a sensible idea.

But to stay here?

Gabby looked around and saw, in different glass containers, spiders and scorpions and snakes. One of the snakes immediately caught her eye and, pointing, she said, "Is that a ringer there?"

"Aye. It's how I make the antidote," Oreg told her. "Please, have a seat. Would you like some tea?"

"Oreg makes the best tea," Lizzy said. "The trick is you have to ..."

"Hey now!" Oreg quickly cut in, interrupting her before she could spill his secret. He impishly waggled a crooked old finger at her and said, "Won't be much of a trick if you tell everyone about it."

Lizzy smiled guiltily, then looked at her mom and said, "Sorry."

Gabby was not at all pleased by the playful interaction between her daughter and the spooky old mystic. Lizzy had a mind all her own and a rampant, rebellious curiosity for the kind of things that led to danger. And Oreg? Well, he might have been a frail old man on the fringe, but it was rather obvious he lived the sort of life that would interest Lizzy. That spelled a kind of trouble that Gabby could not abide.

"I'll make a fresh pot," Oreg announced, and shuffled across the room, his awkward stride and hunched shoulders making him look very old.

"Thanks, but I don't want any tea," Gabby said to him obstinately.

"I wouldn't mind a cup," said Ferdo. He felt the force of Gabby's eyes on him and looked at her. "We might as well stay the night, Gab. I'll keep awake if you like, and you and Lizzy can rest."

"I won't be able to sleep here," she said. "Not with snakes and spiders and wild animals all around me."

"Ma," Lizzy groaned in embarrassment. "They're tame."

"Aye. Until they're not. And what then, girl, when your face is tore up and bleeding?"

"I understand your reluctance," Oreg said politely. "I know I don't keep a normal home. But my animals, they keep me sane. Better listeners than conversationalists, obviously, but you know what they say about beggars." Then he said, "There's a room and bed in back, if you like. Small, but no animals. Hardly ever used."

Gabby looked at her daughter.

"Ma," Lizzy said. "It's fine."

Against every thought in her head, against every instinct she possessed as a mother, Gabby agreed. Though she hated to admit it, staying was the sensible thing to do. At least Ferdo was there to protect them. That made the decision a bit more palatable for her.

"We'll stay the night, leave first thing," she said, forcing the words out through gritted teeth. Then, turning a stern eye on her not-so-little little girl, she added, "And when we get home, you can expect to be doing chores for the rest of your young life. And longer."

"I know," Lizzy said. "I'm sorry I made you worry."

Gabby had plenty of admonishments for Lizzy, and plenty of fire in her belly, but she didn't want to appear overly harsh. Also, she fully expected Yondo to lay down the law when he got back from his trek.

That in mind, she tempered her anger and went with, "I'm just glad you're alright." Then, remembering her manners, she turned to the soothsayer and said, "Thank you, sir. Truly. I can never repay you for what you've done. You saved her life. We are forever in your debt."

Oreg nodded graciously. Then he said, "You can pay that debt now, if you like. A one-time offer."

These words caught Gabby by surprise, as well as Ferdo. They each assumed that Oreg was speaking about gold or trade, but the soothsayer cleared his throat and said, "Relax and know that you are safe here, Gabriella, despite the chaos and ratty look of me. I mean no harm to you or yours, and am too old to have motives. Accept my hospitality, and we are square. On my word."

Gabby had a suspicious mind, and, despite all he had done, she still did not trust the soothsayer. He seemed nice enough, and he had saved her daughter's life, but she hoped this would be the last time she and Lizzy ever saw him. Especially Lizzy, whom she could tell was thoroughly enjoying herself in the strange and captivating environs.

Once again, though, etiquette came to the fore. "Of course," she said. "I accept your hospitality. And please don't hold my attitude tonight against me. I was worried for my girl."

"Understood," Oreg said. "No offense taken. Now, how about that tea? It really is quite delicious."

**Eighteen:**

The soothsayer's back room was comfortable enough, though the best Gabby could manage under the circumstances was intermittent sleep. She may have gotten a total of two hours through the night before waking for good well ahead of the sun. She did not rise, though; instead, she stayed in bed, lying next to her slumbering daughter, staring down at her intently, making sure that her breathing remained normal, that her cheeks were a good color, that her forehead wasn't too hot or sweaty.

Lizzy wasn't as young as she used to be, but she was just as wild. No, it wasn't wildness that defined the girl; it was fearlessness. She had no fear; or, if she had any, she had a dangerous way of casting it aside.

Gabby had fear. She feared that one day soon she would not recognize her little girl. She barely did now. Gone was the precocious child who loved to read and write, cook and dance, swim and climb trees. Lizzy still did those things, but she had developed other interests, too; interests of a more adult and risky nature. She now preferred to fish and hunt and throw daggers, and she loved to practice fighting with her fists and Yondo's unique blades. The terrible part, at least for Gabby, was not that Lizzy liked to do these things (it was actually nice to see her bond with her father), it was that she was rather good at them. Better already than Jonno.

Mix skill with want and bravado, especially in a young girl who did not yet know the world, and serious cause for concern is what you got.

Gabby knew that better than most, just like she knew that punishing Lizzy wouldn't stop her.

Gabby ran a hand through her little girl's hair and tried to convince herself that it was just a stage. A 'tomgirl stage' is what they called it, and it struck a lot of young ladies. It had struck Gabby herself, many years ago. Perhaps one day soon Lizzy would snap out of it, which was what had happened to Gabby. One day she was playing Traps and catching crawdads in the creek with her brothers, the next she was embroidering dresses and flirting with boys.

She hoped for the same transition for Lizzy.

But if that never happened, which seemed more a possibility every day, Gabby knew it would be her will that eventually was put to the test. She had always told her children, emphatically, that they could be whatever they wanted to be, that once they were of age their lives and decisions were their own. Like all words, those ones had been easy to say. But to actually live up to them? That was the trick.

Jonno wanted to be a Herder like his father, which flew dead against Gabby's wishes for the boy. As for Elizabeth? Well, Gabby doubted whether the Angeloi themselves could control such a girl.

Guide them, teach them, support them, and always love them, no matter what – that was a mother's task.

Lizzy snuffled, and her left arm twitched.

Gabby shifted her weight for comfort, and kept a close watch on her daughter's breathing. It appeared normal.

A moment later, Lizzy's eyes fluttered and a soft, sleepy sigh drifted out of her. A moment after that, her eyes opened and she yawned.

"Mom?" she said groggily.

"Morning, honey. How's your leg feel?"

Lizzy spread her arms and arched her back in a stretch that would have been physically impossible but for the flexibility of youth. Gabby nearly pulled a muscle watching her. While she stretched, her eyes firmly closed, her wiry arms and legs strung tight, she let loose a long, raspy moan of contentment. When finished, she looked at her mom and said, "What?"

"Your leg?" Gabby repeated. "How is it?"

Lizzy pulled down the covers and looked at her leg. "Feels fine," she said, moving her foot around. "No pain."

Gabby got up from the bed, and Lizzy sat up some. "Let me see," Gabby said to her. She carefully undid the bandage while Lizzy watched, and together their eyes focused on a wound that didn't look so bad anymore.

"Swelling's down," Lizzy noted.

"Seems so," said Gabby. She studied the bite closely, surprised by the lack of redness and inflammation. Even the two puncture marks from the snake's fangs seemed to have faded. "It doesn't hurt?" she asked.

"Not really. Maybe when I try to walk. That's when it hurt before, when I put my leg down. That's when the blood rushes down."

"Do you want to try it?"

Lizzy swung her legs over the bed and let them dangle, but the pain that had struck her only yesterday did not return. She then put her feet on the ground and stood.

She felt … *Something*. It wasn't pain; it wasn't even discomfort; it was more along the lines of recognition. She knew the bite was there, she could feel it, more or less, but there was no accompanying pain or limitations.

She hazarded a step. A slight thump touched her ankle, but then nothing. She tried another, and this time there was no thump at all. "It feels okay," she said, somewhat surprised. "Feels like new."

"Don't overdo it," Gabby told her. "We've a long walk home."

"Oreg's medicine is amazing. I told you."

Gabby groaned, but inwardly. Outwardly she smiled and said, "Seems so. You're still going to see Doc Morris."

There was a knock at the door, and Gabby called out, "Come in."

It was Ferdo. He looked at Lizzy, who was walking around with a smile on her face, and said, "You're feeling better, I take it?"

"Square as square," she told him.

"Oreg's got breakfast cooking. And I need to get back."

"We'll be out shortly," Gabby said.

The door closed, and Gabby, her impeccable manners taking over, got to work straightening up. She made the bed with care, and cleared the nightstand of the water and crackers Oreg had brought them. Then her and her daughter went out into the main dwelling.

There they found Oreg hunched over an open fire, his one good eye glinting. Above the flames, eggs mixed with vegetables, peppers, and shrooms sizzled in a black iron pan.

Ferdo was sitting in a chair, sipping at a cup of tea.

"Good morning," Oreg said to the Carpana women. "A fine day it is for breakfast, as all days are. Remember, if you're having breakfast, that means you survived the night."

"Yes. Good morning," Gabby said.

"Morning, all," said Lizzy. She then bent down to greet the onrushing Baba. "Hey, boy," she said as it arched its back to accept her fingers. Lizzy scratched, and the beyo pup waggled and snorted.

"Accommodations were acceptable?" Oreg asked Gabby.

"Fine," she replied. "Thank you."

"And how's the leg, girl?" the soothsayer asked Lizzy.

"Better," she told him as she continued to pet Baba, who was quite delighted with all the attention he'd been getting. "Swellings gone and there's almost no pain."

"That's good."

"I have you to thank for that," Gabby told the soothsayer. Then she

185

said, "What is that smell?"

"Breakfast," Oreg told her. "For you and Miss Elizabeth. Ferdo and I have already eaten."

"Mighty tasty," Ferdo reported. "Even with the lack of meat."

Gabby took a seat while Lizzy scratched Baba's belly, Oreg finished cooking, and Ferdo enjoyed his tea.

Oreg filled two plates and set them on the table, and Gabby, just now realizing how hungry she was (she hadn't eaten anything in almost a full day), dug in with abandon. Lizzy left Baba and made her way to the table, though Baba followed close behind and took up residence at her feet.

"It's good," Gabby reported between bites.

"Some tea?" Oreg said, and poured them each a cup. His hands shook a little as he poured, but he didn't spill a drop.

"Thank you," they told him in near perfect harmony.

Gabby took a sip, and instantly a smile curled her lips. It was quite tasty, and just the right temperature.

"All fresh ingredients," Oreg declared. "Try the bread. Please."

Gabby looked at him. "I must admit," she said, an apologetic tone to her voice, "I think I badly misjudged you."

Oreg waved off the comment. "No worries. Part of the territory. My sort have a sketchy reputation, and for good reason. But me, I'm mostly just a medicine man. I see things, but not nearly as much as I used to. Getting old and slow, I'm afraid."

Gabby said to him, "Whatever you put on Lizzy's bite certainly worked like a charm."

It was then that Lizzy thought about the necklace Oreg had given her, and she instinctively checked to make sure it was still hidden. She liked how Gabby was getting along with the soothsayer, but she wasn't about to risk the charm. There was still a good chance, despite everything, that Gabby would take it from her if she saw it, and Lizzy couldn't allow that.

She glanced at her ma before her eyes traveled to the soothsayer, who favored her with a smile. It was a conspiratorial smile, a smile on a shared secret, and Lizzy smiled back.

Gabby said to Oreg, "Will she be okay to walk?"

The soothsayer hobbled over to his desk. "I'll check her before you leave, with your permission, of course, and give you medicine to take with." He opened a drawer and pulled out a small jar filled with gray salve. Then he removed what looked like a small white stone.

Gabby continued to eat, biting off a chunk of fresh, warm bread, but her attention had shifted to the soothsayer. Lizzy, meanwhile, reached a hand down and scratched Baba behind the ear.

Ferdo said, "I can carry her for a spell, if the leg acts up." He then smiled at Lizzy and added, "You've gotten so much taller, but you're still as skinny as a skiachtro."

"My pa says the same," she replied.

"I'm still going to take her to see Doc Morris," Gabby said. "Just to be on the safe side."

"Understood," said Oreg. "If that's so, perhaps you can make a delivery for me. Some basic tonics and remedies only. Worry not, I'll collect the next time I see him. We have a good arrangement. And it'll save his girl a trip out here."

"Sure." Gabby scooped up the last of her breakfast and shoveled it in her mouth. Then she looked at Lizzy's plate, which was still more than half full, and said, "Come now, girl. We need to get home. Jonno's no kind of sitter."

Thinking of poor little Dalla in Jonno's care, Lizzy took a bite of bread and chased it with a drink of tea. Then she scratched Baba behind the ear again. She loved the feel of his soft coat and the way his little muscles twitched whenever she hit a ticklish spot.

After she finished her plate, the soothsayer propped up her leg and had a look. The bite had healed nicely through the night; there was very little redness, very little swelling, and when he pressed an experimental finger near the wound, he discovered that it caused Lizzy very little pain.

Even so, he applied a fresh poultice.

He gave the rest of the salve to Gabby, along with the chalky white stone he'd taken from his desk. He told her it was for pain. "She might have some after such a long walk, and this'll help numb it."

"It's not made from the flower buds, is it?" Gabby asked with a note of concern. The flower buds had more than just medicinal properties; they had potent hallucinogenic ones as well. And they were highly addictive.

"Fret not, it's nothing like the flower buds, or any of the other sopors. It's quite mild, actually. Made primarily from tree bark." Oreg wisely left out some of the other ingredients, which included ground leaches, bee pollen, and a mild toxin extracted from poisonous frogs. "The medicinal properties of nature are astounding," he added. "If you understand them."

Gabby took it, but decided she would hide it away ... unless the wound swelled considerably or Lizzy started screaming up a storm. No point doling out medicine not needed, especially that of a questionable nature.

She gave it to Ferdo, along with the salve, and he put it in his pack. Gabby then told Lizzy to put on her boots.

Ferdo accepted a package from the soothsayer containing medicine for Doc Morris, and Gabby finished her tea.

"He's going to miss you," Oreg said to Lizzy, speaking of Baba.

Lizzy petted the beyo pup's back and said, "I'm going to miss him, too." She wanted to ask her ma if maybe it would be okay if she visited Baba sometime, after she served her punishment, of course, but she had a pretty good idea what the answer to that would be. Gabby was being pleasant and respectful, and Lizzy was smart enough to know not to press her luck.

Oreg said, "I'd take the road if I were you. Seems to be a nice day."

"That's the plan," said Ferdo.

"We really should tidy before we leave," Gabby said, and went to clear the plates from the table.

"Please, leave it," Oreg told her.

"Are you certain? It's no trouble."

"I'm sure. You worry about getting your girl home. And have her rest when she gets there. Leg up, head down."

"Oh, she'll be in her room for quite some time," Gabby said.

Lizzy timidly looked away from her ma. She gave her attention to Baba instead, who gladly accepted it.

"Come, Lizzy," Gabby said. "Time to go."

Lizzy bid goodbye to the beyo pup, then stood and made her way over to Lolly, who was resting comfortably on her perch, those big orangish yellow eyes of hers closed. "Bye Lolly," Lizzy said to the owler.

The bird turned its head, opened its eyes, and hooted contentedly.

"You got a good way with animals, girl," Ferdo noted. "They can tell character."

A grin touched Lizzy's face. "Oreg said the same thing."

"Thank you again for everything," Gabby told the soothsayer. "I'll be sure to make it known to my husband. He's a Herder, away on a trek."

"Aye. Lizzy said. And you're welcome. You've got a good girl there, Gabriella. Feisty, but good-spirited. Don't be too hard on her."

"You don't happen to have a tonic that'll make her easier to control?" Gabby replied, only half-kidding. "I'll pay top dollar."

Oreg laughed.

Ferdo did, too.

Lizzy bashfully looked at her feet.

"Sorry," said the soothsayer. "If I had, I'd be rich."

Ferdo opened the door and went out on the porch, while Gabby waited for Lizzy. At the door, Oreg said to the young girl, "It was nice to have met you, young lady." Then, waving a playful finger at her, "Watch out for those ringers. They're all through the wild corn."

"I will," she said. "And thanks for ... *everything*." She gave him a look, and he returned her a sly wink.

"Come," Gabby said, laying a gentle hand on her daughter's shoulder. "I'm sure Oreg wants rid of us."

"Bye, Baba," Lizzy said, and scratched the beyo pup's back one last time. "I'll miss you."

"Tell Doc I said hello," Oreg told Ferdo, who replied with, "I will. And many thanks for the pouch of spiced tobacco."

Gabby, Lizzy, and Ferdo left then, picking their way through the woods at a slow but steady pace, and the soothsayer shut his door and went back inside.

The charade was over.

He had work to do.


Gabby waited until they got home to lay into Lizzy.

The trip from the soothsayer's hut to the Carpana homestead had been a quiet one, with Gabby keeping to herself, and Ferdo and Lizzy talking only periodically, mostly about the dangers of ringer snakes.

On the road, Gabby had asked her daughter a few times if her leg was okay, but other than that she hadn't bothered speaking to her. She was saving her words for home, and as soon as Ferdo was gone and the front door was locked, she let them out in a torrent.

"I cannot believe you did that," she began in an understated but undeniably angry tone of voice. She paced back and forth while Lizzy sat at the table, her hands decorously folded in her lap, a shy, contrite look on her face. "First, you lied to me. You told me you were going fishing. You took your pole and bucket. You took bait. And it was all a lie. All so you could go to the soothsayer's hut! To ask him of Largo, no doubt. Because when you get something in that head of yours you can't let it go. No matter how ridiculous. No matter how dangerous. No matter what anyone else thinks. And what did your new friend tell you? I'm curious.

What did he have to say about Largo Kelsman?"

"Nothing," Lizzy said.

"Don't give me that, girl. Come now, I know when you're telling lies. You're not that clever."

"I didn't ask him," Lizzy said, flat-out lying.

Gabby stared hard at her little girl, studying her for signs of deceit.

"I woke up only a few hours before you got there," Lizzy said. "First, I didn't think to ask him, because of the bite, and then, when I finally thought about it, I was too nervous."

Despite her claim of being able to tell when her daughter was lying, Gabriella Carpana had always had trouble reading Lizzy. She could tell on a word when Jonno was lying, and young Dalla had yet to develop a sense of deception. She could even tell when Yondo wasn't being straight with her. But Lizzy? Lizzy was honest by nature, but she was also smart. Too smart for her own good sometimes.

Gabby quit trying to decipher her daughter's comportment and instead went back to scolding her. "That's neither here nor there," she said. "It matters not whether you asked him. It's why you went. You went, by yourself, to see a strange man who lives alone in the woods. He could be psychotic. He could be a rapist. He could be anything. You don't know. Nobody knows him. All anyone knows of him is that he lives in the woods and claims he can *see* things."

"He's nice," Lizzy said.

"That's not the point, Elizabeth. You didn't know that. You didn't tell me where you were going. I was worried sick. You lied to me, you disobeyed me, you deceived me. And, on top of that, you nearly got yourself killed. Have you forgotten that already? Do you have any idea how heartbroken Yondo would've been had he come home to find you dead?! Or what Dalla would've gone through? Or me? The guilt. The pain. We would have been crushed."

Unable to hold her mother's blistering stare, Lizzy hung her head. The uncompromising sting of shame constricted her chest and seized her heart, making it hard for her to take a full breath. She hated herself for having put her family through such trouble. She especially felt bad for Dalla, who was young and innocent.

"I'm sorry, ma," she said quietly, in a voice wavering with sorrow. "Honest, I am. I never thought this would happen. I ... I was only ..."

"You were only disobeying me," Gabby cut in, much of her anger still with her. "Your father, too. We explicitly told you, numerous times, that you were never to go see *that man*. Yet you went. On a lie. Wait until Yondo hears it. My punishment will seem like a swim in the pond."

Lizzy sniffled, and said, "Sorry."

"And don't think I couldn't tell how much you liked it there," Gabby went on, her cheeks burning red with emotion. "Playing with that beyo pup, saying Oreg makes the best tea, calling an owler by a name. I could see the stars in your eyes, girl."

Lizzy would have liked to deny that, but her mother had bore close witness to her time at Oreg's, and she didn't think she could get away with another lie.

She had thoroughly enjoyed her time at the soothsayer's hut, and those memories had occupied most of her thoughts on the way home. She couldn't wait to be alone so she could think more about it. She couldn't wait to be alone so she could take a long look at the charm Oreg had given her. She could feel the rough texture of the rope against her neck and the smooth, cool touch of the stone against her heart. It thrilled her to have it. It thrilled her more to think it was magical.

"Two months!" Gabby declared, her voice bringing down the hammer. "Two months of all chores here. Dalla's chores, your chores, even Jonno's chores … the ones you can manage. And no fishing, and no going into town, and no leaving the house except to work. And when Yondo gets back, I'll let him decide if he wants to make it more."

Lizzy nodded sheepishly.

"Fourteen years old and walking through the wild corn by yourself, where there are wild animals and snakes and who knows what else. Vandals and killers lay in wait in those parts. They wait for foolish little girls like you. There are clans out from town that we know nothing of. I thought you'd been kidnapped. I thought you'd gone to confront Largo. I thought the worst."

"No," Lizzy said. "I wanted to talk to the soothsayer about Largo. I was worried about what I saw."

"Largo aided us while you were off trying to condemn him as possessed. He helped gather the town together for a search. What do you think of that, girl?"

Lizzy had her mind made up about Largo Kelsman and nothing was going to change it. She knew what she had seen, and Oreg had all but confirmed it. She had to say something, though.

191

"I'm sorry, ma," she said again, sounding truly apologetic. "I knew you wouldn't let me go if I asked you, so I lied."

"Damn right I wouldn't have let you go. Not there. Not ever. And I thought we had decided to wait until Yondo returned before we confronted Largo. Do you remember that?"

"I remember. But I had worries."

"Yet you didn't ask the soothsayer about him? Went all that way with questions and concerns, and came home with nothing but a ringer bite? Not very likely, I would say."

Lizzy realized too late that her ma had shrewdly circled around on her. Gabby had always been good at getting the truth out of people, but Lizzy wasn't about to fold.

"No," she said defiantly. "I told you true. I was unconscious most of the time. I really don't remember much. When I woke, I was hungry, and in pain, and scared."

"Didn't look scared to me, girl. Had time to have tea and make friends with a beyo pup."

"I *was* scared," Lizzy cried. "At first."

A brief moment of silence cropped up between them. Then Gabby held up two fingers and said, "Two months!"

Lizzy nodded in a way that said she understood and accepted.

"And if your pa wants to add on more, or tan that hide of yours, or both, I certainly won't stop him."

"Yes, ma'am."

Another bout of silence held the room.

Gabby took in a breath, and when she let it out, most of her anger seemed to go with it. Her features softened some, as did the tone of her voice when next she spoke.

"I worry on you," she said to her headstrong little girl. "So much. It's a dangerous world and sometimes I don't think you understand that. You're still a child."

Lizzy hated being called a child, but she wasn't about to say it. Gabby's anger had abated; there was no point setting it back on edge.

"You do these things and it scares us. I was terrified we'd never see you again. You have to think about more than just yourself."

"I know, ma. I'm sorry."

Another tick of silence.

Most of the tension had gone from the room, and from Gabby, too; it was replaced by a deep and fearsome solemnity that brought to mind a funeral proceeding.

After some time, Gabby motioned to her daughter, and said, "Come here, girl."

Lizzy stood and went to her.

Gabby hugged her tight and told her that she loved her, and Lizzy hugged her back and said that she was sorry and that she'd never do it again, even as thoughts of the soothsayer's exotic, forbidden hut tickled her imagination.

"I love you," Gabby said to her when they broke their embrace.

"I love you, too."

They both had tears in their eyes now, and nearly at the same time they both wiped them away.

"Now go to your room and rest," Gabby said. "I'll bring you some bread and tea."

"Thank you."

"And as soon as you're healed, it's to work."

Lizzy nodded once, then turned and went off to her room, where Dalla was waiting for her with a big smile, a big hug, and a thousand questions.

**Nineteen:**

"It feels we've been walking for days," Peck complained.

"We have been," replied Kelt. This was now day three of their search for Peck's father and uncle; three days of walking in circles in the haunted wood known as the Dark Forest.

Early the prior evening they had come to the last place where Peck and his kin had made camp, in that small grotto in the Strawlands, the same place where Peck had wandered off from. They had made camp there themselves, hoping that Titus and Loman would return to a familiar place. They had not.

The ground there was cold, the ashes of their fire had been washed away by the rain, and there was no sign of their sled or gear. Peck had barely slept.

Perhaps inspired by Kelt, or maybe it was the direness of the situation and the ever-steepening odds against them, Peck had tried something that he hadn't tried in ages: he had prayed; he had prayed to the Angeloi for help; he had prayed to find his father and uncle alive and well.

As of yet, his prayers had not been answered.

His hopefulness was waning.

"The Dark Forest is a seemingly endless web of trees and bush," Kelt mused. "If you don't know it, you can get lost forever. End up walking in circles for weeks, until something finds you."

"My dad and uncle are not first-timers," Peck said curtly. "They've hunted the Dark Forest before, when they were younger."

"I've spent years in these woods, boy, and even I get lost here. The old timers used to say that the forest changes, and that any attempt to map it or learn its ways is foolish. In these woods, it's more about faith and feel than direction."

"What does that mean?" Peck replied, his voice keeping a sharp edge. "That it's hopeless? That my pa and uncle most likely are dead? That we're wasting time and energy looking for them?"

"I said nothing of the sort, boy," Kelt shot back at him. "Don't give me lip, and don't make your thoughts my words. All I meant is that it's easy to get lost here, and near impossible to find anything you're looking for."

Peck wanted to argue, he wanted to say that his pa and uncle were alive and well, that they'd find them soon, and that they'd all escape the Dark

Forest unscathed, but the words never made it to his lips.

Perhaps because he didn't believe them.

He continued to walk.

"Maybe we could leave the forest and walk the edge for a spell," Kelt suggested. "Might be they're looking for you there."

Peck thought on that, and responded with a grunt. It was an ambivalent reply, but one the Monk correctly interpreted as agreement.

"We should clear the trees in half a rote," he said.

"What of the Dark Forest?" Peck inquired.

"You want to stay here? Fine by me. But eventually I have to go home, to Lockhead. I must tell my kind that we lost another."

"We didn't lose them yet," Peck asserted. "They're still out there."

"Wasn't talking about your kin, boy. My partner was killed the other day. I told you that. His skull crushed by a Sarkofagos."

Peck cleared his throat with a cough. "Sorry," he said.

"This world is wicked and wild, and this wood much more."

"Which way are we going?"

Kelt turned his shoulders and pointed to the right. "That way."

"So we've been walking ... What? South?"

"West. Remember what I said of direction here."

"I just don't want to go the wrong way."

The Monk strode ahead and overtook Peck, saying to him, "I'll lead for a spell. Get us on the right path. You stay back and keep a wide eye."

Peck fell behind, and Kelt veered right.

The rain had stopped some time ago, but the ground was still slick. Peck had slipped a few times already, nearly falling twice. Because so, he had been picking his steps carefully, watching his feet as much as the woods, making sure he kept on balance.

That way of walking had been fine when he was out in front. Kelt had resigned himself to follow Peck's lead, walking slower than he normally would have. But now that Kelt was in the lead, Peck began to lag behind.

After a hundred steps or so, Peck was ten back. After another hundred, he was twenty-five back. Kelt hollered at him to keep up, that this wasn't an afternoon shally, and Peck proceeded to make double-time.

He was nearly caught up when Kelt stopped dead in his tracks and held up a hand for Peck to do the same. Then the Monk turned to his young companion and, with a finger held up to his lips, went, "Shhhh."

Peck swallowed his breath and did not move a muscle. Part of him was curious about what it was that Kelt had seen or heard, but that part was decisively shoved aside by the part of him that thought to fear whatever it was that had put such a charge in a Monk. His mind rifled through all the possibilities: a demon; a flesh-eater; a bear the size of a boulder; a pack of wild boar with tusks that easily could gore a man.

His uncle Titus had nearly suffered such a fate as a boy.

Kelt got down on his hands and knees and crawled through the bosky growth of the forest. He went up a low grade and sought cover in a cluster of bare shrubs. After a few quiet moments, he turned and signaled for Peck to stay put. Then he crawled through the shrubs and disappeared over the hill.

Peck stayed perfectly still, even more still than the tall pines that surrounded him. His eyes remained active, though; they darted around like angry bees, searching for danger in every dense tangle of green, every dark corner and tree-shadowed patch of ground, every limb above him, every root below. He didn't see or hear anything, but that only heightened his fear.

He slowly pulled out the short-blade that Kelt had given him, making sure not to let the steel scrape the scabbard. The weapon seemed small and worthless in this huge, dark place, no more threatening than a stick or a stone, yet he wielded it in front of him like a warrior, ready to use it if need be.

Time passed in silence.

Peck's eyes had forsaken the impenetrable shadows of the forest and now were fixed on the last spot he'd seen Kelt. He was waiting for him to return, for him to walk, not crawl, over the hillock and say that everything was okay.

More time passed.

Peck was about to start up the grade and have a look for himself when Kelt finally returned. Walking low, with a quick step, the Monk topped the hill and slid snake-like between the pines. He had his knife in hand, and when he got close enough to Peck, he shook his head back and forth in an ominous way.

"What is it?" Peck asked with a whisper. "My pa?"

Kelt shook his head again. "No. The demon and flesh-eater that killed my partner. They're near, maybe three-hundred steps that way."

"Were there any men with them?"

"No. Now come, we need to move."

"But ... Where?"

Kelt pointed left. "That way. Follow me. And keep up and keep silent."

Peck didn't have to be told twice. He followed Kelt, keeping so close on his heels that the old Monk was forced to crack a faster stride. And they didn't slow down or speak one word until they were far away.

"You think we lost them?" Peck said, finally breaking the silence.

Kelt stared into the thick copse in front of them and said, "I suspect. But we can't rest here. We have to clear the woods."

"We can walk the pines that way," Peck said, pointing more west than south. "The tree line will appear eventually. It has to."

"Does it?" replied the Monk shrewdly.

Peck didn't know how to respond to that. Thankfully for him, Kelt spoke again. "It's a longer walk, by some time."

"Aye. But better safe than sorry."

"I agree."

"And we can continue to search for my pa and uncle."

There was hope, tenacity, and raw courage in the boy's voice, and that pleased Kelt. Peck was only a boy, but he had already lost his ma and two sisters to unspeakable violence, violence that he had witnessed firsthand. He had been there that day, he had seen the abuse and heard the screams. And though he had survived that tragedy, the scars remained. They were scars that opened and bled from time to time; they were scars that would never fully heal.

Peck would bleed and scar often, Kelt believed. Some were made to carry that weight.

The Monk could feel the pain in the boy's soul; it cried out like a sick animal, like a winter wind through a forgotten boneyard.

Peck would bleed tonight.

But that time was still a ways off, and Kelt had no intention of losing another friend to the Dark Forest. Not so soon after Manly.

"We'll walk among the pines," he said, "but we can't call out. And we must walk fast and quiet."

Peck agreed, and they started off, walking south and west among the high pines, which blocked out most of the sky and all of the sun. They walked quickly and they walked quietly, their eyes darting into the deep woods now and again, picking through the branches and brambles for a clean line of sight.

Peck searched for his pa and uncle, while Kelt searched for the demon and the flesh-eater. The Monk didn't expect to see the demon-girl or beastly cannibal, but he was quite certain that Peck wouldn't see his pa or uncle. No one would ever see those two again.

Peck was silent for a long time. The flames of the campfire lapped at the air and threw off radiant orange light and soothing heat.

The squirrel they had eaten had made for a fine supper, and afterwards Kelt had told Peck the terrible truth about what he had seen in the Dark Forest. He now was waiting for the boy's response.

It was the calm before the storm.

"How do you know it was them?" Peck asked reasonably. "You don't know my father or uncle. It could have been anyone."

"It was them," Kelt said, certain of it. "They were your kin."

Peck nodded, accepting that as truth. Who else would be walking the Dark Forest on such a day? It had to be them.

That settled, he moved on. "You should have told me then," he said. His voice was quiet, composed, yet edged with anger, and there was a piercing look in his eyes. "We could have helped them."

"No," said the Monk plainly, "we couldn't have."

"You don't know that. I can fight. You're a Monk. It's what you do."

"I lost my partner to them. I'm not going to lose you, too."

"So you left them there to die!" Peck said, his voice rising.

"They were dead already," Kelt replied calmly.

"So you left them there to be eaten?!" Peck's voice was now a shout, and there was no doubt his anger was directed at the Monk.

"If we had attacked them, we'd be dead now, too."

"Coward!" Peck spat at him. He stood with a jolt and reached for the short-blade the Monk had given him.

"What are you going to do with that, boy?" Kelt said.

"I'm going to find them and ... and ..."

Grave uncertainty stole Peck's words but not his thoughts.

What he would do was attack the demon and flesh-eater head on, go in swinging like a red-eyed maniac and either save his pa and uncle from the indignity of becoming some evil thing's dinner or join them and become dinner himself. Either way, he wasn't about to stand back and do nothing. He had done nothing when his ma and sisters had been attacked and murdered; he would not repeat that mistake.

"Sit down," the Monk told him.

"Turn away, coward!" Peck cried out. "Hide your face in shame." He began collecting supplies to take with him: a waterskin, dried jerky and nuts, the short-blade and sheath.

Kelt stood. "Sit down," he said again. "You'll get yourself killed."

"What do I have to live for?!" Peck shouted. "I have no family. I have no friends. I have nothing and no one."

"You have air in your lungs and blood in your veins. You have food in your belly. You have life! That's what you have to live for. There is nothing greater than that."

"I don't care if I die."

"And die you will if you go into the Dark Forest alone at night."

"I will not let that thing eat my pa and uncle. I won't!"

Kelt displayed a passive face while inside he cringed with disgust. That would not be an easy thought for anyone to reconcile, but it would be especially hard for someone like Peck, a boy who had endured so much already. It was one thing to suffer death, to die in battle with dignity and honor; it was something else entirely to be killed and eaten by something monstrous. But the boy would have to come to terms with that horror on his own. As for Kelt, he was not about to let him march into certain death.

"You're not going anywhere and that's final," he said in a stern voice. "Now sit down or I'll sit you down."

"You're not the boss of me!" Peck thundered back.

"You're going to fight Kin and a Sarkofagos all by yourself with that little blade? Ha!"

"Only because you're too much of a coward to join me."

"With a knife and a couple daggers? We wouldn't last thirty seconds."

"I don't care. I have to do something."

"There's no way to help the dead, boy. Your pa and uncle are gone. They're not in this world anymore, and the meat that remains of them is no different than that of an animal. Going back there will only ensure that you won't be here anymore either."

"I don't care!"

"Well I do!"

Peck already had his pack over his shoulder, his blade and sheath on his belt. All his belongings were the Monk's belongings, but he had decided to claim them as his own. He would need them in the Dark Forest against the demon and flesh-eater.

Kelt moved around the fire and cut off Peck, stopping him in his tracks.

Peck attempted to deftly sidestep the old Monk, but Kelt cut him off again. "There's no nobility in sacrificing your life for revenge," he said. "The dirt is full of those bones."

"Out of my way coward or I'll cut you down," Peck shot back.

Kelt glared at him. "Okay," he said. "Show me. Show me how you're going to cut down a demon and a flesh-eater with your little blade there. Show me, boy! Let me see."

"Don't test me," Peck said, trembling with rage. "And stop calling me 'boy!' I'm no boy!"

The Monk slapped Peck across the face. "Show me, boy," he challenged him. "Beat me and go."

The slap stunned Peck. It stung his cheek and his pride, and he drew his blade and recklessly stabbed it at the Monk.

Kelt turned to the side, effortlessly plucked the blade from Peck's hand with a quick grab and pivot move, then spun and struck the boy on the jaw with an elbow. Peck went down in a heap.

"We are no match for the two of them!" Kelt said as Peck tried to blink the stars from his eyes. "My partner and I confronted the beast because we did not know the woman was Kin. We thought she had been captured by the flesh-eater and soon would be eaten by it. Two trained Monks against one Sarkofagos is a bad idea. They're huge and strong and fast, and they don't die easy. Add in Kin, even one, and you might as well take that sword and fall on it."

The faint metallic taste of blood warmed Peck's mouth. He wiped his lip and pulled back a hand streaked red. "You hit me," he said, his anger washed with surprise.

"You're worried about being hit? Ha! You go there, boy, and I guarantee they'll do a lot worse. They'll kill and eat you, or leave your meat and bones for the animals. Or they'll turn out your soul and put you to work for them."

Sorrow twisted Peck's face and tears welled in his eyes. The firelight cast a dark, ominous glow over him, making the blood on his chin look as black as tar.

"You've suffered a great loss and I know you're hurting, but getting yourself killed is no solution. You may not care if you die, but I do. I fight for life, and all are valuable. Monks aren't trained killers, boy, despite what folk say and think. We dispossess people, we exorcise demons, we chase off the evil things that torment this world. Aye, occasionally we're called to fight, but that's not our way. We'd rather save one soul than slay ten Kin."

The Monk stopped for a breath, but he was not yet done. "You can't beat them with violence because violence is a part of who they are." His voice was a mite kinder now, and on his bearded face rested an expression of sympathy, yet there was fire in his eyes. "They are violent and vain and heartless. They look not just to kill but destroy. They want to ruin the spirit. That's their aim. Flesh and bone means nothing to them. Male or female, old or young, dark or light, big or small – we're all worthless meat in their eyes."

Peck heard every word, but not one of them eased his pain. The only difference was that his anger had changed to anguish. "They killed my pa and uncle," he sobbed, tears rolling. "They killed them, and now they're going to eat them. Because of me."

"They killed them because that's what they do," Kelt replied.

"But it was because of me! They never would have been in the Dark Forest if I hadn't wandered off. They were looking for me. If not for me, we'd be near home now. I'm cursed, I tell you. Cursed!"

The Monk wanted to offer the boy words of consolation, but he didn't feel comfortable doing so. Only time and love could heal sorrow; words had no effect on it at all. Words had very little effect on any matter of import, so far as Kelt could tell, which was why he rarely depended on them. More often than not they created strife and discord, and most of the time they were entirely unnecessary. They were little more than empty noise for folk too afraid or too apathetic to act.

Beyond that, and much more worrisome, Kelt had an idea the boy was right: the demon and flesh-eater had killed Peck's pa and uncle because of Peck, but not by happenstance. The Monk suspected that it hadn't been a random occurrence at all but a carefully planned and executed attack. And the more he thought about it, the more he was convinced. If that was true, he needed to get Peck to safety as soon as possible.

Reaching out a hand, he pulled the boy to his feet. He then handed his short-blade back to him and returned to the campfire.

Peck unshouldered his pack and set it down. He sheathed the blade and unattached the sheath from his belt. He laid that down, too, and reclaimed his seat. He had stopped crying, but his face was a mess, streaked with blood and dirt and dried tears. In the strange orange light of the campfire, he looked terrifying and malicious.

Kelt removed the tobacco pouch and leather-bound cask from his pack. He unscrewed the lid of the cask and took a drink, then handed it across the fire to Peck. "Take some," he said to him. "It'll relax you. Help you sleep, too."

Peck downed a couple swallows before the sting of the booze caught up to him. He coughed and hacked while the liquor burned his lungs and warmed his belly. It was a peculiar feeling of nausea and comfort, and Peck added to it with another pull.

The Monk, who was busy rolling tobacco, said to him, "Careful now, boy. Don't take too much."

After one last sip, Peck handed the cask back to the Monk, who capped it and put it away.

"Not very tasty," Peck said, grimacing.

"It's not for taste."

Kelt sparked his tobacco roll with the end of a burning twig. His first exhale sent a cloud of smoke over the flames.

Peck said, "What now?"

His voice was soft, fragile, the voice of a scared, hopeless child, and the pitiable look in his young, tear-swelled eyes would have brought a hungry bear to its knees.

"You have any family left? Uncles? Aunts? Anyone?" Kelt asked him.

"I have a few aunts and uncles in Greenhorn," he said. "That's where I'm from. Where I live."

"We must go see them."

"But I don't want to live there anymore. I can't live there anymore. Not after this. I can't."

"That's well and fine, boy, and I understand, but you still have to tell them what happened. You have to tell them that your pa and uncle were killed. It's what's right."

Peck's eyes started to well up again, and he sniffled and turned away. He wasn't ashamed of his emotions; he just wasn't keen to share them.

"Tell them only what they need to know," Kelt instructed him. "They were killed by a flesh-eater during the hunt, and that you only escaped by luck. Don't mention the Kin, and say nothing of the Dark Forest. You can say you were near the forest, but not in it."

"Why?"

"Folks have a funny way of acting when it comes to Kin. They hear a tale like yours and get to thinking that maybe the demon is in *you*. They start thinking that's why you escaped. They have the same reaction to the Dark Forest. They believe it's cursed land and may think you're cursed for having been there. Trust me, leave the Kin and the forest out of it. It'll only bring suspicion."

Peck nodded. He wiped away his tears with the back of his hand, smearing his face even more. "You'll come with me?" he asked the Monk. "To Greenhorn?"

"Of course. I'll tell them I found you after it happened. I'll tell them you were hysterical."

"A Monk that lies. Isn't that against your vows?"

Kelt smiled at the boy. "Surely. And a habit of it I will not make. But some truths need to be kept. People have a way of mishandling them."

Peck was silent for a while.

The Monk, too.

Finally, Peck said, "What then?"

"We'll figure that out when the time comes," Kelt told him. "Until then, get some sleep. It's a long walk home."

Peck did not think sleep would be possible, not after everything that had happened, not with such anger and grief in his heart, yet his eyelids felt heavy and a long, gaping yawn unhinged his jaw. His vision got a little blurry around the edges and his mind began to fade in and out. Was it the liquor, he wondered, or the blow he'd taken to the head?

Maybe it would help if he laid his head down and rested his eyes for a bit, he thought to himself.

Mercifully, that turned out to be the last thought he had that day.

**Twenty:**

Lizzy fetched another pail of water from the well and carried it to the fire she had going in the pit. She put down the pail and put on her gloves. She took the water that had reached a furious boil in the iron pot over the flames and poured it into a third pail. Then she took the cool water from the well and dumped it into the iron pot, causing it to hiss and throw steam. She hung the iron pail on the hook over the fire, then picked up the pail of hot, steaming water and carried it into the house.

It was bath time for Lizzy, and the chore of drawing a bath was not near worth the feeling of freshness and cleanness that came after. Not to her, anyway. Twelve pails fetched, heated, and dumped, all so she could scrub herself clean after a long day's work.

The snakebite had heeled nicely in just two days; the swelling and pain were gone, and she had no restriction of movement. She felt perfectly normal again. But for two small puncture marks on the meat of her calf, just above the ankle, no one would have suspected that she'd been bit by a ringer only a couple days ago.

Ringers killed little girls. They killed fully grown men.

Yet here it was, two days later, and she was walking around without pain, carrying bucket after bucket of water from the well to the fire to the house without so much as a single limp.

"That's enough," Gabby told her after the twelfth bucket had been dumped. The entire process had taken more than a rote and had produced just enough water for a full and proper bath. Gabby gave her little girl a rock of soap, a dish of jasmine petals, and a small vial of vanilla oil.

Lizzy carried the items into the back room and shut the door behind her. She opened the vial of vanilla oil and breathed in its wonderful scent. If there was one thing about baths that Lizzy truly enjoyed, it was the smell of vanilla. She dumped it in carefully, drizzling a little here, a little there, and swirled it around with a gentle hand. Then she scattered the jasmine flowers on the surface of the water. The pure white petals stood out in the steam that rose from the water's surface, and the scent of the flowers fused nicely with the vanilla oil, sending forth an aroma that Lizzy imagined the Garden smelled like on a perfect Spring morn.

The water was hot, but not so hot that it burned her skin. She got in slowly, carefully, sticking one foot in first, then the other. By the time she was fully submerged, her skin welcomed the sweltering temperature, though she did begin to sweat. She breathed in the heavenly scent of the flowers and oil, and laid her head back and relaxed.

It had been a long couple of days and Lizzy was exhausted. Gabby had started to lay on the punishment, making her fetch not only her own bath but Dalla's, too. Just today, Lizzy had collected the eggs, cleaned the chicken pen, milked the goats, cleaned the dishes after breakfast, and helped make dinner.

It was a lot of work, and according to her ma it was just the start. Gabby and Jonno would need baths tomorrow, and there was knitting and darning to do, and making the beds, and soaping the floors.

"There's an endless variety of work to be done in a home," Gabby had told her, "and you're going to do it all before Yondo gets back."

That would be fine, thought Lizzy, only she knew it wouldn't end there. Yondo would have chores for her when he got home, and maybe even the tail end of a switch.

Worst of all, she knew she deserved it.

No. That wasn't the worst part. The worst part was that she wasn't allowed to do it again. She gladly would suffer any punishment, do any penance, if only she was allowed to visit Oreg whenever she wanted.

She reached over the edge of the tub and riffled through the pockets of her leathers until she found the soothsayer's gift. She had kept it hidden from Gabby thus far, taking it from around her neck whenever she thought her ma might see it. At night, she slept with it under her pillow, clutching it tightly in her fist.

She stared at the small black stone through the steam rising up from the water. Its surface held on to some of the moisture from the bath, which caused it to dull. Lizzy wiped away the film with her thumb, but it clouded right back up again.

Suddenly the door swung open, and Lizzy quickly dunked the amulet under the water.

"I do love that smell," Gabby said as she breezed into the room. She closed the door behind her and sat on the chair at the tub's side. "Let me see your leg, girl."

Lizzy covertly slid the necklace under her other leg and lifted the wounded leg out of the water. "It's all healed, ma," she said. "Look."

Gabby inspected the bite with a keen eye. Faint rings of red could be seen around the puncture marks, but any swelling that had been there was gone now. And that was after a full day's work on her feet.

"Does it hurt any?" Gabby asked. It was the umpteenth time in the last two days she had asked that very question.

"Not even a little," Lizzy told her. "If I press on it I can feel it, but even then it doesn't really hurt."

Gabby was amazed, but refused to say it. What she said was, "You must be a fast healer, girl."

Lizzy nodded and let her leg slide back under the water.

"Wash yourself clean. Use the soap. I'm going to check."

Lizzy said she would.

Gabby left then, and Lizzy quickly removed the amulet from the bath.

She thought about Baba and Lolly and Oreg, and she wondered if Oreg would still be alive when she was grown enough to make her own decisions. She hoped he would be. She really wanted to see him again, wanted to talk to him about the strange, wonderful, and seemingly endless mysteries of Hinterland, wanted to ask him the questions her mother and father never answered for her, or answered only vaguely. Chief among those questions would be the origin of her birth. She suspected the old soothsayer had seen and done just about everything, and that stoked the fires of her curious nature, setting it ablaze.

Thinking about the cabin and the greatest adventure of her young life, Lizzy washed herself clean. She did her hair, too, lathering it with soap and rinsing it by dunking her head under the fragrant water.

Her fingers became wrinkly and pale, while the rest of her skin turned a bright pink color. She felt utterly relaxed and at peace.

The steam stopped rising and the water lost some of its heat, but Lizzy made no move to get out until her ma came back in with a handful of newly washed clothes, a small wooden cup with a brush for her teeth and some fresh mint paste, and a brush for her hair.

Gabby dipped a hand in the water and, finding it only lukewarm, told her daughter it was time to get out. "That's plenty," she said to her. "You're pruning up. Now, towel yourself off, brush your teeth, and get dressed." She left again.

Lizzy toweled off, got dressed, combed her hair back with the brush her ma had left her, and cleaned her teeth. The last thing she did was fasten the amulet around her neck. Then she tucked it into her nightshirt, where it couldn't be seen.

She didn't realize how tired she was until after she left the back room.

The accumulation of the day's chores coupled with the hot water from the bath had her body feeling wonderfully numb and slacked out.

"Let's have a look at you," Gabby said when she saw her. She ran a hand through Lizzy's wild hair, making sure the girl had combed it through, then told her to open her mouth.

Lizzy did as told, and Gabby inspected her teeth. They looked clean, and her breath smelled fresh.

"Can I go to bed now?" Lizzy asked. "I'm tired."

"So soon, girl?" The sky had only been dark for a rote, and Lizzy liked to stay up late.

"It's been a long day. And baths always make me sleepy."

Gabby hesitated a moment, then nodded and said, "Yes. Go. And get good sleep because tomorrow's going to be another hard day. And the one after that. And so on."

Lizzy nodded lazily and went off to bed. She climbed under the covers without saying her prayers and drifted off to sleep almost instantly. And she did not stir when Dalla came in a short time later and somewhat noisily went about her bedtime routine.

**Twenty-one:**

The demon Mar, who was now Alde of Meridon, but whose real Kin name was Amaros, gazed through the eyes of Largo the Herder and viewed with great delight the incredible foolishness of humanity spread out like a field of rotting carrion.

Largo didn't know the Old Kin Elder was peering through his eyes and listening with his ears, just like he didn't know the demon could feel what he touched and smell what he smelled. He had a sense of mystification, a sense of numbing vacuity, but not a sense of the Kin.

He was in a wakeful stupor. He could speak and see and hear, he could feel and smell and touch, he could drink until he was drunk and share flesh with a woman, but all of it was superficial. The Kin had command of Largo; he was but a surrogate on borrowed time.

He presently was at Sana's Saloon, which was where he had spent every night since returning home from his fateful trek. Sana's place was a den of iniquity hiding behind a thin guise of revelry and community, and many of the menfolk in town, single and married alike, went there often to indulge their basest desires. Booze and eager young women kept dry under that roof, and there was faro and dice and other games of chance to play. There was music and dancing, mayhem and merriment.

Amaros loved the sounds, the sights, and the smells of Sana's Saloon. He loved the cackling, half-dressed sallies and the drunken, slavering men. Meridon had had many such places before its demise, and Amaros had appreciated them all.

But tonight the demon had work to do.

The place wasn't overly crowded, but there were enough people there to make it feel like a party. Ava and Eva weren't yet on stage, but Jules was up there, slowly picking at the strings of his guitar.

Sana was holding court behind the bar, as usual, and her sallies were busy working the crowd, picking pockets one smile at a time. They batted their eyes and played their games for a drink, for a dance, for a romp upstairs, and they all made money.

"They found her at the soothsayer's place," Eton said over the sound of the music. He was one of the men who had searched for Lizzy the night before. "You believe that? Ferdo said she'd been bitten by a ringer in the wild corn. Nearly died."

A man named Berra, bearded and broad-shouldered, shook his head. He was from one of the clans on the outskirts of Vernon, in the lands at the foot of the Grand Steppe. He only came to town to sell his goods. A hunter and furrier, he and his boy had stopped at Sana's for a few drinks and some company. It had become a favorite tradition of theirs.

"What is she now?" Berra asked. "Nine? Ten?"

"Fourteen, methinks," said Eton, who had also told this story to Horace, Gregg, and a few of Sana's girls.

Lizzy's exploit was all the rage.

"Fourteen!" Berra exclaimed. "Damn I'm getting old."

"Aren't we all," said Levis, a local farmer with far fewer days ahead of him than what lay behind.

"Some more than others," piped Sana, and those who heard her snorted laughter. Even Levis laughed.

Horace, the High-Sheriff of Vernon, had missed all the excitement. He had gone up north to Coppen with a few of his men to guard a shipment of ore and gems. "Yondo's gonna tan her, I know that," he said. "Fourteen and running alone in the wild corn. She's lucky."

"I heard she was going to see the soothsayer," Largo heard himself say.

"Don't know of that," said Eton. "But the soothsayer's hut was closer than her house, and I heard she barely made it there."

"How else would she know where the soothsayer's hut was unless she was going there specific?"

Eton shrugged. "Don't everyone know."

"Roundabouts? Sure. But it's not easy to find, not unless you've been there before."

"That girl's a wild one," said Horace. One of Sana's sallies was sitting on his considerable lap, flirtatiously twirling a finger through his crop of curly ginger hair. "Yondo says she's fearless. More than his boy. I could see her going to the soothsayer."

"Kids," Berra grunted.

His boy was upstairs with Lessie, Sana's most popular and expensive girl. Berra himself had plans to defile a pert young sally named Gianna, as soon as Gianna was ready for defiling. He and his boy would stay the night and head back to their womanless homestead in the morn, financially and sexually satisfied.

"She went when Yondo was off," Eton noted. "I don't think she would have pulled such a stunt if he was home."

"No chance of that," agreed Horace.

"Gabby's got a soft heart," said Sana. "She lets those kids get away with too much gruff, you ask me."

Horace snorted a laugh. "Soft heart? Maybe. But she used to be a wild one, too, back when she was that age."

"I don't recall any stories like that."

"She weren't born in Vernon. Her clan was more up north, in the lands bordering Boreal. The town of Novan. I knew her father well enough. Apparently she was a handful."

"Boy crazy?" Sana asked, thinking about her own misspent youth.

"No. Fighting. Running off. She had two older brothers."

"What of Lizzy?" Largo said, interrupting them. "Is the ringer bite healed or does she have a fever?"

"Ferdo said she looked fine," Eton reported. "Soothsayer's got some potent medicine."

Horace took a sloppy drink of ale and wiped his mouth dry with the back of his hand. He then gave a look to the sultry young woman currently occupying his lap. She smiled back at him, a tacit sign that she was ready to go whenever he was.

Largo said, "Girl like that, you gotta put her in line straight away, elsewise she's gonna end up dead."

"Or in here," Sana chimed, drawing raucous laughter from the crowd at the bar.

Even Largo laughed.

"Yondo would burn this place to the ground if that day ever came," said Horace.

"Aye," said Eton. "That he would."

Sana had nothing clever to say about that.

"You don't have to look for trouble to find it in this world," said Largo. "I know it. We all do."

"That's a truth," agreed Eton.

"Well said," added Berra with a tip of his mug.

Sana said, "You don't *have* to look for it, but sometimes you just get bored. And thank the Angeloi, or else I'd go out of business."

The others laughed again, heartily, Largo included.

Even Amaros laughed, which created a far-off echo in Largo's head, making him feel kind of dizzy. He attributed the dizziness to his wounds and the hard rye in his glass, and wisely took a seat.

When next he stood, near twenty minutes later, Amaros was gone and he felt … Clearer. Stronger. Better.

Horace and his sally were gone, too; they were upstairs, in bed, doing perverse and wonderful things together.

Largo looked at Sana, knocked his empty glass on the bar, and said, "Another drink, my dear lady. And tell me what young damsels you have available tonight to care for an old lout like me?"

"You been randy a lot lately, eh?" she replied with a smile. She filled his glass with whisky. "Cara's working. She's a snapper."

"Had her the other night. How about Lessie?"

"Lessie? Ha! She'll cost you, old man. And she'll need time to wash up after Berra's boy. You know how sloppy youngins are."

"I can wait," Largo said, hunkering down on his stool. "High breasts and a firm ass are what I need to warm these old bones tonight."

"Hard rye and young breasts are a good tonic most any night," said Berra, about to get his with Gianna.

"I'll drink to that," Sana happily exclaimed, and with a deft hand she poured herself a shot of rye and threw it back.

Laughter and cheers followed, and Sana called out, "Jules! Play something festive, will ya? I'm tired of your sad tunes. Let's get the mood up in here. It's not a wake."

Jules stopped slinging mournful blues and put his fingers to work on something more upbeat, and Berra and Gianna finished their drinks and went on their way, laughing and smiling and touching each other.

Largo, meanwhile, waited for Lessie with a fresh pipe and a full glass of hard rye. He gave a passing thought to his kids, whom he'd barely seen since coming home, but that thought faded quickly, overwhelmed by the amoral ambiance of Sana's Saloon. And later, in a chamber upstairs, sweet Lessie laid it to rest for good with her unique charm.

**Twenty-two:**

The desert trek was going smoothly for the lead group. The stragglers were good folk, and though they had many concerns and questions, they walked a fairly steady pace. In the case of Franklin, the old curmudgeon, it was the enticement of Gabby's cider each night that kept him on the march. But Yondo was already running low on the heady mixture; he only had enough for two more nights, and they were still at least seven from the Great Stone Temple.

There had been one laka attack, the night after they left the Croppings, but Yondo and Dock had taken care of that quickly and decisively, cutting through the sand-creatures with ease. Yenas were always about, heckling and hunting, their whitish-gray eyes like tiny ghosts in the night, but so far they had kept their distance.

In addition to his harmonica, Molt was in possession of a signaling glass, a device used by Herders to send out alerts in the daytime, when the sun was high and bright, and a pair of waft paddles, which were used to send messages at night. Waft paddles were long, flat, hollow, wooden rods that when struck together produced a unique vibrating echo that traveled for miles across the flat waste of the desert.

The trek was going about the same for the second party. Led by Olvin, they were mostly in possession of weapons and supplies. They were walking the western tract, a seldom used path anymore due to its harsh terrain and proximity to the Basin.

But they weren't shepherding souls; they were hunting.

Unfortunately, they weren't having much success.

They had yet to catch wind of any vandals, and they had gotten to use their blades only once, and that had been on a feeble pair of lakas. Olvin had also killed a yena with a crossbow bolt, an act meant to serve as a warning to the rest of the pack. But the remaining yenas hadn't taken it as a warning as much as a dinner bell; they had eaten their fallen friend, flesh, muscle and bone, leaving nothing for the desert. Food was scarce in the deep sand; you took what you could get.

Mengin carried the signaling glass and waft paddles in their group. He and Molt could not have in depth conversations with one another, but they could send vital messages back and forth, messages that possibly could save lives and avert tragedy.

So far there had been nothing interesting to report.

Perhaps they would have better luck over the next couple days, in the desert grass and cacti fields east of the dunes.

With Olvin and Mengin were Darv, Chatt, and Devid. Together, they were five of the most experienced Herders in Vernon. They were men as comfortable in the desert as they were with steel in their hands.

"This is a waste of time, you ask me," said Darv, the resident cynic. He was a large man with a large head and a large pair of hands. He had dark skin and black hair, and his beard was as thick as a summer hedge. "What are the chances we run across them? The vandals might be in need, aye, but they're not stupid. And you know they have Kin in their corner."

Devid and Chatt agreed. None of them cared for the plan, and none of them thought it would work. Yet it had to be done. The vandals had stolen life and drawn blood, and that was unacceptable.

Though rare, the loss of souls was not an unprecedented occurrence. Dazed by the shine of the Kin and the heat of the desert, Herders had been known to offer souls to find their way back home. Desperate Herders had sold souls for wealth and favor, giving up a few per trek, believing they wouldn't be missed. Now it seemed the Kin had found a new way to steal living stones: they were using the desperate clans of Meridon to do their bidding for them.

"The vandals are demon chum," said Chatt. He was tall and thin, with sandy blonde hair and a patchy beard that did little to hide the crooked slant of his jaw. A spade to the face from his old lady after one too many late nights at Sana's had been the cause of that. "I know it well. We all do. Our war is with *to skoteina pnevmata*, not the slaves they've made from the men of Meridon."

"Yet it has to be done," said Olvin. This was not the first time they had had this conversation, and it was not the first time he had made this declaration. "They'll either not see we're here, which will allow us to confront them, or they'll see us but won't know which group has what, which will make them leery to attack. Far from a perfect plan, but it should do the trick."

"And what of the Kin?" Chatt replied. "Could be a trap *they're* setting."

"If it's a trap, it's a trap," said Olvin, succinct as always. His thinning gray hair, neatly-trimmed beard, and wrinkled gaze marked him as the oldest of the second group. He wasn't sure of his exact age, though he guessed it somewhere near sixty-five. Even though he was still a fierce warrior with a strong body and deft blade hand, he soon would be made to retire. The desert was hard ground to walk with old knees and an old back. Though proud, though he often told people he would never retire, that they would have to drag his dead body from the desert, he secretly was counting down the days.

"If it's a trap," said Chatt, "and the vandals have the Kin with them, what do you think that means for us?"

"Nothing good," said Olvin. "But it matters not. It's our duty. We didn't say we'd walk the desert only in good times. I don't remember that part in our vows."

"But could be we're walking to our deaths!"

"Aye. But it's the same every time we walk the sand. We shepherd souls when there are souls to shepherd."

"My opinion ..." Mengin began, but stopped abruptly when something far away caught his eye. The sun was high, but the horizon had yet to be affected by the sweltering heat. He squinted into the red vastness of the desert and saw, if his old eyes could be trusted, two scant figures. Whether they were coming toward them or walking away from them, Mengin couldn't tell, but they were moving. He pointed them out to the others, saying, "Look. There."

"Lakas?" said Devid.

"Likely not in these parts," replied Chatt.

"Vandals?" Olvin wondered, staring fixedly at the far-off stick figures, their bodies nothing more than wavering black vapors in a sea of red sand.

"Approaching so plainly? And only two?"

"We can handle two vandals easy enough," said Devid. Like Darv, he was a fighting man of good size and strength. His skin was mixed (his mother had been dark, his father pale), but his hair and beard were black and bristly. He had more than a few scars marking his well-muscled body, and he wore them proudly. "I can do it myself."

"Might be they're hoping we give away our position," said Mengin. Like Olvin, he was older, more mature. He had an even temperament and a good mind for strategy, and could still handle a blade.

"Might be they're trying to get us to look one way so they can attack the other," Chatt replied.

Devid watched the slow, uneven movements of the far-off strangers, unsure of who or what they might be. He was very interested in finding out, though. "I don't see the problem," he said, his gruff tone adding grit to his words. "This is what we're here for."

"Aye!" said Darv, a note of excitement in his voice. He liked action, and was keen to find some. "Let's go introduce ourselves. Shall we?"

"No," said Olvin. "I think we need to keep with the plan."

"And I think we should scrap it," replied Mengin. "We're Herders. Honored Voukulos. Since when do we play silly games."

"Agreed," said Darv.

"Aye," said Chatt.

"The Council has spoken," Olvin reminded them. "I don't like it either, but the Council gave their word."

"The Council doesn't walk the desert. We do."

"Me, Chatt, and Darv could check it out," Devid suggested.

"Split up? No," said Olvin. "We're stronger together. And safer."

"What if it's just two lakas?"

"Then it's two lakas. Nothing to fret on or concern ourselves with. But do you really think it's two lakas?"

Devid shook his massive head. "No," he said. "Just the same, we can handle two vandals."

Olvin considered the idea, but never was his mind in doubt. "No," he said at last. "I think the time has come to be wise, to do what we wanted to do from the start." The Herder clapped Mengin on the shoulder. "Send word to the others, tell them we've spotted something coming our way. Tell them we've decided to join up with them. Tell them not to wait on us, that we'll catch up by nightfall or early tomorrow morning."

"Come now, Olvin," said Devid. "We should at least check it out. It's been six nights and we've seen nothing."

"We're here to track, lest you forget," added Darv. "It's likely nothing. Or maybe it's something. Only one way to find out."

"What if they're trying to lure us farther away from the others? What then?" Olvin reasoned.

Devid had no good response for that. The prudent move would be to meet up with the lead group and go in force, like Olvin and Yondo had wanted to do from the start. They were still seven or eight days from the Great Stone Temple and the most dangerous paths lay ahead: the high rocks; the hillocks and fields of cacti; the looming, treacherous bulk of the mighty mounts. The smallest misstep could lead to disaster.

"Mengin, send word," Olvin said. "Let them know we're coming." He turned to the others. "Breakfast is done, men. We need to pack up our gear and move out. Now."

Mengin removed the signaling glass from his pack and unwrapped the leather cloth protecting it. He carefully lined it up with the angle of the sun, aiming it in the general direction of the lead group, and began sending the message. Flashes of light darted across the sand in rapid motion.

"This makes little sense to me," Darv put in. "If you want to meet up with the others, that's fine. I take no issue with that. But first we should check this out." He pointed in the general direction of the approaching strangers. "What's the harm?"

"We could be there in a rote," said Devid, adding on to his friend's pitch. "Be back before lunch."

"And we'd have something to tell the Council."

"They ordered us to track, so let's track. This is the first honest sign we've come across."

"Of its honesty, we have no idea," said Olvin. "And forget not, no matter the words and wants of the Council, we're here for the stones and stragglers. They are our primary concern. Our sacred duty is to the Angeloi, not the Thirteen."

"Tell the Thirteen that," joked Mengin, drawing mild laughter from the others.

"If the vandals see our true number, they'll be off like the wind," said Chatt. "And what will we tell the Council then? They'll not be pleased."

"Hopefully we'll tell them we delivered every last soul to the Great Stone Temple on the other side of the desert, and all are safe and accounted for. We can hunt the vandals while we wait for the next trek. We can hunt and track them on the way home. It's what I wanted, and what Yondo wanted, too. It's the wise course."

Devid shook his head again. He appeared genuinely disappointed by the decision. "I was hoping to work up a sweat on this trek … other than sweating my ass off in this heat."

"Sometimes boring is good," said Mengin, who had just finished signaling the lead group.

"Aye. For an old man with old bones."

"That's how you get to be an old man."

"Who says I want to be an old man, old man?"

"He's an old man with a young, fit wife," Chatt pointed out.

Darv and Olvin laughed at that.

"True," said Devid, smiling. "Might not be such a bad deal after all."

"Quite a good deal, actually," said Mengin. "Most of the time. She can certainly nag like an old *glyko*."

The others laughed.

"I imagine that's a fair enough trade, especially for those old bones of yours," Olvin told him.

Brief flashes of light returned from the distance, and after the last one, Mengin said, "Message received."

"Come," said Olvin. "We need to move."

"Look! Where are they now?" Darv called out.

The others stopped what they were doing and stared out at the desert, their eyes trained in the direction where the two stick figures had first appeared. There was nothing to be seen but sand and rock and dead earth for miles, and Chatt said, "Where did they go?"

"Lakas?" Devid said. "Could be they fell to the sand?"

"Strange," said Olvin. "They were there just a moment ago."

The five of them scoured the desert in every direction, looking east, west, north, south, squinting into the shine of a new sun to see farther. The stick figures did not return, but that did nothing to change their plan.

"We go on the quick," Olvin commanded. "If it was nothing, it was nothing. We'll be together and strong soon enough."

As the others got back to work, Darv continued to sweep the desert landscape with his squinting eyes, working steadily from left to right, then from right to left. He thought he caught a glimpse of something, but it evanesced before his eyes … if it had been there at all.

It would get even harder to see in an hour or so, when the heat started to rise off the rock and sand, covering the low horizon in dense, blurry waves. That hot air played tricks on the eyes, revealing things that weren't there, concealing things that were.

"Better safe than sorry," Chatt said, tossing his pack over his shoulder. "Hope the Council agrees. They don't take kindly to disobeyed orders. And Esai was especially proud of his plan."

"Who says we must tell them," replied Olvin.

"Not I," said Devid.

"Nor I," agreed Darv.

Mengin finished packing and turned his gaze to the desert. Something didn't feel right to the old Herder, but he didn't want to be the one who brought a curse down on them.

'Speak ill and ill happens,' the old adage went, and Mengin Prat was a superstitious fellow, a man who believed in omens and the wisdom of old.

"Energy is alive and everywhere," he remembered Oreg once telling him, long ago, back when he was yet young and free. "Put fear out there, Voukolos, you'll get fear back. Put anger out there, you'll get anger back. But the same goes for goodness and kindness."

Mengin was one of the few townsfolk in Vernon who openly consulted the soothsayer. It was Oreg who had predicted that Mengin, an aging, life-long bachelor without any heirs, would marry a young woman from Boreal and have a son with her, and six months later the Herder met his bride-to-be, Cara Ann, who was less than half his age and twice as pretty. They had yet to have a son, but hadn't they had fun trying?

The old Herder had little doubt of the soothsayer's mystical abilities after that, as he had little doubt of his own instincts. And right now his instincts were telling him that they were being watched. The only thing that presently was of comfort to him was the soothsayer's forecast for the end of his life. "Your bones are one with the desert, Voukolos, and shall be buried there," Oreg had told him during one of their most recent sessions. "But rest easy, you shall not die there."

"Come, old friend," said Olvin, clapping him on the shoulder, jolting him from his worrisome ruminations. "We need to make time. I'm sure Yondo and his are already on the move."

Mengin nodded absently and pulled his gaze from the red rock and sand of the desert. Had he turned and looked back over his shoulder, he might have seen two stick figures far on the horizon, slowly moving towards them. But he did not look back. None of them did. They marched in the opposite direction on a swift step, and those faint, vapor-like silhouettes far in the distance followed after them.

The Dustbowl was a large, oval-shaped valley that dominated the eastern rim of the Great Desert, spreading out in a seemingly unbounded expanse that defied size and direction. There was only sand there, mounds and hills of endless sand; no cacti, no rocks, no straggly yellow grass. Lakas could be found there, but they could be found everywhere in the desert. Other than them, there was nothing but sand and wind, and that wind blew the sand around like a storm.

Herders avoided the Dustbowl, knowing the many dangers it held. This was easy enough to do because it wasn't directly on their route to the Great Stone Temple. It whirled and hummed about ten miles east of their normal path, but on clear days they could see the sand bustling around the outer edge of the bowl and spiraling up into the sky. The few people who had dared its terrain had never been seen again. They went in, disappeared after a handful of steps, and never returned.

"Get too close and it'll swallow you whole," were the words Yondo's father had told him when he first started walking the desert, and Yondo had listened. Never had he gotten closer than five miles to the Dustbowl, and never had he made camp within ten miles of its foul breath.

It was considered cursed land, far worse than the Dark Forest or the Marshlands. It was a ground of certain death.

"What is that?" Jacko asked, pointing to the gusting sand to the east. He could see it swirling in the air and blowing around.

"We call it the Dustbowl," replied Yondo. "Only the dead go there."

Jacko thought to ask what he meant by that, but assumed he must be talking about lakas. Instead, he said, "Have we gone off course?"

"Aye," said Yondo. "We have. Good eye, boy."

"May I ask why?"

"We're meeting up with the other group."

"The other group? Another group like us? What for?"

"Because we need to."

Yondo had never been much of a talker. When it came to words, he was like a scrooge with gold. Yet he had a way of getting his message across as plain as a slap to the face.

Jacko heard it clear enough and knew not to ask on it more. Even Franklin, the old curmudgeon, knew better than to pursue it further. Yondo's stoic demeanor frightened him.

In back, Edgar said to Molt, "Something's wrong, Uncle. I feel it."

"How many treks have you been on, boy?" Molt replied.

There was an awkward pause as doubt and embarrassment spilled into young Edgar's mind. Then, in a tone that matched, he said, "Twelve."

"Twelve? And you know of trouble?"

"I suppose not. Not like you. But … I feel something."

"The other group probably needs water or medicine. Maybe food. I'm sure it's nothing to worry on."

But even as he said it, he didn't believe it. Trouble was brewing; it had been brewing for some time now, long before this ill-fated trek had begun. Like his nephew, Molt could feel it in the air.

He had taken well over a hundred treks through the desert and most of them had gone by without so much as a hint of danger. Sure, he had encountered plenty of lakas and yenas, but they were easy enough to handle. As for Kin? He'd seen exactly seven in twenty years. They had made the hairs on his arms and neck stand up, had made his head thump and his blood rush faster through his veins, but ultimately they had had little effect on him. It was all in the mind: keep the door firmly shut and they couldn't do a thing to you; open it a crack and you might as well hand them a knife and present your neck.

Yondo felt trouble in the air, too, but the stragglers were listening, and they had begun to get anxious. It wasn't wise to give them cause to lose their cool. They had adjusted nicely so far to the song of fate that awaited them; to give them reason to fear was not only foolish, it was dangerous.

"You'll learn well of the desert, boy," Yondo called back to Edgar. "It's mostly empty. Thank the Angeloi."

"Aye," agreed Molt. "And hot."

Yondo and Dock laughed.

In a low, humorless voice, Franklin said, "You're telling me." The old man was dripping sweat.

Audrey looked back over her shoulder at Molt and caught him with an easy grin on his face. "Not much farther and we'll break for bread," he said to her. "Another rote should put us at a good time for lunch."

"A rote is an hour," Audrey said with a note of uncertainty, seeking clarification.

It was Dock who would give it. "Aye. An hour. Though I think ours are a little longer."

"Out here it makes more sense to measure by time than distance," said Molt. "I don't believe anyone has ever tried to gauge the full scope of the desert. It's too big an area. Takes at least fourteen full days to cross from Vernon to the Temple. Takes longer from Grim Gorge to the sands east of Mount Dorsette."

Meanwhile, in the trail group, Darv and Mengin had their eyes set on watch. Darv was looking for the stick figures they had seen earlier, while Mengin searched the horizon for signs of the lead group. The sun was high up in a cloudless sky, its intense, unrelenting rays creating a glare that was hard to see through. Almost all Herders had a perpetual squint. The older ones, like Mengin, had eyes marked by them.

The heat had picked up, leaving them with a powerful thirst for water. They maybe had two days' worth left in their skins, but that was near how long it would take them to reach the Lost Caves. There, they could take ease and replenish their supply. There were numerous freshwater ponds and streams in that warren of caverns west of the mesas, and usually you could find something to eat there, too, so long as you weren't too picky.

"Watch the rocks," Olvin said. "This is sidewinder territory."

He was not wrong; the viscous serpents were rich in this area, and their bite was deadly. The Herders carried an antidote for it, made by Oreg, the soothsayer, but a single bite nevertheless cost at least three days.

They were walking east and south, taking a sharper angle to catch up more quickly with the lead group. Yondo and his were walking due west now, going away from the Dust Bowl. This would cost them half a day, perhaps even a full one, but no one was going to complain.

"My uncle was bit by one," said Devid. "Thirty years later and you can still see the scar. He shows it to me every time he's had a few snorts of whiskey. I think it's his most prized possession."

"*I* was bitten by one," said Mengin. "On my third trek. A baby got me. One of its fangs broke off in my leg. My damn foot swelled up like a melon. I couldn't walk for three days and I didn't shit for five."

Devid and Darv found this humorous. Mengin did, too … now. Back when it happened, he had thought he was going to die.

"There," said Chatt, pointing left. A small sidewinder was weaving its way through the rocks, its reddish-brown body nearly invisible in the sand. "They're everywhere."

"Nasty buggers," said Olvin, and the others agreed.

"Any sign of our unknown friends," Darv asked Mengin.

"No. Could be we were seeing things."

"All of us? Doubtful."

"Lakas," said Devid, certain of it. "Had to be lakas lost on the plains."

"Maybe," said Darv. He unhooked his waterskin, unstoppered the cap, and took a long, greedy drink.

"Go easy," said Olvin. "We don't want to run dry."

Mengin saw a flash in the distance, and then another, and then more after that. Molt was signaling, letting them know about a slight change in direction, and Mengin took out his square of reflective glass and sent back word that they understood and would adjust.

"This way," he said when he had finished, leading them more east than south. "At this rate, we should meet for dinner."

Chatt kicked a rock, sending it skittering across the hardpan. "Good.

Away from the snakes and skorpious," he said.

They picked up the pace a step or two.

In the distance, directly behind them, the stick figures reappeared.

Now there were four of them.

The two groups of Herders met on a lonely patch of desert chocked with short, shabby cacti and mounds of black slate. Nobody could say where the black slate had come from, and it looked badly out of place among the cacti and red hardscrabble. Some believed the tarnished black stones were the dead souls of Kin, and it was said that anyone who dared touch one was courting disaster.

Yondo had never believed such nonsense; nor had he ever touched one. Some beliefs were better left untested. His father had taught him that, and he still believed it.

They enjoyed a quick meal and made introductions as the desert sun began its slow descent. They then struck a path due south, wanting to get in a couple more rotes on foot before calling it a day. They were heading for the Lost Caves. They would not make it there until midday tomorrow, and it was likely they'd spend a night in the underground caverns, which offered shelter, protection, water, and even the possibility of food.

Those two rotes went by quickly.

The sun grudgingly gave way to the moon, its red shine turning gold in the nascent moments of night.

They made camp in a clearing that provided a long view of darkness in every direction. They were twelve strong now, and they built two fires to accommodate everyone.

The stragglers were curious about and somewhat wary of this change, but they remained silent, choosing instead to be content with their nightly allotment of bread and cider.

Darv, Chatt and Devid joined together with Edgar and Molt, and the five of them kept the stragglers company while the other Herders spoke.

Olvin explained the need to meet, and Mengin gave his word as well. "We saw them," Mengin said. "They were out there."

"Have you seen them since?" Yondo asked.

"No. But that doesn't mean they're not there."

"You're sure it wasn't lakas?" said Dock.

"Almost certain. They moved different."

"Vandals then?"

"Perhaps. Or Kin. Or those possessed by Kin."

"Or figments," Yondo put in. "The desert plays its tricks."

"Not likely," said Olvin. "We all saw them."

"Either way," said Mengin, "we felt it best to join. The Council wants us to hunt the vandals. That's all well and good, and likely necessary, but first the souls must be delivered. That's our duty."

"Agreed," said Yondo. "The vandals aren't fools, and if our suspicions are right, they got Kin behind them. That very well may have been a trap."

Olvin agreed. Then he said, "This whole trek has been off kilt. We have too many souls in the bag to play games."

"The most important thing is getting to the Great Stone Temple with all accounted for," said Mengin. "And it's best to do that together."

"Agreed," said Yondo.

Olvin said, "We go together from here. We're seven days out. Once we've met our task, we can worry on the Council's wants. We can hunt and track until the next moon."

The others agreed. All except Dock, that is, who kept silent. Yondo looked at his friend and said, "Dock? You with us?"

Dock knew that Olvin and Mengin were right, that they were speaking good sense, but he had another idea. "Yours is a short-term solution," he said. "One not likely to work. Aye, the vandals may not take the bait this time, or next time, or even the time after that, but they'll still be out there, watching, waiting, planning. I can't help but think that forcing their hand would be the better play."

"There's truth in that," said Olvin, who was a good man and a good Herder. "If you want to continue the ruse, we can vote on it."

"I just think they'll likely not attack us on the way back, when we have no souls," Dock said. "Then what? We're in the same spot. And we can't take ten Herders on every trek."

"Who knows what they'll do," said Yondo. "Whatever the Kin wants them to do, I imagine. They've attacked Herders on the way back to Vernon, taking coin and steel."

"Aye. The first couple times," said Dock. "But since they've attacked on the way there, near about these parts. It's the stones they want, and we won't have any on the way home."

Yondo nodded. Olvin, too.

"All I'm saying," Dock said, going on, "is that if we don't track them now, here, where they like to attack, we're not going to find them on the way back. They'll be gone."

That certainly made sense. It was the same point Daglan had made when they were planning this trek. He, Esai, and Stu all believed that if they were to catch the vandals it would be on the way to the Temple, not on the way back.

Yondo thought the same, but he didn't like the idea of risking the stones and stragglers. They were top priority, and he believed everything should be done to protect them.

This was one of those conundrums not easy to solve without the aid of compromise and violence.

And just how often was that the case?

The people of Meridon had been trusted allies not long ago, before the flower buds had led their people to ruin. Thousands were dead. Thousands more had been stricken sick and feeble. Fields of crops had wasted away and their once plentiful game was all but gone, having either died off or migrated to more fertile lands. Their ponds and streams were no longer able to support life.

Meridon had once been a hub of trade and wealth, a vibrant, flourishing land full of promise and possibilities. Their merchants shipped goods to Boreal and Vernon, and the merchants of Boreal and Vernon shipped goods back to them. One of Gabby's favorite dresses had come from the town of Portwich, in the lower western quadrant of Meridon, along the shores of Potami. Yondo also had gifted her a necklace from there.

And now ...

Murdering. Thieving. Slaving for Kin.

Life in Hinterland was hard enough without having to worry about your own kind turning on you.

Hinterland had known no other war than the Great War, and that had been fought primarily between the Angeloi and the Kin. Sure, there had been quite a few family skirmishes over the ages, and even a couple deadly village against village scraps, but never a full-on war betwixt lands. There had always been raiders and vandals, just as there had always been poachers, scam artists, killers and rapists. You couldn't get everyone in line, no matter how hard you tried; there were always outliers and troublemakers, thieves and bullies, and in their wake a string of poor, downtrodden victims.

It was the way of the world.

But this ...

"Yondo?" said Mengin, subtly calling him to attention. He had been silent for some time and the others were waiting for him to speak. "Do you have more to say?"

Yondo looked around at his fellow Herders. These were men he had supped with, drank liquor with, and fought alongside. They were good men and good friends.

"Aye," he said at last, nodding. "The stones and stragglers are our main concern and we shall not forget that. But Dock speaks true and the Council gave word. Yet I do not believe anything we do on this trek will make a difference. The Kin is behind it. It's them we're at odds with. If they have a mind to attack, they'll make the vandals attack, whether we have two groups or one. If they don't, we won't see hide nor hair of the vandals, nor any other sort of trouble."

"I agree," said Olvin. "Yondo is right."

"Aye," said Mengin. "We all know it."

Dock nodded, though it was plain to see he had more on his mind.

"No matter our thoughts," Yondo said, going on, "we must put it to a vote. We are the only Council out here, and every man's word is equal. We must be of one mind. That is the way it has always been and must be."

"Of course," said Olvin.

"Agreed," said Dock.

Mengin went first. "I believe we should join," he said. "The stones must make it to the Great Stone Temple."

"That is my vote, too," chimed Olvin.

Dock spat on the ground. "Nine of us walking three stragglers?" he said. "It's heavy-handed and against the Council's wishes."

"Aye, so it is," said Yondo. "But forget not the near two-hundred stones we have. They count, too."

Dock offered a pensive nod, but his mind had not changed. "I'm not forgetting the stones," he said. "They are the reason we walk the desert. Quite honestly, I don't like this anymore than you. But orders are orders, and a vote was taken."

There was honor and wisdom in that statement, and the sober looks on the other Herders' faces showed that. When the Council handed down an order, it was expected to be followed.

"You have another idea, old friend?" Mengin asked Dock. "Speak it if you do. That's why we're here."

The Herder spat on the ground again. "Joining up is well and fine," he began, "and safe, too, but it will give us no advantage. Neither, I believe, will tracking and hunting them after we deliver the souls. Their wants, whether theirs alone or the Kin's, are clear now. They'll take our steel and our coin, but they *want* souls."

"So what do you propose?" said Yondo.

Dock glanced around at his fellow Herders. "Yondo, Devid and Chatt are the best we have when it comes to blows. I think they should not only track the vandals, but hunt them. We're in the high rock of the desert now, near Domboll and the Lost Caves, where there are many places to hide and take shelter. If they attack, this is where they'll do it. This is where they've done it before."

The others knew this to be true.

Dock went on. "Darkness has to be our friend. When they've attacked, it's been either at night or early morning. They use the night to their advantage. We must do the same."

"Track them at night?" said Olvin, a note of interest in his voice.

"Why not? We know the desert better than they do. We can track at night, rest during the day. They'll not be expecting it."

"I'd be willing to try that," said Olvin. "Six men to shepherd souls and stragglers is plenty, you ask me."

"I agree," said Mengin.

"What was the number of those who attacked Largo and Aglan?" Yondo inquired. "Three? Four?"

"Three," said Mengin. "At Domboll."

"When we were attacked, there were four," Olvin said. "It was after we left Domboll and the Lost Caves, near where the petrified tree stands. There was a boy with them. Big lad. Didn't speak. Looked like he might have been the son of one of the men."

"From word, we can assume there are at least ten vandals," Mengin put in. "They seem to travel in groups of three or four."

Yondo continued to think on it.

"Six of us can handle a trek easy enough," said Olvin. "Most of the time we have only two or three."

"We're likely clear of yenas from here to the mounts," added Mengin. "Not lakas, but there easy to kill."

"True," said Yondo. "But you forget the Kin."

"Not me," said Olvin. "I never forget them."

"They see and hear what we cannot. Could be they're listening to us as we speak."

"Not likely. We'd feel them if not see them," said Dock.

"But if we split up to track the vandals, the Kin will know, and they'll feed that information to them. Only makes sense."

Mengin nodded. "Yondo's right," he said. "We're damned either way."

"Aye, we are," agreed Dock. "They can see us when we can't see them. They know what we're doing and we're none the wiser. But what else should we do? Who knows, maybe we'll catch them asleep."

"I doubt it," said Yondo. "The Kin never sleep."

"I just think it worth a shot. At least until we reach the mounts. We were apart, now are together. They might not expect us to split up again."

Yondo agreed with that sentiment. Mengin and Olvin did, too.

Yondo didn't like the thought of tracking the vandals like dogs, but Dock had made some valid points. Once they reached O Megalos Naos tou Petrou and delivered the souls, there would be no reason for the vandals to attack, and any chance they had to catch them would be lost.

"I can go, too, if you like those numbers better," said Dock. "Five to trek, four to hunt. A more even split."

"Which is what we started with," noted Olvin.

"Aye. But now the hunting party will lead the way. At night."

That idea made more sense, yet Yondo remained hesitant. Defending oneself showed courage and character; attacking favored anger and violence. Anger and violence eventually turned on you, no matter your intentions. But the vandals had to be stopped, and presently there were no better options available to them.

"We can leave soon after the stragglers go to sleep," Dock said, laying out a plan. "We should be able to make it all the way to Domboll and the Lost Caves by morning. And we'll be coming in from the north and west, a direction they'll not expect ... neither the vandals nor the Kin. And once there, we can hunker down and wait for the second group, keeping an eye out for vandals."

Olvin considered the idea, and soon started to nod.

Mengin turned to Yondo and said, "Not a bad thought."

Yondo agreed. It was good plan.

Dock went on. "If there's no trouble through the high rocks, we can join up at the mounts and hike the last leg together. And if we want, we can track them on the way back. Break up into two groups and hope to draw them out. Probably won't work, but we can try."

"That makes sense to me," said Mengin.

"A far better idea than what the Council set forth," added Olvin.

Dock looked at Yondo. "What say you, old friend?"

"I like it," Yondo said. "Not that it will work, but I think it worth a try. We need to put it to a full vote first."

Mengin nodded in agreement. "Aye," he said. "Majority rules."

Olvin said, "It likely won't get us anywhere for the Kin is everywhere in the desert, but I'll vote for it. And the Council's decree will be met."

"Precisely," said Dock.

Yondo agreed with the decision, yet he still had doubts. The vandals were strong and skilled, and they were crafty, too, and since the fall of Meridon they had little to lose. Need is a powerful tonic, and the vandals, sons of Meridon, had many needs. So many needs they had a deal had been struck with demons. A blood-deal, most likely.

"If we do this, we must be smart," Yondo said. "Tracking is key."

"If it's tracking you want, Molt's the best we got," said Dock.

"I take exception to that," Mengin was quick to say.

"Do you want to go, old friend?" Yondo asked him. "You're welcome."

Mengin shook his head back and forth. "No. Not me," he said. "I'm too old to go hunting in the desert. But I'm damn sure a better tracker than Molt. I'm better than him with my eyes closed. I want that on record."

The others laughed.

"Noted," said Olvin.

Mengin shook his head. "Molt? He gets lost in his own back woods."

The others laughed again.

When that laughter died down, Yondo said, "Okay then, Molt will go and Dock will stay back." He then looked at Dock and said, "If you don't mind. I know it's your plan."

"Fine by me. Wherever I'm better needed," Dock replied.

"Let's put it to a vote then," said Olvin.

They did, and it passed unanimously.

Only Molt had a complaint: he had promised his brother's wife that he would not leave her son's side. Edgar was a strong and capable young man who had walked the desert a dozen times, yet he was no match for a mother's worry.

Darv, always thirsty for action, volunteered to replace him, and all put their hands in.

That night, after the stragglers went to sleep, Darv, Devid, Yondo and

Chatt loaded up their gear and walked off into the seemingly endless darkness of the desert, heading south and west, traveling against the tide of the moon.

That moon saw everything that happened at night, silently observing the ways of man from its gentle arc in the sky.

Tonight there would be much to see.

**Twenty-three:**

Yondo did not like walking the desert at night. The desert was vast and mostly empty, but not completely so. Sooner or later they would run into lakas and yenas, even out past the plains, in the high rocks and cacti. The Kin, too, were more active in the dark. And they were everywhere.

Yet they followed the plan and struck out two hours after dark fall. They walked south and west first, then, after two rotes or so, they turned eastward, planning to arrive at Mount Domboll and the Lost Caves from the west; the same way the vandals would likely get there.

As they walked, they searched the black horizon for the golden shine of campfire light, which could glow as far as ten miles in the distance.

Chatt said, "I know I voted for this plan, and I voted for it because I like it, yet I fear it will not help us."

Darv agreed, though he was glad to be doing something. "It's better than walking stragglers," he said.

"Hunting in the desert is a fool's game," Chatt said.

"Depends what you're hunting. And whether or not you kill it."

Devid was young but well-tested. His size, speed, and natural instincts made him one of the best they had when it came to battle, and he was still at that age when battle was what he wanted most.

Yondo remembered those days. He had matured since then, coming to realize that when all counts were tallied, battle, like the gambling wheel at Sana's, always claimed more losers than winners.

"We're nearing the Red Rock Path," Darv announced. He stopped, crouched down, scooped up a handful of sand and small rock. He smelled it, then let it sift through his fingers. "Nothing," he said. He inspected the ground some more, running a hand through it. "If they've been this way, it hasn't been recently."

Yondo looked around. The desert wasn't just dark at night, it was black. The sky was black, too, freckled here and there with the occasional star. Hinterland's ancestors had believed the stars were holes in the roof of the world; they believed that's how the souls and stragglers got in, and how the Angeloi traveled from one world to the next. But that was a long time ago, before the stragglers had started sharing other ideas. They spoke of science and physics, biology and astronomy. They spoke of the cosmos and of life, and did so with great ardor, intelligence, and conviction.

So far as Yondo believed, the truth, while it would have been nice to know, really didn't matter. Balls of fire in the sky or holes in the roof of the world? Either way, at the end of the day he was still Yondo Carpana, and he had a life to live, a job to do, a family to support. That was the only truth that mattered to him.

Some of those same stragglers had tried desperately to keep from going to the Great Stone Temple beyond the mounts, what they called, often with amazement, The Great Pyramid. They had offered their knowledge and wisdom in exchange for freedom, but none had ever swayed Yondo's mind. The loyal Herder might have been surprised to learn that there had been a few who *had* won their freedom over the years. Their lineage still existed in Hinterland today.

"A scenic tour of the desert at night," said Chatt, gazing into the surrounding darkness.

"Beats walking in the heat of midday," replied Devid.

Darv stood tall, hitched up his pants, and started walking again.

The others followed.

"It's worth a shot," Devid reasoned. "We get out in front for a change, then lie in wait for them."

"Aye, worth a shot, but unlikely to yield anything," said Yondo. "The Kin won't let them walk into a trap unless the Kin wants them trapped."

Chatt grunted in agreement, while Devid gave a sarcastic snort.

"You think too much," he told Yondo. "And too deeply. Sometimes things are what they are and nothing more. And sometimes you get lucky."

"Not when you're dealing with demons," Chatt put in. "Everything is sideways when you match wits with them."

"As for luck," said Yondo, "there's good and bad."

"A waste or not, we have to try something," Darv said, hammering home the unfortunate truth, the same truth the Elders had based their decision on. "Something has to be done. We have to let them know we're not going to stand for it."

"Aye," said Yondo. "Something has to be done. And here we are, doing it. But for the good of what?"

"I get it," Devid said. "But it'll just keep happening elsewise."

Yondo knew that Devid was right – if they did nothing, it would just keep happening; and undoubtedly the attacks would increase in both frequency and aggression. But he also knew that he was right – the Kin was pulling the strings, and they had something larger in mind.

The winds had changed and darkness had begun to overtake the light. He felt it as sure as he felt the rock of the desert below his feet. Lizzy felt it, too; that had been apparent the day he had left for the trek. She had sensed trouble in the air and had tried to warn him. He had told her not to worry, that it was just another walk in the sand, but he had known better, and he suspected that she had as well.

That girl had a sense about her that frightened him. He was beginning to think he should have listened to her. He was beginning to think he should have voiced his concerns more boldly.

"Halt! Listen."

Everyone stopped on Darv's command, his anxious tone instantly catching their attention. They remained silent and still, listening to the quiet of the desert.

And then …

In the near distance, the sound of lakas wailing could be heard. It was a dreadful sound, a low, moaning drone that echoed on and on, like a cold wind in a cave.

"Lakas," said Darv.

"About time we get some action," said Devid.

"Time has nothing to do with it, Voukolos. It is cyclical. It goes in circles, not unlike man."

This voice was new to the conversation … and it was Kin.

All four Herders spun around at the same time to find a true demon spirit hovering before them in a cloak of black shadows.

"Evening," it said to them pleasantly. "Herders out for a stroll, away from the flock. Leaving their sheep amongst wolves."

"Demon!" Darv shouted, his voice booming out.

The demon laughed. "Man!" it shouted back. Then, with an air of cordiality: "Now that introductions have been made."

Yondo remained calm. This was not his first encounter. "What are you here for, Kin?" he said to it. "You know better than to play with us."

"I come bearing a message. Will you hear it?"

Yondo stared at the dark spirit with unblinking focus. "What is your message, demon? Speak it, and be gone."

"Daimonas!" Chatt cried out in the ancient language. "Sto onoma …"

The demon evanesced before Chatt could get out another word. It reappeared a few seconds later, almost in the same spot. "This is how you treat an emissary?" it said.

Yondo held a hand up to the others. "Quiet," he told them.

The demon's eyes flashed on the dark-skinned Voukolos. "You're their leader," it said to him.

"Say your peace, demon, but try to possess and we'll stop you."

"No need to possess," it replied. "Here to converse. Will you listen?"

"So long as it's not nonsense."

The demon laughed. It sounded like a snake hissing.

The moans of the lakas seemed to be getting closer. Farther away, somewhere in the black distance, the whinnying laugh of yenas could be heard. This sound was savage.

"It's not your fault, you know," the demon began, its voice one with the dark, one with the desert. "Only a matter of time. Time again. Time running in its great and perfect circle. Time running out for some, beginning for others. Time and all it holds."

"Is that your message, demon?" Yondo said. "Babble."

The demon laughed its hideous laugh. Then it said, "Meridon fell first. That took time, effort, cunning. Its fall opened the door for more of my kind to come here. It opened the door to a darkness you've not yet known. You will know it soon, I say, and you'll not like it."

"Make your claims and threats, demon," Devid sneered with youthful bravado. "But do not think you will ever have dominion here. Not while I have air in my lungs and blood in my veins."

"Only until then?" the demon shot back at him. "I would say 'deal' to that, Voukolos, for you haven't long to live."

"Say the word, demon. I am here."

The demon's eyes flashed yellow, and again it laughed. The sound traveled in the dark like a curse. "Arrogance is a gift we are grateful for, boy," it said. "It enlivens us."

"I am no boy," Devid replied, offended. "Try me and find out."

The dark spirit ignored the challenge and turned its attention back to Yondo. "It's over, Voukolos. You know as well as I. You feel it. I know you do. I sense it in you. Been on the horizon for some time now. Better, more evolved worlds have already fallen. Hinterland is soon to be next. It will become a wasteland of dead men, forsaken women, and enslaved children. You are no match for us. You have no idea what is coming. What is here already. Throw in now and I promise that you and yours will live."

Yondo's eyes narrowed on the black surging cloud that was the demon. "Ever since I started walking this desert it's been the same song," he said in a calm but austere voice. "Your kind telling us to throw in and stop fighting. Your kind talking about taking over and laying all else to waste. Well, my father never threw in, and neither his father before him."

"They faced no real danger, Voukolos, and time was on their side. Now it's on ours. It has already begun. We are ready to reclaim our birthright and you are in our way. You bear the fruit of what we need."

"Aye. Always have. The vandals won't change that."

"*Vandalia* are spoiled meat, barely worth more than lakas and yenas. But like all, they have a worth."

"Impotent ghost!" Devid shouted, venom in his voice. "You tempt and trick the weak. But you won't find any here."

The demon's eyes flashed yellow, but Devid was almost as strong of mind as he was of body. He felt a slight wave of doubt mixed with fear, but valiantly pushed it away.

Yondo cried out, "Daimonas!" and the demon stopped trying to work its way into Devid's head. It looked at the Herder, and its eyes flashed yellow again.

"No cause to die, Voukolos," it said. "It's a fair deal that promises life across generations. Your children and theirs, and theirs, and theirs."

"Never," said Chatt through clenched teeth.

Devid echoed him: "Never."

"We don't deal with your like," said Yondo. "Your words have been wasted."

"Waste and want are woven with the same thread," said the demon. "Send me away and die. Deal and live. The choice is easy, and it's yours to make."

A smile lifted the corners of Yondo's lips. His beard did well to hide it, but the look in his eyes gave him away. No matter the situation, no matter the consequences, no matter the truth, there was only one answer for the Kin.

"No!" he said, staring boldly into the fiery depths of the demon's eyes. "We care not for your words, and your wants make no difference to us."

"You sense the truth, Voukolos, I feel it, yet you would give your life and all you have for pride?"

"Aye. Before I ever side with you."

The demon's ghostly form billowed angrily. The yellow shine of its eyes darkened. "So it shall be," it said. "Instead of kings immortal, rulers of Hinterland, you'll be blanched bones in the desert. Instead of eating, you shall feed. You have guests."

To the Kin's left, the silhouette of a single laka appeared, moving in a lurching, disjointed way. Two more emerged a few moments later, and then four more after that. Then, from the right, the glowing whitish-gray eyes of a dozen or more yenas pierced the darkness.

They were surrounded.

The Kin was gone.

Yondo peered from side to side, calculating the numbers against them. "I've got six lakas and maybe fifteen yenas," he called out.

"Eight lakas," Devid reported. "No. Ten."

Darv said, "Yenas attack methodically. Waste the lakas first."

This was common practice for Herders when confronted by lakas and yenas at the same time. Only tonight the yenas were under the sway of the Kin. They would attack as the Kin wanted them to, fiercely and at once, and they would not stop until they were dead.

Growling mad, their bloodthirsty teeth bared, they charged in without hesitation. The Herders stood in a circle with their backs to each other, as was the way, and began cutting them down.

Yondo got one, and it let out an agonizing howl.

Darv slashed one and then another.

Chatt kept several at bay with his whip.

Devid cut through one of the beasts, but another bit him on the leg before he could gash it. He let out a cry of pain, and Yondo turned and stabbed the thing in the neck, killing it instantly.

More attacked, and Darv was bitten. He managed to kill the beast with his knife, but another latched onto his arm and began to tear at his flesh. He cried out manically, swinging his arm and stabbing at it. He finally got it in the leg, and it let go and scampered off.

Yondo killed another, and then charged forward, breaking formation to strike down the first lakas. He got two in the blink of an eye, taking their heads with clean cuts, making them spit and bleed sand.

Smelling fear and blood, the yenas closed ranks and attacked in full. Devid was bitten again; one of the beasts got him on the ankle, another attacked his hand, causing him to drop his blade.

Yondo swung in and cut one of the desert dogs in half, severing its spine straight through. The one attached to Devid's ankle he kicked hard in the ribs and away it ran, yelping and squealing.

Yondo was then attacked from behind. A wild dog jumped up and bit him on the shoulder, and he whirled around and flung it off him, sending it skidding across the desert floor. The bite had broken the flesh and drawn a good spurt of blood, but Yondo hadn't the time to think about it.

Darv was in serious trouble; a yena was tearing at his leg while two lakas drew near, their stiff, outstretched arms reaching for him wantonly. They moved cumbersomely, but possessed just enough agility and speed to make them tricky to kill, especially when they were in a group.

Darv knew that he was in real trouble and screamed for help. Devid spun around and stabbed one of the lakas through the chest, then pulled back to swing at the desert-dweller's head. But a yena leapt up and dug into his wrist before he could strike, causing him to lose his weapon, lose his balance, and fall to the ground.

There was nothing worse than being on the ground in a fight with yenas; they swarmed fallen prey like flies on a carcass, the smell and taste of fresh blood inciting their savage nature.

Before Devid could find his short-blade, three of the wild dogs were on him, tearing at his arms and legs. One of the beasts went for his face but got a knife to the neck instead.

Yondo chopped at one, killing it instantly, and Devid somehow managed to get the last one, thrashing at it with his knife until it finally ran off, screaming and leaking blood.

"Son of a bitch! Help!! Help me!!"

That frightened cry had come from Darv, and when Yondo looked that way, he saw a laka draped over the Herder's broad shoulders, its rough, sandy-colored face digging into his neck.

Yondo reacted at once. He grabbed the laka from behind, pulled it off Darv, and stabbed it in the back of the head with one his double-bladed knives. The blades sliced through the laka's skull, and it sunk to its knees and fell face-first into the sand.

A yena, its teeth bared, lunged at Yondo, trying to bite his arm, but he knocked it away with his free hand. It hit the ground with a thud, rolled, and got up looking for more. A dagger thrown with force struck the beast in the side of the neck; blood sprayed, and it whelped and fell to the ground, its hind legs twitching.

Then Chatt cried out, "Yondo!"

Two yenas were on him and a laka was moving in for a taste. Yondo hurried that way, but a yena cut him off and made him fight.

Devid quickly stepped in and killed the laka before it could lay teeth on Chatt, and then killed one of the yenas.

Darv cut down a laka, but then was bitten on the ankle by a yena. He cried out in agony, and stabbed at it until it let go.

Yondo slayed the yena in front of him, but got bit on the back of the leg by another. He lost his balance and fell to his knees, and the wild, ravenous dog let go of his calf and went for his neck. Yondo managed to grab the beast before it could bite him, and he slammed it on the ground, hard. Dust and sand flew, bones snapped, and the yena let out a terrible cry. It tried to scamper off, but Yondo fixed his grip around its head and twisted. More bones snapped, and the animal went limp.

Chatt cried out again. A yena had him by the leg and a laka had him by the throat. Devid was busy fighting off two lakas, while Darv was battling a couple yenas, one of which was missing a hind leg.

Yondo rushed to Chatt's aid and killed the laka with one swift blow from his short-blade. Then he killed the yena.

Devid killed one laka and started on the next, but Darv was in trouble again. He had been bitten multiple times and wasn't moving well. His knife and long-blade were on the ground, and he was lunging and swinging wildly with his short-blade, struggling to keep two yenas at bay. One of the beasts got him by the leg, and while he was fighting it off, the other leapt for his neck. It dug its teeth in, and Darv sounded out a gurgled cry of terror as blood gushed out of him. He fell to the ground and tried to pull away from the beast, but it kept ripping and tearing at his flesh.

By the time Yondo made it over there it was too late. Darv was yet alive but as good as dead.

Yondo killed the remaining two yenas, and Devid cut down the final laka. The fight was over. For now.

For Darv, the fight was over forever.

He lay flat on his back, his arms outspread, his face and neck and shoulders covered in blood, with more pumping out. He was trying to speak but his throat had been torn out. Desperate gasps and wet gurgles were all he could manage.

Yondo knelt and said a brief prayer over the fallen Herder in the words of old, and Devid and Chatt joined in.

Darvel Alleck took his final breaths in the Great Desert of Hinterland, choking on his blood and spitting it up.

Devid lowered his head in sorrow.

Chatt turned away and wept.

Yondo crouched down and closed Darv's sightless eyes.

After a few quiet minutes, Chatt said, "I'm afraid I don't have much time left here, my friends. My fate shall be the same as Darv's – a grave in the desert. One of those sandy bastards got me."

Yondo looked at him. "Where?" he said. "Let me see."

Chatt showed his friends the wound on his neck. It was a small wound, and there was very little blood, but mixed with that blood was the reddish-gray grit of a laka.

"Are you sure it was a laka?" Yondo asked him.

Chatt nodded, said he was sure.

Devid turned away in anger and frustration. "Vlasfima!" he cried out, his voice an explosion of sound.

"You've got weeks," Yondo said, trying to be positive. "Maybe longer. You're a Herder of strong character."

Chatt heard the words, but they meant nothing to him.

It was certain death if a laka bit or scratched you and drew blood. They called it *Klimaka Ammou*: Sand Scale. You might live a few days or even a few weeks, but eventually it would take your life; your skin and bones turning to sand; so too the air in your lungs and blood in your veins. There was no remedy for it, and nobody had ever survived longer than a month.

"Devid?" Yondo said. "Any lakas get you?"

"Yenas only," he replied, showing blood and bites on both his arms. He had a couple on his legs, too. "You?"

Yondo shook his head. "No. Just yenas." The bite on his shoulder hurt, and he reached up and touched it with a gentle hand. There was a good amount of blood around the wound and it was quite sore, but it would heal easily enough with some salve and bandages.

He took a deep breath and looked around at the carnage. Twelve lakas, seventeen yenas, and one Herder lay dead on the desert floor. The lakas would eventually turn to sand and blow away, becoming part of the desert forever. The carcasses of the yenas would feed the vultures and smaller scavengers that called the sandy waste home.

Darv's body – that they would burn.

**Twenty-four:**

Molt stared into the darkness and saw nothing. It was a clear night, so stars could be seen above, but the desert expanse was as empty and dark as ever. There had been no moans from lakas or bleating laughs from yenas. It was eerily quiet, and had been that way all night.

The sound of someone clearing their throat got Molt to turn his head. It was Olvin. The old Herder propped himself up on his elbows and looked around. He rested for a brief moment, letting his eyes adjust and his mind awaken, and then he slowly worked himself to his feet, issuing a series of grunts and grumbles after every movement. It was tough work to get his old bones to cooperated after sleeping on the hard desert ground.

He grabbed his cup, his pipe, and his tobacco pouch, and moseyed over to Molt. "Tea made?" he asked in a scratchy voice.

Molt lifted up the kettle. "Still warm."

Olvin held out his cup and Molt filled it with a warm mixture of steeped tea, herrim root, and berries. The aroma was a treat, and Olvin drew in a deep, satisfying breath, letting it pique his senses.

"Been quiet," Molt reported, a soulful look in those deep brown eyes of his. "Too quiet." He was a man who had been on more than two hundred treks. No one knew the desert better than him.

Olvin took a drink of tea and went, "Mmmmm," in a way that suggested he really liked it. Then he set to packing his pipe.

"I don't much like it when it's this quiet," Molt went on.

Olvin gazed out at the darkness. "I haven't liked anything about this trek," he said.

"Me either. You think anything will come of it?"

Olvin put a spark to his pipe and puffed away. "Nothing good," he said.

"I agree. It's a wild goose."

"Big haul, though."

"Had to be done, I know. But the Kin don't play to lose, and I feel it's their game we're playing now."

"I agree. But what are our options?"

Molt shrugged. "We don't really have any. But the more I think on it, the more it's apparent to me that they baited us."

"Aye," said Olvin, nodding. "Feels that way to me, too." He gazed into the darkness of the desert, thinking for a moment about Yondo and the others. Then he sighed and said, "But it's who we are. We're Herders. We shepherd souls to the Great Stone Temple of the Angels. That is our duty, and what is most important."

"But to do so safely, we need to get rid of the vandals," Molt said. "We should go on to Meridon after delivering the souls, search for them there. And not leave until we have them."

"The Council would never allow that."

"Why not? They're the ones behind the violence. Why shouldn't we be allowed to demand justice?"

Olvin drew in a gust of smoke and gradually let it out. "Because that could be considered an act of war. The desert is open territory. Aye, the vandals are from Meridon, but as we know it's not Meridon that's sending them out. They act on their own."

"No. It's the *Kin* that sends them out."

Olvin looked over at his friend. "Aye," he said, giving his pipe a break. "The Kin. But *not* Meridon."

"There's nothing left of Meridon from what I hear," Molt said. "No Council. No marketplace. No law. It's chaos."

"So going there would make little sense."

Molt hated to agree, but Olvin was right. Still, they had options.

"We could offer a reward for their capture," he said. "A rich one. Land, money, steady work. Someone would take up such a bounty. I know it."

Olvin nodded pensively. "That's a fine idea," he said, "and it might soon come to that. But for now we need to hold to reason. We have a way. And remember, if we're right, we're not just fighting them, we're fighting the Kin, too. There's nothing easy or straightforward about that."

"Aye. The *Kin*." Molt's voice conveyed true disgust.

Olvin peered to the left and to the right. Then he stared straight ahead for a long time. Molt stared with him.

"We saw *something*," the old Herder said, breaking the silence. "Dark figures across the desert. Black sticks in the heat."

"Think we're being followed?"

"Perhaps. But by what? That I do not know."

"Nothing good, I'm sure."

"Twelve times I've come across Kin in this desert," said Olvin. "Twelve times in thirty-six years."

"Nine for me," said Molt. "No. Ten."

"Of those twelve times, seven were in the last five years."

"They're around more now."

"Aye. It's getting worse."

"Getting worse everywhere," said Molt. "One of Sana's girls, Dari, told me her uncle and brother saw a flesh-eater a few years back. She's from up north, up in Boreal, beyond Wey's Pass."

"The flesh-eaters are gone," said Olvin. "Been so since the Great War."

"That's not what she said. She swore it."

Olvin slid a wry look Molt's way "What are you doing at Sana's, old friend?" he said to him. "Only trouble there."

Molt smiled sheepishly. "I'm a single man since my Trudy passed and not fit for another wife. Yet some nights I need the company of a woman."

"Understood," Olvin remarked without judgement. He took a sip of tea and returned to his pipe. After a couple tokes, he said, "The word of a sally is as light as a feather. And be wary their deltas, too."

Molt laughed. Then he said, "How many folk would you say are in Vernon now? Twenty thousand?"

"Closer to twenty-five, I'd wager."

"And Boreal?"

"I suppose double that, if not more. They've got a lot more land."

"And Meridon at its peak?"

"I reckon near the same as us. Twenty-five thousand, give or take."

"Now how many?"

"Last I heard? Ten, maybe. But many of them are old and unwilling to leave. Not many young people call that land home anymore. Can't blame them. Everything's dead there."

"I've heard it's cursed land," Molt said. "On the Kin. And now they walk with them. It's madness."

Olvin shrugged ambivalently. "Perhaps. But cursed or not, it's on the people, not the Kin."

"I don't understand what the vandals are doing. They're strong enough and young enough to move on and start over. Why resort to thieving and killing? Why side with Kin?"

Olvin gave the question a few moments of idle thought before saying, "I don't rightly know. Don't understand it myself. But possession is real. The Kin is real. We know it. We've heard the tales and seen it with our own eyes. They tempt and turn the weak, making men mad with rage and women wild with lust."

"Women wild with lust don't sound too bad to me," Molt joked. "I'd say there are worse evils to face."

Olvin cracked a smile. "Depends on the woman," he said.

Molt laughed. "Aye. Suppose you're right."

The two men sat in silence for a spell, staring out at the barren desert and mulling their thoughts. Olvin finished his pipe and his tea, and turned his gaze skyward, to what his father, a former Herder himself, used to call, 'the endless black vault of forever.' He had always liked that turn of phrase, and had often used it himself.

"Why don't you get some sleep, my friend," he said to Molt. "My turn on watch. Rest. The sun'll be up soon."

Molt said, "Sure," and with a protracted groan he stood. His bones weren't quite as timeworn as Olvin's, but they had seen far better days. "Call out if you see trouble."

"I'll call. Worry not," Olvin said. "Though I doubt I'll see anything. Not much to see out here."

Molt set up his bed, which was nothing more than a thin pocket of woolen fabric barely big enough to fit his body. It didn't provide much protection from the elements, but it was better than sleeping on the hard crust of the desert. For a pillow he used his pack.

Herders had to lug everything they took on their treks: food, water, sundries, medical supplies, weapons, the living stones. That didn't leave much room for bedding and pillows, or more than one change of clothes.

Many generations ago, before the Great War, there had been mules in Hinterland; slow, sturdy, amiable beasts, they were built for transporting goods from one place to another. They, along with oxen, had been used by farmers and furriers, builders and hunters, miners and traders, but the desert had proven to be too harsh for their easy nature. More died than survived the walk across the rough, infecund terrain, becoming food for hungry scavengers. A plague set forth by the Kin during the Great War had claimed the species; horses, oxen, and cows had also been eliminated. These were not the first species to suffer such an ignoble fate on the shores of Hinterland, and would not be the last.

Man would be the last.

The last to come, and the last to go.

## Twenty-five:

"You have to do it," Chatt said. "I can't wither. I won't."

Yondo and Devid had burned Darv's body, as was custom when a Voukolos died in the desert; you burned their body so the yenas and lakas and buzzards didn't get them.

They had walked off after setting his body aflame, but the smell of it in the air, even from more than a mile away, was unmistakable. It seemed to be following them, like the darkness and the spirits that dwelled there.

Now Chatt, who was badly injured, in great pain, and certain to die, wanted the same kindness and respect bestowed on him.

"Yondo," he pleaded. "I can't do it. The same happened to my uncle. You remember Toban? In two weeks he wasted to the bone. His skin turned to rock, his insides to sand, and he was gone."

"Two weeks is two weeks," Yondo replied. "What if we need your help? What if we need your sword?"

"I can barely walk let alone swing a sword."

Chatt was stumbling along on stiff legs, his stride slower than the morning shadows that creep over a mount. He was dropping blood all over the desert floor and his twisted shroud of a face held almost no color.

"I'm dying," he said. "I know it and you do, too. Look at me."

Yondo looked at him. "You yet have life. There is air in your lungs and blood in your veins."

"More blood out than in, I'd say. Please, Yondo."

Devid looked at his friend. They had trekked together often over the years and had become close. They lived next to each other, and Chatt had promised his oldest girl to Devid's younger brother. Both kids were close to sixteen in age, and the match had been approved by all. When the wedding happened, they would be family.

"You can beat this," Devid said to him. "You're the strongest man I know. You're my brother."

"I'm meant for the grave," Chatt replied.

"We're all meant for the grave," said Yondo. "But we don't get to decide when. That means you, too. Had you died, we would have burned you with Darv. But here you are."

"Yondo, please!"

"We do not get to choose when we leave our bodies. Those that do, they go on cursed. I want that not for you."

"Devid?" Chatt pleaded.

"Yondo's right," Devid said, though he was unable to look his friend in the eye when he said it. It would be an act of mercy to kill him now, but, by law, also an act of murder. "We can't."

"Held together by bone, dried blood, and patchwork bandages," Chatt groused. "Can barely walk. Can barely breathe. And with a laka bite on top. I can feel the grit of sand inside me already."

"We have medicine at camp," said Yondo. "Mengin knows what he's doing. He can take care of you."

"Medicine does no good for a laka bite."

"We'll be at Domboll in a rote. We can take rest in the caves below and wait for the others. Before nightfall tomorrow we'll be one again."

"One minus Darv," said Chatt with a mixture of misery and anger.

Yondo offered no reply to that, but Devid said, "May the Angeloi guide him to the next world," and he made the sign of the cross.

Yondo did the same, silently offering up similar words.

But Chatt refrained; he presently had no love for the Angeloi.

It was then the demon returned, appearing before them in a shadow-flash. And this time it had friends.

Three dark spirits hovered above the sand of the desert floor, their black, billowing forms like suspended clouds of smoke from the netherworld. To see one demon was rare but normal; to see two together was highly unusual; to see three joined as one was unprecedented. Then, impossibly, a fourth appeared.

"Cannot survive a laka bite, Voukolos. No man can," one of the demons said in a harsh, crow-like voice.

It was impossible to know which one had said it, nor did it matter. They were Kin. They all may have said it at once, or they all may have taken a word or two.

Yondo ignored them. He looked over his shoulder and said to Chatt and Devid, "Don't let them in."

"Not wanting in, Herder," said the Kin. "Only to talk."

"Then speak and be gone," said Devid, snarling.

"That was a true battle. Lots of blood and death. Yenas and lakas alike. And one of yours."

Yondo kept moving. He showed no reaction to their taunts.

Devid and Chatt stayed in stride a few steps behind him.

"It's over," the Kin said. Its voice was louder now, traced with a sibilant echo that scratched the inside of the ear. "As it must be. For time and fate have come together. We'll not lose. We did not lose in Meridon. Nor did we lose in Arctaris, Tartaros, Bouvo."

The Herders kept walking. They all had heard of Meridon, of course, but none of them had ever heard of the other places. Devid was going to ask the Kin to elaborate, but wisely thought better of it.

The Kin went on, undeterred. "You will die in the desert, Herders, where your bones belong. But who will burn you?"

Yondo said, "The sun'll be up soon and you have no more tricks. Leave us, Kin, or we shall chant the old words."

"The old words do no good against yenas and lakas."

"They work fine on you."

"The end is nigh, Voskoi, but you shan't see it. Bones in the sand and meat in the bellies of beasts you'll be."

Yondo summoned his voice and began to chant. "Daimonas! Na Fygei! Sto onoma tou Theou kai Christou! Na Fygei!"

Chatt and Devid chimed in, perfectly in tune and rhythm, and the Demon Kin disappeared before the Herders could finish the second verse.

"What if they send more yenas and lakas?" Chatt inquired as he limped along, struggling to keep pace with his friends.

"Then they send more yenas and lakas," Yondo replied, concise as ever. He added, "But I don't think they will."

"Why not?"

"Call it a hunch."

A single demon reappeared, taking shape out of thin air. It faced them, but moved with them, backing away as they marched slowly forward.

It said nothing.

The Herders said nothing.

Then Chatt cried out, "Yondo! It's trying to get in. It's working on me. I can feel it. I can feel it calling me!"

Devid and Yondo began chanting again: "Daimonas! Na Fygei! Sto Onoma Tou Theou Kai Christou! Na Fygei!"

The demon disappeared, but then another took form. The two Herders started up yet again, their voices joining together like a song, but this time the demon fought against them.

Then a second demon appeared.

The Herders chanted louder and faster, with greater conviction.

245

A third demon took shape, black and furious.

"They're getting in!" Chatt cried out. "Yondo!"

"Chant!" Yondo shouted at him. Then he started back up with Devid, crying out the words of their ancestors.

Chatt started to chant, too, but quit before finishing one verse.

Yondo yelled at him to keep going.

The fourth demon rematerialized and united with the other three to form a diamond-shaped pattern around the Herders. Together they fought against the power of the old words while trying to push through the fragile shell of Chatt's mind.

They were beginning to succeed, and Chatt cried out, "Yondo! Do something! They're getting in. I can feel them. I'm too weak to fight them. Dammit! Yondo!"

"You fight them!" Yondo shouted back at him. He turned, grabbed Chatt by the shoulders, stared dead in his eyes. "You fight them, Chatt! You hear me! Fight them with all you have. Don't let them in." He began to shake him as he yelled at him. "You fight! You fight for your boys! For Milly! For your father!"

Chatt fought; he fought with all the strength he had remaining in his soul. And Devid and Yondo chanted the old words with intensity and purpose, shouting them into the emptiness of the desert, battling to chase away the Kin.

It finally worked. The demons evanesced, and the Herders once more were alone.

In a voice weakened by pain and exhaustion, Chatt said, "They'll be back. I know they'll be back. They almost got in, Yondo. You can't let them get in."

"No!" replied Yondo. "*You* can't let them get in. You want your end to come by Kin? There's no shame dying against man or beast. To die in the flesh is normal. The flesh must die. But to give away your spirit to the Kin! No! You'll not allow that. You are a Herder!"

Chatt nodded. "Yes," he said. "You're right. I'm sorry. I'll not give away my spirit."

"We need to get to the caves," Devid said. It was still pitch dark, and the moon had not yet begun its descent. By his estimation, they had two rotes before dawn.

Yondo started walking, desperation and determination quickening his stride. Unfortunately, Devid and Chatt couldn't keep up with him. Devid had sustained numerous yena bites to his legs and was moving a step slower than normal, while Chatt was struggling merely to maintain his balance.

Devid called out to Yondo. "Not so fast, Yon. My leg is throbbing."

Yondo stopped, looked back, waited for them. They had traveled nine or ten miles from camp and were maybe three more from Foster's Cave, a small grotto on the eastern side of Mount Domboll. Named for the Herder who had discovered it, Foster's Cave was the first of the Lost Caves. There they would find shelter, water, and something to eat.

"At our pace, I'd wager we're about a rote away," Yondo said. "Maybe a rote-and-a-half. But we have to keep moving."

"By the look of those clouds, I'd say were in for a storm," said Devid. "And soon. My guess is not long after dawn."

Yondo gazed upward, taking in the serene night sky of the desert. He then threw a shoulder under Chatt's arm and said, "Come. I have you for a while, friend."

Chatt was thankful for the help, and tried his best to pick up the pace.

Devid walked beside them, shouldering more than his share of weight with their packs and water. He was big enough to handle the extra work, even with a wounded leg.

"This was a cursed walk from the start," Chatt noted, wincing in pain with almost every step.

"Fear not. We'll make it to the Great Stone Temple," Yondo said to him. "Have faith."

"But will we make it home again?" Devid replied.

"I'll not," moaned Chatt. "I know it."

They all turned silent after that woeful bit of truth, choosing instead to keep their thoughts to themselves, and for a long spell the only sounds to be heard were their mismatched footsteps on the desert hardpan and Chatt's deep, wheezing gasps for air.

Then Yondo said, "We must deliver the souls to the temple. Nothing else matters."

Other things mattered to Devid.

Other things mattered to Chatt, too.

But more than both of them, other things mattered to Yondo.

His words had been the strong, uncompromising words of a leader, hard words of circumstance and necessity, but they also had been a lie. He had a family that he loved, that he desperately wanted to see again; he wanted to kiss his wife and hug his children; he wanted to break bread with them, play games with them, sit around the fire and tell them stories.

He wanted to go home. And he would, he assured himself, by the hand of the Angeloi. If the Angeloi were still around.

There was much debate on that topic.

There were some who thought the Lightbearers of old were hiding in plain sight, biding time, watching and waiting, while others believed they were gone for good. An ever-growing faction were of the opinion the Angeloi had never existed, that they were a myth, a ridiculous folklore meant to fill lonely and fearful hearts. No one yet alive had ever seen one before, and all tales of their exploits had ended generations ago.

But Yondo believed in them. How could he not? He was a Voukolos. He felt their gentle but undeniable presence in the barren waste of the desert ... and when he held the living stones ... and when he recited the words of his ancestors ... and when he climbed the stairs of the Great Stone Temple. He still bent the knee nightly and asked them for protection and guidance.

Something told him that he would need their help now more than ever.

They all would.

"Come!" he shouted, and with an extra kick he dragged Chatt ahead, pulling him along. "We'll not die in this blasted desert. Not if I have anything to say about it."

Behind them, Devid fought to keep up.

## Twenty-six:

Peck's entire clan, save a few aunts, uncles, and cousins he barely knew, were dead, all of them having been slayed by evil in some way.

He was cursed; of that he was sure. The Monk could preach whatever words came to mind, but Peck knew he was cursed. It was the only explanation that made sense. In only fourteen years he'd had his entire clan wiped out by murder ... in two separate instances.

Yet *he* was still alive. He still had air in his lungs and blood in his veins. He couldn't understand how that was fair.

The birds had roused him early, before the sun had ascended, and he had awakened to a headache and a dry mouth. All he'd had was a couple swallows of the Monk's heady tonic, but those swallows had done the trick, knocking him clean through a dreamless slumber.

The Monk was catching up on some much needed rest now. He had kept watch all night while Peck had slept, and when the birds had chittered Peck awake, the Monk had been there with tea and bread.

Peck glanced at the slumbering man who'd been nothing but a friend to him. He had met a few Monks before (occasionally they passed through his village, on their way here or there, wherever there was trouble), but had never spoken to one. He'd once shaken hands with of one of them, but that was the most interaction he'd ever had with their kind.

The tales of Monks had always fascinated him. They lived on the land, traveled everywhere, fought evil things. They were beloved, they were respected, and they were feared, and Peck had often daydreamed about joining their ranks, especially after what had happened to his ma and sisters. He was thinking about it again.

It wasn't like he had anything else in his life to live for. He had almost no family, only one friend, Jaston, who was sort of a dolt, and no trade or job to work. By law he would inherit the land and dwelling of his father, but he could not imagine living there. Truth be told, he hated the Lett family homestead. There were many nights when he heard echoes of the desperate screams for help and mercy his mother and sisters had let loose during the attack that had ended their lives, and there were times when he glimpsed their faces after turning a quick corner.

Beyond that, there were more than a few in Greenhorn who thought him evil. They thought he was cursed, and they thought he was crazy. This latest incident, he knew, would serve to confirm those opinions. There might even be some who accused him of being possessed. It wouldn't be the first time, and he didn't know if he could honestly deny it.

Kelt had been right to suggest that he not mention the Kin or the Dark Forest to those in his village. People tended to overreact when it came to strange occurrences, and Peck wasn't a favorite son.

He would have more than three days to work on what he wanted to say to his remaining kin, and he was glad to have someone like Kelt with him. The word of a Monk was more valuable than gold. Then, after the funeral service, if there was one (not easy to hold a service with no bodies), he'd ask the Monk if he could go with him to Lockhead. He needed a new life, preferably one far away from his old one. It would be the best thing for him, and ...

The world blurred for a moment, only a moment, and in that moment Peck's thoughts evaporated. The whole world turned silent and still. The breeze stopped blowing, the birds stopped chirping, the flames of the fire stopped crackling and throwing off light, and the ethereal glow of the stars above winked out, leaving a slate black sky.

Peck wondered if what he was experiencing was real, and he quickly concluded that it most likely was only a figment of his imagination. Then, at once, the stars reappeared, trailing light behind them, and the sounds of the birds and the glow of the fire returned. The buzz of life echoed in Peck's ears, and its colors exploded in his eyes.

And then ...

The song was the same as before, and it canceled out every other sound in the world. The fire licked at the air, its serrated, orange-yellow tongues hungrily lapping up oxygen. Faces appeared in the flames, demon faces with closed eyes and closed lips, with burnt orange skin and hideous scars, with sharp yellow teeth and peeled lips. Behind the crackle of the flames, humming soft and low and continuous, was the song that had led Peck from the safety of his father and uncle to the dangers of the Dark Forest. The sound that had caused their gruesome demise and his guilt.

He knew what it was, he knew of its nefarious devotion, yet he felt himself giving in to it again. He could feel it crawling over his skin and whispering in his ear, whispering sweetly and temptingly, whispering for him to leave, to come, to follow, and Peck felt himself start to move.

One step, and then another, and another. He knew he was in a trance, but he could not break free from it.

In his eyes, everything was dark gray set against black. There were no colors, only shapes, and the lone sound was the song. It carried him gently through the spiritual ether, through the murky gravelands and evil relics that haunted all. This was where the Kin hid from sight. This was why people were afraid of the dark.

He wondered how long it had been since he'd gone under, and he wondered if he'd wake up in the Dark Forest again … only this time, instead of being found by a talking white bird and a kindly Monk, he'd be snatched up by the demon and the flesh-eater that had killed his pa, his uncle, and Kelt's partner.

Perhaps that would be a fitting end.

But before he would let that happen …

He cried out at the top of his lungs, frantic with fear, but his voice held no volume, and the song played on. Soft, mellifluous, beautiful; it caressed his mind and eased his pain. It told him that everything would be okay; all he had to do was listen.

Then something struck him, hard, and he felt himself falling. His body was thrown forward by an invisible force, and then it crashed to a stop.

A flash of white broke through the endless tarp of black and dark gray that had engulfed his vision, and from somewhere far off, perhaps from another world, he heard the call of a voice. This voice was strong and fast and desperate, and it broke through the song of the Kin, first interrupting the melody, then drowning it out for good.

He felt another jolt, saw another flash of white.

Then he heard his name. "Peck! Wake up! Open your eyes, boy!"

Peck did as he was told … and saw the face of the Monk in front of him. "Where am I?" he asked, blinking his eyes, which moments before had been locked in a trance-like stare.

"On your way back to the Dark Forest, I assume," said Kelt.

Peck propped himself up on his elbows and looked around, utterly confused. He didn't see the camp, nor did he recognize the lay of the land. "The song," he said with a rasp. "I heard the song again." He looked around some more. "Where are we?"

Kelt pointed to a patch of shrubs and flowers. "Our camp's about two hundred steps that way."

"You heard it, too? The song? You heard it?" Peck asked his questions in a pleading voice, a look of desperate hopefulness scrawled on his young face. If the Monk had heard the song, too, then perhaps he wasn't cursed.

But Kelt shook his head. "No. I woke up and you weren't there," he said. "Luckily you hadn't gone far."

"But how?" Peck wanted to know.

The Monk nodded to the right. When Peck looked that way, he saw the large white bird from the Dark Forest perched on the lowest branch of an oak tree. He was stunned.

"You have a guardian, it seems," Kelt said. "Damn thing woke me up with a squawk that'll probably still be ringing in my ears on my deathbed."

An expression of awe shaped Peck's young face. "I don't understand," he said. "How did you …"

"He led me here."

Kelt had never told Peck about the role the large white bird had played in their initial meeting, though he planned to tell him now. Maybe not today, but soon. It was a mark of real power when someone had an animal guide. Kelt was beginning to think that finding the boy had been an act of divine providence. Perhaps Manly's death had not been in vain.

He reached down a hand and pulled him to his feet. "Come," he said, "we need to get you back to camp."

"It happened again," Peck said, visibly shaken. "Is it going to follow me everywhere I go? Will I ever escape it?"

The Monk sighed. "Depends where you are," he said. "Haunted lands like the Dark Forest and the Marshlands may always cause you trouble. Other places not so much."

"I'm cursed," Peck muttered under his breath.

"You're not cursed," Kelt told him.

"I am. It's the only explanation. I'm cursed."

"You're not cursed," Kelt said again. "It's a hard world, boy, and bad things happen. They happen to all. You needn't blame it on anything more than that. Now let's get back. We have a long day ahead."

Kelt set a fast pace, leaving Peck and his burgeoning consternation a few steps behind. More questions would be forthcoming, the Monk knew; hard questions that had hard answers, and hard questions that had no answers. But right now he wanted to pack up and get moving.

For Peck's sake, he believed a great distance between them and the Dark Forest was needed, and he was determined to cover that distance as swiftly as possible. They could work through Peck's many issues at a later time and date, when there were safe.

Until then …

**Twenty-seven:**

Mengin spotted them first, soon after breakfast. Dawn had crested, and while the amber glow of the sun had yet to pierce the clouds, there was enough light to see a few hundred feet ahead.

The two bent and broken figures were perhaps three-hundred steps away when they first appeared. They were walking in the general direction of the camp, moving slowly, awkwardly.

Mengin saw no one else on the horizon, and immediately alerted Olvin and Dock. Dock then told Edgar and Molt.

All five Herders watched intently as the two figures approached in a sluggish march, their amorphous bodies slowly growing against the unchanging panorama of the desert. One of the figures stumbled and dropped to its knees, and there it stayed for some time. The other one helped it up, and together they started walking again, leaning on each other for balance and support.

"Lakas?" said young Edgar. It was more of a guess than a question.

"I think they're moving slower than lakas," Dock replied, his eyes darting about. "And lakas don't stop to help another up."

"A trap then?" said Molt.

"Here?" Mengin put in. He looked around. They were on the plains, in a field of scrub grass and squat cacti, more than a full day from the Lost Caves. "Not much of an ambush spot."

Dock said. "We can see them coming. We can see everything."

"I don't trust it," said Edgar. "It's not right."

"What is it?" asked Jacko, squinting into the distance. "Is that Yondo and the others?"

"No," said Mengin. He pointed to the left. "They went that way. And we're not supposed to meet them until tonight or tomorrow morning."

"And there are only two of them," added Dock.

"Lakas?" the young man inquired.

"We don't know," said Edgar, not thinking.

Olvin quickly jumped in for him. "Yes. Most likely lakas," he said. "Not much else out here but us and them."

Herders never mentioned the Kin to stragglers, though occasionally a demon would force their hand by manifesting in front of one, looking to tempt them and lead them astray. Herders also never mentioned the vandals. It was those kind of stories that caused panic and mutiny.

"There're only two of them," Molt said after thoroughly scanning the horizon. "I see no others. You want to meet them?"

Mengin shook his head. "No. We're not splitting up."

"Then what do we do? Wait for them?"

Franklin and Audrey had finished their breakfast and now were standing with the others. Franklin said, "Look like men to me."

Audrey agreed. "Any other people out here?" she asked.

Both Olvin and Molt said, "No," at the same time. Molt then added, "None that we know of."

"What do we do?" asked Edgar.

"We pack for the day," said Mengin calmly. "We've got a long walk ahead and the terrain's gonna start to get rough." He gave Jacko a friendly pat on the shoulder. "Come," he said to him, leading him back towards the camp, "let's get to work."

Audrey went with them, but Franklin stuck around, his squinty old eyes peering in the direction of the advancing strangers. "Those are men," he said, certain of it. "And they look hard-up."

"Lakas look like men," said Dock. "You'd be surprised how much in the light. Now go pack. I need to speak with my brothers."

Franklin returned Dock a sharp look. "That's not a good sign, is it?" he said to him. "Like when a woman tells you she wants to talk. Get ready for the other shoe to fall … right on your genitals."

"It's nothing," Olvin said.

Franklin's sharp eyes drifted from one Herder to the other. "Don't tell me it's nothing," he said. "You can feel the bad in the air. It's as thick as the humidity and the heat."

"You're paranoid," Molt said. "Now go pack up."

Franklin made sure to set his cynical gaze on each of them one more time; it was a gaze that said he knew better, and that he knew they knew better, too. Then he said, "Sure. I'll go pack." He turned and started away, then stopped, turned back around, and added, "Any law against stragglers bearing arms in these here lands, should it come to that?"

"It won't," said Dock. "Don't worry on it."

But Franklin wasn't buying their line. He may not have understood the desert of Hinterland, and he may not have known where they were or where they were going, but he'd been around the block enough times to know when trouble was in the air and people were on edge.

"If it should happen," he said, a serious expression occupying his raison face, "don't you leave me with no way to protect myself." He pointed a finger, and swung that finger back and forth between the Herders. "That ain't something you do to a man."

"We wouldn't do that to you," Molt said. "But it's not going to come to that. You have my word. Now go pack up, or your last nights in the desert will be sober ones."

Franklin still wasn't buying, but he had said his peace, and that, he believed, was good enough for now. He turned around and started across the camp on a good step.

When he was out of earshot, Olvin said, "We need be ready for an attack. Even at their current pace, they'll be near enough to fire arrows and bolts before we finish packing."

Dock agreed. "I suppose we could give old Franklin a sword and send him out to meet them," he joked.

Olvin threw him a look. "Last thing we need is that old hoot swinging steel. He'd most likely kill one of us."

Dock laughed. "Or maim himself."

"Aye. And I'm not carrying him."

Olvin and Dock stayed to watch the oncoming pair while the others packed up camp. They were only three-hundred steps away now, and though their faces could not be clearly seen, there was no doubt they were men. Lakas moved differently, abnormally so, with a slouching, stuttering gait, like something just learning how to use its body. The figures in the desert moved slowly and awkwardly, but there was a naturalness to their movements that was purely human.

"Could be vandals?" Dock put forth, not really believing it.

Olvin sniffed and said, "What else? They're not lakas."

Dock scanned the surrounding desert and found it empty. "Two of them," he said. "Could be a trap."

"Never used one before. Not like this. They like to wait in the rocks. That's their way."

"Perhaps their way is changing."

Olvin stared up at the sky. Dark clouds had rolled in overnight, all but canceling out the sun. "We need to get a message to Yondo," he said.

"They'll be too far gone to see or hear, I imagine."

"Aye. Most likely. But that don't matter none. Gotta try."

Dock lifted his eyes. The clouds were full and solid across the morning sky, spread out in every direction. On the far northwest horizon, where the sun was efforting to blast through, a slight amber glow could be seen, like a dim, far-off candle shining on a foggy night. The rest of the sky was the dull, flat color of wet stone and looked to be just as dense.

"It's not even worth a try right now," he said. "Clouds are too thick to catch the sun."

Olvin knew his friend was right. He also knew that Yondo and the others were probably too far away to hear the vibrations of the waft paddles. Nevertheless, he told Dock to tell Mengin to slap the paddles together a couple times. "Might as well try," he said. "You never know."

Dock nodded obediently and started off.

Olvin, meanwhile, stayed behind to watch the cumbrous march of the two strangers. They didn't appear all that threatening, but that somehow made it worse. It made him think the Kin was playing games with them.

The bad feeling that had been in the pit of the old Herder's gut since the start of the trek rose up like a sickness. It worked its way deep into his mind and touched his soul.

The Kin, he thought, looking around, taking in the full scope of the morning. He could feel their dark energy like he could feel the rush of an oncoming storm. It was undeniable.

And today it was as strong as ever.

The packs were packed and the stragglers were ready to walk when the first words were called out. They were weak words, spoken in a sandy, raspy tone. They were words for help. They were words for mercy.

The two figures were no more than thirty steps from the campsite now, their arms stretched out before them in a sad, beseeching way, their feet scuffing the desert hardpan, kicking up sand and dust.

Olvin told Mengin and Edgar to guard the stragglers and the stones.

"I don't understand what's happening?" said Jacko, his eyes locked on the approaching men, both of whom appeared close to death.

"We take all precautions," replied Mengin, crossbow in hand. "We are entrusted to get you to the temple and we take great pride in that."

Up front, Dock, Olvin, and Molt drew their weapons and waited.

The approaching men lumbered forward with very little speed and balance, their knees mostly stiff, their feet turned in.

The one on the left nearly tripped and fell, and when the other tried to catch him, he stumbled and went down on one knee.

Olvin looked around and saw nothing but empty desert on the horizon: no people, no animals, no demons. He pointed his blade and said to the men, "That's close enough. State your name and want."

"Water," one of them croaked. "It's been more than two days."

The men looked like death. Their faces were red and rough, and they were breathing in great heavy gasps. They didn't look capable of causing trouble, and they certainly didn't look capable of taking on Herders.

"Who are you?" Dock asked them.

"Water," the same one croaked again.

"You'll get water when we get names," Dock replied.

Olvin's eyes narrowed on the men. "I know them," he said. "They're the vandals that attacked us a few moons back. Two of them, anyway."

"Names!" Molt demanded.

The one on the left said, "Dol Fellet of Meridon."

The one on the right said, "Calrick Malone of Meridon."

"They're vandals," Olvin said. He pointed the tip of his blade at Calrick. "That's the one who split my lip."

"We need water," Dol said. "Please."

"Why should we help you?" Molt asked. "You stole from us. You assaulted good men. One of ours is dead because of you."

"We never killed anyone," Calrick said, his voice brittle and broken.

"Wounded them and took their steel, left them defenseless in the desert. That's near enough murder for me."

Dol slumped to one knee. "Water," he said again, his voice sounding like the moan of a laka.

They weren't just broken and exhausted, drained by the desert, they also were badly beaten; their faces scarred and bruised, their arms marked by gashes and welts, their knuckles bloody and swollen. They had caught a beating and surely wouldn't make it much longer without water, food, and medical attention.

"Confess," Olvin told them in a blunt voice. "Confess your crimes and you can have water."

Dol began to nod.

Calrick said, "I confess."

"We confess," Dol added breathlessly. "Please."

"Where's the rest of you?" Molt asked, looking around. "We know you've got more men."

"Just us," Dol managed to say before he started coughing and hacking, spitting up sand and bile.

"What's the trick?" said Molt.

"There's no trick. They took my boy. They took him." The wounded vandal broke down and began sobbing. No tears fell from his dry, swollen eyes, but he moaned sorrowfully and his lips trembled. "No!" he said, pitifully, agonizingly, "I gave him up. They didn't take him. I gave him to them. It was … It was me. I gave him."

"What was you?" Olvin asked. "Tell us everything, vandal."

But it was no use; Dol had gone over the edge. His abject misery led to a violent coughing jag, one that seemed to put him in peril of death. He slumped over on his hands and knees, dry heaving like a dying yena.

"Give us a drink, one drink," Calrick begged, "and we'll tell you all. I swear it on my name."

"The promises of vandals mean nothing," Dock said. "Your kind has seen to that. Fear not, though, you will drink … but not until you're bound as prisoners."

"Anything," Calrick said.

Molt called out, "Edgar. Bring rope. And the warmest water we have."

Edgar took his pack off his shoulder and began picking through it.

"Many thanks," Calrick said.

"Many thanks," Dol echoed, his face an untidy portrait made of sand, tears, bruises, and dried blood.

"On your knees," Dock commanded them. He stepped forward with his short-blade drawn.

Molt kept his crossbow aimed on them just in case.

Edgar brought over two lengths of rope and a dented canteen.

A short while later, the near-dead vandals were shackled by their hands and feet. More importantly for them, they'd been given water; not nearly enough to meet their need, but enough to stave off death.

Then, with Mengin and Edgar keeping watch, Olvin demanded the vandals tell their story. "Leave nothing out," he told them, "or we shall leave you here for the yenas and lakas."

Dol started and did most of the talking, though Calrick cut in here and there, offering details his partner had either forgotten or overlooked. When the story swung to Dol's boy, Alde, who now was meat for the Kin, Calrick had no choice but to take the lead. Dol couldn't get through the account without breaking down. Even Calrick got a little choked up when he spoke of it.

The ceremony conducted by the demon had been frighteningly dark, and when it had ended, the boy Alde was gone, forever replaced by something evil.

"The demon isn't in him, it *is* him," Dol sobbed. "It has ... It ..." Unable to go on, he covered his face with his hands and wailed.

"Alde is gone," Calrick said, picking up near enough where his friend had left off. "The Kin has his flesh."

Across the camp, Franklin said to Mengin, "What the hell is going on here? And don't tell me it's nothing. I know nothing, and that ain't it."

Mengin returned the old curmudgeon a serious look. "You ask a lot of questions for a man who knows so much," he said to him.

Franklin shot back an evil eye, but his tongue remained silent. Mengin walked away then, content that he had won that one.

But the stragglers were ill-at-ease and it showed. They knew something was wrong, and they discussed it amongst themselves in hushed tones. Franklin went as far as saying they should think about stealing supplies and running off on their own. He told his fellow travelers that if indeed they were on their way to purgatory, and he fully believed they were, then it might be better if they died in the desert.

"It's a place of great suffering and atonement," he told them. "A place where you pay your debt of sin with pain."

But the other two weren't so keen to side with him; especially Audrey, who didn't much care for Franklin. She found him to be annoying, abrasive, and chauvinistic.

"I don't know where we are or where we're going," she said, "but I know I don't want to die in the desert. I'll take my chances at the temple, thank you."

Jacko agreed with her, but the seeds of Franklin's words had taken root in his mind. He had doubts both ways, and decided, privately, to remain open to all possibilities. If it ever got to the point where running away looked like their best option, then he would run away, and he would make no apologies about it.

Meanwhile, the Herders gathered to discuss the vandals. Their tale had been one of woe and loss, though it had done little to garner sympathy. These were the same men who had attacked them, who had stolen from them, and the tall one had not only struck a deal with the Kin, he had freely given his son to them. They were detestable, and, at least in Dock's opinion, not worth the trouble.

"We're already short on water and food," he said. "It's not worth the risk to take them on. Do we really want them around the stragglers? Who knows what they might say."

Molt agreed. "Might be better we leave them here bound," he said. "Let the desert serve them justice."

But Olvin would not consent. "That's akin to murder. Leaving them for the yenas and lakas? No. We take them back to Vernon and give them a proper trial. That's the way, and the law."

Mengin nodded in agreement, though part of him liked Molt's plan better. Young Edgar wanted to slit their throats, burn their bodies, and be done with them, though he didn't dare say that aloud. He merely agreed with the others.

In the end, the vandals were made to join the trek. They walked roped and slag-footed between Molt and Mengin, a safe fifteen yards removed from the stragglers and the stones, just in case they had either larceny or mutiny on their minds.

Overhead, angry clouds threatened. A flash of lightning struck in the distance, and the mighty clap of thunder that followed rolled across the desert like an omen.

A storm was coming.

**Twenty-eight:**

There were six mountains in the Great Desert of Hinterland: Elgod, the tallest, its snow-capped peaks more than 11,000 podes high, Athenos, often called the Wolf because its peak resembled the snout of a wolf, Dorsette, the sheerest of the five, Marlekti, and Warnimii, the baby, only 6,400 podes high. Called the five brothers, they shared rock and dirt and shingle, and together guarded O Megalos Naos ton Petrinon Angelon.

If necessary, you could walk around them to reach the temple, but that added at least three days to the trek. The mounts were much longer than they were tall, stretching more than a hundred miles from end to end, covering land from Meridon to the southern tip of the Dustbowl. On the western side, the Meridon side, which was the faster way around, you had to contend with rocky terrain and deep crevasses. One wrong step and the desert swallowed you up like a snack, leaving nothing behind. More than a few Herders and stragglers had met their demise that way.

It was easier and faster to go over the mounts, specifically Warnimii, the smallest brother. The first Herders, with help from the Angeloi, had carved stairs into the rock to make the climb less treacherous. It yet remained a terribly grueling undertaking, especially for stragglers, who weren't used to walking such steep and rocky terrain. The unremitting desert heat didn't help matters, either. Most stragglers lost a good deal of weight on the walk. Yondo usually returned home from a trek lighter in his boots. There was no way around it.

And then there was Domboll, sometimes called the Red Rock Mount because of its rocky face and ruddy complexion. Also referred to as the Orphan, it sat all by itself on the southwestern rim of the mesas, more than twenty miles removed from the five brothers. Only three-thousand podes high, it was better known for the underground caves that spread out beneath it like the roots of a mighty tree.

Its northern face was cracked and rugged, and though it was easy to climb, you had to be mindful of rockslides, especially the higher up you went. Its western and southern sides were too steep to scale, which made going over the mount an impractical choice.

You went around Domboll and under Domboll, never over it.

Beneath its heavy red beard of stone could be found the Lost Caves, the first of which was known as Foster's Cave. An underground warren of

261

small, interconnected grottoes, they went on and on, stretching from one end of the Red Rock Mount to the other.

From the southern side of Domboll, the five brothers could be seen in silhouette, their gray towers standing out against the interminable ecru of the far-reaching desert, connecting the land to the sky in jagged, upside-down V-shaped patterns. To the west, the edges of the Red Gorge could be spied, its rocky depths reaching more than a thousand podes. Nothing lived down there; not even Kin.

Yondo, Devid, and Chatt reached Foster's Cave a rote after sunrise, three weary, wounded Herders seeking shelter and safety. The morning sky in the desert was usually a masterpiece of colors ranging from red to gold, but this morning there was a storm threatening. Thick, dark clouds blotted out the brilliant red hues of the morning sun, leaving the desert in a prolonged night.

Yondo and Devid were walking slowly, cumbersomely carrying all their gear, while behind them, dragging himself along on stiff legs, huffing, grunting, and wheezing, was Chatt. His blood marked their uneven trail across the desert, and the smell of it had piqued the interest of a number of scavengers. Vultures could be seen circling overhead, and some smaller critters, sand hogs and desert rats, were quietly following a safe distance behind, their small animal brains bristling with excitement at the thought of meat for dinner.

Chatt stopped walking when they arrived at the entrance to Foster's Cave. He was slouched over and exhausted. "Halt," he called out in a breathless voice.

Yondo and Devid stopped walking and looked back at him.

"We're here," said Devid. "You made it, old friend."

"Aye, I've made it, but I can go no farther. I'm spent."

"Nonsense. All you need is rest."

Chatt staggered, and then fell.

Devid dropped his gear and rushed to his friend's aid. "Chatt?! Chatt?!" he called out to him. He lifted Chatt's head up from the ground and laid it in his lap. "Chatt?" he called out to him again, gently tapping his cheek. "Do you hear me?"

Chatt's eyes opened, barely.

Yondo dropped his gear, too, and went to check on the fallen Herder. Chatt's breathing was weak and labored, and the pallor of his complexion nearly matched that of blanched bones.

Looking up at Yondo, Devid said, "His heart is weak. His blood is barely pumping."

"I tried," Chatt said, looking up at Devid with tears in his eyes. "I gave it all I had. But I'm at my end."

"We can't stay here," said Yondo. "A storm's coming."

"Storm came for me already," Chatt replied, his voice barely audible.

"You need rest. We have to go into the caves. We're almost there."

The Lost Caves were home to numerous underground streams and ponds, with water that was not only fresh and cool, but teeming with life. Snakes, frogs, baggers, turtles, even sand hogs and desert rats could be found there, living well in the darkness. It was the perfect place to take sanctuary, and it was only a couple dozen steps away.

"I've got nothing left," Chatt said. "It's over for me."

"You'll think differently after a good rest," Yondo told him. "And some of Gabby's cider."

Chatt snorted disdainfully. "Look," he said, aimlessly gesturing to different parts of his body. His clothes were soaked with blood; his face and hands painted with it. "I gave all I could. I'll be dead in a rote. Just do it. Please. It'll be mercy."

"It's not the way," said Yondo in a quiet, almost remorseful tone. "We know not what will happen. You could live another hundred years."

"Pah! Walk the desert in my boots and tell me what you know," Chatt shot back at him.

Yondo's heart went out to Chatt, but his mind remained unmoved. He had always liked the Herder, liked him still, but he wasn't going to kill him … even if killing him would be an act of mercy.

"I can't make it down into the cave," Chatt said as he lay on the ground, his head in his friend's lap. "If you don't remember, the grade is very steep near the bottom."

"Then I'll carry you," Yondo told him.

Chatt glared at him. "No one's carrying me anywhere," he said angrily, and with a grunt he picked himself up off the ground. "I make my own way or I don't. That is my word."

"Now's no time for pride, my friend."

"Now's no time for arguing," Devid piped, interrupting them. "We need to stay together. We need to be one."

"I'm saying I can't make it any farther," Chatt said. He looked at Yondo. "I can't walk. I'm dizzy, I'm tired, all I feel is pain. This is not pride, and it is not pity. I'm dying. I'm firmly in the hand of death."

"You want an end that bad, do it yourself," Yondo told him. "You have a knife. Take it across your wrist."

"You know what old lore says about taking your own life: punishment waits in the Void."

"Aye. And I know what it says about someone else taking it for you." Chatt looked at Devid.

"No, old friend," Devid told him, shaking his head. "Don't look at me. I can't do it."

"Give me my tobacco," Chatt said, reaching out an unsteady, blood-stained hand. "Leave me my tobacco, some jerky, some of that cider, if you don't mind, and a day's worth of water. I'll be fine right here."

"You'll be dead before sundown," said Yondo.

"I'm dead already. You just don't want to accept it."

"You still have ..."

"Yes! Yes! Yes!" Chatt cried out, surprising them both with the crack of his voice. "I still have air in my lungs and blood in my veins. Though I'm not so certain about the blood. The desert has most of that. But no matter. I'm dying. You know I'm dying. Why prolong the inevitable?"

"I'm not prolonging anything," Yondo replied. "I'm not doing anything at all, as is my right."

"And I'm not moving," Chatt said stubbornly. "As is mine." He looked at Devid again. "My tobacco, please. And a canteen of water."

"No," said Yondo. "Don't give it to him."

"Don't give it to me?! Don't give it to me?!" Chatt was apoplectic. "I fought bravely and now am doomed because so. I've been a Herder for many a year, have made many a trek. I'm a good man dying, an honored Voukolos, and you won't favor me with my own tobacco and water? What sort have you become Yondo Carpana?"

Guilt struck Yondo then, even though he knew that had been Chatt's intention. The wounded Herder was trying to goad them into killing him so that he wouldn't have to do it himself. But as guilty as Yondo felt, as much sympathy as he felt for his friend and fellow Herder, he was not about to draw his blade and take an honest life.

Not waiting for Yondo's consent, Devid gave Chatt his share of tobacco and water. The fading Herder took a long drink, sloppily spilling the water into his mouth and over his face, letting it wash away some of the sand and grit and blood that had gathered there. "Curses!" he huffed. "Everything hurts." He reached for his tobacco.

Soon, they all were smoking.

They stood just outside the entrance to Foster's Cave, with vultures circling overhead, their huge wings effortlessly riding the wind, their shrieking caws echoing for miles in every direction. Dense black clouds continued to swarm, getting ready to burst open with a deluge.

"I can't make it, Yon," Chatt said quietly, breaking the silence between them. "It's not want or courage that's lacking, friend, but strength. I can't feel my feet, and my eyes have started to blur. I'm cold, inside and out. I'll be dead in a rote from my wounds. I know it."

Yondo said nothing. He was thinking.

"It's not the laka bite. That's a death sentence, I know, a terrible one, but if that was all it was I'd wait it out. I could make it home if that was my only hurt. Could see my family again, make my wishes known, put my house in order. But I've lost too much blood." The Herder pinched his pipe between his lips and rolled up his left pant leg. Semi-dried blood covered the whole lower part of his leg, while more blood, black and thick like tar, oozed out from one of the many wounds he had suffered. Then he rolled up his left shirt sleeve to his elbow, revealing a bandage soaked through with blood.

"I'm dead but for time. Don't make me beg. Please."

"I'll do it," said Devid softly. He was tired of hearing his friend moan, and, more than that, he thought it the right course.

"We're not to decide when a man's life ends," said Yondo, holding steadfast to the beliefs of old. "What if there should be a miracle? They've happened before. You know it as well as I."

Chatt issued a dreary sigh. "I can't make it any farther," he said. "I'm at my end. Don't make me beg."

"You can last, Chatt," Yondo said to him. "I believe it. You're one of the toughest bastards I've ever walked the desert with. We'll help you. We'll patch you up in the caves. You can rest there for a full day and night. And you can eat and drink your fill."

"No," said Chatt, shaking his head. "I can't make it."

"What about Milly? The kids? Don't you want to see them again?"

Chatt's head lolled and tears rolled from his eyes. "More than anything in this world," he sobbed. "I want to be with them now, and forever. But I'll never see them again." He began to sob even harder, knowing that to be true. "I've seen them the last time, and they me."

"Don't say it," said Yondo. "Don't think it."

"It's a fool who can't accept the truth, and the truth is I'm spent."

Staring out at the barren span of the desert, which seemed more empty and endless than ever, Yondo Carpana retreated to the privacy of his own thoughts. Killing a man who meant to kill you was not only allowed but expected; but killing a man to kill him, be it for mercy, or revenge, or sport, was considered murder. There were strict laws against it in every village, and old lore was specific about the mark such an act would leave on a man's soul. A black mark that never could be washed away.

Yondo knew enough about death to know that Chatt was nearly there. The only problem with being *nearly* there was that sometimes the end dragged on. Chatt might suffer for another week, or he might fall in the next rote. It was a question of when not if, and Yondo wondered if maybe Chatt had a point. The badly-wounded Herder could not go on with them to the mounts; the walk would be too long and arduous for him, and the stragglers would be appalled by his condition. That meant he would have to stay in Foster's Cave, and someone would have to stay with him. And in his present state he would be an easy mark for the Kin, who, like all scavengers of the desert, preyed on those close to death.

"I don't want to die," Chatt said, his voice the voice of a man who knew his days were over. "Truly, Yon, I want to live. But it's not meant for me. We all have a time. Mine is now."

Yondo looked up at the dark clouds overhead. Could he abide such a decision? Could he ...

"I'll do it," Devid said again, but this time he was speaking to Yondo, not Chatt, and this time he said it with decisiveness. He laid a hand on Yondo's shoulder and met his eyes. "I'll take it on myself. His death will be on me, and I'll accept it."

Yondo looked at Devid, then at Chatt.

"It's sacrifice, not murder," Chatt said to Yondo. "You can't carry me over the mounts, and to leave me behind to fight yenas and lakas and demons would be cruel. This trek was cursed from the start. If you have any chance, I can't be part of it."

There was wisdom in those words; courage, too. Yondo didn't care for what they meant, but he recognized the logic. He said to Devid, "You do it, for I cannot. And I'll never tell a soul. That is my word."

Devid nodded once, and the two men shook on it.

"It's square, old friend," Chatt told Yondo. "Thank you." Then, to

Devid: "You've always been a brother to me, and now I make you one. I ask you to look after my family. Teach my boys the way. Show them how to be men. Look in on Milly, too. Don't let anyone take advantage of her."

"It'll be done," said Devid.

"You'll be true family when your brother weds my girl. Our blood will be one. Forever."

"I know."

"Family takes care of family."

"I will watch them, brother. Worry not. That is my word."

"Yondo?"

Yondo laid a reassuring hand on the dying Herder's shoulder.

"It was an honor," Chatt told him. "I'm proud to call you my friend."

"You as well, friend."

"Do not think less of me. Please."

Yondo shook his head and said he would not, yet he deliberated. Did he think less of him? Would he in the future? He thought it wrong for a man to choose the time of his death, no matter if his death was imminent or not, and regardless of whether or not it was a selfless act. But he would not stand in Devid's way, and he would not make Chatt feel guilty for his choice. It was not his duty to judge.

"Say the old words for me," Chatt said, tears welling in his eyes. He knew the end had come, yet it was no easier to accept. He had a family, and he had love; those were hard things to leave behind.

Yondo removed the cap from the small amount of whiskey they had remaining and took a drink. He then handed it to Devid, who did the same. Chatt went last. He took a drink, then another, then finished it.

"It was an honor," Yondo told him.

"You will be missed," said Devid.

Chatt was crying, and nodding. "Thank you," he said.

Yondo lowered his head, and Devid and Chatt did the same. Yondo then began to mouth the old words, those to be said over a Herder's death: "O Theos, chairetizoume afton ton anthropo os pistos filos. O Theos, chairetizoume afton ton anthropo os pistos filos."

Devid drew his short-blade. "Last words?" he asked his friend, tears now streaming from his eyes, too.

The Herder didn't have to think long. "Find the others and get the souls to the temple," he said. "And tell my family that I loved them. Tell them I'll be waiting for them on the other side."

Chatt took a knee and closed his eyes for the last time. Devid's blade cut fast and pierced the heart, and Chatt let loose a terrible croak of pain. His entire body stiffened, and fresh blood pulsed from the wound. Then he went limp and slouched to the ground.

Devid was too broken up to burn the body, so Yondo took on that chore. He emptied Chatt's pockets, planning to give anything of value he found to Milly and the kids, then laid him out in a peaceful funeral pose, crossing his hands on his chest and pointing his boot tips to the sky. He drizzled holy oil on him, praying silently as he did, and then, after a brief moment of silence, struck a match.

The flame took a moment to catch, but when it did, a fire broke out and began to roar. And there they left him, outside the entrance to Foster's Cave, at the base of Mount Domboll, in the Great Desert of Hinterland, with a storm looming overhead.

The storm hit the desert hard and fast, dumping a couple inches of water in less than a rote. Lightning lit up the sky in magnificent flashes, and thunder shook the ground.

The storm allowed the Herders to partially refill their canteens and wash off some of the grit and stink the desert had pasted on them the last ten days. All were thankful for that.

The stragglers didn't much care for the deluge; they wanted to take cover until the storm passed.

"Take cover where?" Olvin questioned them as they slugged through the rain. There was no cover for miles. "We're in a desert."

But the storm went as fast as it had come, and two rotes later not a trace of it remained. The clouds were gone from the sky, and the ground had thirstily swallowed up all the water.

They walked on through the heat and red glaze of the afternoon sun, past the rocky dunes and knee-high cacti that dominated this part of the desert. The cacti looked more green now because of the rain, but the red sand and rock looked the same.

They pushed two miles farther before spotting a good place to break for their midday meal: a patch of hardscrabble and rock with a solid floor and good visibility in all directions.

Molt and Edgar went off to find kindling for a fire, whatever sticks and twigs they could rummage in these parts, while the stragglers took rest on the hard desert ground. Mengin and Dock shackled the vandals together hand and foot, and told them they wouldn't be gagged so long as they kept their tongues flat.

There wasn't a lot of food left, but no one was in danger of starving. Dinner consisted of sheep jerky, bread, and the scant remains of the prairie rats Devid had killed the day before. They were surprisingly tasty little critters, all agreed. And because of the storm, they now had enough water to drink liberally.

The stragglers were curious about the vandals, mostly because they had been kept separate from them on the walk. But at lunch they sat together and broke bread.

Jacko and Franklin stole occasional glances at them, but Audrey held her eyes away. She didn't like the looks of them, perceiving them to be dangerous criminal types.

Why else would they be bound?

For their part, the vandals paid little heed to the stragglers. They talked to each other quietly, and graciously consumed what was given to them. After their meal, Mengin, Olvin, and Dock took them aside for more questioning. They wanted to know about the deal the vandals had made with the Kin, and they wanted to know what had happened to the stragglers that had been kidnapped and the stones that had been stolen from them.

While that was going on, Jacko asked Molt and Edgar about the strangers. Franklin and Audrey joined in, too, saying they felt they had a right to know.

Edgar wisely deferred to his uncle, who, after a moment's hesitation, kindly obliged them.

"The territory south of Vernon is called Meridon," he began in a hushed voice, as if telling a dangerous secret.

From there, he delved into an abridged history of the once-prominent land, touching on how the crops had failed and the waters had dried up, and how the mumba buds had caused so much madness and strife.

"Addiction, disease, and famine put the land in ruin, and most of the inhabitants either perished or moved away."

He said nothing about demons and never would. There were some things the stragglers didn't need to know.

"So," he said, moving on, "some from their land have taken to thieving for a living, like those two over there. For their crimes, they will be tried by the judge in Vernon. If found guilty, they'll be made to pay."

"Death?" inquired Franklin. He had a notion that this was the type of primitive culture that would send a man to his death rather easily.

"Perhaps," replied Molt. "But most likely not. They are thieves. And while their actions contributed to the death of one of ours, they themselves did not kill him. In such cases, the guilty are usually made to work off their debt in servitude."

"They are made slaves?" Jacko asked. It was plain to tell by the look on his face that this idea did not sit well with him.

Molt, however, did not pick up on that. "Aye. So to speak. Usually for a sentence of five to ten years. After, they are set free."

"Do you think that is just?"

"Punishment is necessary to serve justice."

"It is different where you're from?" Edgar asked.

"Yes," Jacko said plainly. "We don't allow slavery."

But then Franklin said, "It's no different."

Jacko turned a harsh eye on the old man. "Slavery?" he said to him. "That's what it is. We don't have slavery anymore, in case you forgot."

"What do you call prison?" Franklin countered.

"Not …" Jacko hesitated, seeming stuck in his thoughts. "It's not the same," he said after a long pause, though most of his anger was gone. He wasn't even sure why he was so upset.

"They are not abused or beaten," Molt told him. "They are given food and billet, and on occasion are allowed drink and companionship. There are worse fates to be had here."

"Billet?" Franklin asked. He had never heard that word before.

"A room and bed," Molt explained.

"I see," said Franklin. "Exactly like prison."

A look of resentment flashed on Jacko's face.

The tension in the air sparked Audrey to action. She was not one who liked confrontation or harsh words, so she took it upon herself to change the subject. "How big is Hinterland?" she inquired. "I've heard talk about Boreal and Vernon, and now Meridon. These are like countries?"

"You call them countries in your world, I believe," said Edgar. "We call them territories. And there are three."

"That's all?"

"That's all," said Molt. "Boreal, Vernon, and Meridon."

"So it's not a big place then?" Franklin said. "Hinterland? Only three territories. That's small."

270

To be honest, Molt had no idea how to accurately express the size of Hinterland. He knew of miles and acres, but he had never thought to do the math or learn the measurements. And though there were maps out there detailing all the territories and their borders, Molt didn't much care to learn them. He knew Vernon, he knew the desert like the back of his hand, and he knew the lands he hunted and fished. That was more than enough for him.

"We don't really put much stock in measurement here," Edgar put in. "There are differences between our ways and yours, and sometimes it can be hard to explain."

Molt then added a phrase that many Herders had used before when speaking to stragglers. "Things here are what they are, and we know them well enough."

"You don't measure your land? Franklin asked, astonished.

"A Monk once told me that it takes 156 days to walk from one end to the other, top to bottom, from the northernmost reaches of Boreal to the southern tip of Meridon. And 114 days to go west to east. So … however big that is."

"Probably about the size of America," said Audrey, only guessing.

Jacko said, "How many people live here? Do you know that?"

Molt almost laughed. "Olvin and I discussed this very matter a couple nights ago," he said. "We settled on ninety thousand. Perhaps as many as a hundred. But it's hard to say exactly."

"And you don't really measure time, either, do you?" Franklin said.

"We measure time," said Molt. "A day is a day and a year is a year. What else do we need to know about that?"

Once again, Edgar spoke up for his uncle. "Some measure these things, like the Monks at Lockhead. They measure everything precisely. Others not so much. It's become more popular the last couple generations. We have timepieces now, and understand the units placed on them. We just don't think much on it. Out here it really doesn't make a difference. Same thing with miles and plots of land."

"What makes one day different from the next? Or one hour?" Molt said. "What is the point of naming a day?"

Audrey shook her head. "How do you know when you're supposed to meet someone or go somewhere?" she asked.

Molt seemed confused by the question.

Edgar said, "We get by. Most families have a timepiece, though our hours are different here. Our days longer. Mostly we go by the sun." He gestured to the huge red sun of Hinterland, now blazing in a bright blue sky. "We can tell how much of a day is left by its position, and how quick the night is coming. That's all you really need to know."

"But you don't name your days?" Jacko said. "That's crazy. How do you make appointments? How do you … schedule things?"

"Only one day has a name here," said Edgar. "The Sabbath. Every seventh day is the Sabbath. That is the only day with a name. And there are fifty-six Sabbaths in a rota, or year."

"I don't know how that works," Jacko said to Audrey.

She shrugged and said, "I know. It's crazy."

"We get by," Edgar said again.

"What about money?" Franklin asked. "You have to have money. Every culture that has ever existed has had money. And they all measure it down to a penny. That's a certainty."

"Aye, we have money," said Edgar. "Chinks of copper, silver, and gold pass for currency here. Copper equals one to five merits, depending on its weight, silver equals ten to twenty, and gold is twenty-five and up. We have different gemstones and metals, too, each of which has a specific value. But a lot of business is for barter. Trade your tomatoes for eggs, your steel for honey, your wine for silk."

Franklin shook his head in disbelief. "We're in the stone ages," he said. "Do you believe this madness? I can only imagine what's next."

"No," Molt said to him pointedly. "I'm sure you can't."

That shut the old buzzard up for once. Shut them all up, actually.

The other group currently was having a more ominous conversation. Olvin and Mengin were pressing the vandals for information, and they were giving it freely.

"So, you kept the stragglers?" Olvin said to them.

Calrick nodded.

Dol said, "They're part of our community now."

"They need to go to the temple," said Mengin. "They're not of this world. They don't belong here."

"The first people were stragglers, according to old lore," said Calrick. "They're our ancestors."

"No they aren't," said Olvin. "That's a lie. Probably from the Kin."

Rebuked, Calrick looked away. He did not know enough about old lore to speak confidently on the subject; he was only parroting back what he had heard before. Rumors from others.

That didn't stop Dol from taking up the word. "I've heard the same," he said. "Where else would we have come from?"

"The Angeloi," said Mengin at once. "They created us to safeguard this land and give safe passage to the stragglers from the One True Living World. That is what the Monks say, and they should know."

"And I've heard different. I've heard the first men were stragglers from the world beyond. So how should we know what is right?"

"Because someone who lived it made the effort to write it down. I have *read* these things, not just heard them whispered from the shadows."

"Writing it doesn't make it so," said Dol. "Just as saying it doesn't. Do not forget, much of old lore has been disproven."

"I care not for your beliefs, vandal, or lack thereof," Mengin said, looking to veer away from discussions on old lore and personal dogmas, which experience had taught him were mostly foolish debates that rarely led anywhere useful. "You made bargain with Kin. You chose them over us. Over your own blood. Say whatever else you want, apply whatever twisted logic, but still you must answer for that."

"There was nothing left of our land and they offered help. I don't remember your kind coming to our aid."

"Some help they gave. They took your boy."

Dol lowered his head in his hands and moaned.

"We didn't know," Calrick said, sticking up for his friend. "We didn't know what they were going to do, what they were going to take, and we needed help. Our people and our land were dying, and the Kin gave us medicine, money, crops."

"They gave what they needed to give to get what they wanted," Olvin said. "And now you're owned. By Kin. They've got your boy already. Next they'll take everything else."

"You don't deal with demons," Dock said in a sharp tone. "They only deal when they know they're going to win."

"I know, I know," Dol sobbed. He thought of his boy, his first born, and a catch in his throat prevented him from going on.

Calrick picked up the thread. "We thought we could get our land back. We were desperate. We needed help and no others would stand for us. Where were you when we were falling?"

"Our borders have always been open," said Mengin. "To all. Many of yours have come to Vernon."

"And got the short end of things. Small parcels of land on the skirts. Limited bartering power. No say on the Council. No freedom to pursue their trades. We heard about it."

"That's not true."

"That's the word we got, and I trust it."

"Even if that's true, it's a better deal than striking gold with demons," said Olvin. "Thieving, kidnapping, assaulting innocent people – these are crimes for which you will stand trial."

"You can kill me now," replied Dol morosely. "I'm finished. I've got nothing left to live for."

"No one's killing anyone until we get back to Vernon. Then you'll be made to answer."

"Fools!" Mengin barked, startling them. "Stupid, bloody fools! Striking a deal with demons. Playing their game for them. And now we're in the middle of a fight. Good people are dead. Souls meant for the temple are walking free. Soon they'll come undone, and you'll be even deeper in debt. We shall have them back. We shall find them and deliver them to their rightful fate."

"What is their plan?" Dock asked. "What do the Kin want?"

"Souls," replied Dol. "They believe the souls belong to them."

"And how is that, vandal? Souls are their own. They don't belong to anyone, Angeloi or Kin."

"The Kin says otherwise."

"The Kin lie and trick fools."

"Forget not, this was their world once," Dol said with a note of scorn. He was tired of being talked down to, tired of being made to feel foolish and small. "You know it as well as I. Old lore is specific about that."

Mengin shook his head. "No. Hinterland has always belonged to the Angeloi. It is *their* world."

"In the beginning, there were Angeloi and there were Kin. They were here together, as one."

"That is blasphemy!"

"It was their world. They shared it. Who do you think got the souls before we came along?"

"The Angeloi," said Dock.

"And the Kin. They both took a share."

"That is not true."

"It is. The Kin said it and I believe it."

"Then you're a fool."

"Am I?" Dol shot back. "Why? Because I have the mind to question things? Because I doubt truths I did not see or hear for myself?"

"Fools lack faith," said Mengin. "They go with the wind and die easy."

"It was their world once. They and the Angeloi together. It is written."

"Whether or not that is true doesn't matter," said Olvin.

He had heard much the same, though he knew that Hinterland had always been ruled by the Angeloi. They had been the dominant race and the Kin had been their subjects. Then had come the revolution, the Great War, and both races had nearly been eradicated. The Kin yet existed in Hinterland, but they were not as powerful as they once had been. The Angeloi, meanwhile, had not been heard from in generations. Many believed them to be extinct; others thought them in hiding. Olvin was among the latter group.

"The Kin are evil," he said, going on. "They seek dominion over this land and all who inhabit it. That means us. We know this to be true." He turned his blazing blue eyes on Dol and finished with, "And you have helped them in that quest."

Dol shook his head angrily. "You don't know all, Herder. No one does. No one here but the Kin. And yes, they lie. But sometimes they tell truths, because sometimes the truth benefits them."

"Aye! Benefits *them*," said Mengin pointedly. "Not you. Not us. *Them*." He fixed Dol with a hard stare, and he held it firm until the vandal looked away, ashamed and sullen. "Think on your boy and tell me the ways of the Kin. Think on that truth, vandal, and speak to me of benefits."

Dol started to tear up again. He sniffed, wiped his eyes dry with the back of his hand, and attempted to reset his composure. But there was nothing he could do about the pain and regret he felt — that he would never be able to rid himself of. Nor would he ever be able to remember the face of his son again without seeing the yellow flash of a demon's eyes.

"We leave shortly," Dock said, standing. "I hope you're well-rested, vandals. We have a long walk ahead of us. If you lag or cause trouble, I'll cut you down myself. There's a bit of truth for you."

Olvin smiled at that.

Mengin, too.

**Twenty-nine:**

Yondo and Devid rested during the day, taking refuge in the caverns beneath Mount Domboll. There, they bathed, cleaned their wounds, changed their bandages, and napped for a few hours. The deaths of their friends remained heavy on their thoughts, but not once did they speak of it. No day was promised, and the desert took what it wanted.

The ponds in the caves were fertile and teeming with life, and they ate their fill of frog and turtle. They drank the fresh, cool water from the underground streams that fed those ponds, and later, after the sun fell from the sky, ushering in another sheet of darkness, they climbed up out of the cave and built a small fire. Sitting aside the flames, they smoked their tobacco and searched the land below for the campfire of their friends.

Devid spotted it first, pointing north and east. "There," he said.

Yondo squinted his weary eyes in that direction. A small, flickering flame was visible, but it was a long way off. "They're not close," he said, sounding surprised. "I thought they'd reach us by nightfall, or be close enough to call to. They're five miles away, I'd venture. Maybe more."

"Aye," said Devid. "I hope all is well with them." Then he said, "Most likely the storm slowed them down."

Yondo agreed, yet remained anxious. How could he not be after everything that had happened? How could he not be with the bones of a respected Herder still smoldering at the base of Mount Domboll, no more than a hundred steps away from them? He couldn't help but worry that perhaps a similar fate had befallen the others. And why not? They had what the Kin most wanted.

He stared for a long time, barely blinking and not once looking away from the small candle flame that was their campfire, searching his mind for a feeling, a sense of their health and well-being. None came to him, and that fashed him.

Were they okay?

Were they yet alive?

Where they were camped seemed logical to him, but to be more than three hours behind schedule was no small thing. What had happened to hold them back so much?

He made his concerns known to Devid.

"Odd, perhaps," said the Herder, "but not unbelievable.

Yondo returned his eyes to the endless black void of the desert night. He packed a second pipe and puffed away.

Devid looked back over his shoulder at him. "You want me to get the paddles?" he asked. "Perhaps we can get a response from them."

"Aye. Good thought," Yondo told him.

"We could always march out there and find them. We should be fine under the cover of darkness."

Yondo had already put some thought to that idea, and he had decided he didn't like it. Roaming the desert at night was a dangerous endeavor, especially after what had happened to them. They were now two men down; if they suffered another attack like the one last night, they most likely wouldn't survive it.

"No. It's too dangerous," he said. He did not care for how that answer sounded, but the truth, he reminded himself, often was uncomfortable. He was worried about the others, but he had to be smart. The Kin would be looking to take advantage of any opportunity presented.

"Mengin and Olvin are wise and battle-tested," he said, going on, "and they are five strong whereas we are two. The morn will be here soon. Let us see if we get a response from the waft paddles."

"Aye," said Devid, and went to get the paddles.

After retrieving them from the cave, he stood tall and slammed them together as hard as he could three times. The sound vibrated out into the night, traveling miles, and a short time later a reply came back. Three notes reverberated from the distance and direction of the campfire, though they were hard to hear.

"Feel better?" Devid said, setting the waft paddles aside.

Yondo looked at him. "For now."

"Good. I'm going back down into the cave."

"For what?" Yondo asked him.

Devid nodded to the right, in the general direction of Chatt's funeral pyre. The fire had long since gone out and there was no more smoke billowing up from the body, but the odor had yet to fade away. "I don't like being out here," he said. "I can still ..." He stopped, not wanting to say what he had almost said.

Yondo understood. He didn't like being this close to Chatt's remains either. "I'll be in shortly," he said. "I want to keep watch a while longer."

Meanwhile, at the other camp, Olvin took a seat by the fire, hoping the heat would take the chill from his old bones. Mengin sat next to him, across from Edgar and the three stragglers. Dock and Molt were off to the left about twenty paces, keeping the vandals company.

"Think they heard us?" Mengin asked Olvin.

"We heard them, didn't we?"

"Aye. But they're likely on Domboll. That's higher ground."

"They should be able to see the light of our fire from there."

"True. But that will tell them little."

Olvin gazed in the direction of the five brothers, which were still more than two days away. They were invisible in the dark, but come tomorrow afternoon their silhouettes would cut an imposing scene. They would have to go around them because of Franklin, who had sprained his ankle on the walk today. That would add at least three days to their trek.

He turned to Franklin then and asked him how his ankle was doing.

The old curmudgeon was feeling better, but that was mostly due to Molt's cider. Not near as tasty as Yondo's, but far more potent. Four shots and he felt no pain; one more and he would sleep fast through the night.

"I'm ripe and jimdandy," he said, his voice slurred with drink. His cheeks and ears were as red as summer berries; his eyes moist and glassy. "Getting weight off it help. I said so when I first did it, remember? And still you made me walk on it for miles. I consider myself fortunate, all things considered."

Franklin was the primary reason why they were so far behind. Soon after making it to the Red Rock Path, his foot had caught the edge of a small rock and his ankle had turned. He had gone down at once, and had stayed down for nearly a rote, whimpering and moaning, pounding the dirt with his hands and shouting curses. He hadn't wanted to keep going, but Mengin and Dock had insisted.

"You guys are real bastards," he said to them drunkenly. "Making an old man walk on a busted ankle. Ha! Bastards!"

"You're going to walk on it again tomorrow," Olvin told him. "And I reckon it'll be worse then. More swelling. More pain."

"You'll have to carry me."

Now it was Mengin who went, "Ha!"

Olvin laughed at that, as did Edgar and Jacko.

Audrey said, "We're close now, aren't we?"

"Not really," said Mengin. "We have two or three days to the mounts, and another three after that. Maybe more, depending on how he walks."

"Screw off," said Franklin, which drew another laugh from Jacko. The old man shot the kid a dirty look and said, "It's not funny. We're in the same boat, you know? And it's a boat going down."

Jacko's merriment went away then, suddenly and completely, and he stared out at the darkness in silent contemplation. In less than a week they would arrive at the gates of a new world, a strange and dangerous world according to Franklin. Purgatory ... or some similar version.

Jacko had heard of Purgatory before but had no understanding of it. The idea was Christian in origin, he believed, and both Franklin and Audrey had told him it was a world of suffering and punishment, a harsh world meant to cleanse the soul of sin. Jacko couldn't remember what kind of man he had been, but something told him that Purgatory wasn't going to be a pleasant place for any of them.

At least it wasn't hell.

Or was it?

He took the bottle of cider from the ground, uncorked the cap, and threw back a mouthful. The sweet yet foul taste of the liquor stung the inside of his cheeks and burned his lungs, yet he welcomed it thankfully. He simply could not get used to the cider and ale they made in Hinterland, though the effect it had on his head was certainly agreeable. It made the desert ... tolerable.

"Easy with that stuff, kid," Olvin said to him, "or you'll be moving slower than Franklin tomorrow."

Perhaps that would be a good thing, Jacko thought, considering where they were going.

"The night's getting long," said Mengin, which was his way of saying it was late. "We should take rest now. Sun'll be up before we know it, and we need an early start."

"My friend is right," said Olvin. He clapped a hand on Mengin's shoulder. "Go see how Molt and Dock are doing with our friends. We'll get started on bed."

Mengin stood at once and walked off.

"Edgar," Olvin said, "you and your uncle will man the first shift of the night. Get yourself ready."

"Aye," said Edgar. With orders in hand, he got up, went over to his pack, and began digging through it.

Olvin set his sight on the stragglers then, giving each one a brief glance. "Listen," he said to them, "the time for bed has come."

"Another day lost to the desert," Audrey said in a soft, doleful voice.

There was confusion and sadness and fear in her eyes, but she kept a strong chin. She wasn't sure how she felt about moving on, yet she understood that there was no other way. The Great Stone Temple of the Angels was where she had to go, where they all had to go, to suffer the trials and punishments of Purgatory, to endure the spiritual pain of the afterlife, to cleanse the sin from their souls. She looked up at Olvin, wanting to tell him that she was scared, that she preferred to stay in Hinterland, that she would do almost anything to stay, but doubt stopped her. Instead, she reached for the cider, undid the cap, and thirstily gulped down a couple swallows of the heady liquor. She winced at the taste, but welcomed the warmth, and, soon after that, the spin it put on her head.

Given that there were five of them and a normal night's darkness in the desert lasted nine rotes by the timepiece that Mengin carried in his pocket, the Herders had decided to man two to a shift and planned to stagger those shifts so that they all would get roughly the same amount of sleep. They were close to their destination and didn't want to take any chances; though the vandals were bound and gagged, they still needed to be watched. It was the best course to follow.

Molt and Edgar, uncle and nephew, took the first shift, with Molt working half a turn and Edgar taking a full three hours. Molt then would work the last half-shift of the night, waking for his watch just before the first rays of the sun hit the sky.

When he went down, Mengin woke for his shift. Nothing of interest had happened the first two hours, and Edgar was certain that nothing of interest would happen all night.

He made this known to Mengin.

The old Herder's eyes were focused on the dark span of the desert. "No telling what may come," he said ominously.

There hadn't been any moans from lakas or laughing barks from yenas, and they really didn't expect to hear any. They were on the backside of the desert now and yenas rarely ventured this far from their primary water source. They weren't expecting any trouble from vandals, either, seeing that they had taken some of them prisoner.

Edgar said, "You suppose Yondo and the others found anything?"

Mengin's hunched shoulders rose and fell with a shrug. "Hard to say. The echo from the waft paddles let us know they're at Domboll. But what they may have seen or come across, if anything, is hard to figure. Most likely nothing. They banged the paddles in sets of one-two/one-two, which means they are well."

"What does it mean that the Kin took the vandal's son?" Edgar asked, changing the subject. He figured that if anyone knew what it meant, it would be Mengin.

But the wise old Herder wasn't sure. "From what they said," he began in soft tones, not wanting the vandals, should they be faking sleep, to hear him, "the boy is dead and his flesh is now home to a demon."

"A demon in flesh?"

"Aye. Flesh like you and me."

"But why?" Edgar wondered. "Why would they want to be flesh? We can't kill them when they're spirits, only send them away."

"We can kill them as spirits, but it's hard. The Monks do it, though they're well-practiced. Anyway, it's hard to kill them when they're flesh, too, and they can hurt you that way. Not just tempt you or possess you, but whip you, cut you, put you down."

Edgar shook his head dismally. "I don't understand any of this. I don't understand why they're here."

"The Kin? They were here long before we were. This is their home. And once they were flesh."

"But it is written and preached that Hinterland is the domain of the Angeloi. And they brought us here and showed us favor."

"The Angeloi ruled here for generations," said Mengin. "They made the Great Stone Temple and carved the steps into Mount Warnimii. They constructed Lockhead, and shared secrets with the prophets and the Monks. And yes, they showed us favor over the Kin."

"That is why the Kin want us dead," said Edgar.

"They want to rule here. We're in their way."

"And the Angeloi?"

Mengin sighed deeply. "I don't know," he said, sounding truly unsure. "Some say they're in hiding, others believe them to be gone."

"And you?"

"I think the Great War took its toll. It is said there were only seventy of them. Seventy of them and more than four-hundred Kin. But who knows if that's true. If they are still around, I can't tell."

"Where would they have gone?"

Mengin shrugged those hunched shoulders of his again. "I haven't a good thought on that, boy. The ways of the Angeloi are not known, even by the Monks, and I suspect they never will be. But if the Kin are stealing souls and taking form in flesh, I can tell you that's a bad sign. Makes me think the end times are here."

"The end times?" Edgar had heard that phrase before, a few times, but never in context. It was always mentioned vaguely, by old timers mostly, as a way of saying that things weren't what they used to be and likely never would be again.

Mengin was an old timer, and with eyes as pale as desert moonlight he gazed at the youthful Herder across from him, idly wondering if he had ever been that young. He couldn't seem to remember. The low flames of the campfire cast shadows on his bearded face, shrouding him with an unsettling depth of darkness. "A lot of old lore is spoken, not written," he said quietly. "My gran used to speak to me about the end times. Isa, the prophetess — you've heard of her?"

Edgar nodded. "A little."

"She wrote volumes on the end times and the war to come."

"The war to come?"

"Aye. The war to come between man and Kin. Souls being stolen, tales of flesh-eaters and other strange happenings, demons in the flesh — to me, these things point to The Tribulation." He smiled wistfully. "My gran used to say it would happen in my lifetime."

"What about the Angeloi?"

Those turned out to be the last words that Edgar Coll ever spoke. The crossbow bolt went clean through his neck and blood spurted out and splashed Mengin's face. There was a moment of thunderstruck silence, and then the Herder hit the deck and cried out, "Attack! Attack!"

He dragged the boy to the cover of a low plot of ground and lied to him. "It's going to be okay," he said as Edgar unbearably spat and gurgled blood. The boy's face was painted savage red, and more blood kept pumping out of the wound, soaking his shirt and pooling on the ground.

No more bolts flew. The other Herders, awake now, went for their weapons. The stragglers, terrified they were about to die, desperately sought shelter, though there was none to find. Instead, they kept low to the ground and huddled close together like scared children.

"Edgar?!" Molt cried out. He saw his young nephew twitching on the desert ground and rushed over to him. By the time he got there, Edgar was already gone. The parts of his face not covered in blood were grossly pale, and his eyes held the hopeless, faraway gaze of death. "Edgar?!" Molt cried out again, shaking him. "No! God no! Edgar!"

"What happened?!" Dock cried out, hustling over to them, mindful to keep his head low. "Where are they?"

"What happened to my nephew?!" Molt shouted at Mengin. "Who shot him? Where are they?!"

"I don't know. I don't see anyone," Mengin said as he frantically searched the desert black. Everything was dark, and flat, and completely empty. "We were talking about the ..."

That's when they first appeared, materializing out of the darkness like walking specters: five men, no more than twenty yards off, coming right at them. They walked five wide and didn't seem to be in a rush. And not one of them was armed.

"What is it?" Dock said, and stole a quick glimpse for himself. He saw them coming, saw they were unarmed, and stood with his sword.

Molt stood, too, and pulled his crossbow. He loaded a bolt, took aim, shot at the one on the far left. The bolt flew true and went straight through the heart. The man jerked back on contact, but didn't fall and didn't stop. Molt loaded another bolt, shot him again, almost in the exact same spot, and got the same reaction.

"Here. Take these," Olvin said to Franklin and Jacko, handing them steel blades. "Stay behind me."

"What's going on?" Franklin cried out, panic-stricken. "I'm not fighting anyone. I'm an old man."

Jacko took the sword and stood without fuss, but he already had plans to flee into the desert. He waited for Olvin to rush off and join the fray before he made it known, though. He told Franklin and Audrey about his plan, and they both agreed.

The Herders, like the vandals before them, were badly outmatched. Molt had put three bolts in the one, but amazingly the man was still alive, and still coming forward. The bolts stuck out of his chest like small, leafless branches; he didn't even seem to notice them.

"The head!" Mengin cried out, realizing that blows to the body had no effect on them. "Aim for their heads!" He drew his long-blade and swung at the first one to attack. The man easily avoided the strike, but Mengin caught him on the shoulder with his short-blade. The man recoiled, and Mengin swung again, missing him badly.

Molt tried to load a fourth bolt into his crossbow but wasn't fast enough. The one that he'd shot three times jumped him, and the Herder drew his knife and stabbed him in the stomach. The man made no noise at all, and the blank, seemingly uncomprehending look on his face never changed. Before Molt could strike again, the man countered with a short, quick left that sent the Herder sprawling.

Mengin stabbed the one that he was battling through the chest, but ate a right hand that put stars in his eyes. He quickly countered with a slash to the man's lower leg, cutting him to the bone. The man stumbled back, nearly falling, and the old Herder wasted not a moment. He raised his long-blade and brought it whirling down, the sound of it slicing through the dry desert air halted instantly by the sound of it slicing through the flesh, muscle, and bone of the man's neck. The head came off cleanly, and the body fell to the ground.

Olvin swung into battle, going at one of the men, then another. They danced around him, moving swiftly, gracefully, effortlessly. He swung wildly and missed with his long-blade, leaving himself off-balance and vulnerable, and a kick to the knee from behind felled him.

"No!" Mengin cried out, running over to help him, his two blades drawn and ready.

But Olvin wasn't the only one in trouble: Dock was down and Molt was losing his fight against the man who had three bolts in his chest.

The man hit Molt with a looping left cross, and the Herder dropped to one knee. Blood pooled in his mouth, and he spat it on the ground. Then he stood with a jolt and stabbed out his short-blade. The man deftly turned away, grabbed the Herder by the wrist, twisted and jerked. The sickening sound of multiple bones snapping at once was immediately followed by the explosion of Molt's scream, which echoed for miles in the quiet, empty desert. His elbow had been disjointed, and sticking out of his forearm was a jagged, blood-covered shard of bone.

With his one good arm, the Herder desperately grabbed for the bolts he'd put in the man's chest, and he twisted them, wrenched them, tried to shove them in deeper. This had no effect at all. Instead, the man grabbed one of the bolts himself, yanked it out, and jammed it in Molt's neck, drawing a spray of blood.

Mengin was being kicked into bloody submission by the man he was battling, while Olvin and Dock continued to flail wildly against the other two, attacking in tandem. Dock struck one of the men in the chest with a death-blow, but death did not come. The blade became lodged deep in the man's ribcage, and as Dock struggled to pull it free, the man struck him in the face with a fist. Dock fell to the ground, and the man removed the blade from his ribs and tossed it aside.

Then, unexpectedly, he and the others backed away.

The two beaten and breathless Herders stopped and looked around the camp: Edgar was dead; Molt was dead; Mengin was either dead or unconscious; the stragglers were gone. The vandals were lying where they had left them, bound and gagged.

Dock and Olvin exchanged a look, and then Olvin said to one of the men, "Who are you?" Then, with more emphasis: "*What* are you?!"

The man did not answer him. None of them answered. They just stared straight ahead with eyes as blank and intransigent as stone.

The Herders realized then that these *men* weren't actually men; they were something different, something evil. The Herders had struck violent blows against them yet had not drawn a single expression of pain.

Nevertheless, Olvin tried again. "Who are you?!" he shouted. "Give your names and wants. We are Herders in service."

This time one of them spoke, in a voice that sounded as old and dry as the desert itself. "We want." That was all it said.

Dock looked behind him and realized that they were surrounded. The man/things had formed a circle around them, and they were slowly constricting that circle, edging ever closer, step by step.

"This trek was wrong from the go," Olvin said to Dock. "A trap set by the Kin and we fell for it."

"Lay down your weapons," Dock said. "Perhaps they'll let us live."

Olvin stubbornly held firm, while Dock made a show of laying down his blades and raising his hands. The man/things didn't seem to understand this demonstration and continued to come forward.

"Don't think that's going to work, friend," Olvin said.

"We can't beat them," Dock replied. "They let the vandals live."

"For what price?"

Dock glanced over at the vandals, and a terrible thought occurred to him: You make a deal with a demon, you end up one yourself. It surely was better to die in the dirt and sand of the desert than to live under the thumb of the Kin.

He crouched down and picked up his blades.

"Valliant."

This voice came from the left, near where the vandals lay. It belonged to a tall, lanky young man with broad shoulders and golden hair. Unlike the others, he looked completely human; there was light in his eyes and color in his face.

"Who are you?" Olvin called over to him. "Give a name."

The young man drew a knife with an ornate bone handle and cut the vandals free. He let them undo their own gags.

"I have many names," he said, sliding the knife back into the sheath on his belt, "and have had many more. Mar. Fate. The Shadow on the Mount. I've been called Disease, Death, The Bone Taker. I am Demon Kin. I am the Wizard. The Desert Ghost. Now, this." He gestured to his new form. "Alde of Meridon. Though, if you must know, my true name is Amaros."

His voice seemed to echo on itself, and the Herders exchanged another look, this one more solemn than the first. This was the vandal boy the demon had claimed as a vessel.

Dol and Calrick stood, dusted themselves off. Along with Amaros, they approached the others.

"Traders!" Olvin shouted at the vandals. "What price did you get for your souls?" He narrowed his eyes on Dol and added, "What price did you get for your boy's soul?"

"They get to live well in their own flesh," said Amaros. "In a new and better world. Just ask your friend."

Olvin said, "What friend? What nonsense are you speaking?"

Amaros nodded to Dock. "Him."

Olvin set his eyes on the only friend he had left. "Dock?" he said, sounding confused. "What is he talking about?"

Dock wanted to deny it, but his face clearly showed his guilt. "Ayna was ill," he said, his normally stoic voice cracking some. "She was going to die. There was no …"

"Trader!" Olvin cried out, and Dock turned away in shame. "You sold out your brothers!"

"I … There …" Dock stepped away from his fellow Herder, moving closer to Amaros.

The demon pulled a small leather bag from his belt and handed it to the traitorous Herder. "As agreed upon," he said.

The disgrace that Dock felt was overwhelming, yet he took the bag of gold; for his family, he told himself. He kept his head down and his eyes away from Olvin, fearing that should he even glance at him, he instantly would die of shame.

Olvin continued to glare at his fellow Herder just the same. Being attacked by vandals was one thing; being betrayed by a friend was something different.

The old Herder laughed angrily, and said, "Go home, traitor. I may be the one to die today, but you are the one who is dead." He then turned to face the boy with the golden hair. "Daimonas!" he cried out, his voice wavering with rage. "Na fygei! Sto onoma tou Theou kai Christou! Na fygei!" He continued to spit out the words of old, those words used to dispel the Kin, chanting them loudly, with desperate conviction. Only like the blades and bolts, his words failed to have an effect. The man/things were unfazed, while Amaros smirked arrogantly.

"Such powerful magic you have," the demon said, still smirking. "Not worth much to me, I'm afraid."

"You can't win," Olvin said. "We'll beat you. Maybe not today, maybe not tomorrow, but soon."

Amaros shook his head. "No, Voukolos, you won't."

Calrick and Dol had retrieved the four bags of souls from across the camp. They laid them at Amaros's feet, though neither could bring himself to look at the boy who now was Kin.

The demon was pleased. "Good," he told them. "Now go and find the stragglers. I want them, too."

The vandals picked up weapons from the ground – Calrick grabbed Molt's crossbow and Mengin's knife while Dol took Edgar's short-blade and Molt's long-blade – and ran off into the night.

"All part of the plan," Olvin said to Amaros. "A plan destined to fail."

The demon chuckled with scornful amusement. "You know not of our plans, Voukolos, and if you did, you still wouldn't be able to stop us. The Angeloi are no longer here to protect you." He kicked the souls at his feet. "These shall help us take full command of Hinterland. It's not as if we don't understand the true nature of ..."

"Shut your damn mouth already!!" Olvin roared. "I'd rather have my bones ground to dust than listen to the words of a demon." And with his next breath he charged the man/thing closest to him, stabbing it in the chest with his long-blade. He then whirled his short-blade over his shoulder and brought it crashing down with ferocious intent. The razor-sharp edge caught the man/thing on top of the head and cut through the bone to the brain. Its faraway eyes stared lifelessly at the Herder, then it twitched, spasmed, and toppled to the ground, with Olvin's short-blade still stuck in its skull.

The Herder, now alone in his fight, charged forward wildly, screaming like a madman. He lopped off a hand of one of the mindless attackers, but the thing made no sound and showed no reaction. Then something hit him from the side, and something else hit him from behind, knocking him to the ground.

Olvin went for a leg with his long-blade but missed, and was promptly struck upside the head with a fist, though to him it felt more like a large rock. A galaxy of stars exploded in his eyes and the whole desert flipped over on itself.

The fight lasted only ten seconds longer.

Olvin Blacke, a proud Herder who had made more than three-hundred treks, who had helped deliver hundreds of stragglers and more than thirty-thousand living stones to the Great Stone Temple, died in the desert sand, under a blanket of heavy darkness, with one of his own standing aside Kin.

## Thirty:

They were still a full day from Greenhorn, but the Dark Forest was well behind them now, more than twenty miles in any direction. That didn't stop Peck from worrying, though.

They ate squirrel meat and nuts in the faint orange glow of a fire, and Peck had a few pulls from the Monk's cask. The liquor, derived from honey and apples, was particularly tart, with a bitter aftertaste that lasted some time. It had a rather strong kick, though, which was most important. It tasted considerably better when hot, and the Monk had wisely heated it to a boil over the low flames.

"I'll not hold back or mix words with you," the Monk said. He lit his pipe. Little whiffs of smoke expanded and dissipated in front of his face. "When we speak, I'll tell you the truth. Take no offense."

"I understand," Peck said. "And agree."

The Monk drew on his pipe. Then he began. "You are curious about your fate, as you should be."

"I'm not curious, I'm cursed," Peck said. "It's the only explanation."

"Aye. Maybe so. But 'cursed' is not the right word. The ancients called it *Markarismenost*. You're *Marked*."

Peck stared at him. "Marked?"

"Aye. Your soul has been Marked."

"Marked for what?"

"For fate, boy."

Peck was confused, and looked it. The Monk tried to explain.

"Being Marked for fate means your soul is powerful. It means you have importance in this world. It means they want you."

"'They?' You mean the Kin?"

"Aye. But also the Angeloi."

That thought fascinated Peck, though he wasn't sure why. "What kind of power do I have?" he asked.

Kelt shrugged. "Hard to say. You saw the wapiti's soul."

"You've seen such things. Does that mean you have power, too?"

"Aye, I see things, but for me it's less about power and more about knowing how to look at the world."

"So you're not Marked?" Peck said.

"No."

"Are any Monks? There have to be some."

"Not anymore. There were some in the past. I've heard tales."

"Do they …" Peck stopped. He could see by the look in Kelt's eyes that the real truth was coming.

Kelt didn't make him wait long to hear it. "Being Marked is rare, and most who are never know it. I can't even say for sure that you're Marked, but the signs are there … the white bird from the Dark Forest being one."

"Ovince?" Peck said. "What about him?"

"He led me to you. Twice."

"Twice?" Peck knew about the most recent event, when the siren song of the forest had called to him and he had, for the second time, slipped into a dark, mindless trance and wandered off. The first time he had awoken in the Dark Forest alone and unarmed. The second time the Monk had stopped him before he could stray into the perilous wood.

"When first I found you, stoned on wilderberries, it was because the white bird led me to you. I was a hike away and going in the other direction. But it found me and led me to you."

"What's that mean?" Peck asked.

"It means you have favor with animals. That's a point of power. Then there are the things that have happened to you. Not random events, I can say with some certainty. The murder of your ma and sisters while you were left unharmed. You heard the song of the Dark Forest, which is an evil song, a song most cannot hear, and it led you astray. It cost the life of your pa and uncle when they went to look for you." The Monk saw the boy's expression change, saw his eyes fill with emotion, and quickly added, "Not your fault, boy. I didn't mean it like that so don't take it that way. They're trying to turn you."

"Turn me? Turn me to what?" Peck asked, fighting back tears.

"To stone. They seek to harden your heart and make you cold. That's what they want. Then they can take you."

Peck took another drink of hot honey cider. The warmth of the liquor soothed his belly though not his mind. He had never heard of anyone being Marked before; so far as he could tell, it didn't sound any different from being cursed. He said that to Kelt.

"Not so," the Monk replied. "We believe there are three sides to the trinity of unknown men: the Cursed; the Blessed; the Marked. The Cursed are destined to be on the side of evil, with the Kin. The Blessed are destined for the good side of the fight, with the Angeloi. Those that are Marked are somewhere in the middle."

"Isn't that everyone?"

"No. Most here live and die, and that's all life is for them. Their fates will be decided elsewhere, in another world or on the scales. Then there are those like you, those whose fates will be decided here. Those whose fates will decide other fates."

"Are you one of those people?"

Kelt's eyes gave nothing away, and his next words came out on an even line. "I'm not sure. I hardly can tell anymore. I used to think I was Blessed, but this world ... nothing is certain."

"So what do we do now?" Peck asked. "What can *I* do to make sure I fight for good?"

"We go to Lockhead, where my Order will put you through the trials."

"The trials?"

"*Dokimes tis Psychis*. The Trials of the Soul. If you pass, your soul will be cleansed. It will be free from the call of the Kin. Then, if you like, you can become one of us."

Peck was silent. If there were words to properly convey how he felt, he didn't know them.

"The truth is that it's usually not a good life for those who are Marked. These days they often fall to the other side and become an enemy. Black souls for the Kin. Monsters made of man."

"You make it sound as if they are destined for the Kin," Peck said. "As if they have no hope. You said the Angeloi want them, too. You said the Angeloi and the Kin want them, though it seems it is the Kin they are most drawn to. Tell me I'm wrong."

Kelt offered the boy a faint smile. "Aye. You're a sharp one," he said. "It never used to be that way. The Old Scrolls tell of the days when the Marked were spoken to by the Angeloi. Many were given the powers of prophecy, wisdom, strength. They were chosen to lead and speak for their people. The great prophet Toman was purported to be Marked. Isa, too. They enjoyed great favor and promise once. But ... the Angeloi are gone. It is the Kin who dwell this world now. It is their voice that calls most loudly to the Marked."

The liquor had Peck feeling flush. The story had him feeling sick.

Marked? It made sense when he thought about it. He considered all the bad things that had happened to him in his life thus far: the savage murders of his ma and sisters; the equally savage murders of his pa and uncle; the death of his best friend, Malcom, who had broken his neck falling out of a tree. Malcom had been the best climber Peck had ever known, and his fall had been called a tragic accident. Now Peck wasn't so sure.

Then there was how he was so different from everyone else: the way he saw and heard things that no one else saw or heard; the way he thought about things that no one else bothered to think about. And his dreams; vivid, savage dreams of violence and death.

Could it be part of some greater plan?

Could the Kin be behind it all?

The idea seemed preposterous, only ...

"Are you telling me the Kin wiped out my whole family just to turn me?" he said, appalled by the thought. His hands were shaking; his legs, too. "They killed *them* to get to *me*?"

"Such is life," replied the Monk. "So is the way of the Kin. And the stronger you are, the harder they'll come for you. They seek the strong, for the strong make them stronger."

Peck finished the last of his drink and set the cup aside. The liquor had gone straight to his head; he could feel it turning his thoughts in circles and breaking them apart, only to reassemble them again, though in slightly different ways. It was very frustrating.

If what the Monk had said was true, and Peck suspected it was, that meant his soul was Marked for Fate, he was a target for the Kin, and his kin had suffered death because so.

"These trials," he said, his young, handsome face locked in an ugly grimace, "what are they like?"

The Monk gave a quick shrug of the shoulders. "Can't say. Never been through them myself. It's been more than two generations since anyone has. Supposedly they're different for everyone."

Peck said, "I don't have to do them if I don't want to?"

"Of course not," said Kelt. "You don't have to do anything you don't want to do." He wisely held back the part that dealt with the consequences of not at least trying to beat the trials. Nor did he mention what would happen to Peck if he tried and failed. Neither was pleasant. Instead, he said, "But I'd try if I were you. It's no life trying to beat this on your own, and you've seen what happens to those closest to you. If you think you can live a quiet, anonymous life in the woods, alone and far removed, think again. They *know* you, and they'll find you."

Peck's head was as heavy as it had ever been when finally he laid it down for the night. Filled with new thoughts and terrors, he wondered how he was supposed to sleep. He wondered if he would ever sleep pure again. He wondered if it was pointless to fight the Kin, pointless to fight the uneven spin of fate, pointless to go on. And he worried, dolefully, that the Trials of the Soul would overwhelm him.

It had been a long couple of days, which had followed a long couple of weeks, and Peck was ready to go home. But home, he knew, would never be the same. After everything that had happened, he didn't think he could ever call Greenhorn home again. He didn't even want to stop there to recount the deaths of his father and uncle.

He had no home, and he had no family.

Lockhead? The village in the northwest mountains that was home to the Order of Monks. That's where they were going, and that's the next place he planned to stay for more than one night.

But would it ever be home? Could he ever think of the cassocked warriors as family? He doubted it.

Lockhead, he imagined, would be nothing more than a temporary stop on his journey, a journey that threatened to take him further than he ever thought possible. A journey of consequence and fate. A journey of the mind and soul. A journey, so far as he could tell, that was doomed to end badly. He felt it in his bones. He knew it in his heart.

Yes, he was Marked.

Marked by death.

**Thirty-one:**

Yondo woke first, and after getting a drink of water from the pond, he grabbed his tobacco pouch and headed for the mouth of the cave. He climbed out into the early morning sun, its orange-red glow glinting off the smooth red rock of Domboll, making it shine.

The land below was desolate and oddly beautiful, especially the pale green field of cacti and scrub grass to the left. Yondo squinted into the distance, looking for his friends. They should be on the move by now, he believed. An early start today would be necessary if they wanted to make it to the mounts by tomorrow evening.

He packed his pipe and put a match to it. He missed his morning mug of tea; the taste and warmth of it paired well with the tobacco, helping to wake not only his body but also his mind. They had lost all their tea, their bread, too, somewhere on the journey, probably during their battle with the yenas and lakas. The second group surely would have some, along with a jug of cider … if the stragglers hadn't drank it all. Yondo hoped there would be some left; he felt the need for a drink, for the pain in his body and the worry in his head.

It had been a cursed trek from the start and they had yet to make it to the mounts. All those souls in their keeping and the Kin on their back. He thought of Gabby and Jonno and Dalla; he thought of his home and how badly he wanted to return there. Lastly, he thought of Lizzy, remembering all too well the ominous look on her face and the blunt warning on her tongue when he had left. She had sensed trouble; something evil in the wind. He had thought to agree, but had not wanted to worry her.

That girl had a sense about her that wasn't natural. Ferdo once had told him it was because she was a straggler. The few number of infants that had come over on the boat – there had been only seventeen recorded through all the generations – were not of Hinterland, so sometimes they saw things that others could not.

Ferdo had gotten that bit of information from an old crone that dwelled in the marshes, and added that the older they got, the less they saw, unless they worked to hone that skill.

Yondo smiled when he remembered what he had told Ferdo that day: "The old crone that predicts the future with her withered tits? Well, it's hard to refute logic like that."

But Yondo could not refute nor explain Lizzy's seemingly supernatural instincts and intelligence. She just seemed to be in the know about things, and a full step ahead of those around her. Even adults.

She was different; there was no denying it. Only slightly, and in ways hard to quantify, but it was evident. Especially to him.

Yondo had known only one other infant straggler who had come to the shores of Hinterland: a boy named of Deelo. Deelo had not possessed a supernatural sense, had not been in the know about things, and had never once been a step ahead of anyone.

Deelo had lived his life a step or three behind, by all accounts. Word was he had died in the Marshlands years ago; he just wandered off one day and was never heard from again.

Deelo would sit and stare at the ground, or a stream, or the stars for hours on end, and he would babble on about things that made no sense, often in a tongue that no one else could understand. If it was a tongue at all; it very well could have been nothing more than extraneous noises and animal sounds. Other times he'd go completely catatonic; he wouldn't speak or move for days. You could scream in his ear or slap his face and he wouldn't so much as blink.

Deelo Hyovan – the lunatic of Vernon.

No one had bothered to look for him when he disappeared, not even his folks. No one had cared to.

Similar rumors had made their way to Hinterland about other infant stragglers. Tales of trouble and dissent; tales of madness and broken lives; tales of strange and unexpected disappearances.

But rumors, like the Kin, could not be trusted.

By decree of the Angeloi, they were not to be harmed, and they were not to be taken to the Temple. They were to be kept in Hinterland, adopted into good families, and made whole. They were to be given names and thought of as indigenes. Even so, they were often looked at sideways, with curiosity and suspicion, and were never fully trusted.

Only one had made a good life in Hinterland, and he had been one of the first. Carlot Biak was his name, and his lineage still thrived today, more than forty generations later. It was a good lineage, too. The roots of the fertile Biak tree ran deep and produced good fruit. As a Judge, one of his descendants had served on the Council of Elders in Vernon. Jeb Moll, the current Elder of the Miners and the richest man in Vernon, was married to a Biak progeny.

Today, Biaks owned marketplaces in Greenhorn and Mun, Cambria and Kittan. They were one of the richest families in all of Hinterland, and their power and reach exceeded their wealth.

An empire grown from an inauspicious beginning.

Only seventeen? That was all? A mere seventeen infant stragglers in more than seventy generations? That seemed like such a small number to Yondo. And Lizzy was the last of them. He wondered if there would be more like her to come. He wondered if perhaps the batty old crone might be right about her. He wondered about her world, where it was, how big it was, what it was like, and he wondered about what had brought her to these shores. Why hadn't only her soul come across? There were always a few small stones in the bunch; smooth, dull, misshapen stones a tenth the size of normal ones. Yondo believed those ones belonged to children. So why not Lizzy? Why not Deelo Hyovan? Why not Carlot Biak?

He thought of these things as he gazed out over the desert and smoked his morning pipe. He wished he would have thought to bring the waft paddles and signaling glass with him; if he had, he could have sent a message to the other group. He watched the horizon for a message being sent from them but saw none. While that alone was not cause for concern, it did worry him, especially considering everything that had happened since they had split up. The second group had the souls and stragglers; their safety was paramount.

Then, in the general area where Yondo was looking, the area where he believed his friends had camped the prior night, he saw a black speck rise into the air. And it kept rising, slowly yet steadily, becoming slightly larger the higher it went.

An ornio?

He was proven right a short time later when, now soaring high in the crystal blue sky of the early morning, the bird began to circle. Then Yondo saw another one. From so far away, the long-winged scavengers seemed to be floating on air. Then they began to descend, coming back down to the earth in slow, meandering circles. And as they descended, they slowly faded from sight.

Yondo tapped the smoldering tobacco strands from his pipe and stomped them out with his foot. He stared off in the distance, in the direction where he had last seen the two birds. They were gone now, and he saw no other signs of life.

Ornioi were scavengers, so they could be counted on to check out the remains of a fresh campsite. It was in their nature. When they smelled burning meat and wood, or the raw, earthy scent of men, or the metallic odor of blood, or the sour-sweet aroma of alcohol, they flew in to have a look. They intruded on campsites all the time, scavenging for food, looking mostly for scraps left behind.

Yondo stood tall and narrowed his eyes to a squint. There was nothing to see but desert in every direction, an endless ocean of sand and rock and sky, as lovely as it was empty. He then returned to the cave to retrieve the waft paddles and signaling glass, even though he had a bad feeling that any message sent would not be returned.

Once again, the Herder sensed death in the air.

"Something's wrong," Yondo said, staring off in the direction where their friends should have been. He saw nothing but desert.

Devid raised the waft paddles, preparing to strike them again. But Yondo stopped him.

"No," he said. "Something's wrong."

Devid had banged the paddles together multiple times, and every time he had gotten a response. Same thing with the signaling glass. He had sent out dozens of flashes of light and had received as many in return. But that had been more than a rote ago, and there still was no sign of the other group. They should be close enough to see by now, Yondo reasoned, and Devid agreed.

"Their camp was maybe five miles off, and it's been three rotes since sunrise." Yondo again repeated his summation: "Something's wrong."

"Aye," said Devid. "This whole trek has been wrong. Out here in the desert with the Kin and the vandals." He turned, spat on the ground, and continued. "Sheep led astray, that's what we are. Led to the wolves. We'll be lucky to make it back alive."

"Speak for yourself," said Yondo. "I'll not die out here."

Devid took a draw of tobacco from his pipe and blew the smoke away. "We need to check on them," he said. "But you know damn well that's what *they* want us to do."

Yondo looked back over his shoulder at the rutted face of Domboll. A bad feeling lay on his skin and in the pit of his stomach. Nothing felt right to him. He didn't know what to think, and, worse yet, he no longer trusted his feelings.

"Up there," he said, pointing. "We'll have a better view."

They climbed up about two hundred podes, traversing a narrow arroyo that split the rock face in two. Up there they found a cradle of large, flat stones that provided them with shade, safety, and a clear view north. They hunkered down and got busy surveying the land.

Once again there was only desert to see.

"Nothing," Yondo reported. "We should see them from here."

"Aye," agreed Devid. "Something's wrong."

Yondo turned his gaze skyward. Hinterland's brilliant red sun lazed in a cloudless blue sky, baking the sand and rock below. Its unfettered heat radiated off the desert floor, giving the empty wasteland a mystical charm. Even with heat-haze blurring their vision, they should have been able to spot the other Herders from this height. But there was no sign of them.

Farther up the mount, perched menacingly on the twisted scarps of Domboll, Yondo spied a number of ornio. They were, as usual, patiently scanning the land below for anything dead or about to be. One of the creatures stretched out its massive wings and took flight, soaring down over the cliffs and coming close enough to Yondo and Devid that Yondo couldn't help but become suspicious.

"Hide," he told Devid, ducking behind a rock.

"What? Why?" Devid asked, looking around. He ducked behind the same rock and buried his head in his arms. "What did you see?"

"A vulture," Yondo said.

"A vulture?"

"Aye. Kin can control them, and see through them."

Devid understood, and crouched down lower.

The bird circled around, flapped its giant wings, and soared high over the mount. Yondo watched it go, then threw a glance at the other birds. They were still perched up there, not moving.

Then Devid said, "Look. There."

He was pointing straight ahead. Through the waves of heat that danced on the desert crust like choppy, fast-running water, a dark silhouette took shape. At first there was only one black clump on the horizon, but as that black clump got closer it began to break apart, becoming two, and then three, and then six.

Six? Only six?

Both Yondo and Devid searched the surrounds for the missing two. Yondo concentrated his gaze to the left, while Devid peered to the right.

"Six?" Devid said. "I only see six."

"I see no others," Yondo reported. "Can you make out the six?"

Devid squinted his eyes, but the waves of heat and the blinding light of the sun made it impossible for him to see clearly. "No," he said. "You?"

Yondo had keen eyes, but from where he stood the approaching party looked like nothing more than a collection of dark, wavering shapes, not unlike Kin. "No," he said. "Six? That means two are unaccounted for."

"They might have stayed back at camp," Devid posited.

"You believe that? After everything that's happened?"

Devid gave quick thought to the question, but then didn't answer, not liking what that answer meant. Instead, he said, "Perhaps the other two are there, but walking behind, so we can't see them."

Yondo didn't believe that. He continued to watch the vapor-like black figures push their way through the desert heat. He reckoned they were about three miles away, which meant they should reach the base of Domboll in less than a rote.

"What do you want to do?" Devid asked. "Stay here and wait for them? Hide farther up and watch?"

Behind them, a few small rocks casually trundled down the slope of the mount, bouncing and skidding and kicking up small puffs of dust. Both Herders turned around and searched the rocky crags above for any shadows or signs of life. They didn't see anything, but that didn't mean there wasn't anything to see.

Yondo slyly tapped Devid on the arm, and when Devid looked at him, Yondo silently mouthed the words, "I think someone might be up there."

"Who?" Devid mouthed back, stealing a glimpse forty or fifty steps up. He saw the dull red bulk of the mount and nothing else.

Yondo turned back around and gazed out at the approaching black stains of humanity. They had begun to taper into shape, becoming tall and thin and human. Then he looked back up the mount.

"We may be surrounded," he said quietly.

Devid kept staring up the side of the mount, his eyes searching for movement. "What should we do?"

Yondo was pondering that very question when the first big rock came barreling out from a perch some seventy steps above them. Another came after that, and then another, and another. The Herders took shelter and listened as the rocks crashed down around them, knocking other rocks and stones from their rest and sending them careening downhill.

Then a boulder, easily twenty feet in diameter, began rolling down the slope. It slammed its way over smaller stones and rocks, loosening them from the mountain's grip, causing them to bounce and roll. Gravity and momentum did the rest, and Yondo cried out, "Run!"

They scurried out from their hiding place, running hard to the left, making their steps in haste, piles of dust and stone sliding under their feet and clamoring around them.

Devid tramped on a rock, his ankle twisted, and down he went. "Yondo!" he called out. "Help."

Yondo was a good six or seven strides ahead, yet he rushed back to help his friend. He lifted Devid to his feet and dragged him away as the huge boulder thundered down the mountainside, threatening to crush them where they stood.

The Herders dove out of the way just in time, barely escaping death. The boulder crashed into some rocks, causing the ground around them to shake. It was as if the mountain itself was breaking apart. The huge rock kept going and disappeared over the edge; a moment later it struck the ground below, and the sound it made echoed across the desert.

One death dodged, but they were hardly out of danger.

Battalions of rocks came bouncing and skidding down the slope in every direction. Most of them were big enough to kill a man if they hit him right. Even the smaller ones would break bones and tear flesh.

The two wounded Herders were under attack from the mountain and there seemed to be no end in sight. Another boulder, easily as large as the first, began a violent descent, and more stones and rocks followed after it, like an army of men following a Trojan horse.

The Herders rushed to find cover, but there was none to find. They were on the side of a mountain that was breaking apart piece by piece.

A rock the size and shape of a human head struck Devid on the leg and he cried out in pain. Yondo was struck on the arm by a smaller stone, and then on the shoulder by another, in nearly the same spot where the yena had bit him. It hurt something awful, but he didn't have time to dwell on it. More rocks were coming, pounding down the slope like an avalanche.

Yondo threw a shoulder under Devid's arm and the two of them hastily made their way down the mount as dozens of rocks rushed by. A few more struck them, but they were smaller and failed to throw them off balance.

Only twenty steps from the crevasse that led down into the caves, Yondo stumbled and fell. He landed awkwardly on his left arm, crying out, "Bastardos!"

Devid went down a couple of steps later and cracked his head off a rock. Blood gushed from the wound and began streaming down his face.

They slowly got to their feet as more stones and rocks caromed past them, bounding down the mount to the ground below.

"We have to make it to the caves," Yondo said through gritted teeth, the pain from his arm nearly unbearable.

Devid nodded woozily. Thick, molasses-like blood had mixed with the sand and grit of the desert to turn his face into a death-mask.

They soldiered on, considerably slower than before, clutching to each other like frightened children in a boneyard. They carefully picked their steps, limping and gimping and stumbling along. They were nearly at the opening of the crevasse when a large rock struck Yondo on the back of the head. He lurched forward without control, and his face smacked the unforgiving stone of Domboll. Then, with a spin, he tumbled down into the crevasse, falling at least fifteen feet.

"Yondo!" Devid cried out. He hurried to the edge, looked over it, saw his friend lying on the ground below, not moving. "Yondo?!" he shouted out again. "Yon?!"

Yondo Carpana did not move.

Rocks continued to slam down the mountainside at a frenzied pace, making Domboll roar. Devid gazed up at the relentless assault and saw three ornio perched high up on the scarps of the mount, just sitting there, as peaceful and still as the sky above them.

A huge stone bounced hard to the left and almost decapitated Devid. He dove out of the way just in time, though nearly ended up falling into the crevasse himself. He caught his balance at the last second and scuttled away from the edge like a crab.

Another large stone crashed next to his head, splashing him with sand and tiny pebbles. He groaned and spit, and jumped to his feet.

More rocks were coming, big ones and little ones, hurtling down the side with great force and speed, threatening to kill him. He sidled around the brink of the crevasse until he came to an opening with a solid foothold. Working quickly but carefully, with rocks and stones bounding all around him, he wedged his way inside and began to climb down.

A large rock followed him in, grazing the back of his shoulder before falling below, nearly striking Yondo. Devid knew that if he didn't get down there and move Yondo out of the way it would only be a matter of time before a stone crushed the Herder's skull.

"Yondo?" he called out, hoping to rouse him. Hoping, he realized with a growing sense of despair, that Yondo wasn't already dead.

He finally reached the bottom, and he rushed to his friend's side, checking first to see if Yondo was still breathing, then checking to see if he could wake him.

The good news was that Yondo had a pulse; blood still moved through his veins and air through his lungs. But there was no waking him. The Herder lay face down on the hardpan, the side of his head split wide and pasted with blood.

Devid shielded his eyes and peered up through the sickle-shaped crevasse. A patch of radiant blue sky met his gaze, and then, a moment later, a stone the size of a summer melon came flying through. It pinballed recklessly off a number of rocks before landing no more than a step away from them.

Devid gave his friend a desperate shake and cried out, "Yon?! Can you hear me? Yon?!" He slapped his face a couple times, gently, and begged him to wake up.

But Yondo remained motionless and unresponsive, a broken man on the threshold of death. There was a lot of blood on him and more leaking out. Devid knew that he had to get him away from the falling rocks before it was too late.

A rock the size of a tomato flew over the edge and thudded Devid in the side, and he fell back and wailed in pain. "Son-of-a-gypsy-whore!" he growled, as angry as he was hurt. Then, desperately, he shouted, "Stop it, dammit! Show mercy!"

That last part was to the Angeloi, should they be listening. But even if they were, and that was unlikely, it wasn't as if they could help him pull Yondo out of danger.

He had no one to rely on but himself for that.

Devid didn't have much left, but what he had he would give. His ankle throbbed incessantly, and that was without any weight on it; his left hip and left arm ached, and it felt like maybe he had a broken jaw. On top of that, his vision was shortsighted and blurry, there was a constant ringing in his ears, and his head felt like it had been split in two. But he called on his size and pure brute strength to lift Yondo over his shoulder and carry him deeper into the cave.

On one leg, he lugged Yondo into the shadows of the ancient cavern, staggering under the deadweight of the unconscious Herder, nearly falling half a dozen times. He took him all the way to the first source of water, a small pond skirted by high reeds and rocks, and laid him there.

He then collapsed to the ground, completely exhausted.

He needed a drink.

He needed to check on Yondo.

But his strength had run dry and unconsciousness stole him away before he could do either.

Outside, the last rocks hit the ground at the base of Domboll.

All was quiet.

That quiet would not last long.

Five climbed down into the cave, one after the other. Amaros led the way. The four soldiers with him were the soul-struck man-things that had killed the Herders and shamed the vandals.

Devid was lying where he had collapsed, his well-made body marked with fresh bruises and cuts.

Yondo lay where Devid had dropped him.

Neither had woken yet, and Amaros cleared his throat demonstrably.

Yondo didn't stir, but Devid did. With his eyes closed, he groaned and rolled over on his side. His head felt like it had been bashed open with a smith's hammer. The bleeding on his brow had stopped, but its rich color stained his face and neck. He shifted his weight, and groaned again.

Amaros edged closer and nudged him with a foot, and Devid's eyes blinked open. He saw ... shapes and shadows, and little else.

"You're awake, Voukolos? Good."

This voice was unfamiliar to him, and he lifted his head to see who it belonged to. A young man stood before him, tall and lean, princely-looking, with long blonde hair and fair skin. Four men stood at his back; they looked like savages, and bore the markings of such. They had scars on their faces and blood on their hands.

"Who are you?" Devid asked in a hoarse voice.

Amaros said, "I'm the one that's going to kill you, Voukolos."

A smile peeled back Devid's blood-soaked lips. "Daimonas," he said. Then he started chanting the old words in a slow, raspy, passionless voice.

Amaros grinned and chanted with him.

Devid stopped, his mouth gaping in silent disbelief.

"The words of old don't work on me, Voukolos," Amaros said. "I'm something different. I am *of* the Old"

303

"Vandal!" Devid shouted.

"Wrong again. I am Divine."

Devid laughed, and then, because it hurt to laugh, he cringed in pain.

"You seem to be in discomfort," Amaros said to him. "I can remedy that if you like. Will take but a moment."

"Divine? Ha!" Devid said with a note of scorn. "You know not the meaning of the word."

Amaros ignored him. "Is your friend dead?" he asked.

Devid glanced at Yondo. The Herder had yet to move, but it appeared he was still breathing. "Not sure."

"Clutching to life. You as well."

"The other Herders are dead?" Devid asked.

"Yes. And no. A couple of them still walk, but they're not themselves."

Devid's bloody lips drew back over his teeth, giving him a feral look. "Evil bastard!" he growled. "What dark magic did you do to them?"

"Only what was necessary," Amaros said, smiling.

"If you're going to kill me, do it. I'm half-dead already."

"Don't be angry, Voukolos. This is mercy. You'll never make it across the desert in your condition. Numerous broken bones. No weapons of worth. You'll be a meal for yenas and lakas, and that's no way to go."

"So quit your talking and do it already. My patience is gone."

Amaros nodded and drew his sword. "Last words, Voukolos?"

Devid tried to take a breath, but that breath got caught in his throat and he began to cough. This jag caused him so much pain that he wondered whether or not death might be a worthwhile alternative. When finally he quit hacking and found his voice, he said, "I'm going to find you and kill you in the next world."

Amaros let loose a husky, full-throated laugh; it was the laugh of a man, not a boy. "Now those were some fine last words," he said rather joyously. "I liked them very much. I wish you luck in the next world, Herder. Truly. You're going to need it. As for me, I'm not going where you're going. Different paths, I'm afraid."

"You think you're going ..."

Devid's voice was squelched by Amaros's blade; the steel slid through the Herder's ribs and into his heart, and he let out a gruff, agonizing croak. Blood spurted from his mouth and flowed down over his heavily-bearded chin. His eyes rolled back and closed for the last time.

"Now for this one," Amaros said, and he poked Yondo in the side with the tip of his blade. Devid's still warm blood dripped from that blade like rain from a leaf. "The best of theirs reduced to death in the desert. Ashes in the sand, forever scattered. I wonder if he'll pass through to the other side or be sent to the Void, where ancestors of mine will devour his spirit?" Amaros poked him again, harder this time, but Yondo didn't move.

"A quick, painless death may be too good for him," the demon went on. He was speaking conversationally, but only to himself; the dead, soul-struck assassins at his back understood his words, vaguely, but were not the type to care or respond. They had not minds of their own.

Amaros sheathed his blade and knelt at Yondo's side, wanting to check him over. The Herder was not playacting; he was certainly unconscious, and seemed near death. There was a deep gash on his forehead and his left eye was swollen shut; his right arm was clearly broken and his left shoulder appeared to be disjointed. His left leg didn't look so good, either; it was bent awkwardly beneath him, in a way that made it seem fractured. And a small pool of blood had seeped into the sand around his head, forming a morbid halo of death. He was sure to have other injuries as well, Amaros believed: broken ribs, internal damage, brain trauma.

The Old Kin Elder looked at the four soul-struck assassins that were his servants, that stood ever ready to do his bidding, the scars and runes carved into their faces the product of ancient Kin magic. "No good can come from leaving a Herder alive," he said to them.

None of them offered a reply; they only stared at their king, their eyes vacant and unblinking.

"But to kill a man like this?" Amaros shook his head back and forth in a show of disappointment. "Not a good death for a Herder. Not a good death for any man. When he can't speak his last words. When there's nothing left of his mind or body."

Amaros put an ear on Yondo's chest. A beat could be heard, but it was slow, uneven, weak. His breathing was the same. How many more breaths could he have left, Amaros wondered? How much more time?

The demon curled the back of his hand and raked it hard across Yondo's face. The sound of the blow echoed softly in the cavern, dampened by the earthen walls and the whispering babble of slow-flowing water.

Yondo did not move, did not wake, and Amaros scoffed angrily.

"I can't do it," he said aloud, again to himself. "It's not the way. Honor abides, as it must. Anyhow, he should suffer, as all Herders should suffer. Speaking the words of old, sending us away like goats. They believe they have power over us, bequeathed to them by the Angeloi. They believe they have dominion here, that this world is theirs, when the truth is it's ours. It's ours and we shall have it. And there's nothing they nor the Angeloi can do to change that. Not anymore."

Amaros glared at the broken body of Yondo Carpana, a look of disgust on his young human face. "He said those words to me, long ago, when he was young and arrogant and stupid. I remember him. And again the other night. Ha! Now look at him. Still arrogant and stupid, though not so young anymore. He soon will die in this cave, alone but for the scavengers of the desert. They shall feast on his worthless flesh."

Amaros pulled his dagger. "They like warm blood," he said. "They'll smell it and come to eat." He took one of Yondo's arms, the left one, the one not broken, and pulled the blade across the skin, nicking a vein. Blood came pouring out at once, running fast down Yondo's arm. With the aid of a couple of rocks, Amaros situated the arm in a raised position, so that the blood would flow slowly. The Old Kin then touched a finger in the blood and scrawled an ancient demon rune on Yondo's forehead. He matched it with a prayer, speaking his evil words in a whisper, and outside the wind howled, stirring the desert sand into a tempest.

"When you go to the Void, Voukolos," he whispered in Yondo's ear, a hint of devious merriment in his voice, "mine will greet you as an enemy. And if perchance you should happen to survive, you'll not be the same. You will be ... *obedient*. You'll know my voice and listen." He stood then, tucked his dagger in his belt, and walked off.

The war had started.

He had much work to do.

**Thirty-two:**

It had been only five days since she'd been home, but Lizzy already was wondering about when she could sneak off to see the soothsayer again. She had gotten an opening that morning, but couldn't bring herself to take it.

Gabby had sent her out to fish and hunt – Jonno hadn't caught or killed anything in four days and Gabby wanted fresh meat for dinner – but the idea of running off again so soon was simply too scandalous. For one thing, Gabby had pointed a stern finger at her and said, "Don't you even think about going back to that soothsayer's hut. You hear me, girl?"

Lizzy had said she would not dare, even though that was what she most wanted to do. It was the one thought always on her mind.

At least she was outside, hunting and fishing.

Five days of doing little but menial house chores had instilled in her a desire never to run her own home. The sweeping and cleaning; the beating of rugs and sheets; the endless food preparation; the cooking, the dishes, the mending and darning of clothes; bringing in water for baths and laundry. It was all terribly boring.

At least she was back doing what she loved to do.

Better still, the fish were biting. Two hours in and already she had five hooked and pailed. Spotter fish and blue-stripes of good size. They would serve well with Gabby's rice and beans.

A familiar rustling sound in the low brush caught her ear, and she set her trawl pole down and reached for her slingshot. She slid a rock in the cup, pulled back on the thick, rubber strap, and waited for the animal to show itself.

A moment later, a fat beyo came bumbling out of the weeds, its black-banded face a clear reminder of Baba. Lizzy had a clean shot, and from a distance of no more than twenty steps. But she couldn't bring herself to let fly the rock.

The beyo spotted her, hesitated a moment, then scampered away, receding in the high grass. Lizzy relaxed her aim on the slingshot and placed the rock back in her pocket.

Beyo wasn't all that tasty anyway, she told herself. She was convinced she would never eat it again. She hadn't been sleeping under her beyo blanket since returning home, either. That she had given to Dalla.

Out of the corner of her eye she saw her trawl pole twitch, and her idle thoughts on beyos were replaced by the prospect of a fresh catch. She carefully picked up the pole and waited for the end to bob again. When it did, she quickly jerked on it, setting the hook. There was some fighting on the other end of the line, but Lizzy held tight and patiently dragged the fish ashore.

It was the biggest catch yet: a fat spotter three hands in length. She pulled it up on the bank, gently stepped on its side, mindful not to crush it's tiny bones, and removed the hook. As it thrashed about, fighting for freedom, for life, she picked it up by the tail and put it in the bucket, which already was full. The sun wasn't even high yet and already she had six fish.

Instead of resetting the hook and bait, she set the pole down and took hold of her slingshot. She wasn't on good hunting ground, but usually small game could be found wandering near the creek, thirsty for refreshment. Squirrels, fieldhogs, and rabbits. You just had to be patient and quiet.

She stood perfectly still and let her eyes do the work.

Time slid by moment by moment, marked only by the wind and the slow rush of water. This was why Lizzy was so much better on the hunt than Jonno: Jonno had the patience of a hummingbird, whereas Lizzy could stand in one spot for rotes, tree-like.

Her patience eventually paid off. Three hares appeared on the far bank, about forty steps away. They were searching for white-tipped clovers, a delicacy in their world.

Lizzy loaded a rock in the cup and pulled back on the strap, taking it past her ear. She set her aim on the largest of the three and then waited, one eye closed, for the little critter to present her an angle.

The hares noticed her but didn't seem overly-concerned. She was so far away, and she was on the other side of the creek. Two of them stopped eating for a spell to watch her, but they lost interest quickly and returned to nibbling the grass.

While she waited for the perfect shot, Lizzy wondered what she may have done had Oreg kept a pet hare rather than a pet beyo. Would she have killed the fat beyo and let the hares live? It was an odd thought to have, she decided, so she put it out of her head. Meat was needed to survive, and she was being counted on to provide it.

Refocused, she set her mark and let go of the strap; only her fingers moved, and they but a dash. The twang and whistle of the shot bussed her ear and caught the attention of her prey. But it was already too late for the hare. The smooth, dense stone struck it square in the skull, and while it hopped on command of its nerves, it was dead before it flopped to the ground. The two smaller hares took off running on instinct and didn't stop until they were safe in the high grass.

Lizzy tucked the slingshot in her belt and started across the creek, agilely picking her way on the slick rocks. She found the hare, made sure it was dead with a nudge of her foot, then scooped it up by its hind legs and toted it back across the water.

Hare was her favorite food. Her ma made a great hare stew with potatoes, carrots, and corn.

Lizzy set the hare on a nearby rock, pulled out her slingshot again, loaded it, and waited.

That's when she noticed a wide bank of storm clouds rolling in from the southwest. These clouds were bulky and dark, and they were moving at a very fast pace, faster than Lizzy had ever seen clouds move before. They filled the sky and blotted out the sun, turning the world an ugly shade of gray.

Lizzy liked rain; she liked the feel of it, the smell of it, and how it made everything look clean. What she didn't care for were violent storms, and that's what seemed to be brewing on the horizon. A real nasty one by the looks of it.

She quickly gathered up her things and clambered over the bank; and when she started for home, she did so on a trot. She made it no more than half way when the sky opened up and began raining down on her.

Thunder cracked like mountains breaking apart, and lightning sparked across the slate gray sky, looking like great tree branches on fire.

One of the bolts struck a nearby oak, and the sound it made rang in Lizzy's head. The powerful vibration of the blast coursed under her feet, nearly causing her to lose balance. Then another bolt hit, striking the ground thirty steps to her left. This time she stumbled and fell. She dropped her trawl pole and spilled the bucket of fish; the dead hare fell from her hand and tumbled across the muddy ground. She gathered everything up as quickly as she could – not an easy task considering three of the fish were still alive – and started off again, running with fury.

The hard rain stung her face and soaked her hair and clothes, and the gusting wind pushed her skinny body this way and that way, nearly making her fall half a dozen times. She persevered, though, and soon made it to the field behind her house. Then she made it to her house, with thunder cracking all around her, with lightning carving up the sky and rain pelting her face, with the wind howling like so many demons.

Into the house she darted, a ragged, soaking, dirty mess awkwardly lugging a trawl pole, a bucket of squirming fish, and a dead rabbit streaked with mud and blood. Gabby saw her and, shaking her head in an incredulous way, said, "I swear, girl, every time you go out it's an adventure. Didn't you see the storm coming?"

"Not until it was too late," Lizzy replied. "It rushed in from the desert. Then she smiled her crooked little smile, lifted up her kill, and said, "Look, I have fish and a hare. We can make stew tonight."

Gabby sighed at her not-so-little little girl. "Go get cleaned up," she told her. "You're filthy."

Just then a crack of sound louder than thunder echoed in the Carpana house, and suddenly it was gusting and raining indoors.

Multiple twisters had touched down on Carpana land, uprooting several trees, badly damaging one side of their barn, and tearing part of the roof off the house.

It had been a violent storm, but also a fast-moving one. It had lasted less than half a rote, but that was enough time for it to seriously damage the Carpana homestead. The main room, the kitchen, the back room, and Dalla and Lizzy's room all had major leaks in the roof. Jonno's room, which faced the opposite direction, and Gabby and Yondo's room had suffered minimal damage.

The back room, which was their bath and storage room, would need completely rebuilt. The door was hanging off its hinges, part of the side wall had collapsed, and a large section of the roof was gone. The floor was covered with water, mud, dislodged stones, broken planks of wood, and frayed stalks of bark and thatch.

Outside, one corner of the barn was leaning inward, and the roof was badly slanted. The whole structure most likely would need reinforced. One of their fig trees had fallen; it lay on the ground like a dead soldier, its branches and leaves strewn about the yard like battlefield carrion. Their lone maple tree had suffered a similar fate; it lay twenty paces to the left, its massive trunk splintered like a twig.

Gabby assessed the damage and sighed.

Jonno looked around in astonishment. "This is unbelievable," he said.

Dalla, who had hidden under Jonno's bed when the storm had hit, couldn't keep tears from her big brown eyes as she looked over the destruction of her room. Her bed was soaked through and her reading books were sopping wet. The rather large hole in the roof gave her a view of the sky, which now was mostly blue.

"What are we going to do?" she asked Lizzy, her words pattering out between sobs. "All our stuff is ruined."

"Stuff is just stuff," Lizzy told her. "It can be fixed or replaced." Then she hugged her and kissed her on the forehead.

Gabby told Jonno to check on the animals in the barn, and she told Lizzy and Dalla to pick as many figs from the fallen tree as they could find. "Get them before they go bad, girls," she said to them. "We'll be eating figgy pie until the next full moon."

"What of the house?" Lizzy asked.

"For now, you and Dalla will sleep with me in my room. Jonno's room is fine enough for him. The barn and back room can wait until Yon comes home. The roof we'll patch up the best we can."

Lizzy and Dalla went out to the yard and began scooping up figs, while Jonno trudged up to the barn to check on the animals. All had escaped harm save one goat. A support beam along the roof, split in half by the storm, had fallen on it, breaking its back.

Jonno hurried back to the house to tell Gabby.

"Kill it," she told him brusquely.

"Kill it? Me?"

"What else would you have me do with a wounded goat?"

Jonno took his sharpest knife and went back to the barn.

"Whatcha doing?" Dalla asked him as he walked by.

"One of the goats is hurt. Ma said to kill it."

Dalla looked crestfallen. The Carpana's kept their animals for milk and eggs, not meat. Because so, they had become like family pets. The goats weren't exactly friendly, but Dalla liked to pet and feed them. Especially the one she had named Dara.

"It's not Dara, is it?" she called out to her brother.

"It is," Jonno replied. He then held up the knife and mocked cutting the goat's throat, a devious, hateful smirk on his face.

Dalla began to cry. "I won't eat her," she wailed as Lizzy once again consoled her. "I won't. Not Dara. I won't."

"Nor I," said Lizzy.

"I will," Jonno called out. "With some potatoes and beets. Mmmm! She'll be tasty, I bet."

"Jonno!" Lizzy shouted at him. "Stop it!"

He laughed and went on his way.

In the barn, the injured goat was bleating incessantly and struggling to get to its feet. Its back was clearly broken, as were its hind legs; jagged little shards of bone could be seen sticking out through the hide and fur. The rather gruesome sight made Jonno feel sick.

The goat continued to bleat in pain, sending out a terrible sound that haunted Jonno's head and added to the sickness in his stomach. In its black, swollen, watery eyes was a look of total incomprehension, of blank animal stupidity and fear. It couldn't understand what had happened to it and why it couldn't get up.

Jonno crouched over the animal, showed it the knife, and said, "Sorry ol' boy, but I gotta put you down."

He grabbed the goat's head with a rough hand, pressed the blade of the knife to the goat's throat, and violently pulled it across. Blood spurted, and the goat cried in pain. Its front legs kicked spasmodically, its head and body juddered. Then it stopped moving, stopped making terrible sounds. Its eyes glassed over, rolling to dead.

Jonno looked down at the knife, and at his hands. The goat's blood was shiny red and thick, and the rich, metallic smell of it stung his nose.

Killing both excited him and caused him to be ill. He liked the primal thought of it, the sense of power it elicited, but not the practice.

He let the animal bleed out, then dragged it out of its pen.

The next part, the skinning and butchering part, he really didn't care for at all. It was hard, messy work, and the smell stayed with you for days, no matter how much you washed. He decided to try to get Lizzy to do it instead. He went down to the house, told Gabby that he really should start working on the roof, that the roof should be priority one, and that Dalla could pick figs by herself and Lizzy could skin the goat.

But Gabby was no fool. She knew exactly what her boy was trying to do, and she told him the roof would hold for now.

"Butcher the animal while it's fresh," she said to him. "That's man's work there. You want to go on treks in the desert, you want to be a Herder like your father, then you need to do what he would do. Don't make me tell him otherwise."

Rebuffed, Jonno skulked away. On his walk back to the barn he shouted to Dalla, "Gotta skin her now. Slice her up nice and good. Not going to be pretty for poor ol' Dara."

"Shut your mouth," Lizzy yelled at him. "Can't you see she's upset."

"It's just a stupid goat," Jonno yelled back.

Dalla cried out, "She's not just a goat! She's my friend."

Jonno walked on, laughing, and Lizzy hugged her sister. "It'll be okay," she told her. "Death is a part of life for us all. Even Dara. One day, a long time from now, perhaps you'll see her again."

Those were hardly words of sympathy to a seven-year-old, but Dalla never wanted to disappoint her big sister. "I know," she said bravely, and wiped away her tears. "But I liked her. She was the nice one."

"I know," said Lizzy. "I know." She broke their embrace, gave her little sister a thin but loving smile, and said, "Come now, let's get back to work. Lots of figs to pick. They'll be coming out of our ears soon."

Dalla smiled valiantly and got back to work.


Dalla and Lizzy had collected eight buckets of figs, and while Dalla and Gabby cleaned and boiled those figs, readying them for pies and jam, Lizzy and Jonno cut limbs and branches from the fallen trees so they could patch the roof. When they had enough, Lizzy climbed onto the roof and Jonno handed them up to her.

There were holes and gaps here and there, but it really wasn't as bad as they had originally thought. Lizzy covered the holes and tied the limbs in place with rope, as Yondo had taught her to do just last year, after a severe thunderstorm had fractured the roof over the main room. She bound the branches and limbs together with creek vine, and secured them to the beams on the roof.

It was tedious, meticulous, painstaking work, but they got the kitchen and half of Lizzy and Dalla's room finished by the time dinner was ready. Lizzy had blisters and cuts all over her hands, her legs ached from walking back and forth on the slanted roof, and she smelled like one of their goats. Twigs and dead leaves festooned her wild brown hair; dirt and sweat shrouded her face.

After fixing the last piece of thatch in place, she stood tall and surveyed the countryside, taking in huge swatches of pristine Vernon scenery. She had always liked standing on the roof of the house; it made her feel like she was a queen and all she beheld was hers. She liked standing on the roof of the barn even better; it was at least twice as high, which gave her eyes that much more room to roam.

She looked at the clouds overhead, now thin and powdery white. The darkening sky behind them had turned a magnificent shade of purple, making them stand out even more. Lizzy looked for the first star of the night, but it had yet to wake. Everything was so serene, so beautiful; it was hard to believe that just a few short rotes ago a violent storm had raged through Vernon, toppling trees and damaging homes.

Lizzy turned toward the barn to survey the damage there and saw Dara grazing in the pen. They owned nine goats, and one of them had died in the storm. Jonno had said it was Dara that had died, but Dara was the only goat they owned with a black face and a black stripe down its back. Lizzy pointed at it and said, "Is that Dara?" She walked to the edge of the roof, glared down at Jonno, and repeated the question.

A grin slid across the boy's face. "Is it?" he said teasingly.

Anger fumed up inside Lizzy. "Jonno Carpana!" she hollered. "Damn you! You know that it is. You made Dalla cry!"

Feigning innocence, Jonno said, "What?" and then quickly yanked the ladder away from the roof so that Lizzy had no easy way down.

"See you inside for dinner, gypsy girl," he told her, laughing.

"Jonno! Get over here and put the ladder back! I mean it! Jonno!"

"What?" he called back from around the corner of the house. "I can't hear you. What did you say, gypsy girl?"

"Jonno!" Lizzy yelled. "Jonno!"

He was gone, and Lizzy was stuck on the roof.

She stepped to the edge and carefully leaned over for a look; perhaps ten podes high and nothing but ground to break her fall. Sure, it was soft ground because of all the rain, but it was ground nonetheless. She thought about jumping, but worried she might turn an ankle or break a leg.

"Jonno!" she hollered again, her temper rising. "Jonno!" Not only had he unnecessarily upset Dalla, he had stranded her on the roof, and after she had done most of the work. When she saw him she was going to …

That's when she remembered the roof over the back room still had a large section missing. She carefully made her way up the slope, watching every step she took, testing each footfall before she applied full weight. There could be weak spots, and she didn't want to fall through.

She noticed a couple of secure planks that ran from the top of the roof to the base of it and followed them down. Moving slowly but smoothly, with uncanny footwork and balance, she reached the edge in no time at all. It was lower here, and Lizzy felt confident she could drop down to the floor without injury. First, she straddled one of the planks; then she set her grip on the other one and agilely swung down to the ground, landing flawlessly. Next, she snuck over to the door to have a listen. She heard Jonno talking, then she heard her mother's voice. They were close by.

Lizzy opened the door a crack and hazarded a peek. Jonno was standing in the entranceway to the kitchen, with his back to her. Gabby apparently was in the kitchen. Lizzy wasted not a moment. She slid cat-like through the door, crept up on her brother from behind, and planted a kick against the back of his right knee, buckling it and sending him down.

Jonno cried out in surprise and pain.

"That was for leaving me on the roof," Lizzy shouted. Then she clapped her hands over his ears, hard, and kicked him in the back.

His world spun off keel and all sense of equilibrium left him. The next thing he knew his face was slapping off the floor.

"Lizzy!" Gabby shrieked.

"And that was for making Dalla cry!" Lizzy said.

"Elizabeth Layne Carpana!" Gabby yelled. "What are you doing?!"

Jonno was dazed, yet he managed to roll over and climb to his feet. "What do you think you're doing?" he said, blood trickling from his left nostril. "You kicked me! Twice!"

"He made Dalla cry by telling her that Dara was the goat that had died when he knew it wasn't true," Lizzy told her mother in a voice that trembled with anger. "Then he pulled the ladder away and left me stranded on the roof."

Gabby turned on her boy with an accusatory look. "Jonno?" she said.

"So I played a joke on her," he said, his voice a bit shrill. "Who cares?"

"You left me up there. After I did all the work. And you lied and told Dalla that her favorite goat was dead."

"Like I know which goat is her favorite," Jonno shouted back. "They're all the same. They're stupid goats."

"You made her cry."

Jonno wiped his nose with the back of his hand and saw a streak of blood. "She bloodied my nose," he said, appalled. "She snuck up behind me, kicked me, and bloodied my nose!"

"You left me on the roof!"

"I don't care!" Gabby shouted from between them, her voice as loud as any thunderclap. She looked at her daughter, and pointed a stern finger at her. "We don't hit each other in this house. Ever. Not for anything. You hear me? We're a family, and families don't use violence."

"It's because she's not blood," Jonno said, further provoking Lizzy. "She's a no-good gypsy bitch and it makes her jealous."

"Jonno!" Gabby shouted. "That's enough from you. Apologize. Now!"

"Me? For what?"

"For stranding her on the roof. And for calling her names."

"She attacked me from behind. I'm bleeding."

"And she will apologize and be punished for that." Gabby looked at Lizzy again. "We do not hit each other," she reiterated. "You understand me, girl? Ever! Say it!"

Lizzy nodded sheepishly and told Jonno that she was sorry.

"Jonno?" Gabby said, waiting for him to do the same.

"I don't see why I should have to apologize," Jonno said, pouting. "It was only a joke. Can't anyone take a joke."

"Apologize, or you can be punished, too."

"This is so unfair!" he griped with such pride and anguish. "I'm sorry, okay? I'm so sorry for playing a stupid joke." Then he turned serious and pointed a threatening finger at his little sister. "And don't think I'm not going to get you back for suckering me like that."

"You won't do anything of the sort," Gabby said to him. "You hear me, boy?! And if I ever hear you call her that name again, you'll be sleeping in the barn with the goats. You'll get to know them all real well." She paused, but only briefly. "Madness!" she cried out, her frustration evident. "Yondo goes on a trek and my kids go mad. And the two oldest." She focused on Lizzy. "You, lying and running off to see the soothsayer. Nearly dying on the way." Then to Jonno: "And you, playing jokes and taunting your little sisters. Both of you fighting like wild animals. Yondo's gone and you think there's no order. Well, I can assure you he'll be made aware of everything you've done. *Everything!* And then we'll see how you act. I'll be glad to see it, too, because you sure don't listen to me."

"I'm sorry, ma," Lizzy said sincerely. "Honest."

"Yeah," said Jonno, "me, too."

They had seen their mother angry before, plenty of times, though never quite like this. Her face was swollen and red with fury, and there was a wet, wild look in her eyes that frightened them.

They both apologized again.

"Sorry or not, sorry you'll be," she told them. "That's my word." She

316

shifted her look from one to the other and said, "Dinner shortly. Go get cleaned up, and try not to kill each other doing it. Mind me, or next time I'll break out the tanning stick. I don't strike near as hard as your father, but I'll keep at it until my arm falls off if I must!"

They nodded together, and did as told.

That evening, dinner at the Carpana homestead was eaten in near total silence, and only Dalla got figgy pie for desert.

**Thirty-three:**

Greenhorn was a quaint village on the banks of one of Potami's many tributaries. It had a bustling market square and dozens of legitimate businesses representing near every guild in Hinterland. That made it a regular stop for travelers and itinerants alike, both by water and land.

Nearly six thousand people called Greenhorn home, making it the third largest settlement in all of Boreal, behind Cambria to the south and Kittan to the south and east. It was the northernmost populated village in Boreal, and a regular outpost for all the clans that lived in the vast and undeveloped lands farther north, lands that skirted the Dark Forest and whatever lay beyond. Lands that had become far more dangerous lately.

Because so, more and more folk were moving south to Greenhorn. Some only stopped there on their way farther south, to Cambria, Kittan, Mun, and on down, some going as far as Vernon.

Peck and Kelt had to stop at Greenhorn to take care of a few matters. They were travelers on their way elsewhere, but first Peck had a number of unpleasant tasks to complete.

They arrived late in the morning and first went to Peck's humble dwelling. It was odd for him to walk into his family home knowing that he no longer had a family of any kind. Signs of his mother and sisters had faded over the years, but hints of his father remained. Loman's favorite pipe – he never took his favorite one on a hunt for fear he'd lose it – sat on the mantle; his work boots, gloves, and hoods, along with Peck's, lay in the cedar box by the door. The blood-red bottle in which he kept his best wine stood on the table in the kitchen; it had been a gift from his father before him, and any time there had been a family gathering or an important event, it had been filled and passed around ceremonially.

Yes, his father was everywhere. And nowhere.

"Excuse me. I need to get a few things," Peck said, and left Kelt in the main room by himself. He reappeared a short time later with a full pack of gear, including fresh clothes, boots, and weapons.

"Wait," he said suddenly, and disappeared again.

This time he went to his father's room, and he searched his father's secret hiding places for copper, silver, gold, and trinkets of value. He took all the chinks and coins he found, and also a silver band, a gold band, and his mother's gold ring. Then he went to his sisters' long-abandoned room and did the same, searching for mementos to remember them by. Not that he needed such things to remember them; he would never forget his family, no matter how many years went by. After what had happened to them, each of them, he doubted whether he *could* forget them, which both comforted and pained him. As for any mementos, he wanted them, and wanted no one else to have them.

He took two of his sister Alise's charcoal drawings, one of them a beautiful portrait of the entire family (Alise had been an amazing artist for someone so young), and a couple of his sister Tama's marbles. She had been buried with her lucky coin or he would have taken that, too.

Then he gave the room one last look.

He knew that he would never return. Nor did he want to.

Going back to the main room, he picked up his pack and secured the rest of his belongings inside. Lastly, he took his father's favorite pipe and the blood-red bottle, which was half full of wine. The pipe he stuffed in his pocket. The bottle he gave to Kelt. "Can you fit it?" he asked him. "I fear I cannot, and I don't want to break it."

Kelt carefully packed the bottle in his bag. "Anything else?" he asked.

Peck took a long look around the old homestead, permitting himself a moment of sentimentality. Then he shook his head. "No."

"If you forget something, we can come back," the Monk told him.

"I'm never coming back here," Peck said in a sullen voice. And he turned his back and walked out of the only home he had ever known.

Peck had a smattering of cousins, aunts, and uncles who lived on the other side of Greenhorn's large and thriving market square. He and the Monk walked through town together, receiving many looks and whispers as they went. A couple people that Peck knew by name called out to him, saying, "Hello," and, "Welcome back," and, "How was the hunt?" One man in particular, a ratty old fellow by the name of Patsy, stopped Peck and Kelt and asked the boy where Loman and Titus were.

"Not sure," Peck said to him.

"And how was the hunt? When'd you get back?"

"Today. And not good."

"Who is this with you?" Patsy asked, giving Kelt a quick glance. "A Monk? Surely, by the robes."

"I am Kelt of Lockhead," Kelt said. "You are well met, sir."

Ol' Patsy flashed a gap-toothed grin and said, "Where'd you find a

Monk, boy? And how? They're known ghosts."

"We're flesh and blood," Kelt replied. "I assure you."

Patsy gave the Monk a suspicious look, and turned back to the boy.

"I have to go, Patsy," Peck said to him quickly. He wasn't rude in any manner, though his voice lacked friendliness. And without another word, he stepped around the old man and went on his way.

Kelt gave Patsy a kind nod and followed after the Peck.

The old man called out, "I'll be sure to see you and your pa later, boy. Tell him I'll be by. Want to see the kill. Cupboard needs stocked for the snows to come, and he owes me. Surely he does."

The Monk walked in silence behind Peck, keeping the boy's fast pace. The only sound between them was the sound of their steps and the occasional clunk or rattle from somewhere inside their packs. Once they reached the short grass on the far end of town, the sound of their steps disappeared, leaving them in almost total silence.

The first house they visited belonged to Peck's favorite aunt, Maria. She was Peck's mother's eldest sister, and she had not aged well. A hard life and a hard husband had left her looking well beyond her years, and her life was about to get even harder. One of the few relatives she could count on for help, Loman, was dead. Titus, too.

Peck told her the news in full detail with a stone face and a soft voice. Maria wept. Her hands trembled.

Her husband, Hovan, wasn't home at the time, but Peck's cousins, Maya and Henny, were present, and Maria called them in and told them the tragic news. They cried, too, and their shrill, womanly sobs nearly caused Peck to scream in anger.

Maria said, "You'll stay with us, dear boy. We could use another man around the house, and you shouldn't be alone."

"No. I'm going with Kelt," Peck told her.

"Going where?" Maria asked, shocked that her hospitality had been summarily denied.

"Kelt has offered to take me to Lockhead."

"But what of us? What of your family?"

Peck had always been thought of as an odd bird, an outsider, yet he never failed to mind his manners. He could have told his aunt that they really weren't that close, and that he had no desire to live in a home with a man like Hovan, who was a crass, angry drunk and a worthless worker. If anyone should have been killed and eaten by a demon and a flesh-eater it should have been him, not good men like Titus and Loman. But the world wasn't fair, and never would be.

What he said was, "I can't stay here. I fear I'm cursed."

Maria turned a glaring eye on the Monk. "Is that why he's with you, sir?" she said to him snappishly. "He's only a boy! He's not cursed. It's a hard world and bad things happen."

"Aye," said Kelt. "They do."

"You don't have to leave," Maria said, tears in her eyes. "I'm your aunt. We're kin. We can take care of you."

Peck glanced at his cousins, two prim, ugly young girls with greasy black hair and mouse-like eyes. Eventually they would probably want him to marry one of them. Cousins wedding was a routine practice in Boreal. Maria and Hovan were second cousins, and some in the family had wanted Titus to marry a cousin from up north.

"No. I have to go," he said again. "There are too many bad memories here. I can't bear it."

"At least wait until Hovan returns. He'll want to see you off."

"He won't care. You can tell him."

"What about a funeral?"

Peck shook his head gravely. "What funeral? There are no bodies to bury or burn."

"Ceremony," Maria told him. "Such things matter."

"We can share a prayer, ma'am, if you like," Kelt offered.

The Monk led them in a prayer, a heartfelt benediction, and all but him wept. Maria and her girls wept, and Peck wept, too, overcome by emotion. Then he said goodbye.

They wanted to feed him, and they begged him to stay the night and leave in the morning, but Peck refused. He still had three more houses to visit, three more somber conversations and tear-filled goodbyes to endure.

He left his Aunt Maria's home after being accosted with hugs and kisses. He left with tear-soaked shoulders and wet cheeks. He promised her that he would return one day, that he would come back to see them after enough time had passed, but he had no intention of ever living up to that promise. He never wanted to return to Greenhorn again, for any reason.

"On to my Aunt Alana," he said as they walked away.

The Monk followed him.

Aunt Alana, who was Loman and Titus's only sister, took the news harder than Maria had. She wailed and sobbed and cried out, "Why?! Why?!"

Her boy and her husband barely flinched.

"A flesh-eater?" she asked the Monk through her tears.

"Aye. Sarkofagos. Twelve-feet tall. It killed my partner, too."

"Where?" Peck's Uncle Jonny wanted to know. "How close by?"

"We were two days from being back," Peck told him. "Walking the barren lands south of the Dark Forest."

Jonny gave the Monk a wary look. "So, flesh-eaters are real?" he said to him. "I thought they were myths, like the Angeloi. I've never seen one. Never known anyone who has."

The Monk decided to let the Angeloi comment pass. Instead, he said, "I've only seen a few myself. But I can assure you they're not myths. They're real, and venturing farther south every year."

"Are we in danger?"

"They don't like crowds, but will go where there is food. I'd keep an eye out. Watch for any livestock missing."

Jonny turned his eyes to Peck. "What of the hunt?" he asked him. "We needed a big one. We're in for a long winter."

"Lost," Peck replied.

Jonny and his boy were hunters, too, and sometimes they went out with Loman, Titus, and Peck. They rarely went on the long hunts, though, only the short ones. "So," Jonny said, "wasted time and wasted meat." He shook his head disgruntledly.

"Jonny!" Alana snapped. "A little respect. My brothers are dead."

He looked at her, then at Peck. "Sorry, boy," he said, though he said it coldly. "Death finds us all eventually."

Peck told them that he was leaving with the Monk, and the Monk said that the boy had potential to join the Order.

"We need good young men," Kelt told them. "And Peck is willing."

Alana said the same as Maria had before her and Aunt Carla would after her: that Peck, only fourteen years of age, should stay in Greenhorn with his kin; that running off to join the Order of Monks was a foolish idea.

But Peck told them, told them all, that he couldn't stand to be in Greenhorn anymore, that the memories of what had happened to his family were too much to bear.

"The house is haunted by them," he said. "I see them everywhere."

He gave the key to the house to Alana and told her that she had first choice, seeing that she was the closest remaining kin of Loman. Also, and perhaps more importantly, Peck trusted her more than any other kin he had left. He believed she would be fair and just when it came time to split the property.

"Go with Aunt Maria and Aunt Carla," he told her. "Pick through things and divvy them equally. But the house and land is yours, should you want it. Do with it what you feel fair. The same holds for Titus's dwelling, though I have no key for that."

"I do," she said. "It will be done."

"Take his woman with you. They weren't married, and she doesn't deserve his things, but she may have things of her own there."

Alana nodded, and promised she would.

They left then, and soon after had near the same conversation with Peck's Aunt Carla and Uncle Des. They had five kids, three boys and two girls, but only Aunt Carla shed a tear. The others barely batted an eye. They didn't know Loman and Titus very well, so their deaths made little difference to them.

Uncle Des was not an emotional man, but he was a good man. He was the only one in the family who agreed that Peck should leave Greenhorn.

"The things that have happened to the boy here," he told his wife. "So much tragedy. How could he ever sleep in that house?"

"He can sleep here," Aunt Carla replied automatically.

"He's nearly a man and has only second kin." Des then turned to Peck and said, "If the Order wants you, go."

Peck nodded, while his Aunt Carla wept.

"Have you enough money and things?" Des asked him.

"He won't need much," replied Kelt. "He will have food and shelter."

"That'll do. For a boy."

Aunt Carla asked about a funeral, too, and Peck told her the same thing he had told Maria: no bodies, no funeral. Kelt then made the same offer of prayer, which both Carla and Des were pleased to accept.

They all prayed together, the whole family, and Carla wept quietly.

This time Peck held back his tears, and when he left, it was with clear eyes and a strong jaw.

"One more stop," he said. "My Uncle Titus's woman needs to know.

She was near enough his wife."

They walked on in silence, and Kelt found himself thinking that the Order would be lucky to claim someone like Peck. The boy handled his business like a man, with respect and authority, with a thought to all involved. He was kind, patient, considerate, and he looked you in the eye when he had something to say, good or bad. Beyond that, he had an innate gift for the supernatural; he not only could see the spirits of animals, apparently he could converse with them.

The Monk had never met anyone quite like him.

If he passed the trials, he could become one of the greatest among them. No, not *one* of the greatest. *The* Greatest. The one who had been written about in To Theiko Kylindro, the ancient prophecies purported to be from the Angeloi themselves.

But if he failed ...

Peck had given his account and his word, explaining to everyone he met what had happened ... to a point. As Kelt had instructed him, he left out the part about the demon-girl and the Dark Forest.

"Some secrets are good for the soul," Kelt had told him.

He also had explained his wishes:

Alana was to stake claim to the lands and homes, while the other relatives would be allowed to pick through the things that had belonged to their first-of-kin. There wasn't much left, so far as Peck knew. His aunts on his ma's side had taken a lot of things after the funeral for Hilde and the girls, and he had taken most of the items of value that had belonged to his father. Any money that Loman had at the house was now in Peck's pack, along with the family's most treasurable keepsakes. As for any money at Titus's home? That, Peck had told Alana, should be divvied up equally.

He trusted Alana to keep it fair more than the others, and when he left his uncle's sweetheart, a buxom widow by the name Kerra, he was certain that he had wrapped up all his affairs in the sleepy hamlet of Greenhorn. He was ready to move on, and ready to leave the past behind.

His uncle Hovan, a short, squat, disheveled man with a poor beard and stringy brown hair, had different ideas. He met Peck and Kelt on the path outside Kerra's place, and he wasn't alone. Two of Peck's dimwitted cousins, Colt and Clive, the eldest boys of Carla and Des stood with him, along with two grown men that Peck didn't recognize.

Hovan's look and stance made it known that this was not going to be a pleasant encounter; his look and stance also made it known that he had consumed quite a bit of drink.

"Well, well, well," he began, a slight whisky-slur to his voice, "whadda we got here? Off again, boy? So soon?"

"Uncle Hovan," Peck replied peaceably. Then, minding his manners, he made introductions. "This is Kelt. He's of the Order of Monks. Kelt, this is my Uncle Hovan, my Aunt Maria's husband. You met Colt and Clive already. The other two I don't know."

Kelt extended a hand to Hovan and said, "Well met."

Hovan looked at the hand like he'd never been offered one before, and then, reluctantly, he shook it, making sure his grip was strong. "So, you're a Monk?" he said. "In the flesh?" He sounded leery, but also intrigued.

"Sorry we missed you earlier," Kelt said. "Your wife is a good woman. She makes good bread and tea."

"So you say." Hovan turned his attention back to Peck. "We have a problem, boy," he said to him.

"How so, Uncle?"

"In terms of property. Ain't fair to give all to one. We got as much right as Alana and her kin."

"You have no right at all," Peck told him bluntly. "Neither Loman nor Titus was kin of yours."

"Kin through marriage is kin," Hovan said. "Always has been."

"Kin, sure, but not blood. Alana is blood. She gets first say."

"And who are you to say who gets first say?" Hovan replied.

"I am the last of my family. That's law."

"Aye. But you're only a boy. And in the case of a boy not yet a man, his time and care is given to the eldest living relative, which is your Aunt Maria, not Alana. Meaning you're now my ward, and what's yours is mine until you're of a proper age. *That's* law."

"I'm nobody's ward," Peck said brashly, offended by the idea that this foul, worthless drunkard was attempting to horn in on his family home and land using half-wit logic. "Certainly not yours."

"Got Fran Rogers here who says different."

A lanky man of middle age with a high forehead and dark bags under his eyes stepped forward. The brass bar on the shoulder of his shirt signified that he was an officer of the law.

"Afraid your uncle's right, son," Fran Rogers said. "As a boy, you need be remanded to the custody of your oldest living relative."

"He needs to be remanded to no one," said Kelt, stepping in on Peck's behalf. "He's a boy by age, sure, but law states that if he's old enough to live on his own, he can. And if old enough for that, then he can make decisions concerning property."

Fran gave the Monk a vacant look. "Not quite sure about that, friend. He looks pretty young to me."

"Old enough and grown enough to be recruited as a Monk. I'm taking him to Lockhead for training."

Hovan laughed, and Peck's good-for-nothing cousins chimed in, sniggering like a couple of dimwitted barneys. "*Him*? A *Monk*? That's a fine joke," Hovan said.

"You insult me?" Kelt said at once. His posture and his jaw stiffened, and all took notice.

"No, sir," said Fran Rogers respectfully. "We're not saying that. But while here in Greenhorn, you'd be wise to heed this." He pointed to the brass bar on his shirt. "Monk or not, the law is the law."

"What of your pa and your uncle?" Hovan said, eyeballing his nephew. "How can we be sure they're even dead? We have your word only, and you could be lying to cover your hide."

"Cover my hide for what?" Peck said.

Hovan gave the boy a drunken look. "Who knows? Could be anything."

"You have *my* word," Kelt said in curt and direct way. "Does the word of a Monk carry no weight in Greenhorn?"

"We only want what is right," said Fran Rogers.

"And what is right is what this young man has already done. To undo it would be a perversion of justice."

Hovan turned his whisky-skewed stare on Kelt and said, "This is a matter for family, which you are not."

"I'm leaving town," Peck said. "The only kin left from my side is Alana, and she shall have her say on goods and property."

"We may need to keep you here until we can verify your claims that your pa and uncle are dead," said Fran.

"They're dead!" Peck thundered back, and the volume of his voice caught them all by surprise. "They were killed by a giant, twelve-feet-tall and crazed. A flesh-eater. And it ate them, I'm sure. So how do you wish to verify that? Tell me! How?"

Hovan took a wobbly step back.

Fran Rogers said, "We want no trouble, son. Just what's right. You can stay in town for a few days until it's settled. That's not going to ruin you. And we can get things straightened away. Properly."

"And you stay with us," said Hovan. "Because it's right."

"If I'm staying, I'm staying in my own house," Peck declared.

"You're still a boy. You need to be with adults."

"What am I?" said Kelt. "You want him to stay here, fine, we'll stay here. Him and I, together, in his home."

"You're not kin!" Hovan blared, drunk-spit flying out with his words.

"Why do I need to be kin to stay in his home?" replied Kelt calmly.

"Well," said Fran Rogers, trying hard to be the voice of reason, and also authority, "until we can verify exactly who you are, sir, I think it might be best if the boy stayed with family. No offense."

"No! I'm leaving," Peck said. "I'm not staying here another day. And I've already made the ..." He stopped suddenly when he felt Kelt's hand squeeze his shoulder. It was a tacit sign that the Monk wanted him to be silent, and Peck obeyed.

Kelt took over then. "I know what this is," he said, his steely gaze shifting betwixt Hovan, Fran, and the rather large man in back that had yet to speak a word. He was well-armed, though, and obviously there to fight, should a fight break out. "It's a showdown. You want the land, the houses, and what's in them."

"We want only what's fair," said Hovan in a voice meant to convey great offense. "Nothing more."

"What's fair is what Peck has already decided, and you should abide by it if you have any honor."

"With all due respect ..."

That was as far as Fran Rogers got before he was interrupted.

Deepening the tone of his voice and shooting the lawman a grave look, Kelt said, "I wasn't yet finished, friend. With all due respect." He then picked back up where he'd been cut off. "I know what is fair, for I have seen both sides of justice across all of Hinterland. Believe me. The law is the law and needs to be respected, but justice is above the law, for the law was made to serve justice. And what this young man has decided is not only lawful, it is just. Now, if you don't abide his noble wishes, if you choose instead to be unjust, I will have no choice but to strike Greenhorn from our map. No more assistance will you get from The Order of Monks, and dark times are coming."

"That a threat?" said Hovan, again spitting his words. His breath stunk of onions and cheap rye.

"No more of one than you bringing full weapons to a talk." The Monk locked eyes with the big man in back. "And if you think you're fast enough to pull that crossbow and put a bolt in me before I can draw a blade and split your skull, you try it. But I would advise otherwise."

The big man looked down at his feet

Fran Rogers took a full step back.

"Now," said the Monk in a full and commanding voice, "if you want young Peck to stay in Greenhorn while the matters of his and his uncle's estates are resolved, that can be arranged. But it'll be up to him to decide who gets what, and there'll be no question of it. Or you can go by the word he put down already, which is fair and just. What say you?"

No one wanted to stand against a Monk, but property was property, and Loman had one of the finest and largest plots of land in Greenhorn. And there was no telling what sort of money and valuables lay hidden in Titus's dwelling. He had been a life-long bachelor, which meant all his money had gone to him and him alone. His plot was large, too, and had a fertile stream on it.

Hovan cleared his throat and made an offer. "Your home and land are yours," he said to Peck. "You may do as you please with them. But Titus's home is not yours to give. Word is you didn't even have a key for it."

"No. But Alana has one. She is his sister. She has more of a claim than I by law. More of a claim than anyone. That house, and all its land and property, is rightfully hers."

Fran Rogers conceded with a nod. Then he said, "Perhaps."

Hovan, who was a bit too drunk to have a convincing poker face, cringed at the decision. He decided then and there that he would not be pushed aside.

"Alack! Now!" he cried out, and the big man in back reached for his crossbow.

"Whoa! Whoa! Whoa!" shouted Fran Rogers, hopelessly attempting to intervene on behalf of peace. He was there because Hovan had promised him a small payoff if things went Hovan's way, and after a few cold ales at Darby's Public House that had sounded like a pretty good deal. But he was not a violent man, and despite the odds and the brass bar on his shoulder, he did not want to cross a Monk.

But Hovan, fired by greed and the whisky in his blood, charged at Peck. Colt and Clive went after the boy, too, while Alack, whose crossbow was already loaded, raised his weapon and aimed it at the Monk, who was standing right in front of him, no more than seven steps away. Fran Rogers was waving his hands in the air and calling desperately for peace, but no one seemed to be listening.

Alack pulled the trigger and the bolt flew from the chamber.

The Monk moved, almost imperceptibly, and the bolt whizzed by him, disappearing into the night. Alack thought about trying to load and fire another bolt, but instead pulled his short-blade and readied for battle. He swung and missed, and a right hand exploded on his jaw, putting a violent spin on the world and knocking him to the ground.

Hovan grabbed Peck by the shoulders, but Peck swung away from him, and the old drunkard stumbled and fell to his knees. Clive tackled Peck, and Colt jumped on him when he was down, yet somehow Peck managed to squirm away from them. He got to his feet, pulled his short-blade, and readied for a fight.

Colt pulled his blade.

Clive drew his daggers.

From behind, with great ferocity and speed, Kelt took Clive's head in one hand, Colt's in the other, and brought them together. The sound was terrible to hear, the result near as dreadful to watch. The two young men went limp and slumped to the ground.

Hovan was up again, and he clumsily drew his sword. "I don't care who you are!" he shouted at Kelt. "I'm not afraid of you!"

"By the law! Stop! Now!"

That command had come from Fran Rogers, who held a knife in a one hand and a mini-crossbow in the other. He had the crossbow pointed at the Monk, but the fear in his eyes betrayed him. He didn't want to use the crossbow any more than he wanted something heavy to fall on his foot. What if he missed, like Alack had?

"That's enough," he added, trying to sound imposing. He missed the mark, but intrepidly went on. "This stops now! Right now! Or so help me the clink will be full tonight."

Kelt pointed to Alack, who had yet to regain consciousness. "He tried to kill me. You saw it. He fired a bolt at me unprovoked."

"I don't need this going any further," Fran said. "I'm the law in this here town since the sheriff is down with the runs and I say it's enough."

"They're trying to rip me off," Hovan cried out. "I told you so."

Fran Rogers recently had had a change of heart. It had started about the time the Monk had knocked out Alack with one right hand. No one had ever bested Alack before.

Earlier, when Hovan had first come to him, ranting about being ripped off, stamping his feet and declaring that there likely was a small treasure to be had at Loman's and Titus's homes, Fran had thought that a play for it might be worth a shot. And Hovan had sworn that if there was trouble, he and Alack could handle it.

Standing there, shakily holding a crossbow on a Monk, Fran Rogers cursed himself for having believed such nonsense from the likes of Hovan Cartron. He blamed the booze in his head.

"You came looking for trouble from a boy," Kelt said, addressing Fran directly. "A boy who just lost his pa and uncle to unspeakable violence. A boy who only survived because I happened to find him. A boy who already lost his ma and sisters to violence. Where is your compassion?"

"I know, I know," said Fran, bending some, about to break.

Hovan groaned exasperatedly and threw his hands in the air. "Franny," he said. "We had an accord. We shook on it."

"I don't want any trouble," Peck said.

"Fran, this is up to you," said Kelt. "But I don't care for weapons drawn on me. I'm not a violent man, but violence is what I do best."

Fran didn't have to weigh that thought very long. There were three bodies on the ground because of the Monk, and he had accomplished that in the span of six, maybe seven beats of time.

The knife went back in its sheath and the mini-crossbow fell to Fran's side. "Sorry for the trouble," he said. "We only want what's fair. It's a shame things got out of hand so fast."

"By the law of Boreal what is fair?" Kelt asked.

Fran Rogers was silent. He seemed to be thinking.

The Monk took that to mean that Fran wasn't too sure about the law despite the brass bar on his shoulder and so he went on. "Oldest living first kin of the deceased decides matters of property," he said. "That's the way not just in Boreal, but across all of Hinterland. And by any account that would be either Peck, or Peck's Aunt Alana."

The deputy nodded half-heartedly.

The Monk turned to Hovan next. "You learned that you lost family today, sir, so I can understand your high emotions. You are forgiven."

Beneath the surface, Hovan Cartron was stark raving mad, so much so that his normally pink face went full crimson. He made no comment, though, and refused hold the Monk's stare.

"I'm counting on you to make this right," Kelt told Fran Rogers. "We're leaving, Peck and I, but his wants should be adhered. I or one of my brothers will check to see how things were handled here. Tragedy must be met by honor and respect."

"Aye," said Fran. "Agreed."

Kelt offered his hand to the lawman. "Thank you," he said to him.

Fran shook his hand. "You're welcome, sir."

It was over then, for the most part. There was some cleaning up to do, and Hovan, by request of Kelt, apologized to his nephew for questioning his rights. Also by request, Hovan raised a hand and gave word that he would abide the law of the land.

Clive, Colt, and Alack were tended to and helped home, and Kelt and Peck went on their way.

"We can bunk here tonight, if you like, get an early start tomorrow," Kelt told the boy.

But Peck wanted to shake the dust of Greenhorn from his boots as soon as possible. "No," he said. "We leave now."

They walked two miles from the village and made camp near a set of small ponds, the same ponds where Peck had first learned to fish.

It was a calm night, yet the boy did not sleep more than an hour. Too many thoughts stained his mind; too many even for the Monk's potent liquor to scrub clean.

Kelt, meanwhile, rested easy, convinced that better times lay ahead.

## Thirty-four:

Largo could walk plainly now, without a limp or hitch in his step. His wounds had healed quite nicely. Even the ugly red and purple bruises on his face had faded away. He looked and moved like his old self, and felt even better. There was a glint in his eye and a jaunt in his stride when he went to visit Esai.

The old Herder with sparse red hair and a soft belly welcomed him with a hearty handshake. "You're looking good, old friend," he said to him. "Good as new."

"I feel like new," Largo said. "Feel *better* than new."

"How are the kids?"

"Fine and well." In truth, Largo had barely spent any time with his children since returning from the desert. Most of his time had been given to Sana and her sallies. "And your family?"

"Grown and gone, aside from Destra. She's of age, and very pretty, but not interested in marriage."

There were many rumors in Vernon that Destra preferred to share her bed with other young women, and Largo rather enjoyed the thought of those rumors. With her red hair and green eyes, Destra was a fine looker, if a bit sullen and unfriendly. But no one ever dared mention such to Esai, who was as respected as anyone in Vernon.

"Make no mention of it, my friend, I know she's a flirty-girl," the old Herder went on, that term being slang for Destra's kind. The casual frankness of the comment took Largo by surprise, though he fought not to show it. Esai followed it up with, "You know the talk. All do."

"Rumors rarely bare truth, sir," Largo said to him.

"These ones do, I'm afraid. It's her mother's fault, really. Not that I care. I'd prefer she marry, bear children, run a home, but what's the difference? A woman is a woman, a whore is a whore."

Not sure what to say to that, Largo nodded uneasily.

A moment of awkward silence followed, and Esai changed the subject. "You're probably wondering why I called for you." He decanted a bottle of rye, poured two glasses, handed one of them to Largo.

"Many thanks," Largo said. "And yes, I am a bit curious."

He figured it probably had something to do with his last trek, but oddly he wasn't even a little nervous. He had only scant memories of what had happened in the desert just eleven days ago: he vaguely remembered the demon offering him a deal in his head, its voice a whispering temptation; he remembered taking the deal; he remembered killing Alain. If the truth should ever surface, he knew he would be hung from the gallows; and he would be left hanging for three full days, while his body rotted, while the ravens pecked at his eyes. Yet he wasn't worried.

"Hinterland has begun to fall," Esai said to him conversationally, in a voice rich with diplomacy and political intrigue. "Meridon is gone. Word from the northern parts is that demons of all sorts are on the rise. And the Angeloi are absent, if they were ever here to begin with."

Largo nodded solemnly and took a drink.

"We have to stay ahead. You are aware?"

"Aye. Of course, sir."

"That means making hard decisions."

Largo wasn't sure what that meant, or what it had to do with him, yet he said, "Yes, sir. Hard decisions."

Esai paused for a drink. Then, with a calculating look, he said, "Like the one you made in the desert."

Panic struck Largo the Herder. His heart began beating faster, and he couldn't find any words to say.

Esai seemed not to care. On he went. "The old tales of the beginning of Hinterland are just that – Tales. Long yarns weaved into a nice tapestry. Threads of truth are there, of course, as they must be, woven in among the lies and the swelled-up stories of the victors. We take truth and edge it this way and that way, and soon it matters not. Before long, you can't tell the difference because there is none."

Another pause followed. Both men drank. Then Largo said, "It's a fool who doesn't obey change."

A thin smile touched Esai's lips. "The Herders aren't coming back from their trek," he said. "None of them."

Largo held his tongue and tried to effect a blank expression.

"It's odd to finally be here," Esai continued. "We've spent so many seasons planning and biding time. The subtleties of revolution require patience and fortitude."

Largo nodded, though he still wasn't sure what his friend was talking about. He thought to ask a question or two for the sake of clarification, but he didn't want to say the wrong thing. Esai was an Elder, a man of great power and repute, and he was a murderer. Given that, he chose silence. To make that silence seem less conspicuous, he covered it with a drink. He was hoping that drink would also help steady his nerves.

Esai calmly went on, not the least bit interested in his friend's behavior. "Hinterland is our home and we must claim it. The Monks have it wrong. The Herders have it wrong. Everyone here has it wrong."

Largo shrugged apprehensively. His head hurt and his skin felt cold. He was running alibies through his head, but none of them made sense.

"I know, I know," Esai said with a gentle little chuckle. "I'm not making any sense, am I? You're probably thinking I've lost my wits. Not sure it matters anyway."

"Yes. I'm afraid I don't understand," Largo said. "If you could maybe give me some ..."

"It's all but over, and we're all but free. That's what's important to know. The days prophesied about have finally arrived. Hinterland is to be ours at last."

Largo was bemused, but then a voice swept through his head, a faint, far-off whisper that spoke words he did not know yet somehow understood. He felt something pure and primal, and then he felt nothing at all.

"All but over, my friend. *Mostly*." Esai stared at Largo, that shrewd, calculating look in his eyes again. "Of course, there's always work to be done."

"I know," Largo said, feeling better now. That voice had steeled him. "It will be done."

"I know you're with us, and I know you can be trusted."

"Thank you, sir."

"There's a man in town. He arrived today. His name is Karl. You will meet him tonight at Sana's."

"Of course."

"You will assist him in his duties and do what he asks of you."

"I will do my part," Largo said.

"Together, you will call on three houses. None will give you trouble. Two old men and a child."

Largo said he understood.

"The girl with *To Mati Fantasma*," said Esai. "Yondo's gypsy daughter. You and Karl will close those eyes and end that Sight forever."

Largo Kelsman nodded obediently.

"After tonight, one step closer we'll be to our goal."

"What about the other Herders?" Largo asked.

"Those who choose to join us we will welcome with open arms. Those who don't we will kill. It's any easy line to draw."

"And the Elders?"

"Worry not of the Elders. They follow more than lead."

Once again, Largo said that he understood.

"Good," said Esai. "Now you may leave. Remember, you will meet Karl at Sana's tonight. Do show him a proper good time. He is a guest here, and he is someone important to our cause."

"You have my word, sir. How will I know him?"

"He's big and black as night, and a stranger to your eyes. You will recognize him at once. And he will know you."

Largo nodded, finished his whisky, and stood. He put the glass on the edge of Esai's desk and made his way to the door. Before leaving, he turned back to Esai and said, "I think ..." But he stopped after only those two words, unable to recall what it was he had wanted to say.

"Yes?" Esai said to him, waiting.

There were dozens of questions queued up in Largo's mind, but for some reason he couldn't seem to latch on to any of them. Simple words were too much for him to speak. If asked, he would not have been able to give his name. Then the fog cleared just enough for him to say, "Nothing, sir. Sorry. I'll be on my way now."

He left then and walked, heated and half-dazed, back to his humble, wifeless home. He wasn't sure what had just happened, and he didn't much care to try and figure it out. He was calm and at peace with his confusion, and more than willing to do what needed done.

At home, he slept away the day, and in his dreams – weird, violent, twisted dreams of a strangely erotic nature – he saw the Herders die in the desert. He also saw the faces of the three people he and Karl would visit: two old men and a little girl with the Sight. He saw how they would die. He saw their blood and heard their screams. Through it all, the soft, scratching voice of the Kin spoke to him, and he listened.

The end was close at hand, and one day he would be a king.

A smile spread across his sleeping face.

## Thirty-five:

Lizzy's punishment consisted mainly of work and time alone in her room. Her work now had nothing to do with domestic chores, which she was grateful for. She despised darning socks and mending clothes, and she hated cleaning the house and preparing meals. Fortunately for her, there was a roof and a wall to fix.

She and Jonno worked together all morning, per Gabby's orders, and did their best to get along. At first they didn't speak much; then, as the day grew longer and the work grew harder, they didn't speak at all.

They made trip after trip down to the creek, loading the barrow with stones and rocks and loam.

They broke for a midday meal when the sun was at its zenith, and soon after Ferdo and his youngest boy, Rand, who was sweet on Lizzy, came by to help. A short time later, a couple of Yondo's friends, Eddy and Lou, stopped to lend a hand. The wall was badly damaged, yet the structural integrity of the house remained intact, making the job that much easier. The men, all of them experienced builders with big hands and strong backs, made quick work of it. The angle was hard to get straight, and it would take time for the mixture of loam and straw to harden, but it was near as good as new when they were done. It was a wall once more.

Lizzy, Rand, and Jonno finished patching the roof at about the same time. Being the lightest and nimblest among them, Lizzy had done most of the work up top. And what fine work she had done. The roof looked better than it had before the storm had damaged it.

When all was finished, they sat together and ate.

Gabby and Dalla laid out a wonderful dinner. Goat stew headlined the menu, with rice and bread and vegetables on the side, and figgy pie for dessert. There was hard cider, too; Yondo's famous peach and apple cider. It was the best they kept at the house.

Around the fire, well after the dishes had been cleared and the last morsels of food had been consumed, when all that remained was the cider and each other's company, Ferdo said to Lizzy, "You're quite the worker, young lady. Your hands must be covered in blisters."

Lizzy gave her hands a cursory inspection. They were red and raw and calloused, but there was not a single blister. "No," she said. "Not like two days ago, when I was darning socks. I must have stuck my fingers a dozen times. It was awful."

Ferdo, Eddy, and Lou laughed. Gabby laughed, too. The cider had put an attractive shine on her cheek, and though the men there never would have thought to make a pass at Yondo Carpana's wife, they all noticed her. She was a beauty, especially when her long black hair was down.

"I guess after you survive a ringer bite," Ferdo said, "a few callouses aren't going to worry you much."

"I suppose not."

"She's a tomgirl, that one," Gabby said.

Rand, who was a shy boy with the same wide ears, wide eyes, and shaggy black hair as his father, leaned closer to Lizzy and said, "That's a nice necklace you have. Never seen one like it. Where'd you get it?"

Lizzy's head snapped down, and her eyes grew unnaturally wide at the sight of the amulet dangling outside her shirt. It must have happened when she was working on the roof, or when she had stooped over to clear the dishes off the table. She tucked it back in her shirt with a quick hand and told Rand, "Thank you," making sure to keep her voice soft and low.

But Gabby's ears rarely missed a sound.

"Necklace?" she said, surprised. She had never known her daughter to wear jewelry of any kind. "Let me see."

"Just something I found," Lizzy told her, obviously lying. "It's nothing."

"Can I see it?"

Lizzy nodded guiltily. "Later," she said.

The conversation swung to Jonno then, with questions centering on his future as a Herder. Being the center of attention thrilled Jonno, and he puffed up with pride and told all there that he'd be walking the desert soon enough.

"I was supposed to go on this trek," he said, "but then there was all that trouble."

"It's hard work," Ferdo told him. "The desert is unforgiving land."

"My pa says the same."

"It's man's work," added Lou, who was a big man himself. "But you look like you can handle it. You carried those stones like a man."

"Thanks," Jonno said, beaming.

While the menfolk talked about the desert and the value of hard work, Lizzy hazarded a glance at Gabby and caught her staring daggers. She quickly turned away and busied herself with a sip of tea, trying to act nonchalant. She could feel Gabby's eyes on her, though, and could still see the stern, condemnatory look on Gabby's face. She knew there would be questions, but not in front of company.

"I remember when you were born," Ferdo was saying to Jonno. "Your pa was busting he was so happy. Had him a little man to carry the name."

"Ha. I was the one busting," said Gabby, "and it wasn't with pride or happiness." She set her hands as if holding a large melon and added, "He had an enormous head for a baby. *Big, big* head."

The menfolk laughed, and Jonno cried out, "Ma!" in that sheepish, embarrassed tone that all teenagers possess.

"What? They're all fathers, boy," Gabby said to her son. "It's nothing they don't know. Trust me."

Ferdo reached over and mussed Jonno's hair, and Eddy clapped him on the shoulder. "It's all right, kid," Eddy told him. "No point bellyaching about mothers. They do and say as they please, and it's best just to listen to them. They're usually right, and they never let you hear the end of it when you're wrong."

"Now that's sage advice," said Ferdo. "Best to heed it."

"You listening, boy," Gabby said to Jonno. "*Heed.*" Then she turned to Eddy and Ferdo. "And we're not *usually* right; we're *always* right."

"Beg pardon," Eddy cried out, laughing.

The others laughed, too. Even Lizzy laughed.

"You're right, Gabriella," Ferdo said, throwing his hands up in surrender. "When you're right, you're right."

Jonno looked at his mom and said, "Yeah, yeah, yeah. So you say." There was a playfully sarcastic tone to his voice, and Rand snickered.

"You boys'll learn one day," Eddy said to them. He snapped his fingers. "It happens that fast."

Rand threw a glance Lizzy's way to see if maybe she was looking at him. She wasn't.

The get-together went on for another rote or so, and in that time Lizzy glanced over at her ma at least thirty times. Not once did she catch eyes on her again, but that only made her worry more. She knew exactly what Gabby was thinking, and she knew that she would have to explain herself when all were gone. She pondered lies she could tell in her defense, but none of the ones she thought up sounded believable.

Eddy and Lou left first, and each took a couple slices of figgy pie with them. "For your wives," Gabby told them. She also gave each of them a satchel of fresh figs; they had so many to spare.

Ferdo and Rand left a few minutes later and got what was left of the pie. They also received a satchel of figs.

At the door, Gabby hugged Ferdo and thanked him again for all his help. "First that night with Lizzy," she said, "now today. We can never repay you. Thank you."

"You needn't thank me," Ferdo told her. "You and yours are family. And you've done at least as much for us over time. Yondo helped build our house, lest you forget."

"Surprised it's still standing," Gabby joked.

"Goodnight all," Ferdo said. He looked down at Dalla. "You are a fine cook for a girl so small," he told her.

"My ma did most of the work," Dalla admitted. "But I mixed the carrots and spuds and onions."

"And a fine job of it you did."

Dalla let loose one of her wide-arcing smiles, her white teeth standing out wonderfully against her dark complexion.

"And you, girl?" Ferdo said to Lizzy, mussing her wild brown hair. "You staying away from those ringers?"

"Yes, sir," she said, a blush and a bashful smile marking her face.

"Good. We want you around for a long time."

"There are a lot of things she needs to stay away from," Gabby said, giving her daughter a sidelong glance loaded with meaning.

Lizzy certainly got the message.

"Well, I'm off," Ferdo said. "You need any more help, Gabriella, you send word. We'll come at once."

"I will. And tell Angela and Carolina I bid them hello. And thank them for lending you men to us."

"Trust me, they were glad to have us gone for a spell," Ferdo said. "It's you who did them a favor."

Ferdo met up with Rand outside, who had been conspiring with Jonno, the two of them making plans to sneak off the following night with the infamous Tandar sisters and a jug of hard cider. Even so, Rand gave Lizzy a bashful smile and told her that it had been nice to see her again. He told her she was getting real tall.

"Thank you," she said. "You as well."

Rand's cheeks turned into strawberries and his bashful smile widened. His father clapped him on the shoulder then and said, "Come on, boy, your ma will be waiting on us."

They went on their way, while Gabby, Lizzy, and Dalla waved goodbye from the porch. Before they exited the gate, Lizzy furtively slipped inside the house, hoping to sneak off to her room and hide the charm before Gabby could make her …

"Elizabeth Layne Carpana! Where do you think you're going?"

All three names strung together, perfectly enunciated. Lizzy knew she was in trouble. She stopped, turned around. "Nowhere," she said. "To my room."

"Which is it, girl?" Gabby asked her.

"To my room."

"There are dishes to be done. And cleaning in the back room."

"I know. I'll get to it before bed."

"And I'm going to want to see that necklace. Didn't think you wore jewelry. Never seen you wear a charm before. Though I have a pretty good mind where you got it."

Lizzy nodded lamentably and slinked forward, her face a portrait of guilt. She removed the necklace from her shirt and showed it to her ma, who looked at it for only a moment before taking it away.

Esai had been right: noticing Karl was no problem at all. He was massive in size and his skin was as black as a walnut husk. He had a shaved head and smooth face, arms that looked like they had been carved from the trunk of a tree and hands that gave the impression they could crush a man's skull like an overripe berry. Every eye at Sana's gravitated to him when he walked through the door.

He strolled to the bar with an easy gait and leaned against it instead of sitting on one of the open stools.

Sana greeted him with a greedy smile. "What's your pleasure, stranger? We have all you could want."

"Ale," he told her. "And company."

"Got plenty of both," Sana said, that smile of hers still in place. A glass was produced, and then a brown jug with a cork in it. The cork came out with a squeak and a pop, and a moment later the glass was filled to the top with a frothy amber liquid.

"You have coin, I assume?" she asked him.

He slapped a large chink of gold on the bar.

Sana looked at it. Her faded blue eyes expanded. She had never seen a gold coin so large. "That real," she asked him.

"Test it, woman, if you feel you must."

Sana picked it up, sniffed it experimentally, then bit it. It smelled real, and tasted real. "Might cause trouble making change for so much coin," she told him, a well-practiced line of hers. The less change she had to make, the more money she made.

"Karl, my friend," Largo said, coming up behind him with a smile. "Good you could make it."

"You know this fellow, Largo?" Sana asked.

"That I do. This here is Karl Tolick. A good man if ever there was one. Met him up near Boreal last season. Hunting."

"Karl, this here is the infamous Sana."

Sana favored the stranger with another smile, this one flirty, almost girlish, and said, "Good to meet you, Karl Tolick. Welcome to my humble establishment. Please feel at home."

"You're well met," Karl replied, his voice deep and powerful. "And I will." He then extended one of his meaty paws to Largo. "Old friend," he said. "Good to see you again."

Largo watched his hand disappear in Karl's hand, and felt his fingers crunch together when the big man squeezed.

"Get my friend whatever he wants," Karl said to Sana. "I owe him that much and more."

"An ale for me, too, dear," Largo said, and handed over his glass.

It was filled from the jug without a drop spilled.

Before Sana could cork it, Karl said, "Leave it, if you don't mind."

"Surely. Any friend of Largo's." Especially one who pays with gold chinks the size of my thumb, she thought to herself.

Alone now, their words silenced by the din of the crowd and the beautiful, sensual warbling of Eva and Ava, Karl turned to Largo and said, "We ready for tonight?"

Largo nodded and said, "All set. Three stops to make. I figure we'll hit the first two at night, the last one early in the morn. The last one is outside town, on the way to you being gone."

Karl said that sounded just fine. Then he said, "Let's enjoy ourselves until then. What say you?"

"I say that's a capital idea"

Karl beckoned Sana with a casual hand and she hurried back to him, dreams of gold playing in her mind. "Yes?" she said. The smile that had helped her get her saloon was stamped on her aging yet attractive face.

She wore it well, especially in dim lighting.

"I'm in want of good company," he told her. "The finest you have. And take care of Largo, too. That chink enough to cover it?"

It was, and though Sana was greedy and thought she could get more, something told her not to push her luck, that this giant of a man was not someone to trifle with. "Should," she said. "Depending on how much ale you drink, and how many women you want."

"Two girls for me," Karl said, and with his huge hand he pointed out Lessie and Marie. "Them two."

Sana shook her head. "Lessie's my best girl," she told him. "My top earner by and large. I'm afraid you might ..." she paused, and chose her next words carefully "... alter that."

Karl's expression did not change. He reached into his pocket again and pulled out another gold chink, this one smaller than the first but still a good size. He offered no words with the gold, and waited for Sana to change her mind.

The greedy saloon owner looked at the gold, then at Karl. That smile broke across her face again. "I think we have a deal," she said. "Lessie's worth it, too. And Marie's no slouch."

Karl took a drink of ale.

Largo patted him on the shoulder and said, "Thanks, friend." Then, to Sana: "I should like to lie with Misty tonight, if she's available."

"She is. And rarin' to go, as always."

"Two shots of rye," Karl said.

Two shot glasses were produced and filled with a swift hand. Sana then called for Lessie and Marie, who currently were spending time with Arman and Pauly, two young men who liked to take up a lot of Lessie's time but not pay for it. There was nothing worse than smitten Joes, and the beautiful Lessie Marts had more than her share.

"What you need 'em for?" Arman called back.

"We're talking here," added Pauly.

"You keep talking, boys," Sana told them. "I got men paying."

Arman, who was desperately in love with Lessie, despite her indecent profession, despite her numerous refusals to date him proper, saw what Sana had in mind and instantly jumped to his feet.

"Hold on," he said. "I got money. I can pay." He rifled around in his pockets, searching for the one small chink of copper he had to his name.

"You're too late," Sana told him.

"But I got copper."

"Copper? Ha! He's got gold, kid, with plenty of weight to it."

"What about credit?"

Sana tossed her head back and roared laughter. "Credit?" she cried out, and laughed some more. "Cunny on credit, eh? That's a new one. I'd be out of business in a month."

That drew a chorus of guffaws from the others gathered at the bar, including Largo and Karl, and Arman went red in the face. He wanted to intercede on behalf of his girl, the young woman whom he loved, but she was already gone, flirtatiously making the acquaintance of her new friend, and he hadn't a coin worth more than a tug in the bathroom. And fighting was out of the question. He was a man of the law but wouldn't be for long if he started a brawl at Sana's over a sally. His old man would see to that. And even with a few heady ales in his blood, he was wise enough to know that he wouldn't stand a chance against the man who had bought his girl for the night. The stranger was a frightening size and possessed the look of someone both familiar and comfortable with violence.

Arman sat back down and sought to take comfort in his ale, which no longer tasted so good. Unable to stop himself, he watched with stomach-churning anguish as Lessie and Marie made nice with the new man in town before kindly escorting him upstairs.

Arman left Sana's a short time later, bleary-eyed drunk and miserable, strung wretched by his imagination. Karl didn't leave until much, much later, not until after he had spent himself twice on Lessie and Marie, neither of whom would soon forget the degrading perversions the tall, powerful stranger had forced them to enjoy. For Karl and his Kin, there was always work to be done.

The moon was pale yellow, the sky black as tar. The stars were out in full force, glinting fiercely in every corner. There were thousands of them; tiny pinpoints of light trailing and circling the pale moon of Hinterland in kaleidoscopic patterns.

"Good young minge gets the blood pumping hard," Karl said as he and Largo made their way across the empty town. "And that Marie, she's a dollop of sweet cream."

"Marie?" Largo said. "You mean Lessie?"

"Lessie's the mixed girl with the perfect body?"

"Aye. Mix of black skin and white. Beautiful."

"Aye. A rare beauty, sure. As fair as I've seen. But Marie? Well, she was a winner. She knew what she was doing, and she started to like it. You could tell. Lessie? She was ten bells, and willing enough to make it through, but she didn't enjoy it. Not like Marie."

"I like Marie, too," said Largo. "But Lessie's my favorite. Everyone's favorite, I suspect."

"That boy's favorite."

"Arman? He's a good enough kid. But a kid."

Karl grunted indifferently.

Largo edged around a flock of bushes and stopped. He pointed out a small log house some thirty steps from them. "There," he said. "Our first stop of the night."

"The Judge?"

"Name of Dale. Lives alone."

Karl said, "Let's go."

Dale Travers lived on a large parcel of land that skirted the northern side of town. He had a nice pond on his property, and spent most of his time these days gardening and fishing. His wife had passed on years back, and his children, three girls, were all married with houses and families of their own.

A cool breeze rustled the leaves on the trees and made the high grass sway. The only other sound or movement came from Karl and Largo, who walked casually, like two men going home after a long night of drinking and cavorting.

They made it to the house with no trouble, but the door was locked, the windows latched. The plan had been to break in if need be, but Largo had a better idea.

"Wait there," he told Karl, pointing to the right, around a tight corner. "I'll give you a sign."

Karl looked at him suspiciously. He was a blunt object, an angry, snarling, grab-you-by-throat kind of guy who had never given much credence to plans or tricks. He left those to the more imaginative of his kind. Personally, he preferred breaking bones and bashing skulls. It worked for him. Even so, he edged around the corner and hid his massive frame from sight.

Largo put his knuckles to wood and sounded out four loud knocks. After some time went by with no answer, he knocked again, even louder.

When the sound of the last knock faded away, a fragile old voice called out, "I'm coming. I'm coming. Who is it at this hour?"

"It's Largo, sir. There's been a development with the trek. They told me to come and get you. We're gathering all the Elders."

The wood shutter over the window opened a crack and Dale's wise old eyes peered out. Standing on his porch was Largo Kelsman, a known and trusted friend. "Largo?" he said. "What time is it?"

"Still dark. My guess would be three rotes before dawn."

"Hold on."

The latch was undone, the lock turned.

The door opened.

Dale stood there in an old dressing shirt, holding a small glass lamp that housed a flickering orange flame. The lamp threw scant light, barely enough to illuminate their faces.

"What development?" Dale asked, standing aside so Largo could enter. "What happened?"

Largo cleared his throat in an obvious way, then sidled past Dale and into the house. "Here. Let me get that for you, sir," he said, taking the lamp from him.

Dale said, "Thank you, my friend," and turned to shut the door.

But a large foot wedged in the threshold stopped the door from closing. Before Dale could react, Karl swept in, grabbed the Judge from behind, and locked him in a paralyzing hold.

Dale struggled and fought the best he knew how. He tried to squirm free. He tried to kick up a foot and catch the man in the groin. He threw his head back violently to try and break the man's nose. But Dale Travers was a scarecrow in Karl's arms, a brittle, gray-haired old man well-past his day. He continued to writhe, continued to fight to free himself, but Karl held on to him, constricting his grip little by little, until Dale's pale, portly face was cherry red and soaked with sweat. It wasn't long before the Judge stopped kicking and fighting altogether.

"The bedroom?" Karl asked Largo, his voice only slightly strained.

"This way," Largo said, leading the way with the lamp. Their shadows went with them, moving silently against the wall; a pair of dark, thorny ghosts haunting a house soon to be empty.

Karl walked Dale to the bedroom. His footsteps padded the hardwood floor while the Judge's feet dangled half-a-foot above it.

Largo pushed the bedroom door open and edged in.

"Largo?" Dale croaked in a breathless voice. "What is this madness?

What are you doing here? Are you with this man?"

"Time has changed, old man," Karl said to him. "Time always does. Your time has run out. It's our time now."

"Largo?" Dale pleaded, his jowls quivering with fear. "Don't do this. I beg of you, friend. Think what you're doing."

For a fleeting moment, Largo Kelsman gave thought to his actions; and in that moment, guilt broke the surface of his consciousness, putting the tips of a frown on his face. But that guilt disappeared quickly and left no mark behind. It was drowned out by the sound of an evil voice whispering words from the other side.

"On the bed," Largo said, and Karl threw the Judge down.

Though hurt, exhausted, and scared, Dale remembered the short-blade he kept under his bed for protection. He tried to go for it, but Largo cut him off, and Karl climbed on top of him, using his full weight to subdue him. Karl then grabbed a pillow, held it over the Judge's face, and pushed down with all his strength.

Dale Travers was a proud and strong man of good stock; he was a man who had survived the trials and hardships of law enforcement to become Vernon's Judge, a position he had held with honor for the last nineteen years. He had been a good husband to his wife, a good father to his children, and a respected town Elder.

He died in his bed, alone, his face twisted in a hideous expression of fear and confusion. It was not the death a man like him should have had, though rarely is death fair in its practice. And in the end, it matters not; that time comes, and it takes.

Karl removed the pillow and stared down at the Judge's lifeless face. He loved seeing the dead; there was something so gentle, so honest, so final about the face and body of a corpse, no matter if they had died violently or peacefully.

A flash of pride struck him, and a childlike smile chased across his face. "That's one," he said. "Who's next?"

"A fellow by the name of Jeb Moll," Largo told him. "A Miner. He lives on the other side of town."

Karl got busy ridding up the scene. With great attention to detail, he tucked Dale's still-warm body under the covers and placed the pillow he had used to suffocate him under his head. When he was finished, he told Largo to put out the lamp, and they left.

Jeb Moll's palatial estate was more than three miles away in the other direction; it was on the eastern side of town, near where the wood gave way to the sand.

"Come," Largo said, waving on his new friend. "We'll travel along the creek. Won't be seen that way."

"Won't matter come the morn," Karl replied. "It'll all be over then, and I'll be gone."

Jeb's house sat just outside of town, on vast acres of lush, fertile land. Jeb Moll, Elder of the Miners, was the wealthiest man in Vernon and one of the wealthiest in all of Hinterland. The mines in Vernon were abundant with rocks and ores and minerals, and these passed through Jeb's hands before they reached the market.

He had a big family, and all his family lived on his land. He had three sons, two daughters, seven grandbabies, and numerous aunts, uncles, and cousins who called Moll land their home. And there was no doubt among them that he was the paterfamilias.

There were eleven homes on the property, and Jeb's was the biggest. It sat atop a sparsely-wooded knoll, above all the others, like a castle over the realm. Made entirely of rock and stone and wood, it was easily the most impressive work of architecture in Vernon.

Largo pointed it out. "We must be careful," he said. "It's not like with Dale. Many people live here."

Karl nodded to show that he understood.

"Come," Largo said. "Follow me."

He cut a wide path around the southwest side of the property, going up and over the hill on the adjoining plot of land, and then back down and across to Jebediah Moll's land.

They walked through the now barren upper farm lot, and looped around the pens where the animals grazed and lazed their lives away.

"Quite the property," Karl noted.

Largo agreed.

"Crops. Animals."

"Ol' Jeb's a rich one."

"Good to know."

Every year come reap, the Molls presented the largest and most diverse crop in town. They grew everything from romas and gourds to peppers, onions, and cabbages, from rice and nuts and figs to carrots, beets, and corn. They harvested wheat and rye and barely, and a variety of herbs and spices. They tended wild vines of grapes and made their own wine (the finest in Vernon), and kept dozens of chickens, goats, and sheep. They were one of the few families in Vernon that never hunted for food; they bred and slaughtered it, which was a custom that had yet to become popular in Hinterland. It was far easier, and the meat often was better.

Jeb's youngest son, Dano, had nearly gotten into a brawl one day for suggesting such to a couple of local hunters.

The house was fantastically decadent, with a carved archway over the front door and the family name – Moll – etched on the door itself. The roof was made of large slabs of timber, as big as trees, and there was a deck on the second level where Jebediah could stand and survey the empire he had shrewdly built on the backs of others.

Karl said, "How many in the house?"

"Four," Largo told him. "Jeb. His wife, Lucy. Her mother. And they have a daughter with … *problems*."

"Crazy?" Karl asked.

Largo shrugged ambiguously. "Got me. She just sits there, staring straight ahead at nothing. Doesn't move. Doesn't speak. She's all wasted away and sickly-looking. Doc Morris can't figure it out."

"No other men?"

"Just Jeb."

Karl sniffed, and moved on.

They were there to kill, yet Karl acted as though they were there for a visit. He strolled right up to the house, walked right up on the porch, and tested the door.

"Locked," he said.

"Can you pick it?" Largo asked. "Tarl, the local Smith, says all locks can be picked. Just takes patience. His boy makes the locks in town. He's got all the keys stashed away somewhere."

Karl lost interest in that idea quickly. Instead, he focused his attention on the house. "I suppose his room is on the second level?"

Largo shrugged yet again. "I'd suppose. I've never had the pleasure of an invite before."

"Well, you have one now."

Karl gazed at the other homes on the property, all of them perfectly spread apart on large parcels of land, some of them separated by fences, others by rows of hedges or trees. There was a huge pond in the center of the property, with a dock and small boat.

The Molls raised fish, too.

"This guy is very wealthy," Karl said. It was not a question.

"Aye. Rich and powerful. And lets you know it, too."

"Which is why we're here. I reckon he's got some gold and silver stashed away in there."

"Most likely."

"We do this right and maybe we make a little something on the side. Unless you have qualms."

"No qualms here, friend," Largo said, thinking that a little extra coin would be nice. He had spent quite a lot at Sana's since returning from his trek and his pockets were a little light. Sooner or later he would have to buy food for his kids.

"Good," Karl said. "Come."

They walked around to the back of the home and Karl tried the door there. It was locked, too; and like the front door, it seemed to be of sturdy construction. He checked the window next and discovered it was open. "Must be our lucky night," he said, and quietly climbed inside.

Largo followed him, and they stood in the kitchen for a while, shoulder to shoulder, both of them looking around in amazement. Neither of them had ever seen such opulence in one place. The table was set for breakfast, with fine porcelain plates and bowls, stemmed glassware, and solid silver flatware at every chair. Numerous pots and pans hung over the kiln, and the grill was easily the largest indoor grill either man had ever seen.

"Pays to be a Miner," Karl whispered.

"I see that," replied Largo, astonished. "I'm in the wrong work."

They crept through the kitchen and into the main living area, which was big enough to hold quite a party. Decorative swords, daggers, maces, and spears adorned the walls, and over the hearth hung a crest of the finest steel with the name Moll over it. Carved in the center of the crest were the Miner's trusty tools: the shovel and pickaxe; they crisscrossed each other at an angle along their shafts, making somewhat of an elaborate X.

"Stairs," Karl said, pointing, and went that way.

Largo took an extra moment with the Moll family crest, eyeing its extraordinary design, wondering how much something like that might cost. Or, more appropriately, how much it might fetch. Then he turned and followed his partner up the stairs.

The first bed chamber they came to was vacant; an unoccupied bed next to a nightstand with an unlit oil lamp on it was all that could be seen inside. The second bed chamber was occupied by what looked like an old woman. She lay sleeping on her back, the covers pulled to her chin, her wrinkled face pointing straight up at the ceiling.

Karl slid into the room, as black and silent as a shadow.

"What are you doing?" Largo asked him with a whisper.

Karl didn't reply. He closed the door on Largo, and then a short time later he opened it. Largo curiously peeked his head into the room, and it seemed to him that the old woman had not moved; the covers were still pulled up tight to her chin and her weathered countenance wore the same blank expression. She actually looked quite peaceful and at rest.

The Herder gave the assassin a quizzical look, endeavoring to ask him, without uttering a word, what had happened.

But Karl ignored him and moved on, easing by a bedroom on the right, heading for the one at the end of the hall. That undoubtedly would be the master bedroom; where Jeb Moll laid his head at night. He tried the knob with a soft hand and to his surprise found it locked. They leave the windows open, he thought to himself, but lock their bedroom door.

He found that to be interesting, and suspected it was because the Moll's kept their most treasured wealth hidden somewhere in their bedroom.

He hitched his head to the left, signaling that he wanted to go back to the bedroom they had passed, the bedroom where the little girl with problems slept. Largo really didn't want to go, but Karl was on lead and not the type to be dissuaded.

The knob turned without resistance, and the door opened with a creaking sound that made Largo cringe. The girl with problems, the girl who never moved or spoke, who only stared straight ahead at nothing, was slowly tottering in a rocking chair, a raggedy cloth doll sitting in her lap. Her hair, a tangled mess of brown ribbons, hung over her face and shoulders like frayed drapery, and her bare feet tapped the floor in rhythm with the rocking of the chair.

Upon seeing her, Karl's heart thumped off beat.

Then the girl who supposedly was catatonic lifted her head and shot Karl a look that sent a chill down his spine. Her eyes narrowed, her mouth opened with an evil smile. Karl feared she would scream and give them away, that she would wake the whole house, yet he couldn't bring himself to act. For some reason he was terrified.

But only a whisper escaped that trembling mouth of hers. The word she uttered was, "Daimonas."

Then her head drooped and her hair spilled into her lap. The chair rocked beneath her.

Karl stood there, motionless, terrified, breathing in big, heavy grunts that stretched his ribs and chest. A cold-blooded demon assassin scared stiff by an invalid child.

But there was something about the girl that was ... that was ...

He didn't know what it was that scared him so, but he knew that he wanted to get far away from her. Fast.

From over his shoulder, Largo said, "That was creepy, right?"

Karl flinched, that big body of his as tense as a locked crossbow thread. Then, slowly, he backed away from the door. "You stay here," he told Largo. "I'll take care of the Molls."

Largo didn't much care for that idea, but the last thing he wanted to do was cross Karl. Then again, the Moll girl scared him, too, and in a much more disturbing way.

Nevertheless, Largo stood watch over the girl while Karl went to work on her parents. The dark assassin kicked the bedroom door open with a mighty foot, sending chunks of wood flying, and stalked into the room. A chorus of screams followed, but they were silenced quickly; first the woman, and then the man.

The demon took his time with what came next. He had questions to ask, lies to tell, and, depending on the level of cooperation he received, bones to break. He employed all three methods before he was finished, and when he walked out of the Moll homestead it was with more than fifty rocks of silver, thirty rocks of gold, and countless gemstones and jewels. He kept the largest share for himself, having done most of the work, but still gave Largo a fair cut.

"For your troubles," he told him.

Largo pocketed the booty greedily, thinking about what, and who, he could buy with it. And as his thoughts whipped and whirled through the seductive pleasures of the flesh, through the moral and physical flexibilities of Sana's sweet sallies, Lessie chief among them, that scratchy whisper of a voice that had plagued him since returning home from the desert began to haunt his ears again. The voice whispered to him evocatively, in words he didn't fully understand, and he listened and agreed.

He was already richer than he had ever been before.

They left Moll land on an easy stroll, not fleeing the scene or rushing off to their next target like two-bit shanks on the hustle. Karl, his hands bloody but his pockets full, wasn't in a hurry, and Largo was too busy daydreaming to move with speed.

"Now for the girl," Karl said.

"Now for the girl," Largo echoed.

"Tell me about them, friend. What can we expect to find at the home of Elizabeth Carpana?"

Largo reluctantly put sweet Lessie aside and focused his thoughts on Gabby and her kids. "A woman, two girls, and a boy not yet a man," he said. "Plum pickings."

"You'll need to help on this one, I'm afraid. Esai needs to know that he can trust you wholly."

Largo wasn't sure what that meant. He asked.

"It means you're going to have to kill her with your own hands," Karl told him. "He wants you to spill the girl's blood. Understand?"

Doubt rose inside Largo Kelsman then, but it evanesced before he had time to think on it. That voice again; that beguiling, inveigling whisper that scratched at his brain like a rat in the walls.

"Surely," he said in a flat, hollow tone, like someone under the thrall of hypnosis. "A no-good gypsy girl not from here. No honest kin to speak of. A miracle she's lasted this long."

"That miracle is about to end," said Karl.

**Thirty-six:**

Lizzy woke in a panic. The dream she had had was a black, twisted vision of barbarity and death, a true nightmare rooted in the mud and muck of the darkest corners of her imagination. Its malevolent remains hung in her room like an evil spirit, taunting her.

She realized she was sweating and breathing heavily.

She looked left and saw that Dalla was deep in slumber. The girl slept like an animal in a cave, huddled into herself and all wrapped up in a clot of pillows and blankets. All Lizzy could see of her was the top of her head, her curly black hair sticking out like so many spider legs. She could hear her, too; Dalla didn't snore, but she took slow, deep breaths that filled the room with sound.

Lizzy laid back and closed her eyes. Strange creatures she had never seen before had invaded her sleep, silently sneaking in from the netherworld to plague her thoughts with fear and confusion. Creatures with human faces and animal bodies; creatures at once human and animal, changing from a young man to a shadow, and then from a shadow to a serpent that stood tall, all in the flicker of an eye. One was a giant bird with wings that blotted out the sun, and when it flapped those wings, the wind-force shook the world.

She had seen demons bent in bone and spirit, with eyes as empty and dark as a starless night. A shadow army of the dead marching on villages, killing anyone and anything that got in their way. She had seen great, monstrous beasts, too, with teeth and claws that could tear flesh like paper. Giant spiders and serpents crawled the land, devouring souls one after another.

The corpses of men and women, girls and boys, even little babies, had been everywhere, lying prostrate on the ground, strewn about like dead soldiers on a field of battle. Their naked carcasses had decomposed before her eyes, the flesh turning blue, then purple, then black, before rotting away completely.

She remembered screaming at herself to wake up, she remembered crying out for help, and she remembered the sound of her voice dying before it struck a single chord. She remembered the fear that had churned up inside her like a sickness, making her skin hot and her body spasm.

Then, from the bone and rotted flesh of the beasts, dark spirits had risen, black ghosts with stone-gray eyes that shined dull and dead.

Lizzy remembered how those terrible eyes had set on her, and how she had been unable to hide from them, unable to move.

They had attacked her in an angry, roiling mob, converging on her at one time, hundreds of dark shadows, so black and endless it was like the night sky had shattered into a million pieces and rained down on her.

They had swarmed her, these evil dream-spirits.

She remembered them trying to tear inside her body, inside her mind, inside her soul, and she remembered fighting them off with all her strength, battling them, kicking them, punching them, refusing to give in.

But there had been too many of them.

They had begun to break through.

They had found the entryway to her mind.

They had discovered the tangled nexus of her soul.

That's when she had woken up, wild with terror and soaking wet.

"It was just a dream," she tried telling herself, though she didn't really believe that. She'd had dreams before, but never anything like this. Never anything so vivid and intense. It had been a ...

What was the word?

A Harbinger! An Omen!

She believed that as she lay in bed, staring up at the ceiling in a dazed but emotional state. There were things coming for her, dark and evil things, and that made her think of the amulet that Oreg had given her. It was for protection, he had told her; demons and evil things would not be able to see her.

But Gabby had taken it away. It currently was residing in her ma's bed chamber, most likely hidden somewhere in the floorboards, or in the back nook of the closet.

"I'll give it back after I know what it is," Gabby had told her. "Wanna make sure there's no hoodoo on it. Your father will see it, too, and we'll decide together."

Lizzy had not wanted to give it up, but had seen no other way. She had thought about telling her ma the truth, but then had decided against it. Gabby would toss it away without pause if she found out it had mystical powers. Not that Gabby believed in magic or mysticism; that didn't stop her from fearing it, though.

Odd to fear something you don't believe in; but many travelled in that boat.

Lizzy believed in it, powerfully, and she wanted it back. It meant something to her, and she thought it important. The night after her ma had taken it away from her she had suffered the worst nightmare of her young life. That had to mean something.

She got out of bed, unlatched her window cover, and peered outside. It was yet dark, but the dawn was near. Soon, morning light would wash the land in bright and wonderful colors.

She was planning on doing some fishing later, perhaps a little hunting, too. They needed meat. The goat had made a fine stew, but Gabby had given away most of the leftovers.

Soon, she thought, and closed and latched her window. Soon after the sun and Gabby rose for the day she would strike out in search of food for the dinner table.

Until then she would try to get one last wink of sleep.

She laid down again and closed her eyes, and almost instantly the dark phantoms from her nightmare swam back into her mind. There were hundreds of them, and they stared at her with their haunting gray eyes, looking for an opportunity, waiting for a chance to take her soul and carry her off to the Shadowlands.

She tried to put them out of her head, then stopped trying altogether, believing it impossible. "Sometimes the mind has a mind of its own," Oreg had told her. At the time, she had thought that a ridiculous thing to say, but now she saw the truth in it.

No point in fighting ghosts.

She climbed out of bed, sneaked out to the kitchen, put on her boots. She wrote her ma a simple note of explanation, then quietly exited the house, closing but not locking the door behind her.

If she was going fishing later, she would need bait, and since she couldn't sleep she saw no reason to lie in bed and stare blankly at the ceiling while bugs and crawlers were squirming above ground. The fresh dirt and mud behind the barn was the best place to find them, and Lizzy tramped up there with her bucket and hand-spade as the first signs of dawn softened the sky.

By the time the Carpana home appeared to them, the sun was level with the horizon and the soft light of morning had chased most of the night away. Clouds hung overhead in ominous shapes, their dark bulk portending a storm to come.

The storm had already begun, thought Largo. Much like in the sky, the clouds had gathered against Vernon, and the first sounds of thunder had already shaken the town. No one would know it until later, until the bodies of the recently-murdered were found, and by then it would be too late. It was already too late.

Largo wondered if he might be suspected of the murders, or perhaps considered an accomplice. He knew Karl would be suspected; the man was a stranger in Vernon, and he possessed the size and menacing look of someone who made their peace with violence.

Largo remembered vouching for him in front of dozens of witnesses at Sana's. He had sat with him; he had drunk ale with him; he had accepted the gift of one of Sana's finest sallies from him.

None of these were a clear confirmation of guilt, though together they could be construed as evidence of it. He thought on these particulars until his mind was haunted once more by the ghostly voice he could not fully hear nor understand.

He looked at his hands and clenched them into fists. They felt foreign to him, like they belonged to someone else. His feet, too. He watched them, step after step, and felt nothing.

He had ...

He was ...

It occurred to him that ...

"Back or front?" Karl asked.

This question yanked Largo from his confounding ruminations, and his benumbed, demon-girdled mind rose to the surface.

"Front or back?" Karl asked again.

"Front," Largo said.

"Any reason not to go in hard?"

"Aye. I know the Carpana's well. I am a Herder, the same as the head of their house. I am known as a friend."

"But he's on a trek. One from which he'll not return."

Largo nodded heedlessly. Though he considered Yondo Carpana a friend, though he had trekked the desert with him dozens of times, had shared ale with him, had broken bread with him, had played cards with him, he felt no sympathy for him, just as he felt no sympathy for Jeb and his family, nor Dale. Everyone comes to their end sooner or later, he mused, and that thought was oddly comforting to him.

"The gypsy girl has *Vlema*," Karl said. "That could cause us trouble. We take our time, she could *sense* something."

Largo thought about that, and said, "Hard it is, then. Should be no trouble this far out from town. No passersby this early."

Karl gave a cynical snort. He worried not about passersby, nor the law, nor any other trivial human enterprise. He had larger concerns.

But before they reached the house, their plan to bust in and spill blood without care or pretense was taken away from them. The front door of the Carpana home opened wide and out came the boy, Jonno. He called back into the house, "I know, I know. I'm going," before closing the door with a strong hand. The sound of wood slamming against wood vibrated in the still morning air, overwhelming with jarring asperity the pleasant sounds of nature: birds chirping; the wind blowing; leaves rustling; the soft, electric hum of a new day coming alive.

Jonno made it only three steps to the woodpile when he saw the two men approaching. He recognized Largo, but not the other. The man with Largo was as large a man as he had ever seen, and it made him think about the extraordinary tales of flesh-eaters, those savage beasts that supposedly lived deep in the forests up north. Those cannibalistic monsters were purported to be twelve feet tall and close to seven-hundred pounds, with gargantuan heads and sculpted bodies. This man was nowhere near that size, though he was terribly imposing all the same.

Jonno normally would have been leery of a stranger that size, but the man with him was a friend. Jonno knew nothing about what Lizzy had claimed to see in the depths of Largo's eyes (Gabby had not wanted to spread gossip and possibly ruin the Herder's reputation, and she knew her son had a loose mind and a loose tongue), so he gave it little thought when Largo threw a hand in the air and wished him a good morn.

Jonno Carpana waved back and said, "Good morning, friend. How are you this fine day?"

"As well as can be expected. You?"

"Likewise."

Largo opened the gate, and he and Karl entered the yard. "Heard you had some troubles here, lad. A storm took off part of the roof. Wanted to know if you had need for help."

"All fixed," Jonno told them. "Ferdo and Rand stopped by yesterday. We got almost all done. Just clean up now, which is what my stupid gypsy sister is supposed to be doing."

"Your mother in?"

"Surely. She's putting breakfast on the table now. Go inside. She'll be glad for the company, I'm sure."

"This is Karl," Largo said, introducing the boy to the demon-assassin that meant to kill him.

"Well met," Karl said, extending a huge hand.

"Well met," replied Jonno. His hand all but disappeared in the stranger's hand, which was uncommonly dry and cold to the touch.

"Chopping and gathering wood is good for the back," Largo told Jonno. "Good work for a Herder in training. Your mum have tea on, you think?"

"That's what she was busy with when she sent me out."

Largo walked away then, and Karl followed him. Jonno cast them a suspicious look from over his shoulder, and watched them all the way to the house. Then he began to gather wood from the pile.

Three knocks on the door brought Gabby. She was in a dressing gown and robe, and she covered herself when she saw Largo and an unknown man on her step. "Largo?" she said with surprise, her gaze shifting back and forth between the Herder and the large stranger. "What brings you here at such an early hour?"

"My friend and I ... Dear, where are my manners? Gabby, this is Karl. Karl, this is Gabriella Carpana, wife of Yondo. You met Yondo once before, remember?"

"Briefly," Karl said in a proper, reassuring tone of voice. He sounded like a well-educated man, not a ruthless murderer.

"Well met," said Gabby, though she wasn't about to move aside and let them in. She again asked Largo what had brought him at such an hour.

"Heard you had some trouble here," he told her. "A collapsed wall and roof. I thought we could help."

He heard himself speak the words but couldn't remember thinking them. Nor could he seem to remember why he had come to the home of Gabriella Carpana, or where he had heard about the storm that had damaged their roof and wall. He could no longer clearly remember what had happened at the homes of Jeb Moll and Dale Travers. It was all in his head, though badly clouded over, like the fractured memories of a long ago tragedy.

"Thank you," Gabby said, "but Ferdo and his boy did most of the work yesterday. Eddy and Lou helped. We're fine now."

"That's good news," said Largo. He peered past Gabby, into the house, his eyes searching for young Lizzy.

A bad feeling struck Gabby. Unexpected visits were not uncommon in Vernon – most everyone was friendly, and folk were always stopping by for a word or a favor – but there was something strange about the way Largo was acting. He didn't seem himself, which made Gabby think about what Lizzy had said of him.

Suddenly, she wanted Largo and his huge friend to go.

"You know," she said to them, using her most pleasant voice, "I'd invite you in for tea, but I'm afraid Dalla's awful sick. She's been vomiting all morning and has fever chills. Wouldn't want to pass it on to you."

"Understood," said Largo. "Poor girl. Just so all is well. Karl and I will head back to town now."

Karl had had enough of Largo's ridiculous ruse and was ready to bust through the door and attack. But the sound of another door opening and closing stopped him.

There was a pause.

No one moved.

For an excruciatingly long moment, everything was silent and still.

Then, from the back of the house, the voice of Lizzy Carpana broke through. "Ma, I'm back. I left a note on the table. Did you see it? Went for night-crawlers. Got a whole bunch of them behind the barn. I'm going to do some fishing now."

She appeared in the back hallway, her hands, feet, and knees covered in the black mud of Vernon. On her young, sun-dappled face rested an expression of youthful contentment. That looked changed drastically, however, when she saw Largo at the door. Her eyes widened, her mouth gaped reflexively, and she drew back. "Mom," she said, her voice suddenly choked with fear.

She could plainly see the men at her door for what they really were: Largo an empty vessel for the Kin, ruined and rotted inside, like the carcass of an animal that had been picked clean by scavengers; and the big one beside him was full-on Kin, down into the marrow of the bones it had claimed, with a hideous monster face hiding behind the face it showed the world. Its inner-face held the markings of evil, with runes and symbols carved into the skin.

The sight of him sent a tremor of panic through Lizzy's entire body.

"Mom," she said again. "Close the door."

Gabby was about to do just that when she saw her boy coming to the house with an armful of wood. She opened her mouth to tell him to run, and Karl struck, backhanding her across the face.

"Get the boy," Karl shouted at Largo.

Gabby tried to run away, but Karl grabbed her by the hair and pulled her close. She fought against him, using the moves her husband had taught her long ago. She slapped his face and tried to kick him in the groin, then in the knee. The slap landed flush, but her kicks missed the mark, and Karl swung a huge fist into her stomach.

Gabby doubled over and fell to the ground, gasping for air.

"Mom!" Lizzy cried out in horror.

Jonno came tumbling into the house then, a nasty gash over his left eye, blood seeping from both nostrils. Largo came in after him, kicked him once in the head to keep him down, and slammed the door shut.

Karl left Gabby and went for Lizzy. He figured she'd run from him like a rabbit from a bear, but she surprised him and held her ground. Her hand disappeared behind her back and a split second later reappeared holding a slingshot. With her other hand she loaded a rock into the strap ... and then the strap was pulled back and released. It took her no more than a single tick of time to complete the entire move, which culminated with the rock striking Karl in the left eye.

The Kin assassin yelped in surprise and stumbled backwards, and Lizzy deftly loaded another shot in place. This one she fired at Largo, who was kicking her brother in the stomach. The rock flew true and thunked off the side of the Herder's skull.

Largo staggered back and fell.

Then, at the top of her lungs, Lizzy cried out, "Run, Dalla! Run! Leave this house and get to town! Go now! Go out the window and run! Get the sheriff! Go! Go! Go! I swear it, girl! I swear it on my life! Run! Run! Run!! Now!!!! Now!!!!" Then, insanely, she charged forward, going right at the half-blind demon-assassin.

Karl was stunned, his vision badly blurred, but he wasn't about to be taken out by a little girl. He closed his swollen eye and stood for battle. He was about to swing a huge fist at Lizzy when she dove to the right, toward the standing cupboard in the kitchen, the bottom drawer of which held some of her father's best weapons. She opened the drawer, pulled out two of Yondo's best daggers, and faced off against the giant.

Karl laughed at the sight. "Brave little girl," he said. "And stupid."

Lizzy's father's voice entered her mind then, much like it had when the ringer bit her. "Use what you have," it said in a crisp, authoritarian tone. "Make who and what you are your advantage."

'Skinny' and 'Fast' was what she was. By comparison, Karl was slow and cumbersome. He was more than a pode taller than her and well over two-hundred pounds heavier. Her plan was to stay low and aim low.

He stalked forward with madness in mind, and Lizzy crouched down, making herself even smaller. He tried to kick her, but she lunged away at the last moment, escaping his giant foot, which likely would have crushed her chest. With him now slightly off balance and off his angle, she dove at his knees and stuck one of her daggers into his leg.

He howled in pain and swatted down at her.

Lizzy tried to duck the blow, but the back of Karl's fist struck her flush on the shoulder and sent her sprawling. The remaining dagger she held fell from her hand and skittered across the floor.

She tried to get up, but stumbled and pitched forward, going down on her hands and knees. Then a foot slam into her midsection and all the wind left her body. She curled into a ball and desperately gasped for breath.

Karl removed the dagger from his leg, drawing out blood and blade. "Mikri skyla!" he said with a snarl. "You'll pay for that."

Largo was the one who had kicked Lizzy in the ribs, and now he stood over her menacingly, a gleeful bloodlust shining in his eyes. "We got her," he said, and grabbed a fistful of her hair. "The little gypsy bitch is ours." He lifted her up by her hair, then dropped her suddenly when Gabby stabbed him in the back with the dagger Lizzy had dropped. The blade pierced the flesh to the hilt, and when she twisted it, as Yondo had taught her to do, the excruciating pain that Largo felt went away. His legs went numb and his body collapsed to the floor. Whining like a wounded animal, he desperately reached around his back to try and pull the dagger free.

Gabby tramped down hard on his arm, which was extended in a vulnerable way, and the elbow bent and popped. Largo Kelsman screamed in agony. He couldn't feel his legs anymore, but the pain in his arm made everything turn white.

Gabby removed the dagger from his back with a quick yank and stepped between the Kin assassin and her daughter. "You'll have to go through me!" she screamed with a mother's fury. There was blood on her hands and blood on her face, and her eyes burned with a savage look.

"Gladly," said Karl, and stalked forward.

Gabby had some skill, and more than enough salt in her blood, but she was overmatched. Nevertheless, she swung at him, and stabbed at him, and tried to kick him in the knee. All good moves, but Karl either blocked or eluded them. He then caught her hand, gripped her wrist tight, took the dagger from her, and threw her across the kitchen. She tumbled over the table, slammed into the wall, and crumpled into a ball on the floor.

Jonno had managed to work himself to his feet, but he was not on steady legs. He grabbed the club the family kept near the door and brandished it threateningly. Karl went for him. On the way, he dropped a heavy fist on the back of Lizzy's head, knocking her unconscious.

"I'm not afraid of you!" Jonno cried out, and swung the club through the air as hard as he could, showing the demon assassin that he had more than enough strength to crack a skull.

Karl sneered at him. "Yes, you are, boy," he said, his smile like a half-curled snake. "I can smell fear like stinking flesh and you've got plenty."

"Come on!" Jonno shouted. "Try me!" This time when he swung the club, he tried to take off Karl's head, but he missed and Karl lunged at him. Jonno swung back and struck the demon assassin in the side, but not with enough force to stop him, and the next thing he knew he was soaring through the air like a bird. He crashed on the floor, and his head whipped back and smacked against the low ledge of the hearth. Stars exploded in his eyes and pain overwhelmed him.

Meanwhile, in the kitchen, Gabby was coughing and spitting blood. She was on her knees, but she was reaching for the edge of the cupboard so that she could pull herself to her feet. She was not yet done fighting, and would not stop until she was dead.

Karl went after her, lifted her up by her hair, spun her around, and flung her against the table.

"For my trouble," he said to her, with her son lying half-conscious on the hearth and her daughter lying unconscious on the floor, "I think I'll have my way with you!" He bent her over, lifted her dressing gown, ripped off her undergarment.

Gabby fought against him wildly, kicking her legs, swinging her arms, squirming and writhing, but he held her down and pressed one of her husband's daggers to her throat. "Resist and I'll bleed you out in your own home, bitch!" he growled in her ear.

Gabby wasn't sure what would be worse: bleeding out in her home or being raped in it by a savage, on the very table where they ate their meals, with her children in plain sight.

She could feel the sharp pinch of the blade against her throat, and she knew it would take only the slightest pressure to open her flesh and spill her blood. But would it be Karl who did it or her?

She felt him move directly behind her.

She felt him undo his pants.

She felt the size of his body and the hardness of his manhood.

And she gave serious thought to shoving her neck into ...

There was a crash and the front door swung open.

The soothsayer stormed into the room carrying only a wooden staff. He was dressed in rags, and that crude leather patch still covered his left eye, yet somehow he looked different. He looked younger, stronger, more virile, and Gabby had never been happier to see anyone in her life.

The Kin assassin sneered at the soothsayer. He moved away from Gabby and laced up his pants.

"Are you alright, Gabriella?" Oreg asked. "Well enough?"

She nodded fearfully, her head going up and down in frantic bursts. Then, as she stood upright, a foot crash into her back, sending her flailing over the table and into the wall.

"You'll pay for that!" Oreg said to the Kin.

"Skyla has too much fight in her. Wouldn't want her interrupting me while I'm killing you."

Oreg glanced around the house with his one good eye. Lizzy was lying on the floor; she wasn't moving, but he could see her back expanding and contracting with every breath. The boy, Jonno, was laid out by the hearth, his eyes glassy and bulging. The man at Oreg's feet, Largo the Herder, was whimpering and saying, "Help me. Please. I can't feel my legs." His arm was disjointed at the elbow and his legs appeared lame.

The soothsayer wondered where little Dalla might be, but he wasn't about to ask. He had more pressing concerns.

"Your time is gone, old friend," Karl said. "Your treachery and treason will be repaid." The Kin added a short-blade from Yondo's weapon cache and moved forward. "Oreg – old and well past your day, yet still clueless. Look at you. When will you learn? Never, I suspect. Not until time is finished with you."

"As it is for you now," replied Oreg.

Karl let out a deep, throaty laugh. "You underestimate us, old man. We're different now. Stronger. And you're at the end."

"Show me the end."

Karl circled to the soothsayer's left, then changed the depth of his approach and stepped carefully to the right. Oreg, his one good eye locked on the Kin assassin, kept his feet in place, though he did shift his weight some. Karl made a stabbing gesture, hoping to goad Oreg, but the old soothsayer didn't fall for it.

"It's been hard to find you," Karl said. "You've been gone for generations. Hiding scared."

Oreg held his tongue.

"Is it the gypsy girl?" Karl edged ever-so-slightly towards Lizzy, who still lay unconscious on the floor.

Oreg took a quick step forward, cutting off his path.

"Aye. So it is." A feral smile stretched the assassin's mouth. A mix of amusement and arrogance sparked in his eyes. "You know how that will end. She must die. It is written in To Theiko Kylindro. And I am here to make sure the prophesy is fulfilled."

Oreg remained silent.

"You confuse me, old friend," Karl went on conversationally, moving back to his right, trying to get Oreg to move with him. "You fight to die when you could fight for freedom. You fight for *them* and not your brothers. You fight for nothing."

"And you don't fight at all," Oreg said, finally breaking his silence. "You dance around the room like a sally."

Another feral smile. Another spark of arrogance and amusement. "Old flesh and bones, about to be cinder and ash."

Oreg now stood directly in front of Lizzy. He held his staff ready and kept his eye on watch.

"Old fool," Karl said, stepping left. "Choosing death in a prison."

It was then the demon attacked, charging forward with unnatural speed and stabbing at the soothsayer with one of Yondo's daggers. But Oreg was on balance and prepared. He avoided the stab and spun away from the swing of the short-blade, which whistled dangerously close to his ear.

"You've gotten slow, old friend. And old."

"That I have. But not yet that slow and old."

Karl laughed. "I'll remedy that. There is no age in death."

Oreg took one step to the left.

Karl feigned another attack and prepared to counter. Oreg didn't make him wait long. The soothsayer's staff whooshed through the air and caught the demon on the point of the elbow, causing him to drop his dagger.

364

Karl spun away, faked a move to the left, and tried to go back for the weapon. Oreg tracked him easily, and jabbed him in the face with the top end of the staff. The blow struck the demon square on the nose and sent him to the ground.

"Vlasfimia!" Karl cried out in pain and frustration. He jumped to his feet and charged the soothsayer, nearly tackling him to the ground. But Oreg's balance was uncanny, and it was Karl that ended up skidding across the floor. The Kin assassin stood quickly and stabbed at the soothsayer with Yondo's short-blade, but again he missed, and Oreg cracked him once more, this time on the knee. The old soothsayer then lurched to the left and smoothly swept the staff behind Karl's legs, sending him onto his back. Not done yet, Oreg twirled the staff and rammed the butt end of it down on the demon's chest, then twirled it again and brought the top end down on the demon's already bloody nose.

By this time, Gabby had regained her feet, if not her wits. She was bloody and woozy, but well enough to move, and she rushed to her daughter's side. She rolled her over and called for her to wake. She then spied her son near the hearth; his head was up and his eyes were half-open, but it was clear to her, even from across the room, that he was barely conscious. Lastly, her eyes moved to the soothsayer. Oreg didn't just look different, he *was* different. Gone was the haggard and hunched medicine man that looked as though he couldn't crush a bug. That Oreg had been replaced by a tall, lanky, powerful man with flawless posture and a ferocious disposition.

He was standing over the strewn assassin, that deadly wooden staff of his poised to strike.

Karl spotted one of Yondo's daggers under a toppled chair and began crawling that way. Any chance he had to survive depended on him making it to that steel.

Oreg tracked behind him, waiting to make his move.

Karl grabbed the dagger, rolled over, and threw it up at the soothsayer with surprising quickness. The move was so sudden and violent that Gabby actually cried out, "Nooooo!" thinking that Oreg was done for.

But the soothsayer dodged left and the dagger sliced by him, lodging in a beam of wood along the ceiling, the hilt vibrating audibly from the force of impact. Oreg then jabbed his staff in the demon's face with such power that its head flung back and cracked off the solid wood floor. He repeated this move again and again and again and again, until the demon's eyes rolled back and its body went limp.

Oreg then moved in for the kill without hesitation. He placed one hand on the back of the demon's head and with the other he cradled the demon's chin; then he wrenched the head with such force that Gabby heard the bones crack from across the room.

The fight was over. The demon assassin was dead.

Gabby and hers were safe. For now.

Oreg stood. He looked at Gabby, who was sitting on the floor, cradling Lizzy's head in her lap, stroking her cheek and begging her to wake up. "She's fine," Oreg said. "I can feel it."

Gabby didn't know what to say.

Her house was destroyed, her children badly injured. And there was at least one dead body in her den.

The soothsayer went over to Jonno, helped him to his feet, and then helped him onto a chair.

"What was that?" said Gabby breathlessly. "What in the hell just happened? How …"

"They were after your daughter," Oreg told her. "Here, let me help you." He took Lizzy in his arms, gently lifted her up, and carried her to the padded sofa. He laid her down on it, taking extra care with her head.

"Help me. Help me, please."

It was Largo, his voice a shrill, pathetic whine. The Herder was still alive but was irreparably broken. Gabby had severed the nerves in his spine, leaving him paralyzed from the waist down, and his left arm hung twisted and disjointed behind his back.

"I should kill you, Largo Kelsman, for what you brought here," Gabby shouted at him. "I should slice you through."

"Leave him," said Oreg. "He can stand for the crimes."

"And what of the other one? Is he dead?"

"Here. Look and see."

Gabby edged around the sofa on yet unsteady legs. She stood at the soothsayer's shoulder and looked down at the man she knew as Karl, a man who had tried to rape her and kill her entire family. Karl lay flat on his stomach, his giant, shaved head facing the wrong way, his eyes open but staring at nothing. It was a gruesome sight.

"He's dead," Gabby said, her lips trembling. "Good." She spit on him, and uttered a curse: "Bastard!"

"Nearly dead," Oreg said to her. "And it's not a 'Him' so much as an 'It'." Then he told her to watch.

From his pocket he produced a box of sulfur-sticks. He took one and struck it against his staff, bringing to life a small orange flame.

"What are you doing?" Gabby said to him. "You can't burn him in here. This is our home. I won't ..."

Oreg turned to her, held a crooked finger to his lips, and went, "Shhh." Then he said, "Watch and learn the truth, woman."

He dropped the match on the demon's body, and Gabby let out a startled gasp. Then her eyes went wide.

It took only a moment to catch, and once caught the flames burned fast and bright. In no time at all the demon's body was engulfed in blood red fire that raged high and hot. The strange light cast an evil-looking gloom in the Carpana home and threw violent stick-figure shadows on the walls. Then, as quickly as it had caught, the fire died out. The glowing red light and shadows vanished. On the floor there remained not a trace of the demon's body except for a small mound of black ash. The jewels and gold that had been in Karl's pockets, treasure stolen from the Moll house just a couple rotes ago, shone resplendent in that ash, catching Gabby's eye. The sofa, which was stuffed with straw and wool, and the hardwood floor showed not a trace of the raging conflagration that had consumed the assassin's body in seconds. The only evidence the fire left behind was the faint stink of sulfur.

Gabby looked at the soothsayer in awe. "What was that?" she asked him, not understanding. "What ...?" She was close to tears.

"That, my dear, was Kin. Old Kin, true in form and very powerful."

"But ... He was ..."

"We'll talk on it more, I expect. For now, you may want to check on your other daughter."

Gabby drew back. Panic turned her face white, making the bruises she had sustained stand out all the more. "Dalla?" she cried out, and rushed to the girl's room. "Dalla? Dalla?" She came back a moment later to find the soothsayer kneeling over Largo. "She's gone," Gabby said to him. "She's not here. She's gone. Where is she?"

"A moment," said Oreg. He gently took hold of Largo's wounded arm, steadied it above and below the joint, and applied a quick jolt of pressure. The elbow popped back into its socket, and Largo screamed in agony.

Gabby seemed to disapprove. "I should do the same to the other arm," she said to him.

"Dalla?" the soothsayer inquired.

There was a groan from the couch, and Lizzy lifted her head.

"Lizzy," Gabby exclaimed, and hurried to her side.

Lizzy rubbed the back of her head. "What happened?" she asked in a quiet, brittle voice.

"You alright, girl?" Gabby said to her. "Talk to me."

"I'm fine. Just … dizzy." Then she said, "I told her to run."

"Who? Dalla? You told Dalla to run?"

Lizzy nodded, but then stopped when she realized how much pain and nausea it caused her. She felt like she might throw up. "I told her to get the sheriff," she said. "I told her to run to town."

Oreg turned to Gabby. "Go get your baby girl," he said to her. "I'll stay here and watch the house." He then nudged Largo with his foot. "And I'll keep an eye on this one."

Gabby paused, drawn by uncertainty. She didn't want to leave Oreg alone in her home with her children; especially Lizzy. A day ago, she would have chased him off with a broom if he had so much as swung open her gate. But now …

They'd all be dead but for him. Not only had he saved Lizzy's life when she was bitten by a ringer, but tonight he had saved them all. That bought him some trust in her book.

"You don't mind?" she asked him. "I don't want to trouble you."

"It's no trouble at all. Truly. While there, you should probably fetch the Sheriff and Doc Morris, too."

"Good thinking." Gabby looked at Lizzy. "You alright, girl?" she asked her. "I'm going to get Dalla."

"I'm fine," Lizzy said. "Just find Dalla."

Gabby turned to her boy. "Jonno?" she said. "You hear me?"

Jonno moaned something, and his eyes rolled back and his head lolled.

"Fret not. He'll be fine," said Oreg. "Got his bell rung is all."

Gabby stood. "I'll be right back," she said. Then, to the soothsayer, with a stern and solemn look on her face: "I hope I can trust you. I am leaving my children in your care."

"Surely you can, Gabriella," Oreg told her. "I have only their best interests at heart. Now go."

Gabby left then, and the soothsayer got to work. There was no time to spare and he had much to do.

**Thirty-seven**:

It all comes down to freewill, making a choice between one thing and another. Some choices are hard, others easy. Some have no consequences, while others affect lives and change the spin of fate forever.

Lizzy had a choice to make.

She remembered waking on the sofa after the attack. She remembered the soothsayer being there and her ma going to look for Dalla. She remembered Largo prone and wretched on the floor, his lame legs hanging from his waist like broken limbs on a fallen tree.

Then she remembered a ... sweet smelling powder and ...

Her eyes opened to the soothsayer's hut, and she felt something furry stir at her feet. She looked down and saw Baba. The beyo pup wagged its stubby tail and scurried up the bed to greet her. She scratched a hand behind its ear, making its stubby tail wag even faster.

Oreg was over by the hearth, packing a bag.

"What are we doing here?" Lizzy asked him, still rather groggy. Her head didn't hurt, but it felt far from clear, and there was a slight blur in her eyes. "How did I get here?"

"I have to leave, child. I have someplace I need to be."

Lizzy looked around. She didn't see her mum, or her brother, or Dalla. "What am I doing here?" she asked. "Where's my family."

"I brought you here. You have a decision to make."

Lizzy looked at him. She made no comment.

"I need to go away. I want you to come with me."

"Me? Where?"

"It has started, child. The Tribulation. The Kin is gaining in strength and number. If not stopped, they will gain dominion here, and then will look to gain their freedom."

"Their freedom?"

"Aye. From the Angeloi. Once and for all."

Tales of the Angeloi had become lore in Hinterland, a ripe fantastical mythology steeped in mystery and magic, with no real proof one way or the other. The Divine Scroll was considered to be the word of the Angeloi, and the old scrolls from the prophets told of their exploits, but over time those words and tales had faded. There were numerous prayers in their name, but not as many people recited them at the altar, and the days of sacrifice and fasting had all but ended.

No living man or woman had ever seen an Angelos; no living man or woman had ever spoken to one. Not even the Monks at Lockhead had familiarity with them. Because so, they were thought to be dead, or absent, or entirely made-up.

Even so, the mere mention of them piqued Lizzy's interest. "The Angeloi?" she said with a sense of wonder. That wonder was all over her face, too, drawing her eyes wide.

"Aye, girl. The Angeloi."

"They're real?"

"They are."

Curiosity rushed through Lizzy like a current, unstoppable and unrelenting. Her young mind hummed with excitement. The Angeloi! The Great War! Then her face fell flat and the light in her eyes dimmed.

"My ma," she said sadly. "She'll never allow it."

"Absolutely not, child," Oreg told her. "That's why I stole you away."

"You kidnapped me? But ..."

"It's not kidnapping. You have your freedom and your freewill. You must make up your own mind. Come with me or stay. The choice is yours. You're the only one who can make it."

"But my ma will worry on me. She'll ..."

"I left a note at the house for her. She knows I have you. She'll blame me, not you, for whatever's to come. As she should."

"What about my pa? He's on a trek. I can't leave without seeing him."

Oreg stopped packing and looked at her. She was so young, so skinny, so vulnerable. Yet at the same time she possessed a strength and a wisdom that most grown adults would never know. Could never know. He knew it the first time he saw her, when she was just a girl of three; those deep gray eyes of hers had shined so bright and seen so far even back then.

"I'll offer you no pretense, child," Oreg began, his normally quick, scratchy voice now eerily emotionless. On his face there sat an expression of care and compassion that seemed out of place. "It's not my way, and it does no good. I'll speak the truth, if you care to hear it."

Lizzy considered that, and nodded.

"I don't know if your father's coming back," Oreg said, his one eye set on Lizzy, watching closely for her reaction. "If the ashes of the demon can be trusted, I'd say there's less than half a chance."

"The ashes of what?" Lizzy said.

"The demon I killed and incinerated in your home. You can read their ashes, if you know how. I got a sense that the Herders ran afoul in the desert. What happened, I'll not pretend to know. But I think they won't be back. Not all of them, if any."

This news hung Lizzy's jaw like a broken fence-slat. Tears welled in her big gray eyes and her bottom lip began to tremble. "But ..." she muttered helplessly. "But ..."

"There's much happening, girl, and much to do. The Kin have gained in power and need be stopped."

Lizzy wiped the tears from her eyes and sniffed. "No," she said, shaking her head resolutely, refusing to accept the soothsayer's dreadful premonition. "I don't care what a demon's ashes told you, my pa won't die in the desert. I know it, with both head and heart. He'll *not* die in the desert." But even as she said it, doubt rose up inside her, swift and powerful, and she realized for the first time that she had seen her father in her dream, in the maelstrom of her dark, demented night-terror, and she could not remember if he had been dead or alive. She remembered his face, and she remembered ...

She fought to piece together the truth of her vision from the mad, chaotic scramble that had left her trembling in her bed that morning, but her father's face, and his fate, eluded her. She remembered the shadows, and the corpses, and the beasts; she remembered the Kin and the monsters made of man. But her father ...

Lizzy's uncompromising faith touched Oreg, but he could sense the doubt growing inside her, digging into her mind, and the last thing he wanted to do was add to that. "Perhaps you're right, child," he told her. "Perhaps he'll return home unscathed. But that changes nothing for me."

"It does for me," said Lizzy. "I have to tell my ma. Whether it's true or not, she has to know."

"You go back there, you can't come with me. She won't allow it."

"But ... Why me?"

"I need help in my quest and someone with the Sight will serve me far better than the fiercest fighter in the land. That's you, girl. You have *To Vlema*. It's raw, undeveloped, but you've got it, and it's strong in you. Now, if you refuse to come with me, and you may, the choice is yours, I'll be forced to go without, and you can return home to your family."

Lizzy was struck speechless. According to Oreg, someone she barely knew yet trusted completely, her pa and his friends had come across peril in the desert. More worrisome than that, the Kin were threatening to take control of Hinterland. Were these things true? There was no way for her to know for certain, but something inside her said that they were … and that it was just the beginning. She couldn't say how, but she felt the rise in power of the Kin; she felt it as clearly as she felt the sun on her face or the wind in her hair. And she had had a bad feeling about Yondo's trek before he had left for it. If that wasn't enough, there was the attack at her house: a soul-struck Herder and a ruthless Kin assassin out to murder her and her family. Lizzy had seen their faces, their *true* faces, and had not a shred of doubt that they were Kin.

She didn't remember the part that Oreg had played in the battle, but she had a good idea that he had saved them all. As he worked on his bag, she asked him as much.

"It matters not, child," he told her without looking up. "A story for another time. What matters is now."

"They came for *me*, didn't they?" Lizzy said, that frightening realization just dawning on her.

Oreg looked at her again, and gave a single nod.

"That's why you gave me the charm, isn't it? But my mom found it and took it away from me. That's how they found me. Because I wasn't wearing the charm."

"Not so, child. The charm *senses* energy, good and bad. I felt the trouble in your house before it was there. It didn't need to be on you, just near. And a good thing it was."

Lizzy was smart enough to know what would have happened to her and her family had Oreg not intervened. She looked away, out the small, soot-stained window to her right. The sun was up and out, but all she saw was darkness. She had been aimlessly running a hand through Baba's thick, luxurious fur, but now stopped. The possible consequences of her decision frightened her, though not nearly as much as the truth did … and where that truth ultimately would take her.

"The charm saved you, girl," Oreg said to her. "Believe it."

Lizzy didn't care about that anymore. "They'll come back, won't they?" she said. The realizations were coming fast now. "The Kin'll send more. They know I've got the Sight. They think I'm trouble."

"You *are* trouble, girl."

"For them? Or for my family?"

Oreg stopped packing again. Lizzy had sense that belied her few years.

Yes, she possessed *To Vlema*, but it was more than that. She not only saw; she understood. In the soothsayer's opinion, that was an impressive talent in someone so young.

"Both," he told her.

"It won't be safe for them if I'm here." This was not a question.

Oreg shook his head. "No. Most likely not."

"Especially if my pa doesn't return."

"I'm sorry, girl. Truly."

Lizzy retreated into the growing depths of her mind once more, where her thoughts mixed not only with concerns and conjecture but also an intrinsic, unexplainable knowledge of which she had just begun to scratch the surface. She stroked the beyo's back, twining her fingers through its soft, bristly fur, while her unsettled mind twined through the possibilities that fate may have in store for her. For them all.

There was a chance that Yondo might not return from his trek. If that was true, the family could be in real trouble. Yondo was their leader, their provider, their pillar of strength. Gabby was the family's heart and soul, but Yondo was its backbone. Without him, the Carpana homestead would wane, perhaps even fall.

Gabby had the intelligence and fortitude to survive, but it would be a hard road. She was no kind of hunter, and neither was Jonno. They would struggle to put meat on the table and money in their pocket. Jonno most likely would have to get a job; perhaps Gabby would have to go to work, too. Dalla undoubtedly would be shackled with more chores, and also the difficult task of having to grow up too fast.

Poor Dalla, thought Lizzy.

How could she possibly leave sweet little Dalla behind?

"Don't mean to rush you, girl, but we haven't a lot of time," Oreg said. The sound of his voice broke through Lizzy's shell of silence and brought her back to reality. "Stay or come with. Either way you'll see trouble."

Lizzy looked at him, a cynical arch to her brow. "That's not exactly a promising statement," she said. "I'm worried enough as it is."

Oreg gave a funny little smile, one that did not fit him well. "I suppose not," he said. "Forgive me. Tact was never a talent of mine."

"I guess there's not a third option, where everyone lives happily ever after, like in the yarns of old?"

The soothsayer finished packing his bag. He strapped it closed and tossed it near the door. "Of course," he said. "'Happily ever after' is not a myth, girl. It's real. You just have to walk through fire to get there."

"You swear I can't go back and tell my ma? There's no other way?"

"What do you think?"

Lizzy knew her mother would never allow her go on a dangerous adventure with the soothsayer. She believed that she'd probably be grounded for even suggesting such a thing. But to leave without an explanation? Without saying goodbye? She didn't think she could do that to them. They were her family and she loved them dearly.

"When will we be back?" she inquired, seeking more information.

Oreg looked at her. "Haven't yet left and you want to know when we'll be back?" he said sardonically.

It was Lizzy's turn to smile now. A wide one broke across her face, lifting her lips and coloring her cheeks. Then, at once, she turned serious again. "A season? Two?"

Oreg shook his head. "I know not, child. But I sense it will be longer than that."

Lizzy sighed pensively and scratched Baba under the chin.

"I have things to get outside. When I come back, I'll be ready to go. You'll either be going with me or staying behind. The choice is yours to make, and I'll not argue it."

Lizzy nodded and said that she would think on it, and Oreg went out, leaving her to her thoughts and Baba's loyal company.

There were so many variables to consider, and so few facts on which to hang her hat. But no matter which direction she steered her thoughts, no matter how many times she played out different scenarios and ideas, one depressing conclusion continued to make itself known: there was no right answer, and no matter what she decided, suffering and death awaited.

But whose suffering and whose death?

That was what she had to consider most of all.


Gabby found Dalla in town, at the sheriff's office. Arman and Horace were gearing up when she rushed in and asked if anyone had seen her little girl.

"Mommy," Dalla cried out, running to greet her. Gabby hugged her tight for a long time, whispering in her ear that everything was all right, that everyone was safe, that there was no reason for her to be scared.

By the end of the embrace, both of them were crying. Even Horace and Arman, two hard-edged lawmen with steely nerves and strong chins, found themselves a little choked up.

"Is Lizzy okay?" Dalla asked, her eyes red and swollen.

"She's fine, child. We're all fine."

"She screamed for me to run so I ran. I climbed out the window and ran as fast as I could, just like she said."

"You did good," Gabby told her. "Lizzy'll be so proud of you."

A smile swept across Dalla's face, but then vanished quickly. She sniffed and wiped the tears from her eyes.

"You're a brave little girl," Horace said to her.

Gabby gave the sheriff a brief summary of what had happened, and he and Arman agreed to follow her back to the house so they could see for themselves. Gabby gave them more details on the way, though she was mindful to keep back some of the more disturbing ones, not wanting to scare Dalla. Neither Horace nor Arman had any reason to doubt her given the fresh bruises marking her normally lovely face. Even so, both were surprised to hear of Largo's involvement.

"Largo *Kelsman*?" Horace said, wanting to make sure. "Kin?"

"I don't know what he was, or is, a demon or only possessed, but his friend …" Gabby glanced down at her daughter, who was listening to her closely, and finished with, "… he was evil."

"Big, dark-skinned fellow?" Arman said. "Yeah, I saw him last night. He was at Sana's. Bought Lessie *and* Marie." There was a note of disgust in his voice for that last part, and a sour look on his young, handsome face. "I hope he didn't do no bad to them. I didn't see Lessie today."

Horace sneered at his boy. "You spend too much time doting on that slattern. She's pretty, sure, but she can't make a wife."

"She's more than a sally, pa. She's …" Arman stopped there, knowing there was no way he could defend the virtue of a whore to his father, who, paradoxically, often took comfort at Sana's himself. Now was not the time to bring up such things, though, so he let it drop.

Horace said to Gabby, "Is Largo dead or merely injured?"

"Injured only, I think. He was kicking Lizzy. I stabbed him in the back and his legs gave out. Then I broke his arm."

"And you said the soothsayer stopped the attack? That old, hunched mystic who lives in the woods?"

Gabby snorted in disbelief. "Crazy, right? But in he came, when things were at their worst, and he stomped that … that *thing* with no trouble. And then he snapped its neck."

"*Its* neck?" the Sheriff asked.

"Whatever it was, it wasn't human. He struck a match and ..." Gabby again glanced down at her daughter, who now was watching her own feet as she walked along the dirt road. Gabby had little doubt, though, that the girl's ears were open. "You'll see when we get there," she said vaguely. "I don't know if you'll believe it, though. I hardly believe it myself and I saw it with my own eyes."

In deference to Dalla, they walked the rest of the way in near silence, only speaking when words were necessary. Most of those words were said to Dalla. The girl's mood had improved drastically since Gabby had shown up; when she had burst through the door at Horace's place, she had been hysterical with fear, her eyes so red and swollen that Horace had worried she'd been struck with poison. It had taken them some time to calm her down enough to coax a story from her. Now she seemed calm and content, almost happy.

When her house came into view, she pointed excitedly and cried out, "Look, ma! Home. There."

"I see," Gabby said to her. "Still standing."

The house *was* still standing, and it looked the same from far off, yet Gabby knew it was different now. They had been attacked in their own home, and for the first time death had breached their walls.

At least it hadn't been one of their own.

"You've had a helluva time since Yondo's been gone," Horace mused as they walked through the gate. "First Lizzy and the ringer, then the storm, now this. That's enough excitement for a year or more."

"For my life," Gabby said.

"Thank goodness for that crazy old mystic."

"Thank goodness for good people. We know a lot of them."

"I thought that old bastard mad," Arman said. "He certainly looks it."

"You're right," Gabby said. "I thought the same. Turns out I badly misjudged him. Turns out he's a decent man."

In the months to come, those words would haunt Gabriella Carpana; they would haunt not only her waking thoughts but her dreams, too. She would hear them echo in her head, in her own voice, and in the voice of the soothsayer. She would hear them in the wind on quiet, lonely nights, of which there would be many. She would hear them in the lazy crackle of a campfire and the cacophonous din of overcrowded gatherings. She would hear them everywhere.

But she would never speak them again, and she would never forgive herself for having trusted the soothsayer.

The man who kidnapped her daughter.

Jonno, who also had gotten a dose of knockout powder blown in his face by the soothsayer, provided a fractured, ambiguous account of what had happened, though it was hard to take anything he said as truth. His head was in a funk, his words slurred and confounding. He twice referred to Lizzy as Liddy, and swore on his right hand that Largo could walk.

Largo had an account, though it was surprisingly short on details. He told them about the powder the soothsayer had used on the kids, and he told them how Oreg had stolen away with Lizzy and a sack full of goods. He claimed not to remember much about the attack, and kept crying that he couldn't feel his legs and that his arm ached like a rotten tooth.

The best account came from the soothsayer's letter, which Gabby read twice before passing it with shaking hands to Horace. She then began to pace around the room and mumble curses under her breath.

*Sorry for the deception, Gabriella, but I believed it to be necessary. I have a quest to embark on and your girl will make for a good companion. She has the Sight, and that's an inestimable trait. She did not wish to come, but I gave her no choice. Yet fear not, I'll watch her closely and see to her health. You have my word. If you need reason, know that you owe me as much. You, your boy, and Lizzy would not have air in your lungs nor blood in your veins if not for me. I collect by claiming the indenture of your gypsy daughter, Elizabeth Layne. I also took the gold and silver found when I burned the demon to ash. We'll need barter for the quest, and gold serves well. I'll stand for these thefts if I must, but I don't believe you will ever see me again.*

*Oreg*

Horace put down the letter and looked around at the mess. The kitchen table was overturned, two chairs lay on the floor, one with a broken leg, a short-blade coated in blood rested near a rather large pile of black ash, and there was a dagger stuck in a ceiling beam. There was little doubt in the sheriff's mind that there had been a knockdown, drag-out fight here.

"Dad? What does it say?" Arman asked.

Gabby grabbed the blood-stained short-blade from the floor and hefted it in her hand. "We're going," she said adamantly. "Now! He's got my little girl, but not for long." She may have been small and trim and pretty, but she had a way about her that made people snap to.

Horace looked at his boy. "Load up," he said to him. "We need to go."

"Dalla, you stay here with Jonno," Gabby said.

The girl looked ready to burst into tears. She couldn't understand what was happening; her ma had told her that everything was all right, that everyone was safe ... only Lizzy was gone.

"I can go, too," Jonno mumbled. But there were clouds in his eyes, and even seated he looked off balance.

"You're in no shape, boy," Gabby told him. "You need the Doc."

"Your ma's right," Horace said. "You stay behind."

"What of the Herder, pa?" Arman asked. "Do we leave him here?"

"Where's he going to go? He's got no legs."

"I'm the one who needs the Doc," Largo cried. "I can't feel my legs. And my arm is busted to hell. Look how swollen. I can barely move it."

"You're lucky that's all you got," Gabby said to him, and poked him in the gut with the tip of the short-blade, making him cry out.

"Easy, Gabriella," Horace said to her. "No more killing need be done here. There's been enough already."

She looked at the sheriff. "He was possessed," she said. "I know it. My girl saw it. Can he ..." She stopped, unsure of how to phrase what she wanted to say without sounding crazy. Of course, the line for crazy had moved considerably over the last ten days.

"Can he what?" Horace asked.

Largo was sitting against the wall in the kitchen, his injured arm cradled in his lap, his lame legs outstretched and slanted slightly to the left. He looked like an unmanned puppet, the kind the traveling players used when they came to town for a show.

Gabby said, "I'd feel better if your boy stayed here while we're gone. I don't trust him."

"He's an invalid," Horace said. "What's he going to do?"

"I don't care. The things I've seen today." Gabby realized that her hands were shaking again. She looked at Arman. "Can you stay here and watch them? Please."

Arman looked at his pa.

"We might need him at the soothsayer's place," Horace told Gabby. "If there's trouble."

Gabby was unsure of what to do, but she knew they had to get moving. The soothsayer had a rote lead on them at least and they had no idea which direction he had gone.

"Fine," she said. "He can come." She then handed the short-blade to her boy and said, "If he moves, if he tries anything at all, if he says something you don't like, you run that blade through him until he's dead. You hear me?"

Jonno's head nodded up and down awkwardly, as if on a broken spring.

Arman said, "You two go on ahead. I'll tie him down and then catch up. How's that sound?"

Horace thought that was a good idea, and Gabby agreed.

"Come," she told the sheriff. "And fast."

"Where to?"

"Oreg's hut. He'd likely go there first. Maybe we can catch them, or find a clue on where he's planning to take her."

"That man in the woods has Lizzy?" Dalla asked, that precious face of hers bathed in confusion and sadness. "Why did he take her? He doesn't want to hurt her, does he?"

Gabby knelt down in front of her little girl so that she could look her square in the eye. "Worry not," she said, forcing a smile. "Lizzy's going to be fine. I promise. We're going to get her back. The Sheriff and I. We're not going to let him get away with this."

Dalla nodded bravely, but she could not stop the tears from falling. "You have to find her because she has to come home so she can teach me how to fish, and how to go to the market, and how to barter with vendors."

"She knows," Gabby said to her consolingly. "And I know she's going to fight to come home. Because she loves you. She loves all of us. A bad man took her, but we're going to find her and bring her back. We're going to bring her back. Now mommy has to go. I have to help the Sheriff get Lizzy back."

Dalla nodded bravely again. More tears fell from her eyes.

"You okay over there, boy?" Horace called out to his son.

"Him?! Is *he* okay?!" Largo cried back. "I'm the one crippled here." Then, to Arman: "You're tying down a cripple, boy. And the real villain, that soothsayer, is getting away."

"Shut it," Arman told him.

"I'll bet he put a spell on everyone, that ol' soothsayer," Largo went

379

on. "Probably put a spell on me. I don't remember a thing. I'm innocent, I bet. It's all a misunderstanding."

"You shut your mouth, Largo Kelsman!" Gabby shouted at him. Her jaw was stiff and there was rage in her eyes. "*I* remember what you did! *I* remember you kicking my little girl in the stomach and knocking Jonno in the head! *Innocent?!* Not at all. You wait until Yondo returns. You wait! He'll hear of it by my word."

Largo had nothing to say to that. He had nothing to say about anything. He remembered stabbing Aglan in the desert and leaving his body for the yenas, and he remembered the look in Lizzy's eyes when she had seen him outside the saloon. He remembered Dale Travers pleading for his life, and he remembered the blank, wraithlike expression on the Moll girl's face when she had mouthed the word 'Daimonas.'

These memories returned to him now, like the remnants of a bad dream, and he hung his head and sobbed. "I'm sorry," he said, weeping. "I'm sorry for everything."

Arman continued to work, binding Largo tight. He told his pa that he was fine, that he'd be finished shortly, and that he'd catch up with them before they crossed the first field.

Horace went to the door, and Gabby met him there. "I'll be back when we find her," Gabby said, looking right at Dalla. "Worry not. You stay here and take care of your big brother, okay?"

She nodded valiantly, yet her eyes were still moist with tears and her mouth showed a frown. "Okay. I will."

Jonno cleared his throat and muttered words that no one understood, words that weren't even words, and Gabby told him that when she got back she would take him to see Doc Morris.

"No. I'm just ... tired," he told her.

Dalla waved her mom goodbye. "Be careful," she said.

"I will, sweetie. I will."

Gabby left then, closing the door behind her. She was leaving her two biological children to go find the gypsy girl that fate had delivered to their home more than fourteen years ago. She wondered whether it was the right thing to do, then put that thought out of her head and concentrated on the weathered, one-eyed face of the soothsayer.

Oreg had saved all of their lives and a debt surely was owed to him for that. But then he had lied to her for the purpose of stealing Lizzy away. Or perhaps it all had been a lie.

That would not stand.

In Gabby's mind, she was now owed a debt, and she meant to collect with the edge of a blade.

Gabby, Horace, and Arman reached the soothsayer's hut in near record time, but it wasn't fast enough. They arrived to find the home deserted and many of the items and strange artifacts gone. Even the owler and the beyo pup were gone. There was, however, another note. This one was from Lizzy. Gabby recognized the scratch of her left hand immediately.

*Ma,*

*I'm sorry, truly, but I have to go away. Don't blame Oreg, it's not his fault. I know you don't believe it, but I have the Sight. I know it to be true. It's not a trick or deception, but it may be a curse. I cannot put you and Dalla and Jonno in any more danger. I love you all too much. The Kin'll come for me again. I know it. I've seen it in my dreams. And if you are in their way, they'll kill you, too. You saw what happened today. I could never forgive myself if something happened to any of you because of me. I love you too much. Tell Dalla I love her and have her with me always. Tell Yondo and Jonno the same. Thank you for everything.*

*With love,*
*Elizabeth Layne Carpana*

The letter fell from Gabby's hand and drifted down to the floor. All the life seemed to go out of her then, and she slouched onto a nearby chair and began to weep. Big, sobbing, ugly tears poured out of her eyes and down her face. The knowledge that her daughter was gone was simply too much for her to bear.

What would she tell Yondo?

What would she tell Dalla?

How could they possible go on as a family?

Lizzy's words aside, Gabby blamed the soothsayer. He had filled the girl's head with all sorts of nonsense and now she was gone.

But what hurt Gabby most of all was that Lizzy seemed to believe that she herself was to blame; the girl actually believed that she had to leave because what had happened at the house had been her fault. Gabby wanted to hold her close and tell her it wasn't her fault, that she hadn't done anything wrong, that everything would be okay.

Horace picked up the letter and read it for himself. He laid a consoling hand on Gabby's shoulder as she cried but said not a word. He wasn't good with words, and crying women unnerved him.

His boy, Arman, was so overcome that he left the hut.

Gabby cried and cried, until she couldn't cry anymore.

That's when anger set in, deep and hungry.

Her strength returned to her, and she stood with a start. Her eyes were yet turgid and red, but behind the swollen, angry redness a look of tenacity glared through. She sniffled and wiped her face dry. Then she turned her terrible eyes on Horace and said, "Can you track which way they went?"

Horace was silent for a moment, then nodded and said that he could. But he was quick to add, "I've no idea how much of a head start they got on us, and I can't go myself. To track proper, I need a posse of men. That takes time and planning."

"No," Gabby said. "I don't want you to go after them. I only need to know which way they went so I can tell Yondo when he returns. Because *he* will go after them."

"Oh. In that case, sure, I'll have a look."

## Thirty-eight:

The first day had been nothing but hills and slopes; up one side, down the other. If they weren't going up a hill, they were going down one; even then, much of the walk took place on a side slant, making balance tricky.

Mostly there had been fields that first day, and that first night they had camped in a clearing of tall grass and bare mulberry bushes. Dinner had consisted of squirrel and nuts, and Peck had drifted off shortly after dusk.

The ground was flatter on day two, and because so their walk was easier. The hills gave way to plains and the tall grass gave way to short grass and scattered brush. A short time after lunch, Peck spied the top of mounts in the distance and asked Kelt if they had names.

"Namumbae." His finger drifted over to a snowcapped mount on the left. "We call that Dorniel. Named after the great Angelos."

"So they are real?" Peck asked him. "The Angeloi?"

"Aye. Why? You don't believe in them?"

"I don't know. I've never seen one. And ..." He paused.

"Aye," said Kelt, nodding. "You have more reasons than most *not* to believe in them."

"But no one has seen one? No one alive today. All we have are stories generations gone."

"We have Kin," Kelt replied. "And if there are Kin, then there must be Angeloi."

"Then where are they? What are they doing while we suffer and die?"

"In the beginning, there were only Angeloi and Kin. We came later. After the Angeloi defeated the Kin in The Great War, they gave dominion of Hinterland to us. After a period of time, after guiding us and imparting all the knowledge we would need to survive, they moved on." Kelt raised his eyes skyward, taking in the soft blue expanse above. "They still watch over us, I believe, and help when most needed."

"I still don't understand," Peck said. "Why are there still demons and evil things here if the Angeloi defeated them?"

"They defeated them, but did not eliminate them."

"Why not? Shouldn't they have?"

"Perhaps. But that's not what happened. We know they left them weak, with only a fraction of their power."

"I think they should have eliminated them for good," Peck said, giving breath to a reasonable thought. "Look at all the trouble they cause."

"Maybe you're right. Maybe they couldn't eliminate them, or maybe they weren't supposed to. I don't know."

They continued to walk, the Monk in front, Peck a few steps behind. The boy wondered idly if walking was to be the bane of his existence. He could not remember the last day he had spent more time off his feet than on them. Days beyond a full moon, at least. He couldn't wait to get to Lockhead and rest. But would his time there be restful?

Trials of the Soul — that was what the Monk had called the tests he would have to endure to rid himself of the call of the Kin, which was shared by all those who were Marked. If he survived the Trials, then all he would hear was the song of the Angels, which had been drowned out over the last ten or twelve generations.

Trials of the Soul.

Dokimes tis Psychis.

He hadn't asked the Monk a lot of questions about what lay ahead for him, mostly because he found it impossible to imagine it could be any worse than what lay behind.

Whatever hardships the Trials of the Soul entailed, Peck was prepared to accept them. If he passed, perchance he'd have a shot at a normal life. A normal life as a Monk. And if he failed, what difference would it make? So what if death came to visit him a little early?

Kelt pointed ahead. "There. That's where we're going."

Peck spied a grove of tall pine trees about two miles off.

A few sparse clouds had gathered overhead and a stiff breeze had begun to blow, putting a chill in the air that reddened Peck's cheeks and tossed his curly hair. There wasn't a storm brewing; it was only a sign that the season had started to change. Before long, winter would lie across the northern parts of Hinterland, turning everything white and icy cold.

Peck pulled a piece of jerky from his pocket, bit into it, and chewed. "How far is Lockhead?" he asked between bites.

Without turning around, Kelt said, "We should be there by this time tomorrow, if the weather cooperates."

"I thought it was farther than that."

"It is. But we're taking a short cut."

Peck gave up on questions and busied his mouth with chunks of jerky. He had always thought his pa had been tight-lipped, but Kelt made his pa seem like a rambunctious kid after too many cakes. Not that Peck was going to complain. He liked Kelt's manner just fine … especially now, after everything that had happened. It was the best of both worlds for him: companionship and solitude at the same time.

The woods they entered were foreign to Peck; he had never been this far south and west before, and there were very few tales from these lands. Not many folk lived out here, so far as he knew, even though the ground was good and life was fertile. Peck could remember passing only a few small villages since leaving Greenhorn.

He asked the Monk why no one lived out this way. "Not here, in the woods," he clarified. "I mean on the land we walked to get here. There were very few homes, very few people."

"Most believe there is safety in numbers," Kelt replied. He said nothing more about it, and Peck let it drop.

A collection of towering pines and cedars dominated the woods; low but thick underbrush and the occasional hyacinth bush added a bit of color to things. The ground beneath their feet was carpeted with thousands of dead pine needles, which softened but slowed their steps. Hundreds of pine cones lay about, and Peck kicked at some while he walked.

In the mighty spokes of the limbs above, birds squawked loudly, as if warning all other life in the woods that intruders had breached their land. Peck wondered if Ovince was up there somewhere, watching over him, like one of the Angeloi. He searched the treetops but didn't see the large white bird. He didn't see much of anything.

What caught his attention was a gentle, continuous rush of sound. At first he thought it the sound of the wind gently sifting through the labyrinth of pine trees that stood watch over this lush green land, but it wasn't long before he changed his mind about that. They had been walking south mostly, but also west.

"Is that the river I hear?" he asked the Monk.

"Megalo Potami Fidi?" Kelt said. "Aye."

"Are we to travel by river? Or along it?"

"I have a small craft."

Peck had never traveled on the great river before; he'd ever only seen it twice, both times from afar. He knew very little about it, though tales of its treacherousness had reached his ears and piqued his morbid curiosity. It was said that many a soul had been lost in the murky depths of Potami. Peck himself knew two people who had drowned in the great river, and he'd heard stories of countless others who had gone swimming and had never been heard from again. Some had been swallowed up by terrifying beasts; others by the water itself.

He couldn't swim a lick, and told the Monk so.

"You don't need to know how to swim in a boat, boy," Kelt told him. "Just need to know how to row."

"But what if we ... you know, go over?"

"'Capsize' is the word. And we won't."

"But what about some of the ... you know ... *things* in there?"

"*Things*? What *things*?"

"I heard there are creatures in Potami that can swallow a man whole. I heard this man was in a boat, and this thing came up out of the depths, bit the boat in half, and ate the man."

Kelt stopped walking. He turned around and looked at the boy. "Sure," he said, "there are some big things in the depths of the river. But we're not going to worry about them. Just like we're not going to worry about the bears and wolves in these woods, or the many snakes that call the riverbank home, or the spiders in the trees. A man can go wild with worry if he lets it have him. But we're not going to do that."

Peck nodded, and said, "But I can't swim."

"Yes. You told me. And like I told you, you won't need to swim. You'll need to row." The Monk started up again, his footfalls silent on the thick carpet of pine needles. "Trust me, boy," he said from over his shoulder, "by the end of the trip you'll be praying to swim ... if it means you can stop rowing." And then he laughed.

Peck had never heard the Monk laugh so jovially before, and he took it as a good sign. He started up again, too, walking swiftly through the silent, beautiful maze of pines and cedars. Before long they reached the mighty river's edge, and Peck's young eyes went wide with amazement. Up close, Potami was monstrous and magnificent, as monstrous and magnificent as any mountain.

"Quite a sight," Kelt said to him.

Peck nodded wondrously.

"It wraps around all of Hinterland and reaches shores never before seen, not even by the river-folk."

Peck nodded again. He was all eyes.

"Come. Help me, boy," Kelt said. "You'll have time to gawk later."

The Monk was over near a patch of bushes, clearing away loose branches, stalks of river reeds, and small rocks. What began to appear was a boat that looked, at least to Peck's untrained eye, much too small to take on the wild waters of Megalo Potami Fidi. When all the camouflage had been stripped away, the vessel appeared only slightly larger and more secure than a farm dray. The sudden bolt of trepidation that struck Peck showed plainly on his face.

The Monk said to him, "Worry not, boy. I've yet to fall into the waters of the great serpent river." He gave the small wooden boat a loving stroke. "She's not the biggest, but she's as safe as they come. And you have my word that we'll not leave sight of the coastline, except when we go through the rapids, and they're hardly anything to fret about. Not this time of year, anyway." That was only a slight mendacity. "Now come, help me drag this thing to the water."

Peck reluctantly did as told, and the two of them, with some effort, worked the boat across the muddy riverbank to the lapping waters of Potami. The Monk promptly threw their gear in, including two long, oaken oars, and hopped over the side. He then looked at Peck and said, "Get in, boy, else you'll be swimming for it. Or sinking to the bottom."

Peck realized then that the boat was already wandering away from shore and if he didn't jump aboard now he was going to get a whole lot wetter. He was still quite scared, terrified actually, but his fears barely had time to take hold let alone squeeze.

He threw his pack in, kicked a wet leg over the side, and clumsily climbed aboard, landing with a thud. He started to stand up so that he could turn around and right his balance, but the Monk grabbed him by the shoulders and held him down.

"One rule," Kelt said as the shoreline slowly drifted away from them, a fact that did not escape Peck's attention. "No standing in the boat. Not until you've got the legs for it. You stand, the boat rocks, the boat tips, we get wet. Understand?"

Peck nodded keenly. "No standing," he said. "Got it."

From his knees, he slowly turned himself around. Then, with the Monk lending a hand, he maneuvered onto one of the hard benches that stretched across the width of the boat. Once firmly seated, he took in and let out a couple of deep breaths, hoping to calm himself. He felt his heart begin to slow and his nerves begin to ease, but then he glanced over his shoulder and saw just how much water lay betwixt them and solid ground. Suddenly his heart sped up again, even faster than before, his palms began to sweat, his mind began to race, and every breath he took came with a rasp of fear.

Sensing the boy's distress, Kelt said to him, "Relax. This here is the easy part. I'd advise you to enjoy it." The Monk rowed a couple strokes and the shoreline edged farther away. The towering pine trees in the distance seemed to get smaller with every stroke of the oars, and Peck couldn't help but wonder if perhaps he had left Greenhorn a bit too rashly.

If this was the easy part …

## Thirty-nine:

Oreg and Lizzy had started off due east, though an hour into their walk, about the same time Gabby, Horace, and Arman had arrived at Oreg's now abandoned hut, they had veered south, toward the Marshlands.

Oreg hadn't wanted Lizzy to leave the note behind; he had wanted to accept full blame so that Lizzy's family couldn't hold her at fault. But Lizzy had told him that she wouldn't go unless she could tell her ma the truth.

"She raised me. She loves me. She's been nothing but good to me. I owe her the truth. I owe them all the truth."

Oreg had been so impressed that he had allowed it.

Even so, he was concerned.

A lot had happened to Lizzy the last ten days, and he worried that she might be too young to handle such privations. Leaving her family. Leaving her home. The guilt of knowing that she had been the reason why they had been attacked and nearly killed. Beyond all that, there was the overbearing weight that *to Mati Fantasma* put on a mind.

She was only fourteen.

The Kin was ancient and ageless.

Oreg looked back over his shoulder at the gangly little girl and said, "You okay back there, child?"

"I'm fine," she told him, but her voice was flat, emotionless, and her eyes were still moist with tears.

"You need to stop and rest, you tell me."

"I will."

Oreg set the pace, traversing the wild terrain with the aid of his staff. Lizzy and Baba kept stride with him, moving together at the same speed. They hadn't seen Lolly for some time now, though Oreg was fairly certain the owler was nearby.

"We'll break on the other side of that hillock," he called back. "I know a place."

Lizzy said that sounded fine.

"We'll eat and rest our legs. Mine are quite a bit older than yours."

Lizzy offered no reply. She already missed Gabby and Dalla. She missed Yondo and Jonno, too. Her heart felt like it weighed as much as a Smith's anvil, and every beat it took caused a terrible ache.

Oreg went on. "From there we'll start back east again. There's a field of squat pines near a small lake that's perfect for camp. I say in three days we'll reach the Marshlands."

That last statement yanked Lizzy from her pit of misery. She had a vague idea of where they were headed, but that was the first time Oreg had said the name aloud. The Marshlands was cursed ground. One of the most dangerous places in all of Hinterland.

In a voice that had yet to recover its full timbre, Lizzy said, "Why are we going to the Marshlands? Nobody lives there. It's haunted."

"Aye. *Kataramenos*."

"Cursed?" Lizzy said, recognizing the word from the ancient language.

"Aye. But the Marshlands is not our destination, child, only part of the journey. A passageway."

"And where's our destination?" Lizzy asked.

"The first?" Oreg said. "Erimia."

"Erimia?" A note of uncertainty could be heard in Lizzy's voice. She wore the look, too. "Never heard of it. Is it beyond the Marshlands? I thought there were no lands beyond the Marshlands."

"There are, child. Quite a bit beyond."

"How far? And where? On the other side of Potami?"

Oreg stopped, turned around, looked at her.

Lizzy stopped, too.

"Erimia is another world, child. A strange and troubled world with lands and customs all its own."

Lizzy stared at the soothsayer. He could see the wheels turning in that head of hers. "Another world?" she said.

Oreg gave her a wink with his one good eye. "Aye. Surely you don't think that Hinterland is the only world? There are others, and, fate willing, you will see them all."

The End.

www.ingramcontent.com/pod-product-compliance
Lightning Source LLC
Chambersburg PA
CBHW020509260626
47156CB00006B/1943